i

First edition, 2024
Self-published
Printed by Mixam

ISBN: 979-8-218-46200-0

****

On the Fringe

****

a novel by

Patrick Grant

8/3/24

This book is dedicated to
my parents, Eileen and John
my siblings, Rosie and Tim
and my friends, too many to list

Fie upon't! foh! About, my brain! I have heard
That guilty creatures sitting at a play
Have by the very cunning of the scene
Been struck so to the soul that presently
They have proclaim'd their malefactions;
For murder, though it have no tongue, will speak
With most miraculous organ. I'll have these players
Play something like the murder of my father
Before mine uncle: I'll observe his looks;
I'll tent him to the quick: if he but blench,
I know my course. The spirit that I have seen
May be the devil: and the devil hath power
To assume a pleasing shape; yea, and perhaps
Out of my weakness and my melancholy,
As he is very potent with such spirits,
Abuses me to damn me: I'll have grounds
More relative than this: the play's the thing
Wherein I'll catch the conscience of the king.

—*Hamlet*

[Act I]

Act II

Act III

Act IV

Act V

1.1 ~ **The Obituary**

Dear friends, family members, and the national security agency. My name is Liam Hawthorne, son of Dr. William Hawthorne. With a heavy heart, I'm sharing that Dr. Hawthorne has left this world behind, survived by his wife of thirty years Greta, his daughter Sofia, and myself. You may have known him as a brilliant neuropharmacologist, an enthusiastic lector at Faith Lutheran Church, an avid partisan of all local sports, or just a familiar and friendly face around town. I knew him as a distant provider, a public recluse, a stupefying genius, and an uncompromising liar. I regret that I never got the truth out of him in time, but I'm writing in tribute to the man beneath the lies.

I would like to apologize for this unusual obituary. You may think that my father is still alive, or you're worried this is a breaking death notice for his recent passing. I'm sorry to say neither of those things is the case.

The truth is that my father departed from us months ago—in my estimation late last year—and has since been replaced by a doppelganger: a biosynthetic, photorealistic reconstruction of the man. Prior to this tragic occurrence, his life's work was dedicated to developing these doppelgangers as a technological method to replace human beings with duplicates identical in all ways except select programming and intentionality. The US government sponsored his work and has featured it in the long arm of US interventionism for years, exemplifying the uncommon depths to which the US empire has sunk to maintain its Hegemonic Power. My father dedicated his life to developing a great and awful technology in secret service of this Power, and upon threat of retirement and the end of his usefulness, this Hegemony used his invention against him, fatally.

I want to be transparent. There is a lot I don't know, and I can anticipate adverse reactions to my claims. I insist that the man we knew and loved is no more, and the one that stands in his place is a shoddy mimicry. I do not know if he is dangerous, only that he cannot be trusted. It is for public safety and concern for my friends and family that I am sharing this information while still gathering evidence. I do not expect anyone to believe me yet, but I ask that you don't fully discount my claims either. I understand reading this raises many questions, including that of my sanity, and all I ask is that you give me the time I need to prove myself. Stay tuned.

Horace dos Santos set his phone on the patio table and leaned back in his wicker chair. Stunned by what he had just read, his eyes drifted until they fixed on the highest point of the tallest tree in his backyard. When they were children, Liam often talked about climbing that tree, and Horace always protested that it was impossible. Neither had ever really tried, and they'd since traded their tree-climbing dreams for the kinds of highs chased by rudderless twenty-somethings.

When Horace saw Liam's Facebook post, he'd already been scrolling on his phone for well over an hour, exhausting every feed. He'd been so close to achieving obliteration, the total thoughtlessness he craved. Just one more refresh, he'd told himself. The post appeared like a painful memory on the verge of sleep.

Before Horace could reject or believe Liam's words, he began sorting them into piles of data. Had Dr. Hawthorne been acting strangely? Could he really be dead? When was the last time he'd seen him? Just over a week ago—coincidentally, the worst week of Horace's life, having flown out to see his ex-boyfriend, only to learn he now had a girlfriend. So much happened over that trip that Horace had almost forgotten how, the night before he left, he happened to observe someone he assumed to be Dr. Hawthorne, only it had all felt terribly wrong. What he dismissed then as a personal psychosis now returned as an inexplicable understanding.

***

Horace was sneaking a cigarette down the hill from the cul-de-sac when he spotted Dr. Hawthorne out for a Thursday evening stroll. Embarrassed to be caught smoking by a local adult, he kept his American Spirit to his side and willed himself to blend into a tree. He was still hiding his habit from the adults of the block. As he waited, he knocked his head against the tree in shame. Embarrassment turned to relief as Dr. Hawthorne passed by and paid him no mind, lost in his own.

Then, Dr. Hawthorne came to an abrupt stop. For a moment, Horace thought he'd been seen, but his neighbor never turned around. Twenty yards apart, the two were buffeted by the bitter March night as the wind howled through the trees in crescendo. With only the buffer of spring buds, the branches writhed and crackled in pain, snapping when it became unbearable. Between them, a streetlight flickered, put up a brief struggle, and cut off. Dr. Hawthorne stood frozen, clutched, like the storm was an omen, like any movement could be his last. Horace adopted the man's guarded posture, as if preparing for the ambush of some terrible beast, hiding in the darkness.

Horace felt a wax, slow and thick like a candle's, not hot but icy cold, dribble from his neck down his spine, crawling and spreading. His stomach churned like a furnace, keeping the icy wax out and producing a cloud of clammy moisture between his skin and winter coat. Panic gripped his heart. His blood surged with the fear of not knowing what was wrong, and anxious thoughts spiraled through his brain, demanding to know why he was so scared.

His vision locked on Dr. Hawthorne, who wavered before him or gave that impression to Horace's trembling eyes. Then the older man broke free, doubling over and heaving, hands on his knees, the silhouette of his chest rising and falling raggedly. The streetlight returned with a flare, illuminating Dr. Hawthorne's face in profile. There could have been tears, but Horace saw no streaks on his cheek whipped red by the oncoming storm. And it could have been the wind, but Horace thought he heard groaning escape from the man's open mouth. He looked like a torture victim, or as if visited by someone he once tortured, the pain returned with vengeance. The cold wax encased Horace and crept under his skin, like an invasion of someone else's sweat, chilling him to the bone, freezing him like brittle glass. Only his mind remained free, trapped inside his useless body, terrified with nowhere to go. The streetlight cut once more, and the wind subsided.

Horace's fingers felt a burn, but only the pointer and middle. His cigarette had reached its butt, ash already scattered by the wind, and it pinched him out of his reverie. He examined his hand, wondering how the cigarette had diminished from nearly full in a moment. Just a moment? Pink and raw, the skin under his knuckle seared and wept. When he looked up, Dr. Hawthorne had vanished into the darkness. The dread lingered as a cloud over the street but dissipated by measures as he hurried home. By the time he crossed the threshold of his door, the feeling floated away as if a dream awoken.

✳✳✳

Clouded by post-travel, pre-sleep, mid-dusk mental fog, Horace returned his gaze from the tree to his phone and read the post twice more for belief. He inspected the burn mark on his right middle finger, ugly and dark as it healed, the only evidence of his recent encounter with the supposedly dead man. Did this revelation explain that spontaneous dread, those cold drips of wax? Had robo-Hawthorne been malfunctioning? What does a bio-whatever doppelganger even mean? It seemed so farfetched that focusing on the mechanics felt like missing the point. Maybe Liam was making things up for a lark, just to shock, but why something so patently ridiculous? Uncertainty not only blossomed off the top but sunk deep down to the roots. He returned to his phone and texted Liam.

"Saw your post, wanna talk?"

"Office hours on my patio rn roll thru"

"Is He home?"

"Nah tg just me"

"Bet, be there in 5"

Horace slid through the back door and bounded carpeted steps up to his bedroom, sandwiched between his younger sister Sandy's and his parents' rooms on the top floor. Despite being the second oldest, he'd always had the smallest room. He magnanimously let Cilla, Sandy's twin sister, take over the downstairs room vacated by Dido, the eldest, when she moved out, assured that his collegiate freedom lay just around the corner. The cramped room made for a good jail cell in the years since he'd dropped out and moved home. Plus, household morale benefited greatly from Horace being the one to share a bathroom with Sandy, not to mention the water bills from the twins no longer taking extra-long showers to spite each other. Upon crossing the threshold of his door, he almost forgot what he had come up here for, but the second drawer from the top of his desk called out to him. He slid it open to withdraw smokes and a lighter from his enrichment box.

Before setting off, he paused within the frame of his mirror. Since middle school, he'd stood in front of it and willed himself to look older, more complicated. What had he to show for it? His same childish curls: dark, short, and so-called adorable. His same barely stubbled, rarely shaved baby face, his mother's wide nose and father's thick eyebrows, his olive skin renewed by his time under the Central American sun like a summer camp tan. Even the bags under his eyes were nothing new. Maybe he'd appreciate his youthful appearance once he was no longer young.

Horace only had a street crossing to consider what he wanted from Liam. They weren't as close as they used to be, but they still hung out almost every week. Despite this, Liam's post underscored the chasm emerging between them, which Horace was nervous to traverse. While it was a comfortable exercise to prepare questions for the hypothetical Liam his mind readily conjured, there was no telling what the real Liam would say and no time to devise a particular strategy of approach. Horace reached through the gate and lifted the metal lock on the other side of the wooden door. By way of hello, Liam blew a cloud of smoke in his direction.

It's a common refrain that the poor waste their money on frivolities, drugs, and other cheap thrills. The racists who say this never meant to implicate pale Liam, but with his resource-intensive upbringing bearing a current dearth of personal income, there can be no debate that Liam spent money like the worst of his generation, and his new, plexiglass tornado bong with ice rack to boot was some of the best he had to show for it. Horace, ever the stingy pragmatist, never saw the need to progress beyond a GB^2 (Gravity Bong x Gatorade Bottle) but was grateful for how his friends spoiled him cannabinoidally. There was no high as fresh as one cooled by Hawthorne family ice cubes.

Horace also appreciated the brazen blazing of the Hawthorne back patio, a privilege won through years of subtextual rule negotiations, conspicuously parallel to the federal treatment of weed. The parental class could never admit to their wrong-headed opposition and the children could never cop to their past indiscretions, so an unspoken tolerance was the best either side could hope for. Alcohol was the drug these parents had been eager to introduce to their kids, dropping many hints of wine and the occasional sip of brandy across their teenage years, and so the pivot to weed around the dawn of legality had caught them off guard. Still too preoccupied with their own, their parents weren't ready for the vices of the next generation (see also the internet).

Horace sat down across the table from Liam, whose soft grin trick-mirrored Horace's flat frown. Their houses faced each other too, built at the same time when William Levitt's disciples tilled and planted white-flight homes across Springfield in the 60s. Sunrise's long shadows would cast from the Hawthorne home to casa dos Santos, which sunset could never reciprocate. Horace had learned to embrace the metaphor, not in the least because it kept his room dark a few minutes longer each morning.

Liam's long blond locks, unshowered and corralled by a basic black beanie, were a weathervane for his vigor. This would be an inward Liam, upkeep having fallen to the wayside. Days late for a shave, dark bags under his bright eyes, these things sent their own messages, but Liam treasured his hair most of all. Putting a lid on that mess meant he might not be his usual, assured self.

Horace's thirty seconds of preparation having failed him, Horace waited awkwardly while Liam lit his bong and dragged on it like he was blowing bubbles in the bottom of a soda. He tried and failed to blow rings with the smoke, then offered the bong over to Horace.

"Long time no see, Ace. How was your trip?"

"Fine. We can talk about it later. I, um, am sorry about your dad?"

Condolences about actual death were hard enough, but Horace had no idea what he should be feeling about Dr. Hawthorne. Now that he was in Liam's presence, he decided to take him seriously, if nothing else to avoid triggering any defense mechanisms.

"Thanks. You're the first one to be. I don't know how I feel yet."

To fill the awkward silence, Horace carefully cornered a hit and set the bong on the patio table. Then, remembering weed would only make the silences more uncomfortable, he fished out a cigarette and lit up.

"Talk to me dude. What is going on?"

"I don't really know, man. It's hard to explain."

"Try me."

"If you insist. Cigarette, por favor? Gracias. So . . . I'm just gonna lay all this shit on you. I don't think I've ever said it out loud before, all connected. You can tell me how crazy I sound at the end, but gimme a chance first."

"Of course."

Horace settled in. He enjoyed being the wall off which Liam practiced verbal volleys. The wall never makes a mistake.

"Okay, where to begin? So last fall...no I'll get to that later. Cuz I mean, this shit goes back to the 50s and MK-Ultra, like this is just more of that CIA mind control stuff. It blows my mind that people think they just stopped, ya know?"

"I know. You've said."

In the catalogue of lectures Liam delivered to Horace to pass the time, forming the curriculum of their friendship, two of his favorite subjects were what the US government had "really done" (which Horace tended to believe) and what his father "really did" (which Horace pretended to entertain), and he loved nothing more than to combine the two. Dr. Hawthorne was a mysterious man, prone to long hours in his firm's lab and long trips "away," so it was only natural for Liam to conflate his father with Big Brother. However, with only his active imagination and without a leg to stand on, Liam's speculations (he's concocting deadly poisons or truth serums; he's developing mind control or telepathy; now, he's creating doppelgangers and may even be one) had always struck Horace as wishful thinking to make up for a mediocre reality. He never wanted to burst Liam's bubble, so he tried his best to offer it a soft landing, letting the bubble burst itself.

"So what makes you think it's doppelgangers? That's a new one, right?"

"I'm getting to that, Ace, hold on. Okay, you remember how my dad's firm got started?"

Horace more or less did, but gestured for him to continue, trusting Liam's methods and wanting his friend to get on with it.

"So the year is 1990, and my dad is finally getting around to marrying my lovely mom in a lovely June wedding. My honorary uncles Jack and Mark, who are not so lovely, and maybe now you'll finally believe caught a ride on the Yale-to-CIA pipeline, choose the wedding reception as the time to spring their idea onto Bill, their big pitch, the one that'll make them all the big bucks to pay for these kids they're having. They corner him away from Greta, tell him he's too brilliant to be stuck in some GI lab wading through GI red tape he can only cut with dull GI safety-scissors, and that it's time for a grand neoliberal turn to government contracting. Jack as CEO has the vision, Mark as COO has the connections, and Bill as CTO would bring the expertise. They'd run a light, specialty outfit fulfilling biotech grants for specific clientele of a highly classified nature. That's the official story of Tyrellius Therapeutics. Just three college buds who were big enough fans of Blade Runner to get their company name from it.

"Anyway, decades go by, my sis and I grow up, and it gets to the point where my dad wants out. If not retirement, at least peace. I think he'd been unhappy with their work for a long time. I remember when I was ten or eleven there was this big breakthrough with CRISPR, remember that shit? It lets us edit any gene we want pretty easily, like it's so sick. I remember hearing about it in school and being completely wowed but also confused by it, so I couldn't wait for dinner that night, since we'd finally have something to talk about. I asked him about it hoping it would light a spark in his eyes, and instead he gave me some dry textbook explanation and then clammed up. I realize now he was totally depressed by it. I think he wanted to be working on breakthroughs like that. Instead . . ."

Liam gathered himself, staring straight at Horace. Having warmed himself up satisfactorily, it seemed he was approaching what he needed to talk about. With communicative silence, Horace matched his posture of attention, the shoe so soon to drop. He tried unsuccessfully to chain-light his second cigarette.

"Look, I still don't have full proof for this, but I'm just going to lay it all out there. A few months ago, my dad announced that he wanted to retire this spring. That's when he started acting weird. Simple cause and effect, right? Retirement sure would bug me out too. But I don't think so. December, he got admitted to the hospital for," adding physical air-quotes, "an irregular heartbeat, and when he came back, I know it's cliché, but it's like he was a different person. He went from taciturn to bounding with questions. I always wanted him to take more interest in my life, but not like this. Like, he would ask me how my day was multiple times over a single dinner, as if the asking of the question was scratching an itch unrelated to learning its answer. He'd hit me with deep questions too, totally out of the blue, like what I hoped to accomplish with my life, or whatever happened between me and Flora. Things that take a serious buildup of trust to be able to answer, and here he was just changing the subject to them while I have a mouth full of linguine. At the time, it reminded me of someone trying to follow a conversation while tripping, but I thought that was just a joke. Still, it got me thinking.

"I decided it was finally time I got serious about discovering the true nature of my father's work. I knew everything classified ought to be stored securely on the computers they had at the firm, but I thought maybe I'd find something interesting on his laptop. He wrote his passwords to everything on sticky notes below the keyboard cuz he doesn't trust digital password managers, so I don't think you can even call it hacking. Just opening some doors with the keys left in the locks."

"Bro," Horace finally cut in, wondering whether his face captured his fear or his disbelief more. "What if he found out? That's so risky."

"Dude relax, I covered my tracks. Plus he'd have said something by now, this was months ago. What's done is done, no regrets. Where was I? Oh yeah. Laptop. So, his personal e-mail had nothing interesting in it, unfortunately. Search history, thank god, had nothing disturbing in it. Last thing, I took a stroll through his files, hoping maybe he had some draft grant proposals or something, anything, that would give me a clue to what he's been working on my entire life. And then I found it. God, I found his *screenplay*."

"A screenplay?" Horace had not seen this coming, and felt a prize wheel cycling through all the possible emotional reactions to such a turn. The needle settled on *spin again*. "A screenplay about what?"

"About what my dad really does." It was strange to see Liam look so serious, but that only contributed to Horace's feeling that he was getting punked. "Now I'll grant that my dad's a huge movie buff, but he's a consumer not a creator. Like he viewed my English major as a total waste of time. So imagine my surprise, my shock, my utter fucking bemusement, to find a professionally formatted 90-page screenplay about what is unmistakably a tale of my father's career with him as the tragic hero. The names are changed, but it's about three ivy leaguers—the idealist, the pragmatist, and the oaf—who start a biotech firm together. And wait till you hear what their big project was . . ."

Horace waited in silence, realizing what this was all building up to and not trusting himself to reply appropriately.

"Doppelgangers. They were inventing a way to replace people with other people. For lots of reasons, but the big dream was to replace foreign leaders with look-alikes who would look after US interests. And not some cheap, Shakespearean dress-up-an-actor routine. It was an all-out scientific assault on individuality from the molecular level. See, with the right 'volunteer,' and better plastic surgery than they've got in Hollywood, they could pull off the look of, say Saddam Hussein, who had plenty of body doubles already. But actors have their limits, chiefly being their own identity lying underneath the character. That incongruity would inevitably surface, and the jig would be up. So my father's character, the reluctant genius, sets to work on the problem of the brain, and consciousness, and everything short of the fucking soul itself. How to destroy an individual, and replace them not just with a carbon copy of a dictator, but one ever so slightly altered to be pro-USofA. 'Slightly' being the key word. As Priest's character points out, if they change their dictator to become a good person, all the viziers would smell the funk and oust him. The change needs to be minimal, a US-friendly pivot.

"So my dad goes about it, and against the odds, he has a breakthrough. He synthesizes a new drug, calling it Chemical X which is literally what made the Powerpuff Girls though I don't know if he knows that, that's some kind of LSD analogue, allowing for the total opening up of the neural pathways in the brain for rerouting. Then, I'll skip the details, but they work out a drug-therapy combination that reforms the brains of carefully chosen, supposedly volunteer agents and soldiers so they become, in the deepest possible scientific sense, their target."

"Liam, c'mon. This sounds like a fascinating screenplay, but there's no way it's true, right? You said it yourself—he's a sci-fi fanboy. Maybe he just wrote it for fun?"

12

"Not a chance, Ace. He's not wasting all that time on creative expression for its own sake. There has to be a better reason. I've been wracking my brain for an explanation, and all I can think is it's my dad's confession note, disguised as fiction to get around classification laws. Like, check this shit out." Liam glanced around for dramatic flair, before fishing in the backpack by his feet and whipping out a packet of paper. "I know it sounds absurd, but you gotta see these technical details. Like, he goes into explaining how he synthesized Chemical X and worked out the brain therapy. Look!"

He was flipping through the pages of what Horace realized was the script and pointed to some lines of dialogue with his phone's flashlight and a finger. Horace moved his eyes along the page as if reading it, but he was too confused and overwhelmed to process any of it.

"Huh," Horace replied, he hoped thoughtfully.

"Yeah, it went way over my head and makes no sense to include in a screenplay, like if he was going to option off the rights to this story, they're definitely cutting out the technical mumbo-jumbo. But these science types can't help but show their work. Therefore, I choose to believe it's real, or at least realer than not. Chemical X, the doppelgangers—think about how insane foreign policy has been in our lifetime! Does everyone just being rational actors putting up with the US make any more sense to you?"

"I kinda never think about foreign policy unless you ask me to. But this is just crazy. And impossible, right? I don't think this is gonna convince people on Facebook. Not without more proof, anyway."

"Ah, now you're with me—me and my dad's old boss. Before my dad founded Tyrellius, he was a just a researcher, hard at work in government labs trying to unlock the brain. Chemistry major, Pavlov fanboy, real optimist that the brain could be 'figured out,' down to a chain of causes and effects, ons and offs, you know, and he earned his PhD working under Dr. Louis Sokoloff, basically the father of brain imaging. Sokoloff had this quote from Lord Kelvin, the temperature guy, that he impressed on my dad and my dad branded onto my brain, quoting from memory here that, '*when you can measure what you're speaking about, you know something about it; but when you cannot measure it, your knowledge is unsatisfactory.*' I mention this either because I think it's important or because my dad conditioned me like a dog to bring it up whenever I hear or say the word Sokoloff.

"How do you *prove* something is infeasible? It's a tautology— lacking proof can't be proof of itself. We're looking for evidence, measurables, to make up for my 'unsatisfactory' knowledge. I'm working with a very small sample size, which ain't great for rigor, but I have devised a test. I emailed myself a copy of his screenplay, and I've been hard at work adapting it to the stage. In fact, I chose to post the obituary today in part because of some great news I received. My three-man play has just been accepted for the local fringe festival. I'll be the director, and the lead of course. My dad will be sitting in the audience, and," Liam's eyes lit up, having just fit a cog of his plan into place, or maybe this was his intention all along? "I want you, Horace, to be sitting next to him when he sees his play unfold. He'll of course recognize this as his own work, but once the trap has been laid, we confront him. It can't be me alone, I need the evidence of his reactions to certain scenes, and I know no one as observant as you, Ace. So, my old pal, what say you?"

This question tilted the conversation, and as the slant of the table pitched toward Horace, he felt a little seasick in consideration. Reason screamed in him at an unintelligible volume, while an unfamiliar feeling, small but resolute, stood its ground. He stopped his brain from thinking. If it was a bad idea, all the better.

"I agree conditionally. I will go along with your plan and watch your dad, but I'm not promising I'll be taking your side. I'm just an observer. It's not my job to pick winners. Deal?"

"Deal."

"So what's the play called?"

"It started as a working title, and based on his dumb name for the drug, but I think I'll stick with it. *Solving for X*. There's high magic in math puns."

1.2 ~ The Party

"Speech!" the people cried.

It started with just one, Horace pointing a mental finger in the vicinity of Al, his excitable father, and, "speech speeCH spEECH SPEECH," the rest joined in. It was a mandate, the resonance of champagne and apple cider glasses, plastic fork and knife drum rolls, suburban pagan noisemaking that Bill Hawthorne couldn't deny. Eventually, he made his way under the basketball hoop, a natural focal point in the asphalt circle. Appeased by the upheld palm of his hand, the small crowd cooled and simmered. Pulling out a folded paper from his breast pocket earned a cheer and some laughs.

Horace figured Dr. Hawthorne's social graces as logarithmic to his audience, negative with individuals but reaching a passable level with a sufficient x-value. The man understood people on average, needing the residual weirdness of each person to converge toward normality. The law of large numbers allowed him to serve as a church lector or give a college lecture, but rendered his dissertation defense a notorious disaster, told as a funny story only to sizeable crowds. It also denied him communiqué with the one person he wanted to speak to at the moment, who was presently truant.

"Thank you, thank you all! Can everyone hear me all right?" General assent sounded from the group. "Alright, if you can't hear me, please speak up now!" This got a scattered chuckle. He deferred from his sheet to continue off the cuff.

"Sorry, can never resist a good paradox joke. But kidding aside, I want to take this moment to appreciate this increasingly rare occasion where we're all gathered together. All those Fourth of Julys and graduations, birthdays and barbecues, Christmas parties and homecomings, at least one citizenship party I can remember and, well, now our first retirement party. Let's just hope the weddings come before we old folks die of senescence! Don't worry, I promise to keep the biology jokes to a minimum viable population. No laughs? Okay. Greta and I moved into 101 King Court the same year I started Tyrellius with Jack and Mark. Amazing how time flies, right? Shame they couldn't join us this evening, but they send their regards and I'll gladly send all yours back." A smile, a final scan of the crowd, and he burrowed into the prepared words.

"The Oxford dictionary—now bear with me here—it defines retirement as 'the action or fact of leaving one's job and ceasing to work.' It also defines it as 'the period of one's life after leaving one's job and ceasing to work.' Well, I don't like either of these definitions, they're both a bit grim if you ask me. After all, isn't everything work? In physics, work means the transfer of energy. If I stop working, I become a closed system to myself, closed off from all of you. That's the last thing I want. I'm retiring so I can keep working on the problems worth working on, which means all of you. I want to give my remaining energy to you all, my family, friends, and neighbors, and to this wonderful little hamlet we each call home..."

Horace could already feel himself slipping away from the disappointingly drab sentimentality, drifting to the edge of the small crowd, thumbing his pocket of turquoise Spirits with an intrusive rush of what if, but no, but really what if he lit a smoke right here and now? How mad would anyone be? Was he too old to get in trouble yet? He visibly shook his head and refocused on the apparent angel haloed by the hoop. Horace had done his best to avoid Dr. Hawthorne since that night when something, possibly, transpired between them, had shared his story with no one, not even Liam, and now carried an unprocessed lump in his breast at the sight of the man cloaked in waning sunlight and conviviality. He resolved that he wouldn't tell anyone about it until he could figure out why he hadn't told anyone yet.

"...moving in here with Greta, the love of my life, my better half, the queen of the King Court. Home here started with you and ends with you. Then, there came the Neufchatels, Paul," looking up briefly, "a-and Edith, followed shortly by Louis and Flora, the perfect playdates for Sofia and Liam. Then Al and Maria and the whole dos Santos clan, you practically doubled the population when you moved in! And what a pleasant sight it is to see the Falcos back on the block, Joe and Hellen, we've missed you dearly. They were just telling me Dylan is due back from Guatemala in a few months' time, so perhaps they will oblige us another block party on their old turf for that celebration too. But what is a community without growth and change, and what a blessing that Mitch and Angie could take their place, since we seem to be getting a new Smithson each year! And last but not least, Brunhilde," whose mention mandated everyone, not just Horace, to glance furtively at curtained, weedy 108, "for allowing us to celebrate in the circle and not calling the cops on us just yet." Another scattered chuckle, certainly more reserved.

"Now that I'm stepping back from the firm, I'm hoping to step up around here. We were lucky to raise our kids on this block, and kids, you were lucky to grow up here, whether you've realized it yet or not. I want us all to hold onto this place, to keep it great for the next generation. All societies, all cultures have coming-of-age ceremonies, and I think we do a great job setting an example of how to live in this world. Look at our kids, and how wonderfully they turned out! Now, I want to set an example of how to age gracefully, be a ceremonial grandfather even while I wait to become a biological one. I may be sad to see my time in the workforce coming to an end, but I'm making room for posterity to take my place."

Dr. Hawthorne paused. His placid lector's mask broke, staring at the page, and resurfaced, scanning the crowd. Was it a residue of cold wax Horace felt at his nape? Had the air gone sour?

"Well, I think I've taken enough of your time. Go eat drink and be merry! Remember this is a retirement party, not a funeral!"

This didn't seem to have been on the page. The irony of his dark expression gave his words dead weight in the air. Al seized the negative space greedily, assuring Horace that his father had started calls for the speech.

"Let's have a toast to Bill! Saúde on three! Um! Dois! Très!"

"Sowed!" cried all, even Horace.

17

The Party

* * *

Three hours earlier, Horace knocked on the Hawthornes' door, thump thump thump with his foot, two hands holding a cutting board dotted with bruschetta al pomodoro, crafted by Santa Maria herself: take one rustic whole-grain baguette from a natural bakery across town and slice it thin; brush it with imported Italian EVOO from an olive oil boutique worth the drive for its International Olive Consortium-approved in-house UV-light testing lab; lightly char the slices before rubbing on freshly minced (not chopped nor god-forbid pressed) purple garlic from a farm downstate by way of the local organic market and be sure to get all the way to the edges; swallow briefly your integrity by dicing Florida-grown organic plum winter tomatoes that are regrettably the best March can get; bowl the tomatoes and add finely chopped basil picked from the plant on your kitchen windowsill, a few dashes of fine sea salt, and some deft twists of a coarse black pepper grinder; dole artfully onto carefully arranged bread and serve . . . fresh?

Here Horace's mother's compulsions yet again were at odds. Uncompromising in her kitchen preparing food, uncompromising in her self-flaying deference to social propriety. The result? Soggy bread.

But dutiful Horace knew better than to question her. After all, he had inherited her tendency to less err than veer on the early side of timeliness. This trait was surely epigenetic, as his maternal grandparents and entire paternal line held Mediterranean passports and attitudes on punctuality. As he waited for the Hawthorne door to open, appetizers already in hand should the gift of his time not be enough, Horace weighed how his mother's behavior bothered him, less because she was so unreasonably early, and more because of how it set them apart from the rest of their family. Was it inevitable, he wondered, that your parents' most bothersome traits are the ones you inherit?

His mother carried the curse of being the eldest. She had five younger siblings to look after and two immigrant parents who never stopped working. Horace's aunts and uncles still teasingly referred to her as Santa Maria, earned for her role as handmaiden and bookkeeper of Lady Justice. It was rare for her to settle scores, but she recorded them fastidiously. She tolerated their jokes, only to grumble in private that she'd been left no choice. The sins of her siblings were signs of her failings in the eyes of their absent parents. Horace was just beginning to see how that neglect still haunted her, in how she refused to pass it on.

As the second of four, Horace could see similar traits in his elder sister Dido, though she administered the role of third parent with far more authority, less like her wise queenly namesake than her tyrannical brother, Pygmalion. Thankfully for Horace, she reserved most of her wrath for the twins—Cassandra (who went by Sandy) and Priscilla (who went by Prissy until she changed it to Cilla)—while Horace learned to skirt by in the shadows of everyone's attention, the unobserved observer.

Standing at the Hawthorne doorstep, Horace felt obtrusive and silly, wanting to explain to the imaginary spirits and probably Brunhilde watching him behind his back that he knew full well the party wasn't for hours, and he was just there at the foot of the door to offer a helping hand. He kicked the door again, but softer this time, wanting to mitigate any perceived rudeness at the cost of efficacy. Then, having had enough of the exposure, he shifted the board to one hand and exercised his long-established right to walk through the Hawthorne's never-locked front door uninvited.

Shifting his attention from made-up eyes on his neck to unseen presences down the hall, he could hear two voices, or two versions of the same voice, pitching higher and louder with each turn. He froze, unable to keep himself from listening.

"Mom, do you have any idea how much work is gonna be waiting for me when I get back? It's a miracle I could come at all!"

"But we never get to see you! Please don't learn the wrong lessons from your father. Work can't be your everything."

"Sorry I can't be like Liam, home alone and making messes for you to fix. Sorry I have a life. What do you want me to do, quit my PhD? Start the whole thing over? The only good econ program nearby is for conservative psychos, so this is just how it's going to be for a while."

"I just want you to be happy, and for your life to have balance. I know this has been your dream, but I'm worried about you."

"Mom, look around you. I'm the last one you should be worried about, Jesus. I'm—I'm going for a walk, so please don't self-harm from separation anxiety while I'm gone."

Sofia Hawthorne walked out of the kitchen and right into a wide-eyed Horace, caught in the act. Horace kept on staring at her, hazel eye meeting blue, as his posture slumped to close the already negligible height gap. Her muscles emanated a tension that could surely conquer Horace, even if finally, maybe, he outweighed her, just by virtue of his male density and mother's cooking.

"Oh, Horace!" Her tone defrosting word by word, skidding out of the stratosphere into almost friendly. "What, uh, are you doing here?"

Unable to form an exculpatory sentence, he looked farther along toward Mrs. Hawthorne, now standing in the kitchen doorway, nostrils flared to the exact same teardrop shape as Sofia's, hair grayer, cheeks redder, muscle tone traded for matronly softness, but for all intents and purposes an aged-up photoshop of the daughter before her. Horace tried blinking away his double-vision.

"Well, Horace," Greta began, asserting control over the moment, "I apologize for my daughter's extreme rudeness. What can we help you with? I see you've got your mother's wonderful bruschetta with you, but you know the party doesn't start for another few hours, don't you dear?"

Who needs paranoia with friends like these?

"Sorry for just walking in, I tried knocking but . . . My mother, she wanted to see if, what with Bill's health and Liam's . . . preoccupations . . . Well, she wanted to see if you'd like my help setting up? And I guess the bruschetta is the bribe in case I wasn't enough." He didn't mean to implicate his mother in the midst of

20

this maternal strife, but it was important everyone knew this was not his idea. "So, well, do you?"

"Perfect, Horace can take over for me. My mother clearly prefers people who need direction. Sorry Horace, that was mean."

"Honey, don't take your anger out on him, and please don't twist my words like that. You need to learn how to take constructive criticism."

"Well, you need to learn how to give constructive criticism! Or do anything other than huff around and disapprove of my life choices."

"Sweetie, I'm not saying you've made any wrong choices. I just wish you would slow down and appreciate life a little, spend more time with your family. It's always rush rush rush with you. Well, with everything except—"

"—Oh my god don't even finish that sentence Mom. I'm going."

She was gone behind the slam of a door.

Horace couldn't tell if the embarrassment or the déjà vu was stronger, each contributing measures to his nausea. These two were notorious for their public spats, in contrast to the cold warfare waged between his mother and older sister. Sofia and Mama Greta, Dido and Santa Maria, all defending the battle lines of intergenerational feminism, of where women like them belonged, of what they owed their families and the world. The less-discussed biological clock was the thirty-year timer set in each mother upon the birth of a daughter, as if unused wombs were an intergenerational trauma. At least Horace wouldn't have to deal with all that. Time to change the subject, so he spotted a task.

"Hey, I see that stack of tables and chairs over there. I can start setting up the cul-de-sac? I just need to put this board down somewhere."

Greta beamed with relief at the suggestion, propriety reestablished, and traded Horace his board for instructions on where to find the tablecloths and how to arrange the tables across the blacktop. She was also content that her argument with Sofia could be paused, played, rewound, or skipped to any time she liked.

Horace wouldn't have been there without his mother's intercession, but he did have a purpose of his own. While setting up the tables and chairs with Greta, who had joined with a pronouncement that she could use a cooling off from the hot kitchen air, Horace calculated in silence how best to bring up Liam. Turns out, silence was enough.

"Talk to Liam lately?" Greta asked, then said without waiting for an answer, "I just can't get through to him. I know it's a tough time for you kids, but I can't help but worry."

"No," he lied, trusting Liam to have concealed their conversation from the week prior. While mostly a straight shooter among his peers, Horace knew Liam prided himself as an accomplished fabulist in P.R. (that is, parental relations). Not like he needed to be, his father unable to pick most of his friends out of a lineup and his mother of firm faith that surely each of Liam's friends sported a fresh pair of wings and a harp to boot, but perhaps the combination of indifference and trust inspired more and more brazen lies about how Liam spent his time outside the home. His magnum opus was the invention of a Keyser Söze figure: Ian Noone, the friend who lived under the bus. Liam crafted Ian's history in such rich detail—his hopes (to be one of those guys who gets hired by the FBI after hacking into their security systems in a join-us-or-else deal), his fears (border collies, due to a literally scarring childhood incident, really unfortunate since the Hawthornes' beloved Moxie couldn't be gentler), his pastimes (urban exploring, the less abandoned the better), and his proclivities (that's his smoke you smell on me, sorry mom, we wish he'd quit)—that he eventually had to write the Noones away to Seattle in order to excuse his innumerable reasons to not ever be available for birthday dinners and other Moxie-free gatherings. Liam certainly could tell tales of various heights, no doubt about it.

"He's been hard to get a hold of for me too, like I reached out after his uh, recent post, just checking in ya know, but he ghosted me. Crazy stuff . . ."

Risky behavior from Horace, less accomplished in perfidy, starting with the truth then diverting hard to a lie. Nothing that would register as deceit on Greta's radar though, not coming from cherubic Horace, son of Santa Maria.

"Crazy is right! I don't know where it came from. Growing up is scary, I know, and watching your parents get old isn't easy. I'm dealing with it now too, my father is in a memory unit you know, and I think Liam was really upset by his father's health scare, but I view it as a blessing. Bill's really taken it to heart, exercising vigorously, watching his diet better, he's like a different person now . . ."

Greta caught herself, realizing what she had just said. Horace fiddled with the tablecloth he was draping, as if he couldn't get it exactly square on the round table, side-eyeing Mrs. Hawthorne with reflexively raised eyebrows, daring her to go on.

"That's not what I meant to say. He's just focusing on himself for the first time in years, finally letting go of his work, and I'm really proud of him for that. Like I said, I have no idea what Liam is talking about."

To see such vulnerability in a guardian figure gave Horace a stomachache. Any other situation and he'd change the subject, but this was why he was here, bruschetta aside. He'd have to get used to familial pain if he was to continue accomplicing Liam's plot.

"I'm sorry, Mrs. Hawthorne. I can only imagine."

"No, I'm sorry Horace. I just wish . . . I don't mean to involve you, but I know you two are close, and I'm too close in all this. Can you please, if you get the chance, talk some sense into him? No need to mention me, but try to get him to back down from this little cliff he's put himself on. I'm worried for him. I think he needs help and I don't know how to help him."

"Of course, Mrs. Hawthorne, of course."

What else could he say?

* * *

"Feeling like communing with the spirits?"

The Party

Flora Neufchatel, out of nowhere. Equal parts persuasive and clairvoyant, a gleam in her dark green eyes, an answer to Horace's prayers. Despite knowing these people his whole life, he sure ran out of things to talk about with them quickly. Maybe drinking more would help, that's what all the adults seemed to be doing, but he still held onto his youthful notion that drunkenness was to be withheld from that generation, and engaging in it with them would be to join them in a way he wasn't ready for yet. A sneaky little vice down the trail behind his house was much more his speed. Providing useful cover for their escape, their parents jockeyed to enter the frame or at least catch a glimpse on screen of Flora's older brother Louis, living proof of the scam that is unlimited PTO. He only had time for a short call-in before getting back on his Sunday evening grind.

Horace lit her cigarette first then his own like a gentleman, and they both took a moment to disassociate, enjoy the peace and quiet and tar, look at each other and laugh, all before exchanging a word. Her face conveyed an ambiguous mixture of pout and mirth, elusive like an optical illusion.

"Shoot, I don't have any breath mints, do you?"

"C'mon Horace, once I came back from rehab, I gave up hiding cigs from my parents. Just felt a little silly."

"Yet you're hiding out here with me?"

"I maintain a deep respect for going through the motions, and I don't want to set a bad example for the little ones, dummy. But sorry, no breath mints. I've got some Le Labo in my purse at home if you'd like to smell floral."

"Maybe I'll take a pit stop at my place to freshen up on the way back. If smoking wasn't enough of a diuretic, I had a couple of Mrs. Hawthorne's pastries too."

"Ew, gross."

They laughed and fell quiet. Low light, the end of wooded twilight and the start of suburban lamplight, distant sounds of the steady-going block party (was that a Smiths song they were missing? Or just Morrissey?), and the burning tips of their cigarettes provided focal points for their own silence, something they both understood. Horace graciously broke it first for once.

"Heard from Liam lately?"

"Heard you have."

"Who told you that?"

"He did. He knew I was back on the block last night, so he threw a pebble at my window like old times, just to get my attention. I never blocked his number. He could've just texted me."

She never looked so adult as when she smoked, but who doesn't. Now with her hair in a short bob curled around her ears, neat bangs cut straight, grown nicely from her shaved-head post-rehab aesthetic, she appeared before him as a tiny but matured woman, capable of holding together conflicting emotions, like peaceful worry or forlorn whimsy. Horace felt the urge to compliment her but held his tongue.

"He told me you've got yourselves a little conspiracy going," Flora continued. "Some scheme to out his dad, but he'd only let me in on it if I agreed to help first. I told him I'd have to be crazier than he is to help him. What an attention whore, as if that post wasn't enough. Maybe his dad will finally care about this one."

Her words were accusatory, but her tone softened them. She spoke as if Horace wasn't really there, and neither was she.

"It's true," Horace admitted, "I've gotten myself wrapped up against better judgment. I don't exactly believe him, but I don't think he's lying either. There's just something not right about Bill of late. It's just a feeling, but look . . ."

He told her about their encounter, and the cold wax, realizing she was the person he was waiting to tell. She listened without judgement, steady eyes and pursed lips, another cigarette for both of them. He was ready for her to laugh off the story as typical Horacian paranoia, but the dying light's blue gravity kept his words grounded.

"Flora, please tell me if I sound delusional."

"No, there's something there. Something not right about Bill. I'm not sure how 'of late' that is either. It's just that Liam's apple didn't fall far from the tree. Back when we dated, there were hints.

The years since, I don't know. Moving back home can't have been good for him. I'm glad you're there to help him, for his sake but not yours."

Horace was surprised, though he tried not to show it. A third person on the same wavelength of delusion? What currents were in the air? Something else too, fear perhaps? Fear of the unknown at the very least, a distinct mass of shadow.

"What do you mean? Tell me."

Before Flora could decide how to answer, a rustling came from further down the trail. Horace nervously stamped out his cig, while Flora enjoyed another drag. It took Horace longer than it should have to recognize the figure emerging from the dark.

"Up to no good as usual I see. Party over so soon?"

"Liam!" The concern in Flora's voice held none of the distance she'd maintained with Horace.

"Speak of the devil," Horace quipped as he dapped Liam up. "Listen to that. Sting. Bet my dad's got aux."

"Well, let's join 'em."

No time to freshen up, Liam was off with Horace and Flora in tow. Disguised at first by the tobacco in the air, Horace noticed in their approach that Liam reeked, not of cigs but of weed at the least, a smell dense enough to implicate Horace and Flora too. As they emerged from the shrouded woods into the streetlight, Horace got a good look at Liam and really did not like what he saw. Fully possible he hadn't showered since their backyard rendezvous, when he already was looking unkempt. He had more of a beard than ever, and while the completeness of his facial hair was impressive, the unruly curls contributed to his wild-man appearance. It was unclear if his eyes were weed-red or blood-shot.

The party hadn't missed Horace and Flora. Liam, on the other hand, was a black hole of attention, bending all sightlines obliquely or directly to his appearance on the edge of the cul-de-sac. Greta looked like she might cry, Bill and Sofia donned masks of Scandinavian iciness, Al laughed aloud, Maria's eyes sent enough accusations toward Horace to make him regret every decision he'd ever made, Dido smirked and muttered conspiratorially to Sandy and Cilla who peaked over their shoulders toward the trio, and out of nowhere with threatening joviality an intolerant Paul Neufchatel wavered in front of them.

"Enjoying the woodsy air have we been?" Paul's skewed teeth had always bothered Horace, something he could mostly ignore while at the office, but with its red-wine-stained lips and a halitotic aura, this was a particularly upsetting mouth chewing them out. "But character judgments aside, I'll grant that marijuana is relatively legal now. Flora, I trust it was just the boys partaking? Remember our arrangement," pronounced arrahnge-manh, obnoxiously Quebecois, "and well Liam, we are so glad you could finally join us! You know this is your own father's retirement party you're hours late to, don't you? Or did you forget that?"

"What. No. I had no idea," Liam's sarcasm dripped as loud as his stench.

"And Horace, I can only say I hope this won't affect your work."

The unfortunate aspect of the modern patronage system was that, when a family friend gets you a job under him, you lose the family friend and gain a boss you can't escape. If he had any alcohol-induced (or better yet, natural) courage, Horace might have quit on the spot. He could always find another menial coding job, but he was finally starting to like his coworkers—one of them, at least—so he held his tongue.

"Flora and I weren't . . . Liam just . . ."

Flora saved the day with a disdainful whisper of French, with Horace only catching the words "tobac" and "détends," before switching to English to say, "I can't speak for Liam. He just joined us as we were walking back."

Détente achieved. John Lennon was telling people to shake it up at a decidedly inappropriate time. Liam moved past the clump.

"You missed a good speech from your father, m'boy. Part about you he didn't even get to read. Waste of my good work."

Liam acted as if he hadn't heard Paul, but Horace certainly had.

"What do you mean your good work?"

"What? What did I say? I meant his good work of course..." Then unable to help himself, "Alright, well I did help him with a bit of it. A consultancy. I was his muse, as they say. Bill's a brilliant man, and it takes one to know one. Not the first time we've collaborated, me as his wordsmith. He's got such wonderful ideas, brilliant like I said. So, we're a natural pair."

Typical Paul, thought Horace, never met a boast he could resist. Only, was Liam staring at him from behind Paul? What was the message in his suddenly clinical eyes? Oh, of course.

"Not the first time? What else have you two worked on together?" Pushing his luck in the affect of a joke, "Should we be expecting a screenplay next?"

"What? That would be ludicrous! No, no...just, you know, speeches, for his investors, or accepting awards. Odds and ends over the years." His entire response was contained in a harrumph. He shook his head and toddled off, downing his glass and grumbling about needing more wine. Horace glanced over at Liam, who was beelining for his back gate, before turning to a nonplussed Flora.

"I'll fill you in later."

"How about right now. Barnum?"

1.3 ~ The Conspiracy

Being open was Barnum's specialty, and for that it was beloved. Late nights, the only time worth going, the waitress and the line cook usually took care of it all, two experts practicing the art of maintenance with the zen of getting by. Its congregants were refugees blown in by the winds of insomnia, seeking shelter from their woes of circadian rhythm and blues: miscreants/ne'er-do-wells/vagabonds; carefree punk kids and their Dorian Gray future-selves; families out of the nearby hospital and nurses on their way in; self-talkers carrying on dialogues; tan men inexplicably in suits; amateur art historians confirming their biases that Hopper beat Rockwell to the American soul; drivers of cabs, trucks, buses, Ubers, and maybe even cattle.

Keeping a diner open twenty-four hours a day is as much a philosophical commitment as a business decision. Always on the margin, always dealing with that last rush while anticipating the next one. Smoke breaks and shift changes were the only kinks in the flat crush of time. No before, no after, only a continuous coming and going, cooking and serving, eating and shitting, clearing and cleaning, paying and leaving—overlapping olympic circles ad infinitum.

As a former math major and service worker, Horace thought of restaurant work like the awkward sketch of a circle on a graphing calculator. Working with only x and y, the best you can do is draw a positive arc and mirror it in the negative below. They meet in the middle to give off a circular impression, but the circuit maintains its component parts, one flowing positive and the other returning negative. The circle of service work behaved similarly, like a clock whose two hands split horizontal custody of its face. One hand started at 9 o'clock when the customer walked in hungry, rose to its noon zenith when the food was consumed, and waned to 3 o'clock with satiation and a paid bill; meanwhile, its mirror hand swung right-to-left along the bottom of the clock, governing the busing and cleaning of dishes, wiping of surfaces, and prepping of cuts and garnishes, handling raw meat as good a nadir as any, all in vain hope of meeting its partner at the 9. But every time a new customer sat down and received a menu, off the hands went again. A polar circle would be too perfect to describe this disjointed series that always added up to zero, but only in the long run. No room for tricks up the sleeve, no pre-open or post-close catching up, no pretense, only slow times and fast times. Witching hour was cleaning hour.

***

Horace came up with this comparison back when he was still enrolled in university math classes and waiting tables for spending money. That restaurant, whose specialty was allowing teenagers to commit identity fraud, closed its doors from 2 to 11 a.m. and therefore satisfied the service equation with only statistical rather than mathematical precision. Close enough for the openers to do the rest was the closer's motto.

Horace enjoyed the work because he liked being useful. For that same reason, he'd applied almost exclusively to architecture programs his senior year of high school, writing personal essays about an alleged affordable housing crisis paraphrased from doses of Liam's sophomoric socialism. Though Horace cared little for social issues, the idea of building something that wouldn't crumble on closing night like the sets he assembled for school theater productions, something that might even outlive him, sounded appealing. He'd somehow convinced himself it was his dream profession by the time the rejection letters came back. His ultimate college of choice was kind enough to release his application to the general pool, and he assured himself he could transfer to architecture (or worst-case engineering) after freshman (or worst-case sophomore) year. When college brought about a convergence of his once-good math grades with his never-that-good other grades, the dream's chances slipped as fast as his single-minded desperation for it grew, like a gambler raising the stakes on emotional bets to break even. Test anxiety infected his homework. Social anxiety infected his attendance. Perfectionism infected his existence.

The final round of transfer rejections arrived only a few days after a notice of academic probation at the end of his fifth semester, so it really shouldn't have been a surprise. Only then did he come to terms with the apathy at the heart of his failure. He'd never really cared about becoming an architect, but it had been the last thing keeping him from caring about nothing at all. With the final seed dying, his future withered in barren soil.

The only way his disgrace could feel worse would be to return home and face his mother, so he left his work schedule open that winter, just coming back for a dissociative Christmas, 48 hours of acting fine being all he could manage. That confirmed his parents hadn't accessed his grades at least, trustful by nature as they were. Then right back to work, such was the scarcity of labor during winter break.

Tuition already paid, he enrolled himself in spring semester classes but didn't bother to buy any textbooks. The restaurant became his life, the one place he could still be useful. Every day was like pressing the snooze button on his problems. He told himself Liam smoked every day and was happy, and his coworkers drank daily and were happy, so why shouldn't he be happy? He did both and let go of himself, not just physically but spiritually, untethered from concepts like time and memory.

He lost his virginity the night before classes began. The guy was a bartender who began flirting with Horace on his training shifts and kept escalating until even Horace saw his behavior for what it was. They'd worked late and drank even later, first with coworkers then just the two of them. The morning after, Horace showed up to open the restaurant feeling cloudy and drained, same as most mornings. An older server, a mother-hen type, stopped by to ask him in private if the bartender had been making him uncomfortable, and what had happened after she left them for the night. He pleaded the conversational fifth, not wanting to discuss personal matters with her, but avoided the bartender in question for the rest of his time there. Only with the clarity of his exile did he begin to wonder about questions of consent, or lack thereof, on his part. His shame told him he'd been asking for it, not exactly from that bartender, but from life in general.

That incident served as an inflection point, recession following a high-water mark for the wash of his life. Slowly, he drank less, lingered less after shifts, and made up for it by smoking alone in his efficiency. The brief calls he'd entertained with his parents now danced silently on his phone. The only texts he got were about work, since everyone knew he'd pick up their shift if they asked. Maybe, just maybe, he'd started some introspection about the concept of forward momentum and the rolling out from the rut he was in when a few jovial raps on his door were followed by a round of semiautomatic door-knocker cacophony. It didn't stop, wouldn't stop, till he let them in. He knew this because he knew who was knocking, that they'd driven hours to come see him, that this was the moment he'd been waiting for. He undid the deadbolt, turned the knob lock, and opened the door to his final judgment. His mother's tears soaked his shoulder while she squeezed the life back into him, bringing him out of purgatory into the eternity of her love.

"I am a failure of a mother," she said over and over.

"She finally opened your mail," his father added with a smirk.

***

"Okay dish, what's my papa been up to with Bill?"

Out of superstitious respect for the conversational effects of Barnum, Horace and Flora had spent the short ride there talking of other things, like his recent trip to Guatemala. Flora was sparing him a proper grilling, but his nonchalant answers resembled a duck treading water, working furiously to appear calm. Yes, the country was beautiful. No, things between him and Dylan had been fine, good, normal. Plenty to see there, nothing to see here, et cetera. Now seated at the booth, they could turn to the business at hand, but before Horace could answer Flora's question, the waitress sidled over to their table.

"Sorry, hi, I'll take a water, no ice, and a coffee, black. And—"

"—Ditto, thanks." Horace watched the waitress walk away. "I might ask the same of you. Do you know anything about Paul writing for Bill before?"

"He's mentioned some stuff. You know my dad. He can't help himself around people like Bill. I remember a keynote speech a few years back he helped with. He wanted me to be impressed. You know how it's supposed to be hard imagining your parents being children once? Not for me. He never grew up, still is a gold star collector. You mentioned a screenplay? If that were true, he'd have been dying to tell me."

"Yeah, that was a shot in the dark, but apparently a screenplay is what kicked off this mess with Liam."

Horace's voice had lowered to a whisper by the end of that sentence because he spotted the waitress approaching with their drinks and for their orders, chugging smoothly along the service curve. Neither had more than glanced at the menu, but they were well past that formality and respected the equation, even if neither had the clout to ask for "the usual" (three-stack with blueberries for omnivorous Horace; side of fries for vegan Flora). After ordering, Flora casually stirred, and Horace sipped his coffee, tongue-burn and all. It was one thing to entertain all this in his head, but he felt silly putting voice to Liam's revelations, even in the anonymous din of Barnum.

"It's where he got the whole replacement theory. He went digging on his dad's laptop looking for trade secrets about his work, like maybe grant proposals? But instead, he found what appears to be a semi-autobiographical screenplay? And what an autobiography it is. It's about a . . . well in it, so Liam claims . . . I haven't actually read any of it myself, but it's about three guys who found a biotech firm to, uh, make really high-tech body doubles, or doppelgangers, of like, Saddam Hussein. Not how to make someone look like him, apparently that's taken care of by other people. They're the ones, I guess his dad specifically, who invent a way to rewrite the brain to become someone else's, like the breakthrough is a brainwashing drug. I don't know, I'm not explaining it right, but Liam seems to think it's all real?"

Horace's cheeks felt as hot as his coffee. Nothing like talking out loud to tell you how little you know. His embarrassment warped any helpful interpretation of Flora's expression, which seemed to be some flavor of suspicious disbelief.

"So, what I'm hearing is Liam's dad wrote a screenplay about inventing a drug that can brainwash people into thinking they're Saddam Hussein. And you think my dad helped him write it. And you also think, or maybe just Liam thinks, it's autobiographical. Did I get that right?"

Horace nodded along to Flora's diplomatic parroting. A new motivation, one of relief at being disavowed of this fantasy, entered Horace's mind, and got him to continue.

"Yes, except I don't know where I stand in any of this. Only, I did agree to help him. He hasn't announced it yet, but he's been accepted to put on a play at the local fringe festival, and it's the screenplay, adapted by Liam to the stage. He wants me to, well I agreed to, sit next to Bill when it goes up and watch his reaction. In my defense, I said I'd watch, but I wouldn't necessarily take his side. I'm not going down with that ship."

"Horace you are such a sucker. I love you. You're a good friend for wading into his daddy issues like that. He's finally going to get one on Bill, and he tapped you because he can't be in two places at once! God, I hope his screenplay story is real, that would make it so much better. It's a good roast either way, but putting his dad's private fantasies on display would be rich. Good marketing too. I'll have to be there on opening night."

"It's not marketing! He swore me to secrecy."

That wasn't actually true, but Horace felt like Liam had shared his plan in confidentiality. A confidentiality he was now breaking, telling her what Liam had not. Flora was still in their inner circle, wasn't she? The Flora he grew up with would never blab. That

Flora he could have told anything, the Flora he thought he was talking to when he shared his windstorm encounter with Dr. Hawthorne. Forged of childhood boredom, their bond had seemed infinite. This Flora sitting across from him had traded a lot for sobriety, forced to shed many childhood notions Horace still clung to. He appreciated her honesty, but did he want her to skewer the fantasy so coolly?

"I agree that Liam's motivations could be suspect," Horace cautiously continued, "but I don't think he made up the existence of the screenplay. He showed me something that sure looked like a screenplay. I guess it doesn't really matter if your dad helped write it. Even if he did, I bet he thought Bill was making it up. Not sure it matters if its it's completely true, like what if just parts of it are? Maybe his dad really did contract with the CIA, and this whole doppelganger thing is just a metaphor for whatever he was too ashamed to actually write about. There must've been some reason for him to write it, and I'm with Liam on wanting to know why."

"I could buy that. It is a little out of left field for him to have written pure fiction for kicks. It also confirms my theory that Liam's the exact same person as his dad. They just have to prove their parents wrong in opposite ways."

Horace could see what Flora was getting at. Liam never met his paternal grandfather, but all the stories he'd received and passed onto Horace involved alcohol, which was as good as a diagnosis. Rather than using drugs to escape his family, Bill turned to work. Liam turned to performance, though drugs played a role, too. Generations of sons making up for a father's inattention.

"I see some Greta in Liam too," Horace countered, "he's not all Bill. He cares about other people, for one. He really took me under his wing in high school and stuck his neck out for me plenty of times. I've never gotten the impression Bill cares about anyone but himself."

"It always goes back to him though. Liam, I mean. Date someone long enough, and you know what makes them tick. You'd feel the same as me if you'd had that privilege."

She had played her trump card. Horace thought he knew Liam well, but friendship only went so far. Not only could Horace not appreciate what it was like to date Liam, he hardly knew what it was like to date at all. His only real venture toward a relationship had shown him the person he thought he knew and whoever he turned out to be later could diverge entirely. Maybe Flora had gotten to know Liam better than he knew himself. On the other hand, Flora and Liam had enmeshed themselves fully then tore apart brutally. When they broke up, she may have come away with only the stickier parts of her memories of him. With the distance of time, those clumps and edges could appear to have smoothed, but that didn't make them a complete picture.

"How did that go? The breakup, I mean. I never heard your side of it."

"What did Liam tell you?" Flora sounded defensive, and Horace realized his mind had drifted toward their breakup more than their conversation had.

"Not much. You know how guys are. We were back for break and gaming, and he just let it drop that you two had split. He blamed 'distance' and left it unclear who really broke up with whom. To be fair, we were high, so I wasn't ready to press for more."

"Distance . . . I guess he's not wrong there, but it was than just the four-hour drive. We both had a lot of problems. Instead of helping each other with them, everything doubled up. I was drowning and all he could do was paddle around me and tell me what I already knew while ignoring his own advice."

Suddenly, the service clock struck noon, and the waitress dealt his pancakes and her fries, finishing with a flourish of refilled coffee. They thanked her, and Horace collected a fry tax. A moment of silence followed, save for background chatter and porcelain squeaking against fork and knife. Horace felt ready to change the topic, but while he chewed, Flora kept the ball rolling, tone changing from defense to quick-tempo offense. She had lots of thoughts about Liam, even still, and few outlets.

"His problem is, he has a way of believing in things so thoroughly they become true. The ideas he planted grew, in his mind, in my mind, in anyone's who listened. Trying to prove him wrong proved him right. Like before my injury, he would tell me about this recurring nightmare he was having, of me landing wrong and shattering my bones in increasingly grotesque ways. I don't think he meant to psych me out, he was just processing his dreams out loud, but they infected me. He got me worried, but more than anything I wanted to keep competing just to prove I'd be fine. He wasn't there when I fucked up that vault and cracked my femur, but in my delirium and pain I could almost hear him saying, 'I told you so.'

"What's worse is when he came to visit me after the surgery. He kept apologizing and saying he did this to me, he shouldn't have told me his dreams, that this always happens to him. Maybe it was the oxy and self-pity cocktail I was hopped up on, but I couldn't believe how self-centered he was taking my injury. Like he had to apologize for manifesting it. As if.

"Then comes my awful injury rehab because they kept fucking up on me, like medically, and that led to the drug one because I didn't have much else to feel good about, and I can't tell you which was worse. As I'm dealing with my pain in doctor-approved ways, he's getting high and telling me the dangers of prescription painkillers, how I'm on my way to being a poster child for the opioid epidemic. Like he's one to judge, I thought, given how much he smokes. But again, he believes something, and I try to prove him wrong, and well, turns out there's an unlimited supply of opioids available to college athletes if you cross-check your contacts with the weekly injury reports. I was the only one in my program who'd gotten there needle-free . . . The constant judgment was why we broke up, but his voice in my head never left me. Eventually, his voice and the one that told me to use morphed into one, and I stayed high to drown it all out."

"Thank you for sharing that with me. I'm sorry. I never knew."

Horace trailed off. He had lost his appetite halfway through her story, and now his plate felt miles away. In some ways, this reminded him of the old Flora, passionate and convincing, but it was only a pond's reflection, quivering and murky. So too was his response. He saw the distance she had traveled since they'd all lived on the same block. He knew she'd gone to rehab not too long after she and Liam broke up, so he'd suspected their split had precipitated her drug abuse. Cause and effect were always swapping places in his head.

"Thanks for listening. We had a good relationship for a while. At some point, we outgrew it, and it ended ugly. We're back on better terms now. Rehab gave me a lot of time to think about my own faults. We've both apologized a bit, and the rest is better left to the past."

"I'm glad to hear it."

Horace chewed on her words and pushed around his pancakes. Was this what forgiveness looked like? She and Liam seemed to have reconciled, but they'd left marks, whether they were scabs or scars. Could he and Dylan reach that point too? Would the four of them ever hang out again? Knowing it would never be the same made him wince and search for a new question.

"So," Horace considered, "you're the expert here. What do you think I should do? I feel like you're telling me I shouldn't get involved between him and his dad."

"Hm. I don't know. I still care about him. Selfishly, I want you to keep a close eye on him, so I don't have to. But be careful. He has a way of willing things into existence. Or maybe seeing things that aren't quite real but can affect us anyway. I've also seen it in his dad. Must be a Hawthorne trait."

"What does that mean? Did Bill gaslight you, too?"

When Flora narrowed her eyes they turned to daggers, and her contemplation in the wake of his question seemed like an unsheathing.

"I don't think it's quite gaslighting . . . more like Greek tragedy? Liam fucked with my head a bit, but I'd been lucky to do gymnastics for so long without getting seriously injured. It's just, what you told me about seeing Bill that night reminded me of something." Horace could tell Flora was digging for a dusty memory in the way she kept her face perfectly still, lost to her interior.

"With Papa always working late on the sandwich lawsuits and Louis off at school, I basically lived with the Hawthornes junior year. All those dinners, sometimes he'd say something that would totally disarm me. One time, there was a power outage, crazy winds, pouring down rain. We sat there eating cold cuts by candlelight, and he asked me what I thought my dad might be doing right then. I knew he should be at work still, so I joked about him reading depositions with a flashlight if he needed to, but Bill said, 'No.' He said, 'Your father is thinking about you, and how dark and empty his home is right now. He's hoping you're here, but that means his home is abandoned. No living soul, and now no electric currents either. Once a home dies it's hard to revive.' Like I swear the candleflames started dancing as he said it. Though of course all the windows and doors were closed. I never could get that out of my head. The feeling his words inspired. It wasn't the only time I felt it, but it sounds like what you went through too? I don't know about cold wax, but definitely a chill, something hiding in the shadows you could feel but not name."

"Did you ever ask Paul?"

"About how he felt at that precise moment, miles away? No. Papa and I don't talk like that. But I did go home that night to sleep in my own bed, and he got home sometime after midnight. I fell asleep to the sound of him listening to jazz on his camping radio, and when I left for school the next morning, he was snoring on the couch, morning talk shows chattering away."

39

Flora picked around at her fries, which were reverting to their natural state of soggy potato. The syrup had collapsed the starchy walls of Horace's remaining pancakes. He pinched a fingerful of fries and ate them condimentless, whole fry at a time. He almost stuck two up his nose to cheer her up, but thought better of it.

"What would it mean if Liam's story is true? That the government can brainwash and replace people like that?"

To hear Flora somewhat-seriously contemplating this surprised Horace.

"They're not brainwashing the people they're replacing, to be clear. I think the idea is that they use drug therapy to brainwash the replacements, who get chosen or maybe abducted and modified with plastic surgery. Then they do away with the original the old-fashioned way . . . But I'm sorry, that's missing the point."

"Yeah, like for now those are just ideas from the screenplay and Liam's imagination, right? I'm talking about big picture. If they have a drug that can brainwash people, where do you think they might've used it?"

Horace considered this for the first time. He'd been so concerned with the roots and soil of the story, he couldn't even imagine the forest it spawned. The last two decades of US foreign policy played from a faulty projector in his head. He waited for the waitress, eager for a subterranean cleaning spree, to pick up their plates and leave the bill before answering Flora's question.

"I hate politics because it's all just self-interest. Greed explains our actions, coercion and self-perseveration explains everyone else's. Honestly? I'm not sure if this changes any of that. It's just a tool, this doppelganger program. We've got battleships, and drones, and unlimited money for war, so what difference does it make if we also are replacing foreign leaders with ones that like us a bit more. They're all already afraid of us, doesn't that accomplish the same thing?"

"You sounded like Liam just now. But I'm thinking, if they could do this, why stop at foreign leaders? Liam thinks his dad got replaced. They invent this weapon of war and then turn it on their own. You could purge dissidents without anyone catching on. You know, there was only one person in Congress who voted against the war in Afghanistan. Could they have put that drug in the Capitol's water fountains?"

People were always asking Horace to think about the early 2000s, all those changes following 9/11. Though he'd been very young, he remembered bits of that day, but sometimes he questioned if his memories were just fictional rehearsals, composited from retellings by his family and eventually himself. Flora was only a year older than him, and so both of their understandings of the fervor following the attacks were constructed post-hoc. What he would never forget was that feeling of alienation, when he learned for the first time that kids just like him could differ so strongly in their beliefs, with their glib desires for death and suffering and vengeance from wrongs none of them understood.

"I don't think they needed to," Horace replied after some thought. "There was enough in the air that they didn't have to touch their water. The people wanted blood."

"What about Obama? Talked a big game about hope and change, and then shows up in office for business as usual. Maybe they got him during the transition?"

Horace shook his head, having reached his fill of this political talk. Dr. Hawthorne's invention could change some whys and hows in recent history, but the what was locked in. Flora had come so close to disabusing him of Liam's theory, then went full circle into taking it more seriously than he did, as if she'd talked her way through Hawthorne-related scar tissue and tapped into deeper feelings.

They got up to pay the bill and walked out feeling neither full nor satisfied. It was past midnight and winter's recession would still grasp these hours for a few more weeks, so they hurried to the car. Flora would drop him off before returning to her apartment in the city. She still referred to King Court as home and her apartment as just that, but Horace suspected this was only for his benefit.

As they listened to Beach House, Horace studied the dark homes they passed on the road. It occurred to him that they'd spent their entire meal talking about Liam, how typical. They could leave him behind in the diner.

"How are you doing? How's life and work and stuff? I feel bad I didn't ask."

Flora had taken a semester off from college for rehab and recovery, but even with the bad grades leading up to her collapse, she still managed to graduate on time. Her collegiate athlete work ethic was now put to use doing communications work for a foundation "lifting up the artistic voices of historically marginalized peoples," something from that weird category of corporate social responsibility left Horace queasy. It didn't help that her dad's company was the foundation's primary sponsor, though Paul was enough of a lowbie that it was doubtful he got her any favors in hiring. She got paid to attend smaller showcases, take pictures, and write posts. It was as legitimate an entry-level job as any.

"It's going really well. I'm interviewing for a promotion, actually...But, I'm sorry, we spent all this time talking about my ex, so now it's your turn. Seeing Dylan was just fine? I know there's more to the story."

"Nope. Me and Falco are just friends now, as we should be."

"You flew all the way out there to visit him as a friend?"

"That's what he expected."

"I'm so sorry."

"It's fine. Let's talk about anything else."

1.4 ~ **The Invitation**

Exiting the chartreuse hallway, Horace entered a kitchenette spilling into a greenhouse: a countertop of living herbs, wall-to-wall carpet for soil, potted rubber and spider and snake plant shrubbery, an understory of ficus and yucca shooting upward, the sword fern and english ivy canopy reaching down to meet them, an expansive south-facing window feeding them all, while a family-sized humidifier vaped thickly in the far corner. Horace couldn't help but take a deep breath in through the nose and out through the mouth at the sight. The threshold of her door felt interdimensional.

"Jena, this is incredible. How'd you get so many plants?"

"I bought them!"

Jena Reus liked to answer questions literally, a German characteristic he supposed. She also found the humor in everything, life not as one big joke but an unending series of small mirth and harmless mischief. On her first day at work, she told him a story about organizing a climate strike just to postpone an exam. She nominally attended college in the US, but spent half of her semesters abroad, each time somewhere new, except for/including a homesick spring back with her family taking classes at Berlin Technical. Anywhere the universal languages of English and Python could take her, she went. When Vein Holdings, their mutual employer with arteries flowing globally, offered her yearly projects and relocations, how could the roving flaneur say no?

She was the only coworker Horace liked, and she was technically his supervisor. On that account, he'd been sheepish about hanging with her outside of work, but needing some distance from his neighborhood drama, he finally agreed to one of her many invitations.

"What are you going to do with all of them when you move?"

"I don't know. Next January feels so far away. Maybe they all die, and I start over. Or maybe you take them?"

43

"Same result in the end. My mom might take some? She's the green thumb of the family."

"Good for her. My thumbs are still normal-colored. I should pet my plants more, so they will turn green. That would be fun! I can paint my nails green to start. Do you want me to paint yours too?"

Horace had never painted his nails before, and he was still standing with a jacket under his arm. He felt overwhelmed.

"Maybe! Can we sit down first?"

Horace got first choice of seat while Jena rummaged for clean wine glasses. Couch, bean bag, hanging chair, rocking horse, ottoman, large pillows from the couch set, all arranged in a circle around an oval wooden coffee table decorated with assorted cups and mugs, a rice-cooker-esque metal cone, and an incense stick tracing cursive smoke in the air. It took Horace a moment to place his disorientation. There was no television. Too hip.

He chose the far side of the couch, and Jena settled in the middle, closer than Horace thought necessary. He didn't want to give her the wrong impression, so he cast his eyes across the room, looking for something to catch hold. He saw suggestion in the LED strips painting shadows of transitioning colors on the eggshell walls, in *Songs About Jane* spinning softly on the turntable and sneaking out of the speakers, in the candles and incense wafting him back to Catholic temptation, in the bottle of red pouring into two stemmed glasses.

"I love that we are friends! It is so lonely moving to a new city."

"Don't you do this every year?" Horace asked, while pondering the German cognates of friendzone.

"The challenge makes it more fun! There are so many wonderful people in the world, and I want to meet as many as possible. I make myself lonely so I can start again. It has been difficult here because your city is unfriendly. Everyone already knows each other, and they are not having room for more. That is why I am glad I met you."

"Likewise," finishing his reply with a gulp of wine.

Horace's social life was cavernous at the moment, and not by design. He admired her exploratory attitude, but preferring making friends to having them was the most foreign thing about her.

"Maybe I will get a boyfriend this time. That way is like cheating to having lots of friends because you get the whole group at once. My boyfriends are always mad at me because I like their friends so much."

"Well, you can add that to the reasons I wouldn't make a very good boyfriend for you. That I don't have many friends, I mean."

He chased his reply with a swig of wine, which carried notes of foot-in-mouth.

"Yes, you are not my type. I like my boyfriends to have nice beards. With you, I would have the beard, or? I just learned that phrase, did I use it correctly?"

"Wait, did you mean that you'd be wearing the pants? Or, oh you mean that you would be a beard. Yes, that is true. Had I told you that?"

Horace knew he hadn't. He enjoyed neither telling people his sexuality nor them assuming it. It wasn't anyone's business but his, especially at work.

"You didn't need to. I have never seen you stare at my boobs, and no straight guy has ever resisted. Relax, I am joking. I can just tell. I have met so many people, so it becomes easy."

So much for worrying she was going to put a move on him, which was egotistical in retrospect. Offering to paint his nails ought to have been a clue.

"I like to keep my life private at work. Not that I'm worried about, like, discrimination. I don't know . . ."

"Then it is a very good thing we are not at work! None of them are good enough for you anyway. Are you single? I bet I can find both of us boyfriends."

"Very single. Sorta recently there was this guy, and we were friends for a while, and then more than friends for a bit, but now he has a girlfriend, so I'm out. I don't know if I'm quite ready to get back in yet. Sorry, can we talk about something else?"

"Oh baby, I am so sorry. Bisexuals are tricky. I have been there. Threesomes are fun until both want to date you instead."

***

Horace and Dylan dated, or something like that, over the course of Dylan's last months before deployment to the Peace Corps and Horace's first spring back home, directly following his parents' extraction mission. As childhood friends who'd grown apart, their coming together both thrilled and discomforted Horace. Having never felt less deserving, Dylan's attention confused Horace as much as it flattered him. He coped with it all by pretending. He hated himself, and Dylan loved himself, so he tried to act more like Dylan, carefree and cool, to forestall the day when Dylan realized Horace had nothing going for him and lost interest. It seemed to work, or at least they continued to hook up and hang out, until Dylan shipped out. With that, the clock struck midnight, and Horace turned back into a depressed pumpkin. Rather than grapple with the reality of their relationship, it was easier for Horace to look back on it as a fairy tale.

While Horace had felt magically better in Dylan's presence, his sudden absence rendered clearly all the work Horace been putting off. It takes work to heal wounds, even if time pitches in too. Summertime's sun stuck around longer, making it harder give up on days so quickly. Calendar time stretched the distance from his winter collapse, an increasingly silly thing in his rearview mirror. Family time with his parents reminded him the stakes of his exile, as the wide berth his parents allowed him gave way to a circling— Al like a subtle shark and Maria an eager sheepdog—both searching for signs of directionality in their son.

Family time with his younger sisters reminded him of who he could be and who he once was. Sandy and Cilla were in middle school when Horace left them behind for college. Hormonal and distraught messes, they were as enigmatic to him as the girls in his grade had been at that age. He returned to find them as cool and composed sophomores, perhaps overly so. Sandy was an athletic workhorse, the soccer prodigy of Al's dreams, and the clarity and determination with which she expressed and pursued her goals made the time he spent taking over Maria's weekly travel-team carpool shift worthwhile and mildly therapeutic. Just like Dido, Sandy took more after Al, a capacity for single-mindedness lightened by a good sense of humor.

A testament to the incomplete destiny of genetics, her identical twin Cilla was clearly her mother's child, which was why Horace related to her more. She blossomed in high school, devoting herself to uncompromising self-expression. It started with her name change, deciding one day that she was not Prissy and never had been. She told their parents that Priscilla was a perfectly fine name they had given her, so they could call her that or Cilla, or wait until she turned 18 and watch her change it altogether.

Tired of being the family doormat, she bottled her preciousness, claimed the biting tongue that was hers by dos Santos birthright, and exercised taste and judgment at will. Like Horace, she recognized traditional popularity was not her game, but rather than following Horace or a Liam of her own into the theater scene, she formed her own clique that dedicated itself to underground music scenes, poetry, and feminism. Horace perceived a veneer, a raw performance of individuality and maturity that overstepped reality a tad, but he never doubted the intensity of her feelings.

Horace and Cilla also helped each other come out to their parents, who accepted him far more easily than her. It didn't help that neither Maria nor Al knew what "pan" meant, though it did provide Al a layup of a dad joke. She told them at the dinner table, like announcing an intention to apply to art school. She hadn't taken steps to pursue it yet, but she knew what she wanted and wanted her parents to know. They received her with skepticism. Dinner ended when she stormed off to her room. As Horace cleaned the dishes with his mother, he took his quiet stand, the words "gay" and "too" slipping out like frogs, small and ungainly and bouncing around the room. Maria told him she already knew that, of course, then she left the kitchen. Stunned numb, he watched as she crossed through the dining room toward Cilla's door and knocked. Still feeling owed, he followed her in when the door opened. Together on Cilla's bed, they came to an understanding.

What shocked Horace most out of his doldrums was how Cilla and Sandy both still respected Horace as their wise older brother, worthy of consultation and eminent in his opinions. Sandy told him she had days she didn't want to train and could easily see that spilling into weeks if she wasn't careful. Cilla already expected college to be bullshit—an attitude Horace tried to discourage—and so she didn't blame him at all for losing interest in it. He was still Horace to them, and through that, he started to remember who Horace was to himself.

Horace would have been content to let time pass like this for much longer than he got. Al, who spent each present moment concocting future schemes, decided of his own volition to craft a deal for Horace. He consulted their neighbor Paul Neufchatel for advice on how to set his wayward son up for success. Having come to the States to study business, Al had never put much stock in liberal arts educations, so he inquired about the career paths opened by and for entrepreneurial disruptors. Paul had just the answer he was looking for. If Horace finished his associate's degree at community college and graduated from a coding bootcamp, Paul could probably hire him for his upcoming project. Except, when Al told Horace, brimming with excitement, the "if" and the "could probably" were omitted. Horace lacked direction? Al would be happy to stand and point. Paul was his son's ticket to the good life, and the train would be leaving the station immediately.

A poster child for late boomer MBAs everywhere, Paul Neufchatel boasted a long career of applying econ 101 to struggling businesses like a stake to an innocent vampire's heart.

Various Wharton influences had put him on the radar of Vein Holdings, a New York-based multinational, multi-industry, private equity, public contracting, and management consulting behemoth whose founder, Tevin Vein, was a fellow alumnus. Paul soon established himself as an effective lieutenant in the company's crusade against insufficiently capitalized entities. A man well-acquainted with boots and their straps, flavors and odors too, he blessed each business endowed to his clutches, for a respectable salary but a salary nonetheless, with a loving kiss of death.

Some bold type on his CV: the Cents and Sensibility Project, in which local bookstores were bought up, gutted, and outfitted as atriums for banks; the Sandwich Diet, in which "less is more" was applied literally to an up-and-coming regional sandwich chain that folded after a class-action lawsuit regarding the length of their footlong sandwich; and now, Paul's finest mission yet, Fitting All the News to Print, a publishing revolution to rival Gutenberg by only printing previews of articles in the paper and providing a QR code to their website with the rest of the story online. The space saved became real estate for more ads, the links were full of redirects and pop-ups that porn sites would consider obtrusive, and to encourage subscriptions ("Receive the full benefits of our journalism dividend!") most articles never appeared in their full form in either location.

Paul wouldn't promise Horace a job; he promised him an opportunity. "An opportunity for a job is better than a job itself," Paul explained, "because it teaches you how to convert future opportunities into future jobs." Horace, color draining from his face every time he thought about the moment, had actually thanked him for this.

Horace did as he was told, though not without fits and starts. A year and a half later, with an associate's degree on his wall and a coding bootcamp completion certificate in his inbox, Horace was finally eligible for the deal he half-hoped had expired, caught between the dread of working for Paul and the misery of applying to other jobs. Paul, who was nothing if not loyal, came through, and Horace started in September as a "software intern," something paid low-enough that Paul had direct authority to hire. Horace got paid minimally to do absolutely nothing until Jena was brought on as lead software engineer that January.

Their project was to design a new template website they could copy and paste to the newspapers Vein was purchasing and gutting. Their primary directive was to doctor clickbait, stop worrying, and love the ads. Horace's coding education had mostly focused on reducing time-complexity in Python rather than web-design in JavaScript, so he wasn't much help at first. Meanwhile Jena was worth a team on her own, suturing the pages together with imaginative syntax, suspending unstable drop-down menus over a sea of spam, making a game of tricky x-outs for pop-ups, auto-resizing ads to occupy the same space no matter the shape of the window, and boldly innovating heretofore unseen frustrations in UX. Having learned the ropes as a swashbuckling music pirate, she enjoyed the challenge of applying the exact opposite of the design principles she learned in college.

She presented her job as amoral rather than immoral. Yes, it bothered her that her performance metrics included ad clicks per day, that the fruits of her labor were frustration and misdirection, that her elegant code resulted in ungainly interfaces, but where else could she get the experience designing her own moderately-trafficked websites? She reasoned that we all work ugly jobs on the way to pretty ones. She might as well be a professional about it. The best thing Jena did was sever her work self from her personal self. A job is a job, not a vocation, not a crusade, just a way to make money to spend on life's remainder.

Taking advantage of the open office plan, they started sitting next to each other, basking in the company of youth among fuddy-duddies and over-the-hill 30-year-olds with, god help them, families. Jena had just turned 30 herself, but something about being European and actually fun set her apart. They traded memes, staged ambitious Wikipedia Game tournaments, and practiced their impressions of Paul. They became work friends, rafted together for buoyancy, hitched by the twine of commonalities to float above dull seas. Horace enjoyed how she kept asking him questions till he eventually answered, demonstrating a dedication to hearing what he had to say. She was easy to talk to and talked easily, neither of which Horace would say about himself.

***

In short order, Jena introduced Horace to the Volcano. Turns out that rice-cooker-like apparatus on her table represented the state of the art in weed vaporizers. As she explained in between puffs, two German stoners began manufacturing the Volcano in the opposite corner of Germany from where she grew up, in an industry town dedicated to medical devices. This medical device vaporized herb in its convection oven base, releasing its cloud into a detachable plastic balloon connected to the top, ideal for attendant nurses to minister the cannabinoid sacrament to their wards and invalids. They marketed its medical uses with a straight face, but the undiagnosed everywhere recognized it as one of the most pleasant ways to get high. She and Horace passed the bag back and forth all night while they chatted.

When you're first hanging out with a coworker in a liberated setting, there are some hallmark topics to hit. The wine and weed spoke louder than words, but what about other drugs? Jena had lots to say on this matter, considering it her culture. You think Germans lack a sense of humor? Well what could be funnier than introducing cocaine to the world as a prescription analgesic? Try to deny the pure comedy of Albert Niemann synthesizing it for his PhD thesis at the University of Göttingen, and Freud's buddy Karl Koller testing its ophthalmological potential by rubbing it on his own eyes and poking them with pins, pain-free as a slapstick comedy. Or consider Bayer's Felix Hoffman acetylating morphine in hopes of producing the weaker, less-addictive codeine, and ending up with an opiate so fantastically strong he named it heroin. Then there's a personal favorite for Jena, its Christian name being methylenedioxymethamphetamine, which she wanted Horace to know was not first patented as an appetite suppressant, like the urban myths say, but rather as an intermediate step to dodge a Bayer-held patent on a blood-clotting agent. It lurked on the fringes of research until the 60s, didn't hit the streets till the 70s, and only got coined as Ecstasy one year before Nixon outlawed it in 1975. Also, while Jena would insist that she's tired of bringing up the Nazis every time she talks about her homeland, no discussion of German drug discovery would be complete without mentioning Pervitin aka Panzerschokolade aka tank chocolate aka crystal meth aka a big reason why Nazi Blitzkriegs could move so fast. Some say the Führer himself was hopped up on Pervitin, although that's a History Channel leap off the curious fact that his physician would mark "X" in his journal for an unspecified cocktail he'd give addled Adolph.

"Hold up," record scratching in Horace's head, "you're telling me Hitler was on some Chemical X?"

"No one knows what he was on. Some say it was an opioid because he got a big dose of it after his generals tried to assassinate him with a bomb. I would need some good pain killers after that. What is Chemical X?"

At last, the ball had been teed up, and Horace was vibing and ready to swing.

"So the other week, my friend posted this thing . . ."

He went on to explain it all—the doppelgangers, the screenplay turned actual play, the vague outlines of Flora's concerns—talking without interruption for far longer than his cross-fading brain was comfortable with. Jena was rapt from start to finish, then launched a flurry of questions Horace felt unequipped to answer. He had to wrap things up.

"Anyway, I still think Bill wrote it to imagine a more interesting life for himself. Like, we'll see I guess, but there's just no way it's real."

"Oh, I hope it is all real, that would be way cooler. What if Liam was replaced too? What if everyone in your life had been replaced, except you? You could only trust me! I am the real deal, or?"

Jena started giggling at herself here, and Horace succumbed to the humor of it all too. But by the time they subsided, Horace could feel distilled paranoiac panic brewing in his stomach and hoped Jena would change the subject to free him from further consideration of this idea. Jena delivered, loving nothing more than a new topic of discussion.

"Ah, this is so fun. We need to hang out more! Where do you go out around here? What is fun?"

"As long as I live with my parents, I don't do fun, sorry. I know there's plenty of bars in the city people go out to, but I honestly don't even remember names of any good ones right now. I'm lame, I know."

"I think I have been going to these bars, and I agree with you, they are not very fun. You have clubs here, but you do not have *klubs*." Playing up the German pronunciation here so Horace, who had been dragged out to discotheques by his cousins in Portugal once or twice as a high schooler, could guess what she meant.

"Yeah, none of das funky beats in this town, sorry. I guess concerts are the closest you can get."

"Well . . . There is a place I want to try. A man invited me last weekend. Get this. I am out at a dumb bar, no fun because it is all rap and no techno. No one dances on their own because everyone has their boy or their group. How do you make friends like that? I am drinking a beer at the bar, and a man sits next to me. He is handsome, and he definitely has good arm muscles under his dress shirt. He looks like a taller version of you, and he smells amazing. But I am just happy to have someone to talk to. He asks if I am having fun, and I say no. He gives me this card, and I am thinking it is his name and number. But no! The card says 'E-D-E-N' and has an address and a date and a time, 12 June at 9 p.m. It is a very fancy card, and it smells like he did, but I do not know what it means, so I ask. He says it is an invitation for the opening of a secret special *klub* in town. I can get in with this card, and I should bring a friend too. I am very excited, and I ask if they play good music. He tells me they have a DJ every night, and they play things like trance, which is so my favorite for dancing. Then I am thinking, is this for real? So I ask if it is some kind of sex thing, because I do not want that. He laughs and says, isn't that all clubs? I say not for me, I just want to dance. He says it will be the best dancing of my life, and he gets up to go. Then he says this was just a free invitation, but if I like it then I can become a member. I am so interested! What do you think?"

She pulled the card out of her purse and showed Horace.

"I think you're crazy! You go out alone? Isn't that dangerous?"

"I don't have many friends here yet, but you could go out with me. My protector, and my gay best friend. It is perfect. Are you free on 12 June?"

"You actually want to go to this place? That guy screams sketchy. I don't want you getting human trafficked, or me for that matter. I'm a better target than bodyguard."

"But I am so curious! I need to find out. If this place plays good trance, I must try it. Please, please come with me. Maybe they serve the Hitler cocktail?"

"Yeah, maybe. Have you looked up the address? What part of town is it in?"

She had not, and so they popped it into Horace's phone. The pin stood in the richest part of the city, not where people typically go out. There was a golf course wrapping behind it, and Horace was pretty sure he'd driven Sandy to some private school homecoming pre-party at a mansion nearby. The building itself appeared to be a former church, a staid Presbyterian affair with a steeple to boot. The street view still had the sign with mass times and a blurry bible quote, but the address was no longer listed as such. Who knows how long it had been since the scaffolded Google car had driven by, but there was no indication it was a club either. They switched tacks and tried searching "Eden club" on Google. The first result was a chain down in Texas with the same name. It was a swingers club. Horace had seen enough.

"Okay, no thank you! Not for me."

"No, this one has a different font! The man told me it is not a sex club."

"I don't know what to tell you. Let's go out together somewhere else."

Horace surprised himself with how firmly he'd stated this. While more of a slow burn than flowing lava, the Volcano had taken its hold on him. He shuddered as a valve that had been closed in his mind turned open, and anxiety slithered in. He had trained himself to accept the snake rather than fight it and risk entanglement, but his guard was down. He didn't like the stranger who had approached Jena, and he suspected that if this one wasn't for swinging, it would offer something even worse. His anxiety thrived on spinning out vague information into concrete fears, but he wanted to be braver.

"I think I will go. I trust that guy. He is not a creep. I know creeps. He was a salesman. He knows I will like this place. I must at least try, and if I don't like it, I will leave. Life is short, or?"

"Ugh, fine. If you're set on going, I'm not letting you go without me. I really hate this, but I guess I'm in."

"Yes! It is a date! A date to find us boyfriends."

As if one questionable scheme wasn't enough. Horace desperately wished he knew how to say no to his friends.

1.5 ~ The Pamphleteer

Horace needed backup, ideally a second version of himself. The falafel balls, guesstimated tablespoons varying widely, required constant attention, each on their own fickle schedule in the coconut oil bath. He'd switched recipes on the fly from "herb-alicious homemade tahini" to "easy-peasy lemon tahini" to skip steps and save time. The rice simmered suspiciously (or suspiciously appeared not to simmer) under the metal lid, tempting him to take a peek, to ruin it (or save it from ruin). The tabbouleh would be a hit because he bought a tub of it at the store, one less thing to worry about, but could he get away with replating it and calling it his own? The pita bread, oh god the pita bread, he only meant to warm the first round up but was looking now, and of course they were burnt. If they'd been more well done, he could have excused just chucking them and starting over, but he hated wasting food. Every surface in the kitchen was covered with his culinary sprawl, so he had to scoot over a mixing bowl and position the pita pan as to precariously overhang the sink. It was about time to change out the round of falafels, and it was past the time he'd promised dinner would be ready. His mother popped her head in from the dining room.

"Horace, sweetie, can I help with anything?"

"No, I'm . . ." he stopped himself there. The salad needed to be mixed, the dressing made, the table set, the dishes bowled, the sink cleared, the floor swept, the oven turned off, his brow wiped, his conscience forgiven, his ego stroked, his crisis averted. It was only dinner, but yes he could use some help. Maria understood this, and didn't wait for permission. She walked into the center of her culinary temple and silently assessed. Her son was stressed out, and talking more would do him no good. He nodded in appreciation at her, then gave his full attention to the falafel. She danced around him gathering dirty bowls and utensils, transferring them to the sink and sliding the hot pan to safety. This unearthed a red onion that Horace had meant to quick-pickle before he started cooking, but (as if detecting regret on his face) she grabbed it, chopped it, and placed it in a wooden bowl that moments later held a resplendent salad.

Anxious on the verge of dinner, the rest of the household all drifted near. Al appearing first, grabbing a beer and testing a falafel in the meantime but finding it regretfully hot for his mouth, then Sandy refilling her water bottle and getting pressed into setting the table, and finally the moment prep finished, Cilla coming downstairs and queueing a jazz trio and lighting a candle. No need to call for dinner, everyone had called themselves. Horace rued that his family could estimate his cook times better than him. They all sat as one, seeming happy, even Horace. Obligatorily, they muttered a quick grace and Horace answered questions about each dish he had prepared, and everyone laughed when Sandy held up the tub of tabbouleh and asked how he'd made the plastic and printed the label. Horace was beaming. Then Maria changed the subject.

"I ate lunch with Greta today. The poor woman, her son is still not speaking to his father. I do not get it. Horace, why have you not talked sense into Liam?"

"Because Horace isn't a miracle worker? Like he's not literally Annie Sullivan? And Liam is a maniac?" Cilla here was only coming to Horace's defense collaterally on her way to disagreeing with whatever Maria was saying.

"Liam is a good boy," offered Al, whose impressions of people were generally locked in from the first, "but I dislike his crazy talk. Why does he not apologize and move on? Tell me, Horace."

"Personally," chimed in Sandy, "I think he did one too many drugs and now he's a lost cause. I don't know why you still hang out with him, bro."

This was an unexpected betrayal from Sandy, preempting Horace from downplaying their friendship of late. But he was tired of denying it. He wanted to protest that Liam was his same old self, but if that were true, that was even more damning.

"I am trying to help Liam, and he needs friends right now. Him and Dr. Hawthorne have always had a weird relationship, and sometimes the only way out is through, I guess. He's really excited to do this play this summer in the local fringe festival, and I think that will be good for getting things back to normal. I'm, well, I actually agreed today to help him produce and direct it, so he can focus on acting and stuff." Horace could tell his family took this revelation poorly and dearly regretted volunteering the information.

"Horace, do not be dragged down with that boy." Maria's words rushed out with concern bordering on pain. "You have enough trouble as is. Why are you looking for more?"

"I didn't go looking for it! He asked me. And I said yes. I'm happy to help him. That's what friends do. Do you not want me to have friends?" Feeling knocked off balance by Maria's reaction, Horace was shoving right back. No chance now of talking this down now, his retaliation made it a fight.

"How could you say that. Of course I want you to have friends. Good friends. Like who Liam *used* to be. People who respect their parents, who apply themselves, who don't just do weed all day and fry their brains."

Horace hoped maybe Maria saying "do weed" would be enough to merit a Cilla tag-team, but she was nowhere near the ropes, recognizing a smackdown in the making.

"Well, I don't have that many good friends right now, so I'll take who I can get. I guess I thought it might be nice to get back into theater, and good for both of us to get outside of ourselves a bit. You know, self-expression? Aren't I supposed to be working on that?"

"Horace," Al interjected, "do not talk to your mother like that. She is right. This idea is a terrible one. What is this play even about?"

Even in a tense situation like this, Horace couldn't help but appreciate his father's inability to be mad effectively. He clocked Maria's flinch of a scowl at the question and blessed his foresight to have discussed this question—the question of a cover story—a few hours earlier with Liam.

***

Horace and Liam observed a new-age religion on Sunday mornings, a polytheistic affair at the altars of Nintendo and Microsoft and Sony. Only dating back to sometime the previous fall after Liam moved back home from Manhattan, it began as a great excuse to not accompany their families to church, to which both sets of parents tried guilting their wayward sons into returning. Easy enough to just roll over in bed and ignore the Sunday morning knock-knock on their bedroom doors, but Horace still felt the guilt seeping under the doorway and disturbing his sleep. He had to find something else to do Sunday mornings, both to assuage Maria and to prevent himself from bleeding out the entire day in bed.

Like most religious practices, the mythos filled in behind a simple habit. In the beginning, there was a biking component, as college had converted Liam to cycling zealotry, and he kept badgering Horace into going on strenuous leisure rides with him. Sunday morning just happened to be the most convenient. For maybe a month of Sundays straight, they rose around 10 and met each other to bike about town, making a point to swing by the Hawthorne's church a few miles away. Liam got more out of the joke of literally going to a church every Sunday than Horace, who just needed the exercise. Afterwards, video games and a couple puffs of weed felt like a heaven they'd earned. Then the weather turned, first an unlucky pattern of Sunday rain then a nasty spell of cold that took hold and never let up, so they decided biking could wait till spring. No reason to give up the gaming however, and thus their modern ritual was born.

What little they talked was never personal. Like anti-therapy, they segregated this time off, disconnecting from their real worlds and plugging their controllers into the matrix. In the few weeks following Greta's request to talk sense into Liam, Horace meekly avoided asking him about anything that could result in talking nonsense about his schemes, fantasies, or family members. This separate peace held until Liam chose to bring those things up himself, which he finally did in the lobby between Rocket League matches. Horace was waiting for Liam to mark himself ready and start the search.

"Ace, I've been thinking."

"Mm-hm?"

"About what I asked you to help out with."

"Defense?" Horace wasn't being thick, just reflexively awkward.

"Yeah that too. No, I mean with the play."

"What is it?"

"Do you believe me?"

"Uh . . ."

"No, it's fine. I just, I feel like I'm going a little crazy on my own. I felt so sure when it was just me. Convincing other people, even the thought of it, just feels wrong, like I'm some missionary. That's why I asked."

"I believe *in* you, if that makes sense. And the play's what's supposed to convince people, right?"

"God, the play. I forgot how much work it could be."

"Been awhile."

"Okay, there's another thing I meant to ask. Can you help me out with it, maybe a co-director situation? I know that's asking a lot, but I want it to actually be good, y'know. A serious, stand-alone project."

"But I'm not a director. Plus, won't that be a conflict of interest for me?"

"Are you not on my side already?"

"No! I mean, yeah of course. I don't know. I'm your friend."

"Got it. I just want your help, Ace. Someone to get me out of my head. Sometimes I feel like a ghost walking around my house."

Horace put down his controller, realizing this wasn't just chatter but a cry for help.

"What do you mean?"

"Like I'm haunting my parents. I'm creaks in the floorboard, and my parents don't have the heart to exorcise me yet. I know I'm living on borrowed time. I can't talk to my dad or even look at him most of the time. He seems happy, but I know it's a mask, and it drives me crazy."

"Damn."

Horace could tell he was serving as these thoughts' first audience after many rehearsals, silently uttered and refined, muffled in the privacy of suburbia. In homes with too much space for their own good, secrets travel sideways over backyard fences, spill with glasses of wine on enclosed porches, while living rooms and dining rooms are climate controlled to deter any confrontations from bubbling over. Liam could avoid collisions with entire floors to himself, even a garage turned guest house. Their home always maintained a visible beauty, inside and out, like makeup on a depressed housewife. Could they kick him out and replace him with interior decor?

"What about your mom?"

"We only talked about it once. They had just left for a weekend getaway when I posted it. Another one of my dad's new personality traits. They came back having conspired, which I expected. My mom took me out to lunch, and not to be too Oedipal, but it felt like I was about to get broken up with. She was calm, like approaching a wild animal. I'm so sick of people tiptoeing around me. She asked me why I had written an obituary for my father. I said because I want people to know the truth about him. She said and what truth would that be. And I said that he's not my father anymore, that he's been replaced. That's not your husband either. He's something else, and it's because of what he did, and that he had it coming. I couldn't tell her about his screenplay or my play because then the jig would be up. I had to stand on belief alone with my compass-gut guiding me, while all the norms and social forces baked into my brain were tearing me apart and begging me to just be normal. But love is a force too. I love my mom and she loves me, so that's the only way we got through that conversation."

"What did she say to all that?"

"Oh, she just mothered me. She's used to me acting out. Rather than talking about the issue at hand, she just went on about how changes in life are scary, and she understands why I'm feeling confused, and she forgives me, but she just wants me to take down the post and apologize to my father. But I can't, I literally can't because he's gone, and I told her that. I even beat her to it and said I'd move out if that's what was necessary, but she wouldn't have that. She said I wasn't going anywhere till I was doing better. Which, fair enough."

"Do they know anything about the play?"

"Oh yes, it's the only thing that's got my mother off my back. Not that I could tell her the real plot of course. I told them it's my adaptation of *Glengarry Glen Ross*, so it's about a couple of unethical businessmen faced with a key decision. Not far from the truth really, but nothing that would tip my dad off either. My mom thinks it's great I'm being creative again, and the one normal thing about my dad is he couldn't care less."

"Can't blame him on that one, given that he's publicly dead to you. I wonder what he thinks about how you got the info in your post, like if he's made the screenplay connection yet."

"Who knows how effective the memory replacement was. Maybe the screenplay slipped through the cracks."

Liam's quick response here challenged Horace, who was trying to operate in a domain of taking him seriously. What would an incomplete memory transfer look like? What was a doppelganger's conception of their past self? Do they know they're a replacement? These questions were filed under "Do Androids Dream of Electric Sheep" and never retrieved.

"But that he's not madder at me I think is evidence for my theory," continued Liam. "If it was totally off-base, he could have denied it convincingly. Just ignoring it the way he has makes me think he doesn't want to get tangled up in it and reveal something."

"I guess we'll find out. Shit. If I'm in for an inch, I may as well be in for the mile. So whatever you need man, direction, production, you name it and I'll try to help. But I need to ask you something in return. Please at least pretend to be normal. Find a way to make your mom feel better and somehow treat your dad like a human. My mom low-key thinks you're possessed, and I get the sense she disapproves of us spending too much time together. Help me make the argument we're bettering ourselves by doing this together."

Liam grimaced at the word possessed, and for a long moment he stroked his short beard while looking out the window. Then he nodded to himself and turned to Horace.

"Okay deal, I can act normal. I'm good at pretending."

At that, he picked up his controller again, and Horace followed suit, uneasy with his response and eager to move on. But Liam still hadn't marked himself ready and turned to Horace once more.

"If we swear to each other, here and now, that we are committed to exposing the truth, no backsliding, then I'll do what it takes, even lying to make temporary peace. And the truth is what it is, not what I want it to be. So we must swear to be true to each other and true to our purpose. Will you swear to me on that?"

Horace felt bound and left without a choice, but his commitment had always been to the truth. Despite misgivings, it was something he could get behind, so he held out his right hand, and the burn on his middle finger caught the light. Liam gripped his hand, smothering the mark.

"I swear."

"I swear as well. Alright, League time."

***

The butterflies in Horace's stomach had taken flight, tailspun, and were now crashing and rolling against his insides. Walking away

63

from the black hole of anxiety that had spawned at the dining room table and would envelop his home, his block, and his mind if it caught him, he yearned for a place to feel lost, akin to a northwest passage on these childhood streets. Tame familiarity manifested on mass-produced yard signs, their posture of politics like Livestrong bracelets for single-family residences. An absent sun watched behind the overcast as the wind desiccated the flowers of early spring. Horace too watched absently, glancing into homes with television sets in the same corner as his, avoiding eye contact with all but a judgment-free golden retriever puppy attended by someone nameless and faceless.

The conversation had spoiled dinner, and having cooked it, Horace felt absolved of cleaning it up. After allowing a few follow-up questions from Al (who came to the defense of unethical businessmen) about the plot of *Glengarry Glen Ross*, Maria pounced again. She decreed that Horace would not be doing this play, and that he should tell Liam he was too busy, and that Liam was a terrible son who brought shame to the neighborhood. Horace stood his ground. He told her he was not changing his mind, that she couldn't change his mind, and that yes, he was sure about it.

They were a household that frequently bickered but were unused to such clashes of deep values. No facts to be introduced, no judge or jury to win over, no verdict or justice to be meted out, only presupposed guilt and willful innocence. The wooden legs of Horace's chair were four gavels screeching mistrial and the end of proceedings. His windbreaker held cigarettes and a lighter. His sneakers smushed under his heel and slipped on. His phone lay charging upstairs, but that was fine with him. He sent his last message with a slam of the door.

At some point, he reached a major road and the end of the sidewalk, a video game level traversable only by unlocking a car. This road ended Springfield, as it bifurcated or bisected so many townships and zoning distinctions along the East Coast. Past it, mirror neighborhoods to his own covered the county, high school rivalries whose similarities drove a fervor for zero-sum superiority. Crossing the road would only bring him closer to the feeling of home again, or some false equivalence of it. Since he wasn't ready to go back, he turned right and ambled along the weeds, bottles, and butts of the roadside. At last, he lit up and slowed down.

A white, windowless van bucked onto the shoulder of the road, veering right up to Horace. A workingman's van, a "free candy" kind of van, a thoroughly unnerving sight. Horace flexed the cigarette in his lips as he made eye contact with the driver, defiance emerging out of the puddles of his self-pity interrupted. The man was long, reaching while buckled into his seat through the passenger window to offer something to Horace. The man was ugly, his round-the-clock shadow muddled with rosacea. The man was ageless in a poor way, equally unfortunate whether he was 35 or 65. Wrinkled off-white skin sagging off his face, a wrinkled jumpsuit clinging to his chest, the man was a freezer-burned lemon. He held out a red pamphlet to Horace.

"Hey! Take this," he said pleadingly.

"No thank you," Horace answered simply.

Horace wanted nothing to do with this man, had no interest in his pamphlet or his presence. There was something wrong, and he could smell it and taste it even through the veil of cigarette smoke. He took a few steps back up the road. The van reversed with him.

"Please. It is important."

There was a cotton-ball quality to the way the man spoke, dry like a deserted man in a drought, each phoneme requiring more work than reasonable. Less like an accent or an impediment than the result of something unnatural, malfeasant. The seven words he'd hefted onto Horace were unbearable. Wary of the road-safety violations this man was willing to commit, Horace backed his way toward the woods flanking the road. Shattered glass crunched under his shoe as he stared the man down. Pain lingered on the man's face, then he moved, reaching back to unbuckle his seatbelt, shift into park, and slink out of the running vehicle.

"Wait, wait," he urged, the pamphlet trembling in his upraised hand as he loped round the car. Horace had seen enough.

"No thank you, goodbye!"

Horace turned and bounded to the tree line, wanting to move as fast as he could without looking panicked. When he reached the bramble at the edge of the woods, against Biblical instinct, he glanced over his shoulder to take one more look. Seeing the man had returned to his van was a relief. As he skipped down into the trees, he listened to the engine spurt into motion, then he heard braking and an adjustment. Horace ducked behind a tree and poked his head out to confirm: the man had moved the van fully onto the grass and turned it off. Not waiting to see more, Horace took off on a jungle run.

After plenty of tripping over ferns and urban detritus, Horace stumbled upon a semi-professional trail, a welcome relief from the ivy and underbrush. It ran perpendicular to his path, so he wasn't quite sure which route he should take. He also wasn't sure if the man had followed, or how close he could be. He paused to listen but heard nothing. Part of him felt he knew the pamphleteer, even if he didn't recognize him. Perhaps it was his future self, trying to warn him, saving his life to come. Switching from speed to stealth, he tip-toed leftwards down the trail.

The light faded in cut time as the sun set and the forest thickened. Low humming winds and the pamphleteer haunting his steps. When was the last time Horace had felt spooked? Was Dr. Hawthorne's double chasing him? Was he the original, kept alive and made grotesque? Or else a religious loon or an anti-tobacco campaigner or a government agent? Was it cold wax he felt dripping down his back?

As he trundled along his path, the dark swallowed up more of his periphery, creeping in on his central vision. Light pollution gave the ground he trod a faint glow, but roots and mud confounded him. He missed his phone for its flashlight, its map, its escape-rope services, modern life's omni-tool. He hated how easily he was unsettled, and how cowardly he always proved himself to be. He wished he'd taken the pamphlet. How would he react to the moment of confrontation with Dr. Hawthorne? Could he carry on far enough to reach that point? Would he even make it home today?

Horace found himself stepping over a root he couldn't see but knew lay across the path. On his left, a stump featured carvings he could read like braille in the dark, having made some of them himself. Kilroy looking down over a muted horn; one game of tic-tac-toe that ended in a tie; "smoking kills" encircled by ash burns; "BUSH SUCKS" in thick, deep letters; a dickbutt; a pentagram; an etching of a chubby finch Flora had watched build a nest overhead; teen folk wisdom like "Quis custodiet ipsos custodes" and "So it goes;" four dates for four birthdays: 9/10, 6/6, 11/3, and 3/27 (years excluded to avoid attracting predators, so went their reasoning as pre-teens); a heart that once contained "L + F" but had been awkwardly amended to "H^{+F}". He dragged his hand lightly over the wooden canvas, mindful of splinters, brushing off the forest's droppings to uncover that changed heart.

When he and Dylan had recarved the stump together, it was already mostly forgotten, a natural relic of childhood, a thing that could age and deteriorate but never grow. Horace wondered, had Liam ever discovered the change? Had anyone else? His heart was thumping, and he knew he should keep running, but he lingered. The world was perfectly still. Tears leaked from his eyes, and he let them dribble down his cheek, as the exhilaration of escape gave way to exhaustion and emptiness. He wished that this wasn't his life, that it was all a dream that would go away so the world could return. A world without scary men and his broken heart. A child's world. The snap of a branch down the path called his attention.

"Hello?" Horace called out, surprising himself with the weakness in his voice.

No response of course. The pamphleteer would be following from behind, while anyone or anything could be waiting in front of him. The choice seemed clear enough. Keep going and he'd be home, this nightmare could end, but he couldn't make himself move, and he couldn't deny the dew of cold, thick wax forming along his spine. The stump was his new black hole that he had to escape, but its tendrils of deadly gravity had already snatched him, and he was tired of running.

A light flickered further down the path, a flame then a glow, reminding Horace of an angler fish in the deep sea. He let it approach him, watching a figure form slowly from behind the flame, smelling of weed, looking familiar. From no one to someone, from someone to Liam.

"Boo," Liam hissed softly, flicking the lighter's flame under his chin. "Did I scare you?"

"Till I saw it was you, yeah. What are you doing here?"

"Was feeling nostalgic tonight for some reason. Wanted a nice little smoke down memory lane." He moved closer to Horace and held the flame to his face. "You look rough."

"I've had a day, man. My mom was not happy to hear I'm helping you with the play. Then this weird, ugly guy tried handing me a pamphlet from his white van—I'm talking pedophile style— on the side of the highway? I cut through the woods to escape him and got lost till I found the stump. But . . ."

Horace caught himself, realizing his tears hadn't gone far, and would surely resurface if he kept talking. Liam handed him his joint and moved to inspect the stump.

"Well, good news, I think you're too old for those types. Though wouldn't it be funny if they lured us with, I don't know, New Yorker articles, like how they get kids with candy? But, bet it was some religious loon, I wouldn't worry about it." Liam paused to light a flame over the stump. "Huh, so you and Falco made it official. Should've learned from me and Flora. The stump is cursed, Ace."

"Yeah," was all Horace could manage in reply, more air than voice, a sound that trembled and quivered and betrayed him.

"Didn't want to press you about it, but I'm guessing your visit was disappointing."

Horace could only nod and cover his face, not to hide tears, but to block out the world, as if maybe it wouldn't be there when he next looked.

"Flora and I are chill again. Maybe you will be too."

"I don't know if I want that," Horace said, taking his hands off his face, sounding pathetic but carrying on. "I don't ever wanna look at him again."

"Jeez man, breakups are tough. Give it time. I mean, he joined the Peace Corps, what could you expect?"

"I expected him to tell me he had a girlfriend now."

"Oh."

"Raquel. Another volunteer. She was really nice and very pretty. And she only knew that we'd been friends, nothing more."

"Shit. Fuck, dude. I'm sorry."

"I'm over it. Actually, I'm clearly not. But I don't want to talk about it."

Liam wrapped his arms around Horace and hugged him with all his strength. Horace let his tears run free. Time passed for a while in complete stillness, then they walked home together with little else to say. Horace approached his yard apprehensively, but he saw no lights on and none of the three shared cars in the driveway. No one called out to him as he slipped into the foyer. No candles burned, no music played, no sinks ran or toilets flushed. No floorboards creaked except under his own weight as he climbed the stairs to his room. His phone was charging on his desk. He yanked the cord, and the lock screen displayed. No notifications, no messages, nothing but LED silence.

By next morning, everyone was home again, like nothing at all had happened.

Act I

[Act II]

Act III

Act IV

Act V

2.1 ~ The Festival

Horace was sucking his breath, sweating, cursing the sun, the unseasonal heat, the betrayal of May. He fought to keep his laptop from slapping his back through his bag as he swung his elbows, hated himself, power-walked and skip-ran past shiny buildings, names with ampersands, bus stop PSAs, and tent residences; evading littered scooters, dodging Nikon caravans, froggering weekend traffic, chasing after lost time. He was late and he was never late.

Horace wished he could blame Liam more, he who foisted this upon him last minute, but it wouldn't have been a problem if Horace hadn't missed his stop, preoccupied by his concern over possibly running late. The walk and the heat were his penitence, and he was really sweating his sins out. His thumb was too moist to unlock his phone and double-check, triple-check the progress of his approach. Instead, even numbers on his lock screen taunted him, time rationed from 2:16 to 2:18 p.m., skipped minutes all pooling in his stomach's pit.

At 2:22, he spotted his target, the Vein Convention Center. 2:24, he put his phone in a bin and passed through the metal detector, twice because of the lighter at the bottom of his pocket. 2:26, he presented the forwarded email to the front desk clerk, who pointed toward the elevator and banished him subterraneously. Around 2:28 (though it might have been 2:29 because he wasn't checking his phone), he saw signs for City Fringe, arrows pointing down hall after all. At 2:30, he approached the unmanned check-in table, scanned the name tags instinctively for his capital letters, spotted "Liam Hawthorne: *Solving for X*," registered the situation, searched and prayed to no avail for a Sharpie, figured what the hell, picked up the tag and a staple of informational pages from a dwindled stack, peeled the sticker back and placed the false name atop his frocket and heart, struggled with the doorknob, gathered it was locked, gently knocked, and was let in by a friendly polo shirt finally, mercifully, at 2:34. 34 minutes late, so Liam of him.

He considered the room, and the room considered him back. A black box theater, dark cement bricks, soft white lighting, and a separate air-conditioning track from the stuffy halls that wasted no time assaulting his damp skin. A circle of folding chairs around a three-foot-high square stage, most of the chairs with eyes regarding him, perhaps a few dozen pairs of eyes, ears, legs, arms, no mouths talking at first, though some were showing teeth, snarling?, no, smiling, those were smiles.

"Ah-welcome! See Julie, you weren't the only one who had trouble finding the place hm-yes, well make your way to the circle, don't be shy hm-hmm, we're just finishing up ice breakers, so sorry you've missed much of the fun yes-hmm, well please have a seat, hm-looks like there's space between Lulu and hm-Kevin, and ah-hmm, your name is Liam I see, a fresh new face, welcome indeed, hmm-yes welcome indeed!"

Horace slinked into the seat to which the tweed blazer and bald head on stage directed him, a modern cut of West African fabric to his left and a Greek-life rush shirt to his right. He took in the sneakers, sandals, boots, and flats that surrounded him, occasionally making it up past statement socks and calf tattoos to a knee visible through distressed jeans or a modestly overhanging floral skirt, but his optical nerves refused to acknowledge the upper halves of the rest of the people in the room, a bid to avoid the reciprocity of being seen. The goateed mouth on the bald head emanated a constant stream of sound, an operatic tenor flowing ceaselessly from phrase to phrase, instructing Horace on the rules of the icebreaker: first name, preferred pronouns, show title, production role, years of Fringing, zodiac sign, and spirit emoji, rattling off examples such as those given by rainbow Tevas and Caterpie ankle tat (Christine, she/they, *The Last Trombone*, writer/director, second-time Fringer, Leo, lady doing a facepalm) and black platform combat boots with white laces (Wanda, they/she, *Shakespeare's Femmes Part Six*, one-person show so writer-director-choreographer-actor-producer-etc., sixth-time Fringer, Aquarius, smiling purple devil). Meanwhile, Horace milked a search through his backpack for his notebook and pen, rummaging every pocket of his Jansport from back to front and marveling at how they possibly could have spent half their allotted hour on introductions. The droning stopped, and in response to the silence he looked up to see everyone expecting something of him.

"Well, Liam-hmm, you got all that? Yes, care to share?"

Barely opening his mouth, "My name is Horace, and—"

"—Speak up Liam! Yes-hmm, years next to timpani have rather shot my hearing you see, oh-ho-yes."

"Horace! My name is Horace, sorry. I'm filling in for Liam, who wrote our play. Well, it's more his play. He's acting in it too. Oh yeah, we're both he/him. And it's called *Solving for X.*"

"Hmm-ah, Horace, Horace Horace Horace. We are but dust and shadow, no? So true, yes-hmm, so true. Well, my poetic friend, you've only broken half the ice so far, no? And on Liam's behalf, no less, when we want to hear about you. Hmm-yes, remember, exempli gratia, I'm scripted to say that my name is Gregory, my pronouns-yes are he/him-hmm, my show is City Fringe itself, my role is artistic director for the program, this will be my decennial Fringe hm-hmm-yes, I naturally am a Cancer, and I am the walking embodiment of the smiling full moon emoji, on account of how the light catches my waxed head. Ho-ho-yes, now back to you!"

"Right. Horace. He/him. *Solving for X.* Co-director. This is my first time," at which half the room broke into whistle-pitched cheers and spastic applause, obnoxiously spontaneous, not even suppressed by Horace's dead-eyed non-reaction, honed through years of avoiding classroom bullies and now turned on a group more bullied than he'd ever been, if he was taking a guess. He waited for the hoopla to die down, took his chance to lie and say, "I don't remember my zodiac," paused just long enough to feel the sucking of breath as several mouths rushed to ask his birthday, and cut them off with an icy, "and my spirit emoji would be the face with no mouth."

Having sufficiently asserted himself as better than the rest of them, Horace granted his eyes a pass to scan the faces safely avoiding his own. Round cheeks, hairdos of various colors, breath-supporting postures, ensembles designed to tell you their exact deal. Had Liam attended instead of Horace, he might well have been the exception that proved the queer rule, Horace noted with a sourness that surprised him. He checked his breath, a moment of mindfulness, to locate at approximately his lower ribs an unwarranted feeling of mild disgust. Dwelling in the disgust softened it, the flavor complicating into its component parts, most of which he could recognize were not their faults but his. He was no stranger to his internalized homophobia, a steady childhood diet of Catholicism and *Friends* marathons that his own attractions might never fully cure, but the real issue was Horace's allergy to theater people, developed by years of overexposure. How quickly he could sink into his high school mask without helping it. It takes one to know one, he mused.

***

Horace emerged from middle school accepting that he was different, even venturing toward an early form of pride for this difference. He joined the alternative haven of drama club because Liam's carpool left after rehearsal, but he could have found another ride home if he'd wanted. Horace would not entertain the thought of performance, so Liam introduced him to that year's stage manager, a Doctor Who obsessive now going by Margaret, who to her credit knew as much about Phillips screwdrivers as sonic ones. He was also taking the laid-back technical director Mr. Rice's art basics class, so he trusted he'd be in good hands backstage. Freshman year swam by on a pleasant current from fall play to spring musical, and he spilled into the summer with no new bona fide friends but a nice identity from 4-6 p.m. as the most capable baby in his class, in the strong and silent mold.

He'd look back on those days with fondness as he started to get sucked into the drama of it all. Sophomore year, rather than develop his techie acquaintances into friends, he exploited his connection with Liam and the other senior leads into an elevated coolness, preferring to watch them smoke weed out of apples over the leg work of mall hangs or game nights powered by Mountain Dew with the spazzes and geeks his age, those tribulations that serve as the trial runs for self-determined social bonds. His first fits of personality in those days came by way of outing the eccentricities of the most socially maladroit in his cohort, and what a rush he got from dishing on Brendon Moskowitz's whispered conversations with Hammy his hammer or Denise LeClair's stash of undelivered love notes for Liam. Near the end of the year—by which time he had started taking hits from their improvised pipes, gotten frighteningly high on several occasions (though all were adamant that no peer pressure had been applied), was known by the whole group as "Ace" on Liam's example, and was no longer bartering gossip for cheap clout—he realized he could be *with* them but was not *one of* them. There were parties to attend to which Horace expected no invite, pre-college road trips planned in his presence without abashment, and a general dawning that he was only getting their kid-glove treatment. They never roasted him as he initially feared, so it took months to acknowledge that among them roasting was a sign of respect, a tool for calibrating their own hierarchy to which he was an addendum. Horace took the ego blow on the chin, but it turned into another lonely summer, which he accepted as the price to pay for punching above his weight all year.

His loneliness was also defined by the elevation of dating and, increasingly, hooking up as forces that governed the lives and waking moments of the upperclassmen. Liam and Flora had been going steady since two summers before and projected a confidence, built upon a foundation of their lifelong friendship, about surviving Liam's jump to college. Among the rest of them, college decisions and prom season culled and reorganized nearly every other relationship. Horace felt himself a noble gas amid a cloud of proto-promiscuous bonding in a suspiciously heteronormative scene, considering theater was their collective's raison d'être. In a cloud of his own sexual confusion, he suspected he didn't like girls the way Liam liked Flora, but it was their single male friends, the unlucky and unsuccessful ones especially, expressing naked lust toward mutual female friends or younger ingenue upstarts and against their own virginity, who most discouraged Horace's understanding of the mysteries of romantic attraction.

In a blink, after a summer of long nights and short weeks, Horace returned to school as a slightly taller, ambiguously dark, and approaching-handsome junior, stage crew's second-in-command and first-in-expertise leader of a body with whom he felt he had nothing in common. That was also the fall of Coming Out. In the vacuum left behind by the patriarchal, exclusive, brocialist men of Liam's year, sophomore Kevin Rodriguez kicked the season off with a Facebook post, words and likes numbering in the hundreds, that surprised exactly no one who had ever spent a moment with him, but then who better to signal a sea change. Knowing that Kevin's family was very large and very Filipino, Horace had nothing but respect for the move, even if he did secretly harbor opinions about Kevin's new behavior involving a tad bit of compensation for lost time. A few other guys and two girls who'd been seeing each other on the low publicly followed suit, exhortations involving it being the current year and about time and all that, and come homecoming season, there were a record number of same-sex asks to the dance, coming mainly from the theater crowd.

Horace skipped out on homecoming that year as he had the previous two, not being one for dances. Riding the excuse of all the AP classes he was taking, and outside of calculus, not taking too well, he scrolled past group photos of the techie weirdos he'd previously rejected, noticing how they'd grown too, their personalities approaching tolerable, but he'd tasted cool and would rather fast than go back on a diet of sleepovers and improv games. Instead, he drifted toward the other sticks and bones from the erudite and masochistic cross-country and crew cliques, and so, when he accepted the inevitable nomination to take over as stage manager for the spring musical, he focused his efforts on doing Mr. Rice's job for him while leaving the social leadership to his assistants.

The fall of Coming Out hadn't passed him by entirely though. He internally evaluated the patterns of his gaze, rated the inexplicable flutters he felt at shirts vs skins basketball games with his friends against his nonreactions to the relatively unabashed changing habits of actresses, caught himself mulling over why exactly long-locked lax bro Sean Harper occupied his mind with such frustration, and concluded the inevitable, the obvious, the truth as he had really always known. If he liked anyone, it was probably men, but he had yet to meet a guy who he liked and also like-liked. Sean Harper sucked as it were, and not in the way he eventually got around to fantasizing about. He was also hot.

As with most matters that needed explanation, the internet provided further proof. Porn had never really done it for him, which he attributed to or at least correlated with a form of moral righteousness, but turns out that was just straight porn. Gay porn, at first an undifferentiated rush, then tailored into more specific tastes, was an inexhaustible gold mine from which he later had to wean himself off. Still, while he came out to himself, he decided there wasn't much point in Coming Out the way the others were. It's not like he was interested in any of them, and last thing he wanted was for one of them to become interested in him. He supposed he felt relief, and being at the peak of his atheistic zeal he denied any concept of residual shame, so he promised himself to tell Liam and some other close friends when the time felt right, but that ended up being awhile.

***

No, Horace couldn't fault these fringe festival folks for wanting to express themselves. Despite cringing at the hokeyness of theatrical ideology, he respected differentiation more than conformity, and he could hardly consider it a coincidence that his repressed ass had wound up back in the theater again.

He was looking forward to it too, these people aside. Liam had assured Horace that the actors he'd recruited to play his father's business partners, two of his college buddies Horace recognized only from social media, were fine actors. More importantly, they seemed like normal dudes. At the thought of Russell and Gilbert, Horace wondered how far along the rest of these shows were in their timelines. Easy to imagine Wanda began work on their next project the very day *Femmes Part Five* had wrapped up, but what about the less auteur-inclined among them? Oh fuck, were they behind schedule? The festival would open two months from today. Nine weeks had to be plenty of time, surely, so just calm down. The cold brew he'd downed on the bus had him wondering whether caffeine was causing more of an anxious effect on him of late. He tuned back into Gregory, who'd been hemming and hawing in legato transition through Horace's daydreaming.

". . . why we're all here, yes? City Fringe started 19 years ago, ah-how time flies-hmm, as a venue for artistic taste without exclusive judgment. We creators in this society know what it means to be told no, yes-hmm we certainly do, and so our founders, inspired by our Scottish kin in Edinburgh, bestowed our region with an unjuried arts festival each summer in July. Yes-hm, the beauty of this festival is that every single one of you is here by merit of simply wanting to be here. No-ho, no tyrannical businessmen asking questions like, will this sell, does this have mass appeal, who wants to watch deconstructed, avant-garde operas despite opera's long tradition as a force for social change, and using their artistic directors like pawns in this brutal game we all know as capitalism. In fact, I'm proud to say that this year, we didn't turn down a single application, ho-yes, and in past years we've only sent denials to some frankly crude and unserious would-be entrants," sniff-sniff, "that didn't pass the old smell test."

Horace let his focus wander again until his eyes fixed on the logo at the bottom of the first page. He couldn't believe he'd missed it. A sanitized geometric of red and blue triangles, separated by clean white lines cutting X's across the square in tidy proportions. It probably took around an hour to design and several years to pass corporate committee muster. The logo was at the bottom of every email Horace sent and most he received. Vein Holdings was that year's generous sponsor. In fact, their generosity was unprecedented in the nearly two decades of City Fringe history.

"Ahem-well, I suppose I must relay the details of importance that have called us to gather on this fine May day, hmm-though perhaps the real occasion was one of camaraderie, ah-yes for this is one fewer email in your inbox and one more meeting of the minds. This is a most fortunate year for our beloved festival-hm, as we have been endowed with quite a gift from a certain philanthropist, Mrs. Petunia Vein. Ah-see, on her direct intercession, the Vein Holdings corporation has bestowed us with five excellent venues for our performances, oh-yes, free of charge, yes-indeed. See-ah, I had the honor of sitting down with Mrs. Vein for a quarter of an hour last fall, and oh what a lovely lady she was, so kind and generous. Yes-yes, she made it quite clear there would be no editorial restrictions from above, no tainting of the spirit of fringe theater, and she even expressed interest in attending some of the shows, ho-yes can you believe it?"

At the mention of venues, Horace skipped to the back to check where they'd be. When he saw it, his eyes didn't exactly pop out of his skull, but he gained a new appreciation for the phrase. Their assigned performance space was Eden: "a multi-purpose community space in the cathedral district." It matched the exact description of the Eden he'd begrudgingly promised to attend with Jena. He braced for the cold wax but was hit with something else. Maybe it was the AC redoubling its efforts on his residual sweat, but he felt unduly chilly, shivery, shrunken. Eden was one of Vein's capillaries, another access point to oxygenate their masses. News to him, and likely news to Jena, though he wondered about that. It felt like a dead-baby joke, funny in how it killed any laughter.

"Hm-ah-bollocks, look at the time, ten minutes to go and I've still yet to get to the meat of our meeting, oh-my. Yes-well, thankfully our wonderful production interns have whipped up a handy packet with all the dry stuff you need to know. If you flip to the back, ah-yes please all do right now, I'll wait for the sound of flipping pages to subside hmm, we have detailed the calendar in-hm basic detail. Nota bene-yes that the technical rehearsal, a-hmph perennial scheduling challenge, is bolded, as one of the few strings attached by our gracious benefactors at Vein was a rather limited selection of early access to their exquisite facilities. For some-hm, it is a week prior to opening, and others-hm, only a day before. They are-ah, well, entirely non-negotiable, but I assure you I tried oh-yes . . ."

Horace scanned the rest of the venues: one at Vein's Galleria of Art, two with the Vein Center for Performing Arts at a local university, and the last at Vein Theater & Cinema, which Horace recognized from the brouhaha a few years back about restoration efforts of the historic theater involving Vein's trademark gutting, this time not just staff but interior infrastructure, supposedly all justified by saving it from bankruptcy and demolition. Each was marked with explicit Vein branding and included in its public empire, while Eden had flown under the radar. Curious that Eden would be spared of Vein's label. Yet, if Vein did one thing well, it was marketing, and a new-age night club might not take off with such a corporate stamp. The risk of adding it to the Fringe menu seemed minimal, since who really cares about off-label theater anyway. The powers that be must have calculated crowd exposure to the space, surely gaudy and eye-catching, was worth more than the revealed linkage's potential to turn a few people off from it. Attendance at his show would serve as advertisement for what

Horace now pictured as an evil place with fucked vibes. Good thing he didn't want friends to come, not that he had many friends to invite anyway. Gregory was still going on about something, but the friendly polo, having attempted a series of escalating hand waves, cut him off.

"Mr. Diggory, your time is over. Please wrap up so we can prepare this space for our next booking."

"Ah-bother, I knew an hour would never be enough. Alas, alack, I'll just speed through the—"

"—No, your time is now up. Another group needs this space. Kindly direct everyone to the exit."

Gregory was, for once, at a loss for words, which was all it took to set off a chorus of bag packing and chair screeching, like a bell ending class moments before the teacher could explain the homework. Horace regarded this polo shirt with approval, and for the first time in that room, he didn't feel alone.

2.2 ~ **The Players**

Horace was not particularly surprised to be first to arrive for their debut rehearsal. Russ and Gil were a package deal commuting from work, and even without traffic they would have been cutting it close to their agreed time. Liam, meanwhile, was always late. What irked Horace was that he was sitting in and on Hawthorne property, the guest suite turned gamer pad above their annexed garage. Not only did Liam have no other responsibilities that could possibly be keeping him from a timely arrival, but given his typical server status was active and his entire gaming setup had been moved into the annex, he ought to have been hanging out here anyway. It simply could not have been made any easier for him.

Unless he was already here and planning to prank Horace. He glanced around the room for possible hiding spots, most of which had been mapped out in their hide-and-seek golden age. Many of those spots, like the ledge behind the shade of the window or the crawlspace beneath the couch, had shrunk over the years to be impractical, while others, like the Hawthorne's massive VCR and DVD cabinet, had disappeared entirely. All that remained were the more temporary and obvious spots from their earliest hiding days, before the meta-game had developed to the point of exhausting creativity and turning it into a game theory exercise of avoiding where the seeker was most likely to check first. Horace felt himself shifting his weight onto his feet in a bid to get up and check, just to be sure, behind the shower curtain in the bathroom and in the closet of the guest room, but why bother? It was wishful thinking that Liam would be so conveniently near.

Some beeping from down the stairs, someone punching numbers on the keypad to unlock the door, reassured Horace, who settled into an aggressively casual position simulating an immersion in his notes. The door creaked open, and heavy feet hit the steps.

"Liam?" Horace shouted down, as positively casual as he could manage. Two laughing voices replied.

82

"No fuckin' way, dude. I told you we'd beat him."

"Damn, but like, he lives here, right?"

"Gil, have you met Liam? My guy is gonna be late to his own funeral."

"That's so facts."

First Gilbert Bartoszcze, then Russell Singh, with a cloud of vape smoke intervening, emerged from the stairs. Gilbert, with a man's body and a baby's face, covered all the basic shapes. Triangular torso, ovular jaw, square hips, a half-moon ass outlined in khaki shorts, clutching a cylindrical Slurpee in his sausage fingers. He moved with the stiff grace of someone who found weightlifting after the critical window for sporty coordination had passed him by. Standing at the head of the stairs directly between Horace and Russell, his dimensions obscured his friend entirely. Russell's head poked out from behind his friend's shoulder, Warby bespectacled, dark hair freshly faded and coiffed, beard neatly trimmed, studs in his ears catching the light off his salesman's smile, as he slid past Gilbert and approached Horace. His stride was a glide, accentuated by Adidas joggers accented lime green to match his kicks.

"Yo Ace, the guy himself! I'm Russ, what's good."

Horace rose to dap him up and was surprised to see his shoulder hit just above Russ's, making him what, 5'7? Horace, an average American male, tried his best to ignore size politics, his nonchalance sometimes earning him tall-guy energy and other times contributing to his vanishing presence in a room. Russ, occupying more space than he was worth, had fooled Horace into thinking he was almost tall in the solo flexed fit pics littering his Instagram (@bollys_lyfe), which Horace now clocked as classic short-king energy. Compensation if not overcompensation. He supposed many movie stars stood similarly, assuring him Russ would make for a fine actor. He had more doubts about Gil, stock-still by the stairs and slurping thoughtfully, who on first impression talked dumb and moved dumb and generally mismanaged the ample space he contained. Horace moved to greet him.

"Hey, I'm Horace. Gilbert, right?" Offering a dap they somehow both fumbled, Gil having just come from handshake world and Horace generally being out of practice.

"Yup! Wait, no. Just Gil."

"Or GB, cuz he loves to rip geeeebs," Russ chimed in with faux-hype voice.

"Hey man, not anymore. I cut that crap out. But nice to meet your Hor, er, Ace? Hor-Ace?"

"Yeah, you can just call me Horace. Mostly Liam calls me Ace." Gil looked concerned, so Horace added, "You can call me Ace, too." Gil continued to look concerned, so Horace moved on. "Seems like we're still waiting on Liam, so—"

The door to the guest bedroom swung open and Liam shuffled out rubbing his eyes and yawning performatively in his signature groutfit, Nike long-sleeve and sweats and socks in a set. Bed-headed and bleary, but looking much better than his recent usual, a healthier complexion behind his de-scruffed beard. Despite the rubbing, his eyes were less red than usual. He held his hand up by way of hello as he made a show of adjusting to the light.

"What the hell, you were here this whole time?" Horace asked, feeling embarrassed and already on the wrong foot. What would have happened if he'd actually searched for him? "I called out when I came in."

"Just took a helluva nap. Must not have heard. Good thing Gil climbs stairs so fucking loud he shook me out of bed."

Liam properly greeted Russ and Gil with collegiate grab-assery and playful chauvinism. He politely fist-bumped Horace. They all settled around the coffee table, with Russ nabbing Horace's spot on the couch. Gil plopped down next to Russ and made himself at home, kicking his feet up on the table while producing from his bag a hefty Hydroflask and a single can of Miller Lite, which he immediately cracked. Horace gathered his stuff from the table and floor and dragged over an armchair. Liam unfolded a director's chair, a high school graduation gift propped against the couch, and took charge.

"Gentlemen! Props to you all for being down to do this. This is the dream team, some of my best buds under one roof. Been a minute since the three of us were on the same stage, and let's just say several minutes since Ace and I worked together. But I've got full faith in this crew. Goal for today is to knock out a read-through then talk through character motivation and shit. Ace will take notes. Let's get to it?"

Horace passed out the scripts he'd printed, three-hole punched, and snapped into binders. Assistant director and assistant to the director both, he knew what he was signing up for with Liam. It's not that Liam's ideas were half-baked as much as that he'd forget to turn off the oven after. Horace enjoyed the role of being Liam's "yes, but" man, assigning his anxiety to cover the flanks around Liam's narrow aperture of inspiration. If only he could apply these organizational skills to his own life, but managing his objective, his approach, and how it could go wrong turned into an unsolvable three-body problem. Liam's fixations simplified things.

For example, Liam's fixation with secrecy meant Russ and Gil were not joining the innermost circle of their conspiracy. That meant no mention of the true nature of the original screenplay. Liam's casting call for "two actors for an original play at City Fringe this summer" had gone out via social media and listservs, and he'd been surprised when Russ and Gil emailed back within minutes of each other. They'd been his acting buddies once upon a time, but not actually best buds, and he hadn't kept up with them after college. He could only assume they'd seen the obituary, so when they asked what the play was about, he mentioned the obit was avant-garde marketing for the project, posted with the permission of his family. Given that Flora initially jumped to a similar conclusion, Liam's lie was believable enough, albeit risky if Greta ever invited them down for cookies. Horace had wondered why Liam didn't fully trust them, but now having met them, he could guess. Despite being actors, they seemed incapable of deception.

"Before we start reading, I'll walk through a general rundown of the play."

"General Rundown," Russ interrupted to say with a mock salute, which Gil belatedly but enthusiastically followed. Liam returned the gesture to dismiss them.

"Russ is the Professor, Gil's the Sergeant, and I'm the Doctor. The five scenes take place over the course of a few years, starting at the Doctor's wedding reception. They're in their thirties, but they're all still pretty fresh and idealistic at this point. I want the Prof's cynicism and Sarge's callousness to build over time. They'll be holding champagne flutes—which is a prop we'll need, Ace—and do some exposition with their toasts. Then Russ will propose his business opportunity to them, keeping it a little cryptic, and how they'll need Doc for his biochemical expertise. After some cajoling he agrees.

"Then it's time for a scene change. The set will have to be light since it's just the three of us doing all the moving." Gil raised his left hand while putting down his beer to take a sip of water with his right. Liam looked at him, pushed some air out of his nose, and called on him. "Yes, Gil?"

"Isn't Horace helping?" After asking this, Gil sucked on the remnants of his Slurpee, which sounded empty. He put it on the table and produced a protein shake from his bag. Horace wondered about the temperature of these beverages.

"Because that goes against the minimalist aesthetic, and I prefer it when actors get their hands a little dirty. Horace's job is to be in the audience and observe. You're a big guy, Gil, you can handle moving a card table. That's as heavy as it'll get. First scene, we'll place some slices of cake and be standing around it, and we'll pipe in some Abba or something in half-stereo to simulate there being dancing in the other room. Idea is y'all stole me away for a minute to have this conversation, and it ends with us returning to the party.

"Second scene we'll be hanging out and mock-playing pool, so Gil takes the cake slices off and Russ brings on some pool cues. Only reason for this is to make the scene more dynamic, since there's gonna be a lot of standing and talking. As we pretend to play cutthroat, nice little metaphor there, Russ as the Prof reveals the contract he's secured for us, if we unanimously agree to go for it."

"Okay bro, I only skimmed the script, but this business plan? I've got *questions*," Russ cut in, then stopped to vape before getting to the questions. His device resembled a walkie-talkie rather than a flash drive, the kind you can refill with custom juices. The vapor was treacly and dark, unnatural like an English dessert.

"That's what we're here for. Let's hear them," Horace replied, wanting to insert himself as a co-authority. He'd already gotten this overview from Liam, theoretically for his input, but Liam had done a thorough planning job and just needed Horace's rubber stamp. Horace would play his part, but he was wary of his role being reduced to production assistant/bitch boy printing scripts and attending meetings. He could at least help these two couch-fellows understand the material.

"Word, Ace, but I think my questions are really more for Liam, y'know, as the writer. Like how'd you come up with this shit? Your dad do any work with spies, tell you some stories?"

Horace found this specificity odd. Liam's answer danced agilely.

"Where do any creative sparks come from? The ideosphere. Society. God himself. Not like there's such a thing as original thought, so I was just tapping into existing currents. My dad's just a normal scientist who did boring government contracting shit, so I tried thinking up the coolest possible thing he could've done instead. Brain washing for the government sounds pretty sick, right?"

"So, you don't think your dad's been working with the deep state?" Gil asked, burping up vanilla protein shake.

"I don't believe in anything at all, mate. It's just fiction."

"That's so deep, bro," Gil said, nodding sagely.

"Okay, I have non-meta questions too," Russ continued, "like, they're offered this grant to figure out a way to wipe someone's brain and replace it with a tweaked copy of someone else's brain. Then your dad does all the work, somehow succeeds, and then suddenly regrets it and wants out. Why? What was he thinking they were gonna do with that tech?"

"We're getting a little ahead of ourselves here, but that's okay. Also, maybe my character is inspired by my dad, but he's not literally him. That would be weird. You have hit on the interesting conflict for my character, though, that he doesn't really know what he wants. He's lured by the scientific challenge and some delusions of grandeur, but once he achieves what he set out to do, the wool is pulled off his eyes and he sees for the first time the damage he may cause. That's the main arc of the show, and he ends up feeling trapped."

After this, Horace stepped in to keep the overview running. He quickly noticed the consumption of vape juice and beer intensified while he spoke, so he kept it brief. The second scene ended with the Prof winning their game of pool and Doc agreeing to the contract. Third scene was a series of vignettes between each of the characters broken up with Doc working solo at his table, adorned with a monitor, a microscope Liam hadn't touched since shortly after his 12th birthday, and some beakers and flasks. That's where the cracks in their operation start to show, philosophical disagreements and questions of their mission, intermixed with Doc announcing bouts of progress in his experimental research.

Horace wasn't sure yet about lighting capabilities but dreamed of something cool. For liability reasons, a City Fringe employee would be manning the switch board, so the commands would have to be kept unfortunately simple.

"And the third scene wraps up with Doc having his final breakthrough, which is that the uh . . . Yeah, Liam I'm gonna pass this back to you to explain."

Horace didn't pretend to understand what Dr. Hawthorne, or at the very least Doc, had allegedly invented. Nor was he sure which aspects of the invention came from Liam's adaptation rather than his father's original work. Better to let Liam navigate those layers.

"Doc really has two breakthroughs, and the scene ends when they're combined successfully. Both come from real things too and I just, or Doc if you prefer, enhanced them. There's this thing called decoded neurofeedback, which is when you . . ."

Gil had raised his hand again, this time so eagerly that he didn't notice the beer in his hand, which splashed out as he waved for Liam's attention.

"Yes Gil?"

"I know this one! Decoded neurofeedback uses machine learning to analyze fMRI-based multivoxel models of the brain and induce fine-grain neural activity through repetitive manipulation of stimulus and response. Wooh!"

Having successfully recited what seemed to be an exam answer from years prior, Gil chugged the rest of his beer and crushed it on his forehead, leaving a red mark. While Horace put little stock in the colleges people attended, this was a useful reminder that at least one point in his life Gil had been considered some definition of smart.

"Very good, Gil. A textbook couldn't have said it better. Point is, you can render a 3D map of the brain, and as you tinker with it, you can see in real-time how it changes shape. As I'm sure Gil remembers from whatever class he just pulled out of his ass, shape determines function in biology. Doc's bet is that if you make one brain look exactly like another, it'll behave exactly like the other. The elegance of this solution is that he wouldn't need to understand how each path in the brain functioned as long as he could perfectly recreate it. But the trick is I mean perfect, not an easy feat. Working with mice, he'd get two brain scans and try to morph one to look like the other. To do so, he'd induce polarities in the subject's brain so the positive spots would attract negatively charged growth factors and vice versa. He programmed it so these hot and cold spots were based on the way the control's brain looked, hoping over time through trial and error the treatment would get the subject's brain there too. He goes through a lot of mice like this, with not much to show for it.

"That's where our good friend LSD comes in. See, psychedelics open up neural pathways in your brain, making it mushy and moldable again, like a baby's. Only, he finds LSD wouldn't do the trick for him. It softened neural rigidity but not enough. He takes a detour to develop various LSD analogues, and tries them out on different mice, rinse repeat, until finally the tenth analogue shows real promise, hence Chemical X. Eureka, boom."

"Damn bro, you put a lot of thought into this," Russ said without apparent sarcasm. "How'd you come up with this shit?"

"Research. Consulted various tomes, primary sources, Wikipedia."

"Nothing from your brain-doctor dad?"

"No. But, come to think of it, there was one crucial source of most of my info for this. Your mom. Over a series of candle-lit dinners. Yeah, I treated her well first. You're welcome."

"Hell yeah," Gil exclaimed, as he slow-motioned a high-five toward Liam till he finally met it. "But wait, so does this thing from your play really work?"

"I don't know dumbass, I made it up. But who knows what's going on in top-secret labs around the world. All those poor, poor lab mice . . . to say nothing of the human subjects the government totally, definitely stopped experimenting on. Which brings me to scene four, where Prof tries convincing them to make the jump straight to humans. Doc doesn't want to and threatens to quit, so they agree to stick to proper course. Only, Prof and Sarge stay on-stage to reveal they're just gonna take his method and go behind his back. More time passes, and we cut to Doc walking in on them celebrating experimental success. He's furious to learn they two-timed him, but when he threatens to quit for real, Prof doesn't push back. Doc storms out, Prof tells Sarge to get the replacement ready, and they exit.

"Bringing it home, scene five, empty stage, and we start introducing some ambiguity. Doc comes on and tells the audience he had a change of heart, that he realized he'd never trust his replacement, and so he's staying with the firm to limit their most depraved impulses. He'll keep prattling on about the passage of time, and with the same lighting trick as before, we'll cut away from his hammy monologue a few times to see Gil and Russ act out example doppelgangerings. What I'm picturing is Russ hiding behind Gil, who's facing the audience and talking about something good like hope and change, then mid-sentence Gil clutches his heart and Russ, from behind, slips on Gil one of those Phantom of the Opera masks. When Gil recovers and resumes talking, his tone is noticeably different, more sinister. We'll repeat that move three times, playing around with each one, like maybe you two are trading places, or they're all done in pantomime. I haven't decided yet. But after the third, Doc wraps up his monologue by saying he can finally retire in peace. He starts to walk off, only to clutch his chest the same way as Gil. Stage goes dark, lights come back up for bows, and Doc's wearing the phantom mask, too. And fin, that's the play."

The readthrough went fine. Russ and Liam foiled each other well, and Gil added moments of humor that weren't always intended by the script. Liam's writing was at times amateurish but usually forgivable, and he was open to changes, rarely sticking verbatim to his own words anyway. Inside this slab of granite was a show to be chiseled. While the other three congratulated themselves on a job well done, Horace couldn't enjoy the emotional high, dwelling on how their opening night plan would likely ruin an otherwise respectable show. They'd signed a contract to perform four times, but would Liam's heart still be in it after confronting his father?

After two hours, they called it quits on rehearsing. Russ proposed gaming. Gil withdrew the nine remaining beers from his

Mary Poppins-esque bag of beverages and placed them on the table. Liam packed his bong. Horace did not protest, while Russ and Gil did not partake, which surprised both Liam and Horace.

"Sorry brah, security clearance, shit sucks," explained Russ.

"I hate asking this question, but what do you two do exactly?" Horace only knew they worked together.

"Consulting." They both answered as one. The perfect conversation ender.

"Yeah, they're both big loser sell-outs," added Liam. "Now gimme your controllers, let's get some doubles going."

With four fiends assembled under one roof, there was only one game in consideration: the 2001 Nintendo GameCube classic, *Super Smash Brothers Melee*. Rejected by its creators for the competitive scene it bred, the last-man-standing fighting game still held sway two decades and three sequels later. Liam rolled over a dolly sporting a massive CRT television set (an essential inconvenience that reduced input lag by 17 milliseconds) and plugged in Gil and Russ's customized GameCube controllers to his Wii, modded to launch the game off an SD card. CRTs were already on their way to obsolescence when Horace, the new kid on the block, had first learned to play.

***

Though they wouldn't know it yet, the gang was all there in the Falcos' basement, eating sweetbread Maria had baked and sipping caffeine-free soda. Liam lounged upside down, feet over the back of the couch, arms bracing the carpet for support, and jaw extending tremulously to snatch a cookie off the table. Flora practiced cartwheels with her shirt tucked in. Her older brother Louis was up by a touchdown in *Madden*, but Dylan Falco, his classmate and their host, was driving with 30 seconds to go. Fourth-grade Horace watched with his feet up on the chair, arms wrapped around his shins, chin on his knees. He hoped Maria wouldn't smell the cola on his breath when he came home. Peyton Manning connected with Reggie Wayne for the score, and then again for the two-point conversion, securing Dylan the win. Louis chucked his controller and said a curse word, both actions anathemas to Horace.

"This game is so broken. I don't want to play anymore," Louis whined.

"Someone's salty," mumbled Liam. The cookie perched in his teeth made it sound like "shumwums shoddy." Louis feinted a punch, and Liam bit down on the cookie as he rolled over into a defensive position, causing the rest of it to fall to the floor.

"How about a game we can all play?" asked Flora, whose arms were getting tired.

"There's five of us, sis, that's impossible," replied her brother.

"What about something other than video games?" she voiced without hope.

"What about Super Smash Bros? That's at least four player," Liam put in, ignoring Flora's plea.

"What's *Supersmashbros*?" inquired Horace, a child so far deprived of consoles.

"Only the greatest video game ever," answered Dylan with zeal. "I can teach you how to play if you want."

Horace met his gaze, a bright face with a guileless smile, and felt warm and welcome, even strangely excited. Maria had sent him across the circle to the Falco's door, Tupperware of baked goods in hand, with one instruction: make friends. He'd met Liam, Louis, and Flora on move-in day a few weeks back—the worst day in Horace's life so far—when the neighbors came by to introduce themselves and lend a hand. Horace wanted nothing to do with them, nothing to do with anything this new life in Springfield might offer. After a parent-assisted meeting and exchanging of names, Liam and Flora ran off to play in the woods while Louis tried lifting heavy things.

Horace didn't meet the Falcos till later because they'd been vacationing in Italy, but not to see relatives, which confounded Horace, fresh off a torturously dull trip to see his decrepit great-grandparents in their sleepy Sicilian town. Upon their return,

Maria caught wind from the other parents of a group play date and secured her children's invitations. His older sister Dido, already crushing on Louis, scoffed at the idea of hanging with her little brother, and Horace pleaded to be spared of bringing the twins along, so off he went alone with her baking. After being shepherded down to the basement by Mr. and Mrs. Falco, he mostly just sat there, watching them, playing dead to avoid predation.

Dylan beckoned for Horace to come sit on the rug next to him and handed him a GameCube controller. Louis joined, spinning out more braggadocious words he'd soon have to eat. Liam insisted Flora take the last spot. They chose their characters from the list of 25. Louis went for Ganon, the bulky, purple warlock. Flora selected Kirby, the perennial favorite of those blissfully ignorant of tier lists. Dylan, by right of his family name, selected Falco, the cocky, gunslinging bird. Liam informed Horace that he "mained" Marth, the sword-wielding, tiara-wearing prince. Horace, overwhelmed with choices, asked Dylan to pick for him.

"You don't mind playing as a girl, do you?" Horace shook his head no. "Because Princess Peach is actually really good. She's very defensive, and if anyone gets too close to her, she can down-smash them away and do a ton of damage."

Horace didn't know what that exactly meant but liked the sound of it. Dylan explained the controls and the rules: hurt your opponents enough that they're knocked off stage and can't get back on while avoiding that fate yourself. He likened it to playing rock-paper-scissors really fast, over and over again until they don't have any lives left.

That's all it took for them to become friends. Dylan and Horace teamed up to beat the Neufchatels with Dylan netting every kill. Horace wasn't any good, but Dylan was a patient teacher, telling Horace he'd be happy to coach him up whenever. Horace didn't want to leave when time came for Maria to extract him, but at least there'd be a next time. Dylan had mentioned taking a knife out to carve a stump he'd found out in the woods. Liam and Flora, thinking they knew the one, excitedly agreed. Louis asserted that defacing public property was illegal, so he was out.

"Trees aren't property!" Flora protested.

Horace, high on soda and friendship, was ready to break any made-up law with them.

2.3 ~ The Question

Liam's birthdays had always been bashes, ambitious, a bar set high by Greta's creative spirit. Scavenger hunts, field days, and Nerf wars gave way to gaming tournaments, camping expeditions, and ragers as Liam's tastes evolved into bacchanalia and away from maternal control. They were loud fun, serving as eventful commencements of the summers to come. This night was different.

Nestled within an early June evening, a small crew gathered around the firepit in the Hawthorne backyard. Liam didn't care much for cake, so Greta had baked a blueberry pie, vegan for Flora's sake. Early in their season, the berries were small but sweet and perfect for baking. The warmth of the fire and the pie mixed with the cool of the breeze and the oat-milk ice cream to spread pleasantly through them, while an arthritic Moxie moseyed around their feet for crumbs and smells. The chilled rosé (for all except Gil, who surrounded himself with beer cans) gifted them cool refreshment and warm encouragement. Nights like these—sitting on lawn chairs, pressing barefoot soles into the grass, smelling carbon reunite with the atmosphere—imbued a temporary bliss powerful enough to repel any thoughts of endings, of inevitable change. This was it, this pie, these people, this feeling. A firefly's glow doesn't look the same in a bottle, but this night they fluttered gaily and free.

They'd rehearsed that day, blocking the final scene. Rehearsals stressed Horace out because, lacking anything else to do, he obsessed over productivity and efficiency. While the three actors clowned around, he played the villainous roles of taskmaster, timekeeper, page-turner, and naysayer.

The process of picking targets to allege as doppelgangers had been especially frustrating. No, they couldn't pull off a Jeffrey Epstein body-double bit, it would lose the audience. No, Gil doing brown-face would not come across as parody. No to school shooters, Jesus. Inspired by some hidden discomfort and justified by Gil's poor impressions, Horace urged them into three fictionalized examples: an anti-corruption politician, an environmental activist, and a patsy for leaked intelligentsia, each singing a different tune after the application of a mask.

Horace had entered into Liam's local conspiracy, an inter-family affair, but the further its reach extended, as Liam's theories attached to specific names and events and narratives, the more troubled Horace became. Replace one man with another, and so what? The structures are unchanged. Loose thoughts about material conditions rattled around in his head, theories far more powerful than their little conspiracy. If not for the birthday plans, Horace would have headed straight home after rehearsal, gotten high, and tangoed all night with his paranoia, that bestie he knew was toxic for him but who never abandoned him.

Instead, they were to dine with the Hawthornes. Liam assured Horace he'd kept his word and made up with his parents, but Horace couldn't imagine how. A dinner with them felt impossibly risky, and Horace had spent days planning for every contingency lie. He felt bound up in a Gordian knot, with Liam knowing more than Horace who knew more than Russ and Gil who knew contrary things to Bill and Greta, who themselves may have known things Horace did not. Opening night would cleave the knot and render the whole thing moot, but he'd be in a tangle until then. Any thought even adjacent to Greta also twanged Horace with the guilt of their conversation before the block party, of her request to save her son from his lunacy. While Horace readied himself for an evening of conversational landmines, Liam entertained no worry. It'll be fine, it'll be fine, relax, was all Horace could get from him.

Horace expected a dinner of surprises, and suitably didn't foresee the ones he got. To start, the table had a seventh seat, and Flora arrived to fill it. Liam had invited her, and she came as the old friend she was, bygones left behind. Casually, yet clearly planned, she mentioned that she and Liam had agreed not to discuss his play between them so she could experience it authentically fresh. Now as for why Liam hadn't informed him of this twist, Horace guessed Liam just liked to watch him sweat. Nonetheless, it cleverly deflected conversation from the matter of the show to the process of rehearsing, a far safer topic.

Later, Greta took a moment aside with Horace to thank him. Relief radiated from her eyes as she described Liam's apology and return to normalcy that had coincided with their public collaboration on the play. They shared only a moment in the kitchen, giving Horace little chance to reply, but she knew he'd taken her request to heart and would be forever grateful. Horace kept himself from calculating the interest on this emotional debt by doubling down on wine.

Finally, and contrary to his general expectations, the dinner passed not just pleasantly but enjoyably. Russ charmed and Gil stayed out of silliness with seltzer water and still water and a glass of milk, not being a fan of the craft beers in the Hawthorne fridge. Flora regaled them with a comical story about an artist she interviewed who was in the midst of a "childish period," in which she not only used only classroom materials like crayons and construction paper to render her art, but also insisted on eating dinosaur nuggets and scheduling nap times and behaving overall like a petulant seven-year-old in order to channel that raw innocence of youth into her work. Liam for his part updated the table on his so far unsuccessful job hunt. He might have been lying, but the work required to maintain these lies seemed to match the work of actually applying. Greta served them all a massive pot of ratatouille, filled and refilled their glasses of wine, encouraged them to eat more bread but save room for dessert, and misted joy at their togetherness. Bill surprised by being exactly the new man Liam had described: attentive, instructive, maybe too easy with his laughter, like a father who couldn't believe his luck at having such a wonderful son with such lovely friends. The context unnerved Horace, watching an old dog perform new tricks, but having steeled himself for a night of tense suspicion, he welcomed the ebullient atmosphere.

Only in the bathroom, washing his hands and rubbing the scarred mark on his finger, did Horace dwell on the layer of film that clung to everyone gathered there. Its distortions angled the light rosily, changing not where anyone was but where they seemed to be. No one, least of all Horace, wanted to peel it back and examine the swirl of motivations beneath their surfaces. The thick film so far had kept any cold wax from crawling down his skin, and for that he was thankful. The night offered a liminal happiness, a picture of old times that weren't quite and a promise of new ones that wouldn't be. It was in this spirit that the younger ones retreated to the backyard and sat around the fire pit.

"Here's a question for y'all," Liam, while scratching Moxie behind the ears, started up from a lull in conversation. "Given the option to either keep your life or switch places and live the life your pet has had, which would you choose?"

"I'd love to be my dog!" Gil, a golden retriever, shouted instantly. "I piss where I want, and people clean up my poop for me. Like, where do I sign?"

"My mom never let us get a pet, so not as tempting an offer," Russ added.

"Doesn't have to be literally your pet then," Liam replied, in a prime drunken state for discourse. "It's your life or the life of a typical, well-treated suburban house pet. Your every need is taken care of in exchange for effortlessly bringing joy to your family by simply existing. Your essence is still you, but you have the desires and problems of dog-you, rather than human-you. You're worried, or not, about meals and scratches and smells and mailmen, rather than bills and climate change and fulfillment."

"My cat might be worried about climate change, in her own way," Horace contributed, stalling for time on his own answer. Who would he be without his anxieties? Not recognizably Horace, that's for sure. "Animals can sense what's wrong with nature, even if they don't understand what's going on. Plus, Cleo's been on anxiety meds since Tony died. She was spraying everywhere cuz she missed him I guess." The dos Santos classical naming convention had not escaped their cats, though Horace had been opposed to naming littermates after lovers.

"I'm not saying pets don't have problems, but we all miss Tony," Liam answered, "and if avoiding loss is a concern, owners watch their pets die, or even choose to put them down, way more than the reverse. Not outliving loved ones is major points in favor of taking the dog pill. What's going to be waiting for you in sixty years?"

"Team dog pill takes the lead!" barked Gil.

"Hey for what it's worth, I'm not sure I'd take it," Liam hedged. "It's just an interesting question."

"Technically," Russ began, exhaling vapor like an impotent dragon, "isn't this question impossible? Cuz our sense of self is bound by our mental and physical attributes and shit. What about me can actually transfer to a pet? Like, I don't believe in fucking souls or whatever, and even if I did, what good are they? Plus, getting spayed? Yeah, that's a no for me, dawg."

"I think this question is impossible because the dog pill doesn't exist, Russ," Gil whispered, tone walking the density line so perfectly it was impossible to tell if he was trolling or contributing.

Flora had been silently passing judgment on their conversation. Horace, philosophically engaged and tipsy, hoped she wouldn't mock them to the point of defeating the question. Were these stoner thoughts below her now? Or perhaps too in the vein of masculine argument for argument's sake?

"What he's really asking," she began once she was sure she could speak without interrupting or interruption, "is whether eating that apple in the garden and gaining the knowledge of good and evil was a mistake. Would you rather live with shallow happiness or know better and live with your choices? If you ask me, Eve made the right choice, and I'm tired of people being mad at her."

This stirred something deep in Horace's Catholic recesses. The sublime ignorance of Edenic man or a half-deaf, nearly blind border collie sounded pretty good right about now, so why did it feel wrong? When had man's original temptation to bite the apple morphed into a temptation to spit it back up? Possibly from the first moment it happened.

From what Horace recalled of Sunday school, God gave Adam freedom so that he could choose to love Him back. Then Adam and Eve, grouped together by feminist Horace, opted into moral knowledge and there was no going back from there. What was stopping him from trading away his superego, that know-it-all conscience of his wielding guilt and shame willy-nilly, for a wagging tail or a purr, if not that guilt-tripping superego itself? His conscious brain would never turn itself in willingly.

But while thought-provoking, Horace guessed Liam was after something other than Catholic dogma. The question inverted the doppelganger process—rather than reconstructing one mind in another, with no transfer of the essential soul, it transferred the soul into a completely different mind and body that were untroubled and ideal. A corollary dawned on Horace.

"I think I'm with Flora, but I'm still working it out. Also, does my cat get stuck with my life then? Or am I replaced by, let's just say, an equivalent of myself?"

"Okay, Mr. Co-Director," Liam replied mock-slyly. "Remember, no show talk around Flora, right? But it's no spoiler to say this is something I've been thinking about. Same with Russ's point. If you're in a new body, a new species, what would transfer about you and what would be left behind? If Cleo took over for you, what would be different about this Cleo-Horace? Maybe some gender dysphoria . . . Maybe we are exactly the sum of our parts and no more, but I don't buy it."

Gil's mouth hung open in what looked like awe but was actually the search for a sentence he didn't know how to start.

"Uhh-so taking the dog pill, that means I'm dying and hoping I get reborn. Dang! But even if something transfers to Fetch, might not be the parts of me I was hoping for."

"Bet your ass Gil-Fetch would still be drinking from multiple dog bowls tho," cracked Russ. "Bro, also that's the dumbest name for a dog I've ever heard. How do you play fetch with Fetch? Like calling a dog Sit, goddamn."

"Don't listen to him, Gil," insisted Flora. "I think that's a very cute name for a dog."

Horace's mind was still circling around, sniffing, digging for something like it had been forgotten, although he doubted ever consciously knowing it. The search patterns in his brain reminded him so strongly of being high that he might've imagined smelling weed, but no, Liam was rolling a joint. Maybe it related to what Gil had just said.

"How much of this depends on the quality of your current human life? Like, terminal cancer, life in prison, anyone's taking that trade. But I'm not trying to get into eugenics here, so for you guys personally. Is there a time where you might've wished you could take the dog pill, and now you see why you shouldn't? And if that's the case, shouldn't that stop you from ever choosing to take it? Speaking from experience here, for me it's a yes."

"Good point, Ace," said Liam, while twisting closed the cone, "I'd definitely have traded places with Moxie a year ago."

Horace understood what Liam was referring to and glanced at Flora, who returned acknowledgement. Russ and Gil seemed unfazed. Returning to Liam's face, he tried to read the scars it might bear, but a smug grin papered over anything deeper, as if he was bragging to Horace about the experience. But then, too drunk to be satisfied by subtlety, he finished the thought aloud.

"Yup, today marks one year suicide-attempt free! Where's my chip?"

***

By the time Liam reappeared on King Court that previous fall, Horace had heard nothing from him in months that were preparing to group themselves into years, like the counting of a newborn's age. Horace had no idea how to maintain a long-distance friendship, in which all one could do was talk, especially once Liam abandoned online gaming in college. They'd see each other over breaks when Horace was still in school, but the stretches both felt and grew longer once he dropped out. Already not a talker, the thought of volunteering updates about the progress of his depressing life was unappetizing to the point of nausea, and it never occurred to him that Liam ought to be reaching out to him too.

The last time Horace had seen Liam was the day he moved to New York, packing his belongings into Greta's Porsche Cayenne bound for an East Village one-bed that he didn't make enough to afford, not that children of wealth are stopped by such things. Having done an extra year of school to soak up a consolation degree in exchange for more of his college town's playground simulation of reality, Liam Hawthorne's life was about to begin at last. Shackled by jealousy on one hand and shame on the other, Horace had barely spoken to him that day, wishing him well from a distance like an onlooker to a fabulous cruise.

When Liam returned in Greta's luxury crossover, it served as his lifeboat. It was apparent to Horace something terrible had happened, a failure so great they were celebrating it having not been worse, but no one would tell him straight. He'd been in treatment, Maria had told him curtly. He'd had a rough go of things up in New York, Al had added. Horace felt like a fool, like his parents were judging him for failing as a friend, but how could he have known? Why did he still not know?

As they waited to surprise him in the Hawthorne living room, he could see what was not being said in how Maria was rallying them to enthusiasm, how Al and Paul were pretending to get along, and how Flora was steeling herself, a placid surface with an empty gaze. Horace had his speculations, but this scene prompted disaster thinking, picturing Liam physically transformed, scarred or broken or ugly. A text from Bill alerted them, and they took their places behind doorways to spring Liam when he walked through the front door. Horace had first guessed Liam's treatment was drug-inspired, but this pageantry felt inappropriate for a newly diagnosed alcoholic or junky.

Bill opened the door and ushered his wife and son in. Feeling acutely sheepish, Horace joined the shout of "surprise!" without looking directly at Liam, but nonetheless caught his genuine surprise. Liam responded with tired grace, a weak but genuine smile, maybe even wet eyes, which he covered behind his mother's hug. He looked himself, better than expected, clean-shaven and short-haired, perhaps a little thin. If there were scars to be found, they'd be within.

Horace didn't have to wait long for the truth, nor did he have to ask. As he embraced Liam, who apologized to him for not keeping better touch, Liam asked his thoughts about a Barnum visit after this. Flora was included in the offer, and with that Horace could relax. Scheduling their reconciliation meant as much as the act itself.

Unable to let a moment last, Greta turned to her shepherding, pushing people into the dining room for a meal Horace was unsure yet existed, offering snacks and refreshment to tie people down. Liam took her aside and asked permission to leave, his manner reminding Horace from across the room of early therapy, stiff and explicit. Overtop his bashfulness, she responded loudly that she thought it was a lovely idea for them to go off and hook up together. Everyone's vernacular grasp was slipping, making Barnum's remedy necessary and urgent enough for a rare daytime visit.

The three of them piled into Flora's car, with Horace watching the two of them from the backseat. Respecting Barnum's sanctity, Liam spent the drive asking them about the far less interesting things they'd been up to, congratulating both of them on the new jobs they were starting, while joking about the dumb job he'd worked (Horace noted the past tense) in New York. At first it seemed like idle talk about the cushy gig he'd scored, but Horace began to see the trap it had laid for Liam and some hints at what was to come.

His former employer, WordVomit, which had quite the logo, was a tech startup that pitched AI-generated solutions to companies suffering from dire content deficiencies. Marketing itself with the slogan, "Just start typing, and let the magic of WordVomit take over," it made decent business selling subscriptions and commissions for corporate-friendly posts and blogs, product descriptions and reviews, job listings and dismissal notices, apologies and double-downs, you name it. Liam was one of a half-dozen monkeys with a keyboard writing content for the express purpose of training the algorithm. Each day, he was to pump out a certain number of original pieces from which the machines could learn and improve. He confessed wondering if, given the bounties of fake work his fellow junior copywriters produced, the algorithm was unnecessary and they could better handle their clients' demands personally. Then, about one month into the job, he realized he was the one who was unnecessary. Each company computer came with WordVomit's proprietary software. For kicks, he submitted a WordVomit-generated post to the WordVomit training algorithm and waited to see if he'd get caught. No one was the wiser, so he did it again, and again, until soon his entire job was automated, the trainer consuming its own outputs Ouroboros-like. As long as he met his content goals, no one cared. He started working from home.

"Everything was the right amount of wrong," he admitted once seated in their favorite booth, having been given their pick of the empty space by their idle server. "A do-nothing job, way too much free time, and a terrible ratio of acquaintances to friends. My most regular contacts were my bodega guy, who sold me weed too, and the liquor store owner beneath my apartment. Both named Mo, nice guys, but not a good look. Still, I was convinced life's currents were about to sweep me around to that hidden corner, like any day I'd tap into some podcaster clique or find myself in a literati illuminati or some other New York BS. I was being really delusional, it's so weird looking back."

Liam paused for the server to take their food and drink orders all at once. None of them wanted interruption, including the server who was collaborating with the cook on a crossword. When he continued, he addressed Horace and Flora equally, suggesting this was new to her as well, although Horace figured she'd had the ending spoiled.

"It's like my life was underwater. It started in my apartment, where I could just float and let time pass with the outside world muffled. Once it got cold and dark in the winter, it was the only enjoyable way to spend my time. Drunk and high, or whatever else I could find. I, um, think you guys can relate. I should have reached out to you."

Flora and Horace nodded in solemn understanding of why he had not.

"It's a two-way street," Flora replied. "I'm so sorry."

"Hey, at least we're all here now," Liam assured her with a relieved look that made Horace feel left out. So far, Liam's experience sounded a lot like his, but his continued existence had never seemed in jeopardy.

"Thinking about killing myself didn't happen for a while," Liam continued evenly, which caused Horace to flinch. "I wasn't exactly unhappy, just bored and empty. So it started as a curiosity, like if this is life, maybe I should find out what's next? Then I'd tell myself probably nothing and move on, till the thoughts came back. I started journaling about it, the first time I'd opened a book in months. It became a mental exercise, like if I were to kill myself, how would I go about doing it? What messages would I send? If it's gonna be my last act, it's gotta be a good one. Keeping it intellectual like that let me think it was okay to consider. And I did survive, so maybe I was never serious about it. I really do like being alive, I promise."

Horace suppressed his reaction and the shame of just now learning. Liam clearly assumed they all knew, and Horace didn't want to make the moment about himself. He receded further and let Flora speak for them, grabbing Horace's hand from next to her and joining it with Liam's on the table.

"It is so good to hear you say that. It's the most important thing, to want to keep trying. We all have so much ahead of us."

Physical contact brought Horace back into the conversation, their bravery spreading to him through squeezes.

"You don't have to tell me if you don't wanna, but how close did you get? My parents didn't want to talk about it, and I've been too afraid to ask."

"It's fine. Pretty close. Like I went through with it, I just survived. Yeah, I know. I ended up with a long note titled 'The Perfect Suicide.' I thought I was being so clever, and if I'd been any smarter or dumber it probably would have worked. I treated it like I was staging a play, so the note would explain all my artistic choices. I chose my birthday so my parents would notice I was missing. I was . . . I wasn't suffering from hidden trauma or anything. No one should feel bad because they couldn't have known what I was going through. I was dangerously stuck in my head.

"The last thing I figured out was how to actually do it. I wanted it to be unique. I also had the idea of using water, like every time I walked by a river I was tempted to jump, but that wasn't enough. Then, on Memorial Day, I took a solo trip out to Coney Island. You know the word 'sonder'? All those people there hit me all at once, the screaming children about to grow up and their parents who already had, the couples who had found love and the loners who hadn't. And just so, so many people. It was a perfect picture, and I brought nothing to it. I was redundant. That stuck with me.

"I came back to the pier the night of my birthday with some dumbbells in my backpack. It was 3 a.m. and raining, so the place was a ghost town. All this time I'd felt so weightless and empty, so going out sinking seemed right. I was wasted of course, but I remember walking to the end of the pier, stepping up onto the railing, and launching myself. I don't remember hitting the water, but I think there was a moment in the air, a feeling that I held onto, of regret because the water looked too far away. Turns out I picked the lowest tide of the year. I hit my head on something, maybe a support beam, and ended up washing ashore without my backpack. Someone found me and called me in."

The server, who had been eavesdropping, took this as her chance to drop off their orders. They ate while digesting.

***

The version of Liam's troubles he gave Russ and Gil was so abbreviated it didn't even last the joint, which only Liam and Horace smoked as they led the group down their favorite trail, with Liam downplaying its severity while insisting on his full recovery. After taking a couple hits, Horace hung back with Flora, and they shared a cigarette in lieu of thoughts, while Russ and Gil came to grips with Liam's story.

The walk had been Liam's idea, and Horace was grateful for the change of scenery. He was bothered by Liam's flippant retelling and wanted to move past it, as if Liam's words were staining the ground they landed on. Even after the conversation lightened, a heaviness clung to Horace's clothes and weighed down his steps. Lingering on the fringe of the group, he kept his thoughts to himself and watched them be happy.

2.4 ~ The Members

"I heard they built nine basement floors and each one is a different circle of Hell."

"After we danced, he gave me this card. He was so hot I wanted to die."

"Now that I'm here, I'm feeling way better about my outfit. The vibe could have been literally anything."

"Well, I heard from my friend's roommate that all the bartenders are topless cuz it's like Bible-themed."

"If I can't buy a beer for less than $10, I'm leaving."

"Friend of mine got hired to bartend here, and they flew everyone out to Hawaii for training, so sick! Hoping I see him tonight, haven't heard from him since."

"If I see the girl he was dancing with after me, I'm throwing hands, I swear to God."

"Not gonna lie, a little disappointed to see how many people are here. Thought it was gonna be more exclusive."

"Jordan's card was for last weekend. She said they're doing it in waves, but just for the first month. Apparently, it's in-cre-duh-ble."

"Do you feel yours yet? Yeah, me neither. Should we take more?"

"Well, what I heard is we better get our drinks quick. This is all just some social experiment, and as soon as someone fucks up and breaks a rule, we all get kicked out."

"Hey, you got any cigarettes?"

"Hey, buddy! Can I bum a cig?"

Fully occupied by his eavesdropping, it took Horace a moment to register a direct address. How did people so consistently sniff him out? Was he such an easy mark? He hadn't even been smoking, yet.

"Oh, um," short of denial, no excuse came to mind, "yeah, here."

"Thanks, I got a dollar somewhere," and the beggar proceeded to dig into the pockets of his jeans.

"I'd rather give it for free. Need a light?"

No, his interlocuter never went anywhere without a lighter. Horace wondered about these people, prepared at any occasion to beg for nicotine, treating strangers as vending machines. Might he be able to chain-smoke from Horace to Horace, preying upon the endless goodwill of suckers? If that's what Horace even was. Suckers part with their possessions too freely because they give too happily, but Horace felt no such benevolence in his heart, only a stooped superiority condescending to join the rabble.

Horace had been standing in line since 9 p.m. on that sweaty evening in late June, waiting to enter Eden and looking foppish. A thorough costume of dark fabrics clung to his body, designer muck suppressed his curls, and new, white sneakers performed brightly like cracked glowsticks destined to fade by morning. By his side, Jena wore a similar fit more naturally. Straightened hair emboldened the oblique angles of her look, dark mascara underscored the playful gleam in her eyes, and the sheer of her top dropped hints of her loosely guarded transparency. Her superiority had no need to stoop or condescend, amply able to bring people to her level, while her generosity gave nothing but a reevaluation of what one already has and is. Yet by casting her spell of ascendance on Horace—picking his outfit, styling his hair, painting his nails, and stoking his potential—he felt less built up than built upon, constructed.

Having been lifted to a false height, Horace felt like every interaction would require looking down, sucking up, or some mix of both. Was he the figure he'd seen in Jena's mirror, or the one underneath who'd nervously asked her to plan his outfit? Did anyone—or everyone—else there feel that same dysmorphic discrepancy? A meaningful connection would have a long way to travel: starting in his gut, filtering through his mask, slotting into another's, and trickling down into their core. Better for the masks to speak to each other, or best of all for his mask to speak for itself, silent and unbothered.

Yet the cigarette beggar had seen through his disguise, or perhaps matched the mask to another type of generosity, that of abundant indifference. Jena wore that same indifference coyly, teasing her exuberance for the occasion like a shirt with just one more button undone. The German rule of cool still governed her, a shibboleth against visible anticipation, but she knew no one was there to enforce it. She allowed herself cracks of a smile, amused glances toward her dolled-up Horace, and a quickening pulse that flushed her cheeks. Holding an invitation that promised entrance, she performed this club line etiquette as a ritual, observing the advent of fun with a broadcast of boredom. The air she breathed and the scene she took in felt electric, but she stored these sensations as potential energy, ignoring them flirtatiously like she would a cute guy. Soon it would be time to dance.

So the two stood with differing indifference, brimming with opposite anticipations, in the unmoving line doubled back and forth along the lawn before the former church's doors. Around them, the crowd hummed a chattering chorus. The scene resembled the entrance to a small-scale music festival, not only in the peacocked outfits and intoxication, but also in the vibrations of expectancy for the something they were about to experience as a private, cultivated ensemble.

There himself by pure accident, Horace tried to reason out Eden's selection algorithm. From his eavesdropping, he'd gathered that Jena's case was typical. For the past several months, Eden's devilishly handsome and beautiful agents had roamed afield with cards aplenty and handed them out with discretion. Reverse-engineering their standards from the crowd's demographic profile, Eden wanted to fill itself with an almost racially diverse crowd of socio-economically identical people. There was no telling who were the invitees and who were the plus-ones, but they were all birds of a feather, a flock with the means to achieve prettiness if not beauty. In daylight and different outfits, they might well have resembled an Ivy League's five-year reunion.

Horace knew there was more to it, and it bothered him that he couldn't place it. Perhaps it was the way Jena had been approached, alone with her beer. Surely, she and Horace were outliers in their isolation. Yet everyone, or at least half the people there, must have been approached and therefore deemed approachable. As Jena liked to complain, that's hard to do for tight-knit circles, nigh impossible for couples (unless they approach you). Looking around, Horace saw some date-like behavior, a few hands held or backs touched, but for a plus-one event, it was minimal. Instead, he witnessed the loneliness of twos. Pairs of friends with only each other, imbalanced by the even numbers. Even he and Jena, both content to people watch, were stuck between the anonymity of one and the equanimity of three or more. Alone together, they had all shown up.

A hush fell over the crowd like dominoes, spreading rapidly enough to suggest that Horace wasn't the only one casting his attention outwards. His view obscured, he couldn't tell if the quiet was a response to a new event at the front or the crowd's request for one. They'd been there for 45 minutes, and by now the line had grown as long behind as before them. Like dress code, timing was another of the evening's mysteries. Did Jena's invitation play by the rules of a party, in which a comfortable two hours could be added to the posted time, or a standing room concert, for which some would show up early and few would want to be late? The real Horace, risk-averse, originally favored a punctual approach, but the man he saw in Jena's mirror told him to chill out, be cool, just roll through whenever. Jena had not given much thought to timing—she never did—but upon dressing them up, her excitement and curiosity compelled her to call a rideshare immediately. On the drive, Horace vocalized mild worries about a long, expensive night waiting for the party to arrive, while secretly basking in relief at their 8:57 p.m. ETA.

The chatter reasserted itself triumphantly as two individuals from the front of the line ascended the steps and entered through the front doors. Horace must have missed the appearance of bouncers. While a curtain behind the door kept the expectants from catching glimpses of the interior, Horace was unique among them for knowing the basic infrastructure of what was held in store. Yet he underestimated the deceptions daylight could perpetrate.

Earlier that day, Gil chauffeured, Liam rode shotgun, and Horace and Russ sat cramped in the back of Gil's Mustang as it zipped through the residential streets that led up to Eden for their first and only tech rehearsal. Much like his acting, Gil's driving was defined by a confidence that either outstripped or made up for his natural abilities. It's hard to take your eyes off a performance that runs yellow lights so daringly and seizes gaps so abruptly. He kept his right foot busy between the two pedals, perpetual escalation and deceleration that rejected the concept of cruising. Current motion sickness aside, Gil had really grown on Horace, emerging as the only professional among the crew. Liam and Russ were better at acting, but Gil was the only one who hit his marks consistently, recited his actual lines, and did his job without creating more headaches and work for Horace. All this despite the steady drip of light beer into his bloodstream, from which Horace prayed their driver would refrain today at their technical rehearsal.

Their show had reached the point of "ready-in-theory," and now hinged only on random elements like Eden's technical specifications, the effects of a live audience, and Liam's mood of the day. That they were in jolly spirits on the drive, bumping Kanye and cracking wise, boded well for that last factor, but the recent anniversary of Liam's suicide attempt weighed heavily on Horace. As he watched his friend drift into increasingly erratic behavior at rehearsals, Horace found it harder and harder to resist the temptation to pathologize Liam's actions into a definitive state of ill-being. The primary mode of expression for Liam's inner turmoil was dissatisfaction, a feeling from which no one was safe. Liam found Russ's Professor too likeable one moment, then too villainous the next. Gil's face looked wrong, and his body carried inadequate intention. He begged Horace to tear his performances apart, and then bristled at minor corrections. He altered words in his script compulsively, sometimes recreating the original phrasings by accident. He ran scenes again and again, unhappy with his own choices for reasons he could not articulate. While Dr. Hawthorne's reaction would not be in the artistic mode of critical, Liam seemed to think the play's execution testified his case, and its merit was his merit. Horace, no stranger to fixating on details as a distraction from what he could not control, acknowledged Liam had plenty good reason to be stressed out.

City Fringe, playing a bad hand with house money, had secured *Solving for X* a total of four hours to work in their space that day, and that was all they would get until opening night. Four hours to work through every tech element from cue to cue, and then run at least one dress rehearsal. Since everything necessarily would go wrong before it could go right, this looked to be an impossible task, even with their forty-five minute runtime. They'd have to squeeze what would normally be a week's worth of trial and error into only three hours and pray for a final hour of perfection. Horace had done all his homework, marked his script with every lighting change, music insert, and set transition, but his test anxiety was rearing its ugly head again. It didn't help that Mint, the stage tech for *Solving for X*, had been responding to Horace's fanatically detailed emails with only curt replies along the lines of "we'll see" and "I can't promise it." Horace was sure that when he met Mint in person, he would either love them or hate them. His heart held plenty of room for bad communicators if they produced good results.

Gil backed into his spot in the empty parking lot, and they unpacked the trunk, distributing between them the card table, set dressings, and prop boxes in such a way that Liam escaped with empty hands, while Gil went full child-carrying-groceries mode.

The address was curiously unchanged from its street view preview. Still just a red-brick edifice with white columns and a tall steeple emerging from the center of the roof; still perched on an unremarkable grassy field that sloped down and away from them; still even the white cross impressed on the wall above the double-door entrance. Only the church's marquee board for mass times and Bible quotes had been removed. Where were the modern fonts, the streamlined aesthetics, and market-tested eye-catchers Vein was known for? Why did it still look quaint? The one notable thing about this place was its lack of surrounding density. Thick woods wrapped around and behind, a golf course occupied the space across the street, and its nearest neighbors down the winding road were set back on sizeable plots. Eden could make quite a ruckus before reaching the threshold of local disturbance, though rich, bored busybodies might have a different say in that.

Locked front doors delivered the first blow to morale, which crumpled under the frustrations of the ensuing troubleshooting experience. Russ went off looking for a second entrance to the four-sided building, finding two more locked doors—one on ground level and another down a cement staircase—before giving up and turning his attention to out-of-reach windows. Gil kept knocking and knocking. Liam leaned despondently against a column, convinced of the futility of their actions. Russ proposed picking the lock, then asked if anyone knew how. Gil switched to yanking and shaking the door handles with all his might. Liam sank to a seated position. Horace, for his part, sought an external intervention. He emailed Mint, who should've been there by then. He called the City Fringe office line, but no one picked up. He tried to find a number for Eden online to no avail. He double-checked the communiques he'd received for mention of a time change or key pick-up he'd somehow missed. 1 p.m. arrived. Their four hours kicked off with a bicker about who to blame while the sun's intensity approached its peak. All Liam could do was stare at the sky, losing himself in the endless blue.

Every few minutes, the sound of a car would raise their hopes and the sight of its passing would dash them. At last, the fifth-or-so car, a mid-aughts beater of a Honda with a frame-rattling bass, pulled into the parking lot. The driver waited for the end of the song, a collection of noisy distortions unrecognizable to the onlookers, before exiting their car. Horace had never met a self-identified punk before, but the driver, with a face of sharp angles and a posture of menacing capability, hair buzzed and bleached, and Latin skin pierced and tattooed extensively, would probably qualify. Or maybe they were post-punk, some genre of person beyond Horace's understanding or experience. He was intimidated.

Mint approached Horace and introduced themself but offered no apologies for their tardiness. They seemed hungover, pained by the demands of existence, and maintained in person the brusqueness Horace had first experienced via email. They shrugged off Russ's "Nice of you to join us," and ignored Gil's affected frowning. Liam didn't even say hello as he rose with effort to wait by the door. Having already lost fifteen minutes, Horace chose to let the matter drop rather than risk further antagonization. Their operation depended on Mint's cooperation, and he knew personally how spiteful techies could be toward performers.

Mint withdrew an insane assembly of keys, a Frankenstein of permissions and trinkets they had earned or otherwise obtained over the years, and pinched a fob between two fingers, letting the rest of the keys slacken and jangle. They pressed it to the handle, waited for a click that opened the door, and passed through the curtain. Eden's interior could've passed for a grade school gymnasium decorated by resource-intensive PTA moms channeling the dying embers of community mythmaking into the creation of a truly ambitious haunted house, if that haunted house was set in a pseudo-Hellenistic, pseudo-Christian anachronism of a church, and that church had a bar running the length of the right side. The sight was going to give his classics-loving mother a conniption.

All forms were divorced from their purpose. Down both sides of the room, arches spanned between Corinthian columns that bore no weight. Along the plaster walls, scatterings of stained-glass mosaics conveyed no light. A taut, matte canvas, cutting off the windows and spanning the vaulted ceiling, created a low, cloud-covered, claustrophobic sky. The architectural lines directed their sights straight back to the stage as a focal point, dark, inaccessible, and aloof. Closed doors on the ground to either side of the stage could offer a way up, but their thickness implied a locking away of something below. Forest green walls and brown hardwood mocked them with their imitation of natural colors, while gold stencils, trims, ivy, and fixtures drove the joke home, as if golden were the building's natural state of being, with more muted colors having been overlaid.

To reach the floor, they descended a half-flight of stairs from the rail-lined perch at the entrance. The ground, artificially depressed, spread wasted before them, mourning its lack of pews. As Mint led them across to a door in the back, Horace felt the sorrow of an empty space longing to be filled.

✳✳✳

Horace and Jena stepped through the curtain into a scene of swirling impressionisms. Waves of golden light shimmered across the crowd, each individual their own point of living color, while the walls seethed and the stained glass danced. The navy sky was backlit with a constellation of red-purple, green-blue stars, seeming to reflect the patterns below that its hidden lights created. Momentum, or attraction, swept them down the stairs and into the mix.

"It smells just like the man did!" Jena yelled into his ear over the music, an ambience flowing like marbles up and down scales and decibels over a driving beat. Intoxication entered into

Horace's nose and stung his eyes, something unfamiliar yet pleasing, like ancestral forests. He tried to check his exhilaration against reality, noting how the crowd moved more than any individual and swelled more than its dozens of members were worth, but he could not hold these thoughts in his mind. The vibes were self-perpetuating. He could no more picture the canvas above his head than a screen hosting a film projection, the illusion of depth insisting upon his vision. Rooted to the floor, his mind briefly turned with the possibilities these capabilities presented for their play. Jena grabbed his arm and dragged him to the bar.

Horace was eager to get drunk and forget about the day. Technically, the dress rehearsal had been a success, Mint having outdone themself in the execution and improvement of Horace's instructions. Disappearing into a booth to the left of the entrance, they orchestrated each lighting change and music cue as if they'd been along for the whole ride, yet also as if they weren't there at all, merely a voice from a walkie-talkie and a presence in a switchboard. They weren't there to make friends, which Horace respected but regretted, for once feeling an impulse to connect. Liam maintained the balance of entropy by trading his languish for mania. It seemed his goal was to be a problem, escalating from new, off-putting line reads into wide diversions from the script, baiting Russ and Gil into frustration. He never broke character, but the character was not a Doc that Horace recognized. The three of them maintained their tacit agreement to just power through Liam's antics for a time, but Russ finally snapped when Liam put him in a headlock, an uncalled-for escalation of their characters' verbal altercation. Horace had to step in and read as Doc for thirty minutes while Liam smoked himself off his edge outside. Just like he'd promised Greta months before, Horace assured Russ and Gil he'd talk sense into Liam before opening night, only this time he meant it. With the rehearsal close in his rearview and that conversation approaching in his windshield, Horace drank to live only in the thin, hazy present, speeding dangerously along.

The drinks were cheap, shockingly so, and the house cocktails they ordered were splendid, vibrant in color and flavor. The bartenders, attractive and vacant, moved with impressive (perhaps performance-enhanced) efficiency. Horace and Jena drank greedily, the great bargain increasing the value of the drinks. Again, pesky thoughts about loss-leader pricing and ulterior motives tried and failed to gain traction in Horace's clouded head. They ordered another round, and then merged into the throng.

They danced with abandon. Jena, in her element and unleashed, Horace, severed from his usual shame, the edge of the crowd pushing in, the center gaining critical mass. The beats spoke to them and the lights guided them, joy spreading like a communicable disease, tossing their bodies about, Jena dancing with people from one to the next, a choreography of free love, a communal body of one purpose. Horace felt his consciousness float upwards, intermix with others, adopting a bird's-eye view, feeling the scene for its mass effect more than his own sensory experience. After all, each attendee was flooded with the same stimulations, one sight, one sound, one smell, individual distinctions collapsing between them, permissions granted from without. There was nothing to sing, only heavy breathing and petting. Physicality crept in as borders broke down, possession of limbs came into question, hands connected to each other like joints in sockets, the sharing of drinks, sweat, and spit. Horace found himself on the receiving end of a kiss, evaluating what it was like for both of them, whether he was grabbing or being grabbed, only for a dying flare of self to emerge and push the other guy away, absorbed back into the crowd. Horace's lips were left cold, like he'd made out with a mirror. Another communal sensation was the irrelevance of time.

On stage, a DJ stood in fog. Hat, sunglasses, masked, misty, mysterious. Occasionally, he would speak to them, issuing commandments that traveled from the external, the making of noise and raising of limbs, to the internal, the bearing of hearts and vanquishing of negativity. Horace felt impossibly light, a feather in the wind, at no risk and of no risk. It was nothing to obey the dicta. He was, is, and will be, all at once. That was all. Sentences without object, ideas fully formed and static, frozen in amber, petrified in action.

Someone was holding his hand, kissing his cheek, a gentle hello in context, someone familiar to him, familiar to many by then, this Jena of his. She'd drifted away and returned, carrying along a flushed and smoky-eyed friend. They had something to discuss with him, and one linked body with six legs snaked out of the crowd back to the bar. Over more drinks, which the friend seemed to receive in gratuity, Jena made her announcement.

"She is telling me to become a member! Do you want to!?"

"What does that mean!?"

"That we can always come back here! We will always be welcome!"

"Okay!"

Disagreement seemed impossible, alien. Why wouldn't he want to be able to tap into this experience again? There actually seemed to be an answer to that rhetorical question, an original thought scratching at the door to be let in, but he couldn't hear it over the music, thoroughly wormed into his brain. Nothing seemed binding, tied to his real self. He'd been replaced, and was content to watch this replacement carry on with living. Anything that happened to him that night would be gone by morning, any progress cached in memory that would wait for his return, his redeparture.

Nicotine saved him. He told them he wanted to get his lungs some fresh air and smoke. They declined his invite, which Horace didn't think was possible. What discretion did they still possess? What ranking of choices that refused one thing for another? Every request had been going to the top of his queue, the whole point being to deny nothing to no one. They were sad to see him go, everyone he passed, watching him swim back upstream, empathies attaching to him like leeches, projections of FOMO foisted upon him. The guard opened the door for him, and he stepped outside.

The flame, the glow, his finger's scar gone pale like a tiny graft. He settled back into his own senses. The selfish thrill of a cigarette, a buzz in his lungs traded for carcinogens in his and others, though no one was around him then. His shoes hit the grass, and his mind descended to Earth. The sky's simple beauty recast Eden's false ceiling as kitsch. Thoughts still weren't coming easily to him, but he had a feeling he didn't want to go back.

Something rustled around the side of the building. Guided by curiosity, Horace found himself looking around the wall at a bald head in the darkness, handling garbage. The body turned to face Horace, a long body with a wide reach. Even in precious little light, the face was familiar to Horace. An ugly face. A pained, ugly face like a freezer-burned lemon. The pamphleteer. He was here.

Horace's high was utterly popped, and its residue clung to him, sticky and cold. This time, the wax didn't drip. It encased and paralyzed him. He waited for the man to move. There was no mistaking it, they were looking right at each other, recognizing each other, waiting for each other. Thoughts finally broke through to him, starting with "RUN!" before tempering to "back away slowly," a translation of survival instincts. He made the same motions backwards as when he first met the man on the highway, but with more respect than defiance this time. Horace detected no change in the man, no reaction to movement, no effort to maintain their encounter. He may have been just as surprised as Horace, who had no way of putting himself into the stranger's shoes, empathy crowded out by fear, two wild animals passing in the night.

Once Horace retreated behind the wall, a new feeling took hold. This had been his second chance to learn about the man, and again he had failed. His fear was justified, but so was his curiosity. He didn't want one to rule exclusively over the other. When would he ever get another chance like this, just the two of them in the quiet air? He hesitated, weighing his choices, one light and one heavy. The lighter option, returning to the dancefloor, appealed to him by minimizing disturbance, the lifted scale only reaching higher into the air. Confrontation, the heavier option, would create ripples, the scales swinging as a consequence, forcing a flipped equilibrium for which he would be responsible. A choice to end all choices or choice to keep choosing. One foot at a time, he decided.

When Horace peeked his head back around the wall, the man was gone. His heart sank, confirming for him he'd made the right choice at the wrong time. Next time, if there was one, he'd be ready.

He walked back up the steps and into Eden. Its sensations assaulted him again, but this time he was ready, disillusioned to its magic. He fetched a drunk and fading Jena. It was time for them to go home.

2.5 ~ **The Thing**

Waiting, pacing, what else was there to do? Standing behind glass, stuck observing. The seats filling slowly; Flora touching up Liam's makeup; Gil rehearsing lines under his breath; Russ, headphones in, practicing Melee tech skills on his laptop, bullying a lifeless CPU, moving choppily, brutally, fearsome yet lacking Dylan's suave control of that character, like seeing your ex with a new partner and personality; Horace's mind coming up with new ways to torture itself, collecting and connecting all of his problems into one. It was opening night.

That night in Eden stirred something in Horace. He woke early the next day with a sensation of realization disconnected from any material change. There were new powers at his disposal that demanded usage, as yet unnamed but there within reach. He felt cheated, having been given a second chance with the pamphleteer but not a second take on that chance. This left in him a deficit like opportunistic bloodlust, but there would be more things to get into, more responsibilities to undertake, reverberations ready to become earthquakes. He prepared for consequences as though he were suiting up before battle. The critical window had arrived.

First order of business, Liam. It was time to give him a taste of his own medicine, fight fire with fire. He clung to these cliches as wisdom, guidance for unfamiliar territory. How else could he learn to stand up for himself? He knew pulling himself up by his own bootstraps was impossible. Ready to be rude, he crossed the road to the Hawthorne's front door, knocked and entered without waiting, and walked straight through the main hall into the kitchen, soaked with morning's light. Across the island countertop, the Sunday paper covered Bill's face, front page news stoking a border crisis between distant lands, while behind him Greta was tending to eggs on the stove.

The Thing

"Morning, Bill and Greta," Horace sticking to first names, unceremonious as his entrance, "is Liam awake? We're supposed to meet up early today and go over some stuff, but he hasn't been answering his phone."

The lie came easily, the first new power to reveal itself. Calm and unapologetic, he waited for them to adjust to his presence. Bill shifted the paper just enough to make eye contact and grunt and nod at him before returning to his shelter and reading, while Greta held court, social stabilization her second nature.

"Good morning, sweetie. I haven't seen Liam yet. Bill, have you?"

Bill grunted in the negative.

"You know, he might be over at Brunhilde's already. Isn't it great he's been helping her out?"

Bill grunted in agreement.

"Wait, helping *her*? Brunhilde?" Horace asked bemusedly. Their curmudgeonly neighbor was hardly a real person to him, more like a feature in his father's scary bedtime stories, an exception to the neighborly spirit, a black cat whose path you hoped not to cross. Not a human being to know and to help.

"Oh, hasn't he told you? I suppose he's just bashful about it. Yes, he's been at it for a couple months now, just a few hours each Sunday cleaning up and doing little odd jobs for her. I've always been telling Bill that poor woman must find maintaining her house an awful struggle. Hardly blame her for it being in such rough shape. We're so glad that Liam decided to do something about it. The perfect kind of thing for him, given his situation."

Horace swallowed two gulps of disbelief. Not only was Liam spending time in the "forbidden forest" (as they took to calling her plot after she abruptly razed the backyard of all its trees), but he also hadn't told Horace about it. What was the point of keeping a secret like that? Was it just an omission? Horace didn't expect to be kept abreast of Liam's every hobby or occupation, but this must have involved some deliberate deception. He was sick of the lies.

"No, that hasn't come up. Huh. That's so generous of him. I'll go see if he's there."

Crossing the pavement to the house at the cul-de-sac's dead center, Horace passed the tame and respectable Smithson (née Falco) home to his left, glanced at the renovated and professionally maintained Neufchatel maison to his right, and turned back to take in his mother's eclectic garden across from the Hawthornes' austere hedges and regal exterior. All five buildings began as a matching set, but their residents, spending their years and money on them, had cultivated for each a distinct personality. When they'd played as children, the stump squad—Liam, Flora, Horace, and Dylan—spoke in hushed tones of a fifth child locked away in Brunhilde's basement, whom they dreamed of rescuing and befriending. Flora spoke of her as a forgotten princess, a Cinderella without the company of evil stepsisters; the rest agreed, until one day Liam added to the legend. There must be siblings in there—every Gretel needs a Hansel—and out of that original idea, Ian Noone was born. Their imaginary friend, equal parts scapegoat and aspiration, broken free at last and covering for Liam's lies as compensation.

Horace approached Brunhilde's front door but froze with several steps to go. He'd never entered her home, let alone as a solicitor. To wit, he was unsure they'd ever spoken directly to each other. Her raspy whispers were saved for the adults of the block, whenever they wronged or displeased her. Yet Liam was spending quality time with her. It reeked of a scheme, though Horace couldn't guess his angle. It wasn't to satisfy Liam's attention cravings, given that he wasn't telling people. Could it just be to get his parents off his back?

Horace added it to the list of explanations he needed from Liam. But first he wanted to explain some things to Liam, tell him off really. Horace could tolerate anything in service of a plan, did his best work as a cog in a machine, but all that depended on belief in the architect, the higher power. Let him critique his wiggle room and he'll never bother the broader structure. Liam, shaking the foundations of their plan with his erraticism and misdirection, had forced Horace into cleanup duty and left him worrying the roof was about to cave in. Today, he would spill his feelings with no regard for how Liam would respond, a reversal of his usual, managed approach. Though harder to name, this seemed to be his second power to unlock, truth telling coming hand-in-hand with lying.

Horace stepped up to the door and rapped the brass doorknocker three times. While he waited, he tapped his foot and drummed his fingers on his pants. Signs of rude impatience, symptoms of strained nerves. Knocking again would be more rudeness, but he prepared himself to do it anyway, only for the door to open and reveal Liam, looking sweaty and self-satisfied. A stooped, scowling Brunhilde loomed in the hall, standing just out of reach of the sun's light, staring them down. Liam stepped through and closed the door behind him.

"What can I do ya for, partner?" Liam asked serenely, as if it was perfectly natural he was opening Brunhilde's door.

"What's this with you doing shifts in the forbidden forest?" Horace asked pointedly.

"Ah, don't worry about it," Liam beamed, already walking back toward his house. "C'mon, let's find a better place to chat."

"Liam," Horace called as he made up ground, "what the hell? Why didn't you tell me?"

"What do you care? Charity don't count if you brag about it."

"That's what this is, charity?"

"Okay, she pays me. Interesting lady, too. Almost feel bad for all the witch allegations."

"This is so classic. Why do you always need to have a secret thing going on? Even the play. Keep stuff from your parents, sure, but I feel like you're holding out on me too."

"Bro, shh."

Horace realized he'd let his voice climb, and the empty cul-de-sac swallowed the sound. You never know who's listening from open windows. He bit his tongue and followed Liam into the Hawthornes' garage. As soon as Horace closed the door, he launched in on Liam again.

"Dude, what is your deal right now? Like what the fuck was up at rehearsal yesterday? I don't even care that much about the play, but you're being a shitty friend. To Russ and Gil too."

Horace had never spoken so directly to anyone before, though he only said it to the back of Liam's head. When they reached the top of the stairs, Liam kept going and plopped on the couch before responding.

"Sorry, I don't really know what to tell you," he tossed out vacantly, picking at his nails, glancing at Horace but not holding the moment, as if inviting Horace to rip further into him. Horace paced back and forth as he unspooled all the words he'd been gathering.

"You swore to me you'd keep things together, at least pretend to be normal. That was our deal. I don't have to confront your dad with you. It's not too late for me."

"Then don't. I don't care. This was all a mistake anyway. It's not gonna work."

"Goddammit, cut the shit. You can't do this. You can't bring us together under you and then bail. You need to see this through to the end. I still want to believe in you. We can do this, but you need to want it. Everything is ready except you."

As Liam affected a silent pout, his eyes narrowed to a specific spot, just below the TV set. He was working through something that he wasn't ready to share. Horace felt antsy, so used to Liam talking through things. He had to fill the silence.

"We need a plan for when we talk to him," Horace continued, going for encouragement, "and there's no point in coming up with one if we can't even get through the play. If you can't get through it. This only works if you seem in control. Don't let him dismiss you as crazy."

"Do you think I'm crazy? That I've lost it?"

"I don't fucking know, dude. Yeah, you're being crazy, but that's a dumb word. It's too dismissive. Until we confront your dad, the whole thing's like Schrödinger's cat. And, the thing is, I don't care if the cat ends up being dead or not. Until we find out, all that matters is taking the right approach."

"And what would that be?"

He sucked his teeth and stared at Liam. Was this how others felt when talking to him? All just casual deflections and reflections, pivots, a lack of forward progress. He was not enjoying the pressures associated with carrying the weight of this conversation. For fear of losing Liam to an inner zone, he tried on another new power, thinking out loud. This one was the least developed by far.

"Well . . . It starts with you gaining Russ and Gil's trust again. And mine, for that matter. Like, all you gotta do is read your lines and play your part. And, an apology for acting out so much wouldn't hurt either. The play is good enough, and it honestly doesn't matter anyway. Now, as for your dad . . . confronting him . . . the best approach is to be direct, right? Tell him you found his screenplay, and you think it's real, and . . . well, I guess you're gonna be telling him he's a doppelganger whether he knows it or not?"

This whole thing was supposed to hinge on a sample size of one, confronting Bill for either a confirmation or a denial, but if it was all true, wouldn't the effective sample size be zero? The real Bill was supposed to be gone. That's how the play ended. The doppelganger factored into Horace's calculations like an imaginary number, bringing with it endless and incomprehensible possibilities. If Doc's method was operational, the minimum memory gap between the target and the replacement would be the event of the switch itself, a discontinuous kink as one life took over for the other. If they knew they were a replacement, they'd be no better than an actor, plagued with literal imposter syndrome. Even if Bill admitted the screenplay was based on his life's work, what possible evidence could exist to convince Horace he'd been replaced? More worrisomely, what could get Liam to believe his dad *hadn't* been replaced? They appeared to be hurtling toward a cliff wall, or maybe a pit, but either way nothing scalable.

"Yeah, there's the rub," Liam picking up where Horace trailed off, "I miscalculated. I zeroed in my dad's replacement, and he can't prove shit. That's why this whole thing is pointless."

"We don't know that. We don't know what he's bringing to the table. That's why we just gotta get our process right. Do the play, confront him, stick to the facts. I'll be sitting next to him the whole time. Oh, god. What if he talks to me during the play? I've got to get through forty-five minutes next to him?" Horace's hold on the conversation was slipping, his grip strength too underdeveloped, anxieties stacking up and spilling over.

"Yeah dude, we're fucked. But at least we both know it."

The lights flickered. All things were in their places. A ten-by-ten grid of folding chairs with a couple dozen scattered butts filling them, reading the festival's thick program, chatting at catty-corners, making plans for after, checking scores and bets, tuning in and out, a multitude of frequencies coexisting harmoniously. Horace twisted around in his seat. Behind him sat Paul next to Horace's parents, ready to be so proud, and several rows behind them the twins with some friends, ready to leave. Down the row from the twins, Gil's family formed a visual blockade, two large adults and three larger sons in a row, sitting upright out of touristic respect for the arts, appreciating Gil's performances like fridge art. Russ's parents hadn't made the trip. Flora had re-joined her roommate on the left-middle edge of the grid. Hm-yes, way in the back, Horace even saw Gregory's bald head catching the light, oh joy. What seemed to be some mix of college friends, high school friends, work friends, and life friends, none of Horace's but some of each of the others', filled in various patches of seats. No sight of Bill's partners at the firm, on whom Liam had briefed Horace with photos just in case. Eden's distortions did nothing to swell what was a decidedly meagre turnout, but that didn't matter to Horace, because there was Bill, elbow-to-elbow with him in the front row, their reserved place of honor, spitting distance from the stage.

Horace had long since sweat through the pits of his button-down shirt, enlisted other parts of the fabric to soak up some excess, and yet still could feel skittish drops racing down his ribs. This fresh sweat and that cold wax shared similarities, but the wax moved with a slow inevitability, while this was an active sweat, one that wouldn't let up till his work was done. The actors behind the curtain had their own sweaty nerves to contain, but at least they could weaponize them by rising to the occasion. To Horace, this last-minute crawl of time could at best only passively filter things from "could go wrong" into "didn't go wrong."

With furtive glances, another skill being tried out to mixed success, Horace tried reading Bill's expression for a baseline. Grave, but not deadly serious, eyes looking nowhere in particular. Perhaps a placid surface masking a tumultuous interior, perhaps suspecting nothing at all. Next to him, Greta had been reading the program with a smile, and put it away as the lights dimmed. Then, total dark, the imminence of dawn.

Lights up on Doc, Prof, and Sarge, smartly suited, stumbling onto the stage, gesticulating with their filled champagne flutes (equally a testament to realism and a desire to drink), making fun with each other, dropping expositional hints about the wedding, the open bar, the extravagance of the evening. "Money, Money, Money," by Abba was piped in from a recording of a recording, intentionally shitty in a way that Horace had convinced himself worked until this very moment, now realizing it created a terrible first impression for the audience. Thankfully, the music stopped as soon as the lights cut to focus on Doc, the other two frozen in shadow.

"Many stories end with the happy marriage," Doc began, addressing the audience. "My story starts with one. I want you to remember, through all my problems that are to come, that I did it all for my family. Everything that happens from here on out comes back to them."

The lights switched back to full, Mint not missing a beat, as Prof put his arms around Doc, and Sarge downed one of his two glasses of champagne with gusto.

"Gentlemen, I must propose a toast," announced the Professor, "before we return the good doctor to his better half. To the next generation! May they may inherit a better world from us!" Three plastic glasses met in the air as each man cheered. Prof continued, and Horace slid his eyes rightwards, straining himself with subtlety. The first reaction would be crucial.

"I want to tell you about another wedding gift I've got for you, one that can't be wrapped. Doc, let's face it, you're too smart to be stuck working for the government. You belong at the top of the pyramid, we all do. The three of us together could accomplish anything, could hold history in our very hands. So, I have a proposal. Something that will help pay for these kids we're about to be having."

"Hey, I've already got two!" Sarge interjected boastfully.

"All the more so. Doc, I must be frank, this is a matter the Sergeant and I have already discussed at length, and we only held off on sharing with you because you were preoccupied with these nuptials. But now time is of the essence. We want you to enter into business with us and lend your generous talents to matters of national security. The future of international conflict is not mechanical, but biological, and we will need your expertise."

"Folks like me are gonna go out of fashion, Doc," added Sarge, "and that's a good thing. We're dreaming of a world without war, and we've got some interested parties who might pay us to help make that dream a reality. It's a moonshot deal type thing."

Bill slowly turned his head toward Horace, whose peripheral vision blurred with fear. He leaned over, opened his mouth as if to say something, then rewound the motion and turned back to the stage with renewed attention. One minute in, he already knew, recognizing his written words. They had each other trapped, but Horace felt like a mouse in a lion's paw. No telling yet how Bill felt, further interactions withheld for the rest of the first scene, which closed with Doc monologuing while the other two changed costumes and set dressings.

"On the same day I gave a definitive yes to my wife forever, I offered a tentative yes to my partners' proposal. There were two tracks leaving the station, and I could only board one train. I hoped they'd run parallel for the rest of my life, never crossing or diverging from each other, but that was a fool's hope. As soon as our next meeting, and the discussion of the work to be done, I could see the mistake I had made. But momentum is a powerful force, and it was already too late to switch trains."

"I liked my version of that speech better," Bill whispered into Horace's ear as the lights briefly dropped, allowing Doc to loosen his tie, lose his jacket, and take his spot for the next scene. Horace tensed and froze, channeling all his nervous energy into the invisible movement of his bouncing toes. Bill had offered wit rather than ire, but that was no less terrifying. Re-exerting control over his feet, Horace focused the rest of his presence on not betraying anything to Bill before the show's finale. He was to be Liam's backup in this fight, not his replacement.

"I don't know what you mean," Horace muttered back, his jaw moving like an amateur ventriloquist's. He side-eyed Bill icily, who side-eyed him back with a smile and an eyebrow raise, uncomfortably at ease. The on-stage action resumed. In short order, Prof was introducing the contract.

". . . They have asked us to do only one thing for them. It's not an easy feat, and success is by no means expected. We will advance our national cause simply by pursuing it. But the dream of a world secured at every corner by our interests, working together for a common goal, that is too sweet a dream to give up without trying."

"Enough of this rhetoric, Professor," Doc interjected, "Please just tell me what it is that we've been asked to do."

Prof soaked in the moment of suspense, while Sarge was giggling with excitement. For a moment, Horace got to appreciate the villainous, bordering on hammy, chemistry those two had developed since the read-through.

"Doppelgangers, my dear friend. They have requested proposals on how to make one man out of another. Only . . ."

At this point, Horace's attention was pulled from the stage in multiple directions, audience reactions not quite reaching gasp levels, but certainly some stirring and grumbling. Save a few like Gregory, everyone in the audience was aware of Liam's claims about his father. Horace could imagine all the eyes at the back of his head, fixed as much on Bill as him, but most target lines would implicate them both. Surely Maria had eyes only for him, sitting near enough behind that he could sense her heat, her anguish. The train had left the station.

The actors carried on. If anything, Liam fed off the negative energy, preferring it to the listless ambivalence of amateur theater-watching. His endless production of new Docs had temporarily ceased in the week between Horace's intervention and opening night, as he turned in a few reliable, almost-tame performances in their final practice runs. Now, tonight, all his divergent explorations and expressions of the character were coalescing into a singular Doc, conveying a sincere optimism strong enough to justify his actions to the audience, while leaving room for self-doubt and falling short of full self-justification. Even Horace, whose past few months were defined by an obsession with identifying the real Liam, watched as his disbelief suspended itself, one eye seeing Liam and the other seeing Doc, each at their own crossroads.

Doc eliminated Sarge in their game of cutthroat pool but failed to sink the fatal blow against the Professor. All their talk was of history—psychological experiments, three-letter agencies, regime changes—scoring points and counterpoints about the ever-elusive just cause. Was not power's only goal to perpetuate itself, Doc challenged. Is that causation or correlation, victims of power without sufficient purpose, Prof countered. What to do with this power was all that mattered to Sarge.

"We will do what we believe is right," assured Prof, as he finished Doc off.

"And if we disagree on what is right?" wondered Doc.

"Then it is not right. We can only act in consensus. Three equal partners with one common vote and one common goal."

As they shook hands to end the scene, Horace felt Bill's breath on his ear, carrying with it unpleasant sounds. However displeased he may have been with the production, it was becoming apparent that he didn't want to miss a word of dialogue.

"I can only wonder where this is going from here."

"It's just a play. Wait and see."

"I'm not talking about the play."

"Then I still don't know what you mean."

While Horace always preferred the aesthetics of quick scene changes, he had never appreciated them so much as now, keeping his exchanges with Bill to a minimum. Guilty as he was, he'd instinctively fallen into the tried-and-true strategy of playing dumb to delay any serious cross-examinations. The wheels were starting to fall off though. He only realized Greta was crying once she got up to leave, just as the lights came on for the third scene. Bill half-rose to stop her but did not follow her out. In the commotion of watching her go, Horace accidentally turned his head far enough to see his parents, and Maria snapped her head toward him milliseconds faster than he could shift his gaze back to the stage. Milliseconds was all he needed to clock the betrayal on her face. At least Al was probably having a better time at this show than any of his previous experiences with live theater, an aficionado of drama such as he was.

The wall between the stage and the audience continued to break down with the third scene's rising tensions. Liam must have seen his mother storm off, as his Doc included new mentions of his paternal negligence, appropriately in character but nonetheless jarring to Horace, Russ, and Gil. All his work was dedicated to them, Doc proclaimed one moment, then lamented the next at how even his successes were failing them, those long, draining hours of toil. The better world for which he worked was slipping away. His eureka moment, back on script now, came just after resolving to quit and return to a normal life should it not succeed. Prof and Sarge were bemused by his anguish as he revealed his triumph.

"I've done it. The tests on Prototype Chemical X have achieved p-values of point-zero-zero-zero-one. Gentlemen, we have found the shape of consciousness and can mold it to our will. God help us."

"Chemical ten," Bill said quite loudly, unable to help himself, not restricting his commentary to Horace's earshot.

Russ and Gil heard and hesitated, exchanging confused looks. Liam cracked the slightest hint of a smile. Had Bill said that to put them off? Was that really what he had called it? Did this mean Chemical X was real? Horace's mind was racing too quickly to settle into any conclusions, each flickering by like strobe lighting. He heard an unmistakable shush shoot out from behind him, the silence of Santa Maria. Whether that meant she was at least somewhat on Horace's side or so incensed as to see enemies all around her, it was too soon to say. Horace was nonetheless grateful, fearing above all else Bill's capacities for destruction.

Scene four started with the vote prefigured by scene two. It was a question of next steps and proper procedure. Still no disagreement on what was right, the advancement of US hegemony unquestionable, but now there were timelines to consider. Were they to continue playing with mice and pigs while men and women and children died needlessly under dictatorial regimes? Or should they press on with human experimentation, readying their divine intervention post-haste? The Professor asked and the Sergeant answered, dancing Socratic circles around the Doctor that were reflected in the staging. Doc was reduced to nothing, defenseless against their higher cause. But every time they called for unanimous consent, Doc denied them. He could not change their minds, nor they his heart. After an impassioned speech, he gave them a choice:

"Either we continue our tests ethically and ensure our method does minimal harm to the subjects, or I resign. I don't care how many lives we lose for the sake of doing things right. My conscience has spoken, so I must listen."

So keenly aware of the foreboding presence seated next to him, Horace wondered if this Bill on stage had ever really existed. This was Liam's portrayal of his adaptation of Bill's suspected memoir, now witnessed by Bill's alleged doppelganger. Who was the real Bill? Had he ever stood so strongly on principle? Or was this all a reconstruction of the principles he had abandoned along the way, a fantasy of his untraveled paths? Though Liam's adaptation was not exactly flattering to Doc, the tragedy depended on his misplaced but genuine good nature. A better man would've never entered this business in the first place.

Whatever Bill thought of himself in writing the screenplay, he thought far less of his partners. It was time for the double-cross, where Prof and Sarge appear to appease Doc's request, only to remain on-stage and reveal their intentions to begin human experimentation behind Doc's back. While this had been those two's agreement all along, Gil's Sarge put in a commendable performance expressing his inner conflict here, having been touched by Doc's defense. Horace wondered if he'd be able to remain friends with them after this unravelling fiasco, a thought full of both hope and doubt. In what was easily the most awkward time cut of the play, they exited only to reenter in celebratory fashion moments later, recycling and refilling the champagne flutes. Horace had abandoned plans to construct a "Mission Accomplished" banner to fly here, but it had been strongly considered. As they caroused, Doc entered from upstage and overheard them. He confronted them, demanding answers Prof was happy to provide. Human experimentation trials were proving successful, and soon to be operational.

As Doc went about telling them off, Horace noted that it had been a while since Bill had side-talked him, longer than Maria's shush should've lasted. He turned his head slightly, more than he'd been previously willing, and saw Bill in an unfamiliar light. What look was on his face? Was he perturbed, despondent, nostalgic? Hurt? Was it by the play, or his memories? Horace had no idea, but he recognized it as an inner feeling and felt safer for it, at least for now. Anything but righteous anger looked good to him.

The final scene began with a dark, empty stage. Doc took his time walking on and getting to his mark. Mint took even longer to get the lights on him. This was all in the blocking, of course, but Horace's nerves about the end of the show, begging for it and dreading it equally, distorted time's effects. Finally, Doc began his monologue that would carry through the scene. Liam cried off and on throughout it, in a manner that Horace couldn't quite call Doc. Gil and Russ's mock doppelgangerings seemed inappropriately comical in juxtaposition, the Phantom of the Opera masks too flimsy to be sinister. Their desired effect had been to leave the audience in a state of unease, and they succeeded, but at the cost of the audience's trust. Even Horace didn't know how to feel about their performance. At last, a broken and hollow Doc reached his bit about retirement and peace, and then clutched at his heart. He fell, and Prof and Sarge rushed to his front, covering him as they helped him up in darkness. When they turned for lights up and bows, hands held high, Doc was wearing the mask.

Applause trickled in from all except Bill, who stood and clapped thunderously loud. Then he turned to Horace, deadly serious.

"We need to talk. Now."

Act I

Act II

[Act III]

Act IV

Act V

3.1 ~ The Confession

The thrill of performance, the power of his words over them, the looks on their faces, their disgusted attention, his mother's tears, how "doppelganger" felled the fourth wall like Jericho, his "dad's" interjection, the pressures of the current moment, his urgency to find and save Horace—all these thoughts and feelings, impulses and misgivings, brawled in a street fight for Liam's attention as he took his bow. Exiting the stage, surveying the damage, regrouping in the dressing room, facing the mirror, admiring his reflection, channeling a deranged look and loving it, softening it slightly and setting it, living with the simultaneous motion of events, still watching from his liminal crevice, the place he first discovered years ago on stage, his squatter's den of many months now, the home of his untransferable self, that voyeur to his own behavior. Someone had to do something, for all their sakes, so he had volunteered to play the part, subletting his conscience to the role, downsizing his identity. Call it method acting if you want, but the cart was going before the horse here, his acted experiences inspiring his lived ones, like a river flowing up to its source, defiant in its anti-gravitational stance. His current impression, one he couldn't yet trust, was that the doors were left open, possibly by mistake, to the rooms of his mind, move-in ready, furnished yet empty, and he could emerge from his den, reassume agency, if he was so inclined. Wouldn't some sunlight and open windows be good for him? But it could be a trap. Was he ready to be real with his dad? with Horace? with all aspects of himself?

Not yet. Still more work to be done. First, a quick bout of emotional labor. He wanted to make Russ and Gil feel proud of their work tonight, since others might feel sorry for them. Strong embraces, one, two, three seconds long for each of them, transferring his gratitude with a deep and steady breath. Actions speak louder than words after all, but he slipped in some niceties, how Russ timed an interruption perfectly, how Gil earned the best laugh line of the night. Then he changed into his "Liam" clothes, designing himself to be who he was expected to be. The light stage makeup needed removal, though he rushed the job, leaving traces of smeared mascara across his upper eyelids. An acceptable flaw, appropriate even.

Out into the world he went, like a mine sweeper searching for open spaces, assessing dangers by proxy. The families and friends milling about in the venue uncertainly, somewhat post-coitally, were none of his concern, but he was of great concern to them. Obstacles to slow him down, question or congratulate him, pretend they didn't know what he'd just done or pretend they understood it perfectly. All sweets and sours when he was out for umami, blood, answers not questions. Pausing outside the stage door, he scanned for Bill and Horace to no avail. Paul filled this window of hesitation with his girth, less a landmine than a heat-seeking missile in his approach. Drunkenness smeared his face.

"What a show, m'boy. Your imagination is truly . . ." Paul searched for the right word, one of sufficient temperature to burn while avoiding self-harm, Liam thought, leaning strongly toward his collaborator hypothesis.

"I couldn't have done it without you," were the words that emerged from Liam's mouth, a useful translation of his interior's "fuck off, fuck you, fuck this."

"I am not remotely at fault for the damage you caused today, young man," Paul murmured while grabbing his arm in false camaraderie and pulling him close. Whiskey poured from his breath.

Flora saved him with a shout and a hug, peeling their bodies away from Paul, creating angles for his escape. She'd broken from her roommate the moment she spotted Paul's charge.

"Where's Bill and Horace," Liam whispered in her ear, a familiar action from a distant time, like a dusty, dog-eared tome of ancient magic.

"I don't know, but they're together."

Back at arm's distance, her eyes transmitted the rest of the message. Bill had a hostage, and the interrogation was already in progress. Liam spun out from the conversation and into wrong-way traffic. Each member of Gil's family wanted to shake his hand, an important measure of worth to their kind, leaving Liam's hand pulsing and the Bartoszczes disappointed by his suboptimal grasp. Then Sam and Taylor, bless their hearts, had he invited them or was it the fault of Russ or Gil? Already engaged, settled, having important conversations, going to bed early, half-proud of being old so young, reminiscing on halcyon days of who they were in college, coming upon Liam like he'd just eaten some shrooms, someone for whom college never ended, it only lingered and metastasized, so he had nothing to say to them. And in place of that nothing, he dealt platitudes of gratitude, two more hugs, two more apologies, spinning off and away, leaving them dumbfounded but assured of his larger mission, that inspired friend of theirs, ineffable as ever. When will he slow down, they asked each other on the car ride home, one with respect and the other with concern.

Where could they be? Liam spun the room around, interrogating his visual search strategies for improvement. There weren't many people in the cavernous room, nowhere to hide, not much he could be missing. They must have gone outside. How dramatic of them. As he jogged away from the stage, passing the rows, nearly bumping into a bald goatee who moved to apprehend him with an outstretched hand, another suburban speed bump failing to understand his right of way and the emergency sirens implicit to his motion, his looping thoughts lassoed around Horace. He was supposed to be his back-up in this fight, not his replacement. Why was he going solo? Or, more likely, why did he let Bill strong-arm him into this private negotiation? Why was he such a goddamn pushover? Paranoia and anger nipped at his heels like hungry dogs, but he raced ahead of them, nimble as a hunted fox, equal parts predator and prey.

Out the door, down the stairs, on the grass, nothing. Well, not just nothing. Mint stood preparing a cigarette, a paper flexed in their mouth, pinching brown flakes with crumbles of suspected jazz. Degenerate sophisticate, they sure were cool, he thought, pissed off. Bordering the parking lot, the dos Santos twins in teenage company, not actively doing drugs, but likely making plans to. Pausing here was dangerous, concern could corner him, negativity could close him in. It was under these circumstances that Liam struck up his first ever conversation with Mint.

"Yo Mint, you seen where Horace went? Nice job tonight, by the way."

Mint slid their eyes over to Liam, then returned to the task at hand, pace unchanged. Not speaking with the paper in their mouth, not speaking while rolling and twisting and sealing, not out of concentration but careless ease, and only after lighting and inhaling did they reply, Liam having approached handoff distance expecting no handouts.

"Yeah."

Liam already knew they didn't like him. He was used to that, it didn't bother him, and he really couldn't blame them. But now he needed something from them, something outside the job description to which Mint had stuck unflinchingly. He was moving like he had to pee, like if he stopped moving, pulsing, clenching, he would separate and fall apart. It was a fear of an interior kind of unknown, a toxic solvent you'd rather not come to know. Only constant stirring could keep it from rising to the surface.

"I need to speak to him."

"I'm sure."

"What's your problem?"

"What's yours?"

"I wouldn't know where to begin."

"I bet." Then, after some calculus, the path to solitude rerouted in Mint's head to telling him what he needed to know. "Try the tech booth. I held the door open for them. It might be locked now."

Liam thought to ask for the key, but he could guess how that would go over. He started back up the stairs. Mint watched him go. So much attention paid to so undeserving a figure, they mused. Better to deprive someone like him of an audience, but it wasn't up to Mint. Not enough was.

Back inside, Liam headed left on the platform and tried the booth's door. Locked. He put his ear against it, but the sound-proofing swallowed all. He knocked and tried to disguise his agitation. People were leaving, saying goodbye to him without stopping, sensing some mission of his they'd rather not interrupt. Maria and Al ascended the stairs, and Liam gave them a nod. Al nodded back. Maria was also searching for Horace but refused allyship with Liam. Could she be why Horace was in hiding? Bill wouldn't have known about this room. The dos Santoses continued to their car. Ambushes were more Maria's style, exercising meticulous control over the conditions, and Horace would have to come home eventually.

Liam knocked again, considerably harder. Only then did it occur to him to call Horace. Doing so acknowledged their distance, was in some way admitting failure and ceding ground to his opposition, but right now Bill was running up the score, and new tactics were necessary. Plus, the impatient stance of a phone next to his ear communicated to the passersby his unavailability. Those remaining on the floor were officially stragglers by this point. Ring, ring, voicemail. Only two, he'd been cut off. He was composing a text when the door cracked open. Liam jumped Horace, blocking the opening like he was preventing a dog's escape, and pushed him back in.

At last, the three of them standing together. Liam, collecting himself breathlessly, indignantly, caught between expectations. Horace, shell-shocked, blank, giving Liam nothing, shoulders forward and down, receding into himself. Bill, facing away, arms behind his back, towering over the switchboard, staring out through the one-way mirror at the floor below. Liam wanted to be the first to speak, to retake the offensive, but what was holding him back?

That it was unmistakably his father standing before him. That he lacked belief. That he had already lost. Horace's vanishing presence all but confirmed it. The silence lasted seconds too long. Bill could win by refusing to play. Liam found Bill's reflection in the glass, and it stared back at him, smiling gently, like he was remembering a joke, or Liam as a baby in diapers.

"Admit it, if you'd been replaced, you wouldn't even know!" Liam blurted out, relinquishing any composure he'd been cobbling together.

"Then why are we here? Why did you put all of us through this?" Bill was still facing away, then turned to his son. "Liam, look at me."

Liam refused on instinct, then forced his eyes to meet his father's. Bill tugged at the scruffy flesh of his neck.

"Where are the scars, Liam? Surely there'd be some physical evidence of an operation. You have nothing but a meagre, unsatisfactory hunch."

"Absence of evidence is not evidence of absence, like you always used to say."

They were speaking past each other. Even this deep in, they couldn't connect. Here stood not just a father's son, but a son's father, two congruent puzzle pieces clashing instead of tessellating, incompatibility born from similarity. Liam had once considered Bill's reticence an asset, a sign that he had something to hide, but that was good for nothing if Liam couldn't uncover it now.

"Liam," Horace started explaining, puttering, unwilling to tip the balance in either direction, "we came here to have a private place to talk. He, well, I told him, I mean, I watched him like you asked, and I only promised to let things speak for themselves. And, uh," he took a breath, "I told him we thought he was, or might have been, replaced, and wanted to confront him about it, and that's why we did this play."

"I had gathered as much," added Bill, serenely.

"And, now I think he hasn't been . . ." Horace continued, making Liam feel double-teamed, "hasn't been replaced."

"Why did you write the screenplay?" Liam countered, trying to get momentum back on his side.

"To be honest? For a lark," answered Bill.

"I don't believe you."

"And nothing I say will change that, will it? You believe whatever you want. If you don't think of me as your father, then that's that. I'll love you as my son forever, but, regrettably, it's looking like tough love is up next to bat."

"Because you've been so generous with your love till now."

"Enough of the sardonics, Liam!" At last, Liam had gotten a rise out of his father, was getting somewhere. "Do you not understand how hard this has been for us? Did you not see your mother storm out in tears? And all this time, we forgave, we maintained temperance, we believed in you. Those days are over. I don't care what mission you think you've been on, the game's up. Your potential can only take you so far. It's time you grew up."

"I accept responsibility for my actions, and all I ask, the whole fucking point of this thing, was to make you own up to yours! Do you have any regret for the career you chose? Can you look me in the eye and tell me didn't make the world a worse place? I just want to know what could've been so important to my father that he'd choose it over his family, night after long night. I'm not the only one who's made Mom cry, but at least I feel bad about it. At least I was there to see it."

"To live is to regret. Maturity is accepting that. Everything you could say, everything you're thinking, I've already thought. I knew the tradeoffs all along. Rather than facing that yourself, you criticize me. I'm inviting you to join the club."

"Dad," the word was massive, hauling the words that followed along with it, "what did you do at work? How much of the screenplay is true?"

Bill released a deflating sigh, dropped the amiability in his face, and sank his body into Mint's chair. It was his turn to break eye contact, to gaze through the ceiling into the past, x-ray vision trained on the skyscraper of his life, quite tall at this point but always growing upward, often inviting a jump, a deadly nostalgia, a desire to return, but he knew it couldn't be in the same form. He would never again climb the steps he built. He could only watch helplessly as his son built an adjacent tower below.

"Only the regret is true. We never created doppelgangers. We never . . . did anything I would be proud to tell you about. We became rich off our failures, and how those failures served certain interests. I don't think I was ever supposed to succeed."

"Dr. Hawthorne," Horace whispered into the silence that followed, "can I ask you a question?"

Liam swallowed the instinctive admonishment that "you just did," and saw his father's Adam's apple move simultaneously to his. Horace noticed too, looking from one to the other meaningfully, perhaps having even triggered them intentionally, before he continued speaking.

"I was out walking some night last March, and I saw you out too, just down the hill from our block. I don't think you saw me, but I don't know. It was pretty cold and windy that night, but right when we were out, the wind starting howling, and the streetlights flickered on and off, and you just stood frozen for I don't know how long, in what looked like a lot of pain. Do you remember that night, Dr. Hawthorne? Can you tell me what happened to you?"

"You're saying I stood still in the middle of a windstorm, months ago on a random night? That sounds like something I tend to do. But hm . . . I think I know the night you're referring to, though I can't be sure I'm not thinking of another windy night from past years. I've had a lot by now. Did nothing else make this night remarkable?"

"Only the strange feeling I had. Like dread, or something haunting me. And you looked haunted too. I think you cried out."

"Horace, I can't tell you what you saw or felt was wrong, but feelings can just be feelings. The two of you suffer from overactive imaginations, and while I appreciate the way you think for yourselves, perhaps a happy medium can be found? I think it's high time both of you join us in the real world."

***

Dr. William Hawthorne, stuck in traffic well after sunset, clouds having covered the sun that whole bitter day in March, felt antsy and incomplete. Keeping the blur of red brake lights in his dulled periphery, he brought his phone over his leg and into the frame of his glasses, perched on the end of his nose. His face, save his eyes, betrayed no movement, much like a student in class or a father in church, while convening with the digital world. Bill had business to discuss with Paul Neufchatel. With fat thumbs and large font, he scratched a mental itch by drafting a text.

He needed someone with whom to flesh out certain feelings. Paul, as not an old friend but rather a friend who was mutually old, would have to serve. Having known each other for twenty years, he and Paul didn't lack history, but they'd met as new fathers already feeling wise and world-weary. The kinds of hot experiences that mold friends to each other felt behind them even then, and neither man was looking to be changed by the other. Instead, brittle, they could lean on each other for support, Bill the taller and mightier, Paul stodgily in his shadow. It was mutually beneficial and transactional from the start, but then decades came and went that left Bill with no one else. Perhaps transactional relationships, with their public ledger and limited services, enjoyed a better viability than passionate friendships, the kind that have a life of their own, some animus co-parented between the two individuals. Bill had fostered his share of those in his days, and where had that left him? With business partners he wished he could divorce, and a wife who, well, he wouldn't blame her for it.

He was workshopping a name for what he was feeling, and the best he'd come upon so far was senioritis. Like a slowing down at the end of the race, a victory lap, but with melancholy there too, vaguely psychedelic in how it all swirled together, evading any close examination. He didn't expect Paul to be much help directly. Retirement, senescence, death—all one and the same to workaholics like him. But Bill appreciated receiving bad advice, since figuring out why it was wrong helped him determine what was right. Anything to get himself out of his head.

For the most part, he was embracing his seniority, comparing Medicare Advantage plans in AARP mailers, seeing which museums have the best senior discounts, researching covertly whether pot gummies would be right for him. If his final days of life were just a drawn-out version of his final days of high school and college, well, he could imagine worse things. But it lacked the rosy tint, none of that playing hooky, drinking beer with your friends, calling authorities by their first names.

He was no longer facing death as some cosmic, distant inevitability. Death would be his next and last friend, someone with whom to coexist. Death as a partner.

Bill often mused through his commute home with thoughts such as these, highways evoking death ceaselessly, herds of living dead in spacious coffins rolling past wrecks and memorials for the fallen soldiers of labor's unending, daily war.

"Bury me in my car in my backyard, so in my big sleep I'll have perfected the American Dream," he composed out loud. "God, I'm depressed," was what slipped out after, less a diagnosis than a mantra at this point.

His consultation with Paul, which took precedence that evening over seeing Greta, dinner already acclimated to the refrigerator and getting no colder, did not center around such amorphous feelings but rather the practical matter of retirement and its execution. Sitting in leather chairs in Paul's Hemingway study, a temple for books and alcoholism and history, some pleasing gestalt of previous eras flattened together, he broached the subject like this.

"I'm thinking of giving up the fight. The only way to win is to outlast them, and I just don't have it in me."

"They're still set on selling?"

"They've signed the paperwork already. It's just my signature left."

"And what about staying on? I've already said that's what I would do. Tevin Vein is a reasonable man, more than you give him credit for. You could be a positive influence."

"I've been telling myself that for thirty years and look where it's gotten me. It's no use. It costs me too much."

"Well, your options are clear, and your mind seems made up. You can't keep it from Vein, and you won't work with him. That doesn't leave much but calling it a day. I admire you for it. I'm not brave enough to retire. I wouldn't know what to do with myself. At least you still have Greta."

"I want to disagree with you, but I know you're right."

"And what are you so worried about, anyway? You told me the process doesn't work. Is there something you weren't telling me?"

"I haven't been lying to you, but there are things we never tried. Without my veto, I expect that to change. What gets my goat, the real joke of it is, I could really use a damn doppelganger right now."

"Without doing away with the original, I hope you mean?"

"Of course, on my own terms. Someone like me to keep a hand on the till, but not me. Hell, he could take my identity, my home, the remains of my life, as long as I could keep Greta and the kids. Well, the kids will find their own way, but you know what I mean."

"You'd have to tell them, in this scenario."

"As I've always wanted to do."

"Yes, tomorrow's the day, isn't it? And tomorrow and tomorrow?"

"When I'm out, like I've said."

"Which is what we're discussing here. Well, I'll be honest, it's in everyone's interests for you to walk away. If that's what you really want. It's a free country, though not free of consequences. If I were them, well, I'd thank you for your service and that would be that. There's no more love between you three, that's clear, so what's the worst that could happen?"

"They're worried about what I might say."

"A well-placed paranoia, you can admit. You brought me in for a reason, after all. Was it just to share your conscience with me, and never a broader audience?"

"I wanted to tell my story to make sense of it myself. Where had I gone wrong? How could I ever explain it to my children? Narrative structures are useful for that, and it was fun to imagine as a retirement project Liam and I could work on together. I haven't been behind the lens of a camera since college. But to imagine it was enough. I knew it could never be made. Doesn't everyone wish they could watch a movie of their own life?"

"I imagine mine would be quite boring. Look, you must promise your partners that you're out without any strings. Bury the hatchet, and the hatchet job. If you're serious about it, I say delete the files entirely. I'll do the same for mine. Then tell them in good conscience you're leaving the past to its own kind. Not that they'd know better, but it's for your own sake. There's a right way to do these kinds of things."

The conversation carried on, but little more was said. The good it did for Bill, he reflected as he crossed the street to his dark home, was give him hope that types like Paul, who, like his partners Jack and Mark, would be invested in the work till their end, could view his retirement as a complete relinquishing of power and an embrace of steady decline. Life after death was a fool's dream, and they were no fools. They believed it was too late to change, and perhaps they were right. Revenge was a young man's game, couldn't they all see that?

Chewing cold lasagna, Bill booted up his laptop, forever plugged in on battery life support and collecting dust. He opened its file explorer, searched "untitled1_final", and hovered his cursor the document at the top of the list. While far from a digital native, his muscle memory was developed enough that, when his eye caught the "Date Last Opened" line as implausibly being only several months prior, it was already too late to stop his finger from double-clicking the track pad and opening the document. It was a blink-and-miss moment, and the dutiful file explorer updated its records immediately.

He couldn't be certain that it hadn't been from the December a year prior, that someone hadn't been snooping on his computer. He could only suspect it. He resolved not to delete the file. After all, there might yet be another copy, a duplicate with its own intentions. He slammed his laptop closed, grabbed his jacket with urgency, and was out the door and down the street before he knew it. He sought relief in the night's cool air, which was taking on a chaotic swirl.

The charged atmosphere did nothing to improve his mood, each a brewing storm. The laptop had triggered in him a pressure change, a collision of systems needing discharge. The wind howled in crescendo as his heart pounded. He feared for his pacemaker, inserted last December to save him in moments such as this, moments of panic and stress that could rewire his body's currents. His heart had grown tired of its own beat after so many years. There were too many stimuli, vibrations internal and external, feeling the cold, hearing the trees, seeing the streetlights flicker under duress. He made it so far as the bottom of the hill before he stopping himself, catching his breath, and yanking on the leash of his runaway imagination. He tasted vomit, felt an upheaval, and desired for claws to pierce his back precisely at the spine and cleave it apart, macro-acupuncture, a fatal solution to this anxious pain.

It had to have been Liam. His son had opened the file and seen his work. Bill felt it setting in—that terrible, obvious feeling of being right against his wishes. His mind was tearing itself apart to find contingencies, anything to delay the problem-solving phase.

A hallucination of Liam appeared in his mind's eye. Loose around the edges, face darkened and blurred and unreadable, but unmissably him and unmistakably saddened. The streetlight flared back to life, and in its transition, Bill saw not his son, but his younger self fade into the light, a look of contempt on his own face.

3.2 ~ **The Intervention**

Her son been deceived her. His best friend had used him. That friend's parents (her friends, too, though she'd been right to keep up a wall) had leaned on her sympathies while being the source of their problems. Her husband found these matters funny. Her twins were going to too many parties, and her eldest didn't call or visit nearly enough. She couldn't help but lump her daughters' faults into the equation, in part by sheer habit but also because grievances fueled her. She was someone you wanted on your side, and she liked to prove that by turning against everyone from time to time. Her care was carrot and stick, the sweetness of the former heightened by tastes of the latter. In these moments she thrived, and in her docile life of late they were increasingly rare. At last, Santa Maria had scores to settle.

Maria spoke with Greta in the parking lot after the show, while both waited out the conversation happening in the tech booth. Caught in a moment of weakness, Greta was uncharacteristically revealing. She admitted to being blindsided, to not knowing where Liam's ideas had come from but suspecting her husband did, and to feeling guilty that her son had roped Horace into this mess. She started sentences about blaming herself that she didn't know how to finish.

Maria listened carefully, as she put the pieces together. She didn't yet know the full picture, but Bill's outburst about "chemical ten" was shifting her anger away from Horace and toward broader failings, the sources of original sin. She found it easy to comfort Greta, who put up no resistance to her misery, letting the tears and assurances wash over her pathetically. It was a disappointing experience. Maria preferred those who put up a fight, even against their own emotions.

She made plans with Greta to talk again in the morning, then joined her husband in the car. She informed him that she'd changed her mind; they would confront Horace at home. No sense wasting their time in the parking lot.

Al agreed with her, as he always did when she spoke with such authority. He understood the mood she was in and that immoveable will of hers. This wife-pleasing enablement often bothered her, but they both knew it was for the best, as it denied her the vice she most wanted to indulge: the hollow thrill of argumentative victory. He was still the man she had married, never having matured the way she might've hoped, but he knew how to be there for her, naturally and effortlessly, as if she was simple to figure out. She wanted to resent him for never taking her bait, but even at her most testy, she could see that as one of love's miracles. An even larger miracle was that he never seemed to tire of it or her. They'd been there and would be there again and again in that car, her with an axe to grind and him with two ears and a suppressed grin.

On the drive home, they relived their experience of the play, an event which was bleeding backwards through time, staining their memories of the things Horace had said and done in the months since Liam's post. Maria's emotions led them on a guided tour, selecting exhibits and providing commentary, to which she gave voice and they both listened. Anger, first in line, reminded her of when Horace had lied about the subject of the play, a premeditated crime committed at their dining room table. Vindication inserted itself to mention how she'd told him then what she wanted to say again now, that Liam in this state was not to be trusted, that Horace would get hurt. That vindication, like a grasp at control already lost, slipped quickly away as sadness moved in, bringing with it tears for Horace, whose progress since his collapse had revealed itself as a mirage, for the Hawthornes, whose scabs were ripped open and scars put on public display, and for herself, whose world was spinning out of control. The sadness settled into shame, for what she had failed to prevent, and hurt, the lasting mark from all this turmoil.

"You know," Al responded, having given proper weight to her silence, "it is a rare thing for a play to produce so much emotion. That means it is good art, no? In bad taste of course, but it cut through. Can I say that I'm a little bit proud of him? This is the boldest thing our son has ever done."

"It's certainly the most foolish," Maria replied curtly, though she didn't dismiss his comment entirely.

As she lay awake in bed that night, long after Al as always, she couldn't stay fixed on Horace's faults because virtues kept popping up—not just any virtues but the virtues she'd instilled in him—like loyalty to friends, boldness in face of opposition, and commitment to a job well done. Unable to resolve these contradictions, caught in the trap where she opposed his choices despite knowing she might've done the same at that age, her murky discontent turned inward, and she fell asleep in a fog. Later in the night, she awoke from a dream, and the only clear image she retained was of her hands stretched out in front of her, one hand wanting to throttle, pummel, and slap, while the other sought to soothe, clutch and worry. She folded her hands together in prayer until sleep returned.

When she rose the next morning, Al was already downstairs watching the Tour de France, reading the *Economist*, drinking coffee, and listening to the morning news. What a silly man, she thought lovingly, never content with just one thing, unable to sit still unless multiple forces pressed down on his attention.

"Happy Independence Day, meu amor!" Al hollered with genuine excitement, the product of his love for all holidays and an immigrant's love of American mythos.

"Hello dear," she replied more flatly, accustomed to his morning enthusiasm but still at times unprepared for it. "I'll be going over to Bill and Greta's for breakfast, to talk things over. Would you care to join?"

"The race is on!" Al said, gesturing to the TV with his *Economist* hand.

"And will be for several more hours. Weeks, even! On second thought, I am not asking. Please come with me. I imagine we'll be discussing the barbecue tonight as well. At least care about that."

Al assented, asserting his intention to commandeer the TV next to the Hawthorne's breakfast table, and they made their way across the street. Greta opened the door and ushered them into their spacious kitchen, where Bill and Paul already sat, listlessly watching the Tour.

Paul's presence triggered Maria, suppressing any conciliatory instincts and flaring her critical eye, which turned to her hosts for having invited him. Meanwhile, Greta was up to her typical tricks, applying busyness like an eraser, rubbing out her worries to craft a perfection—if only one ignored the smudges. The coffee and tea selection, fresh eggs and yogurt, an assortment of berries, matching plates, designer furniture, the kindness and thoughtfulness, Maria saw it all for what it was. She could describe the difference between them in the way they wore their aprons. (She could compare their careers, too, but they were both teachers, even though high school Latin was a boys' club and kindergarten was basically daycare.) Maria tossed her apron on, untied at the waist, home to turmeric and tomato stains, because she had to, knowing that care work was in the cards mankind had dealt her; because she had to, she did it to her very best. Greta wore hers like she was meant to, with meaning and motherhood wrapped up in one. Maria's final disillusionment with popular conservatism came with motherhood when her individualism had hit a wall. There was such a thing as society, and it was fraying, and mothers were and would be its last stitches. Intuitively, so it seemed to Maria, Greta understood this individualism was never for meant her. There were greater individuals to serve, seated around her kitchen table, sleeping above her garage. It bothered Maria that Greta, accepting what Maria protested, had picked the favored side, but even more so it troubled her that this acceptance hadn't brought Greta the peace she deserved.

"Thank you all for coming over this morning," Greta declared, once she had finished her culinary ministrations and assumed the fullness of her chair. "I'm so sorry for Liam's behavior last night. I still can't believe . . . Bill and I talked it over last night, and we agreed that there's no more time for excuses. It's not even the play itself, but the lying, the embarrassment. It just doesn't reflect well on us. Business within our family is just that, but it's all a mess now. That's why we've asked you here. We want to get through to Liam, and some outside voices, if you're all willing, that is, would be of great help, we feel."

"Oh, with pleasure, Greta," Paul chimed in eagerly. "Anything you need."

"What do you have in mind?" inserted Maria quickly, cutting Paul off before he got a full head of steam.

"Liam is a bit too stuck in his own head at the moment," Bill stated delicately, "and we're hoping to do a bit of dislodging. Tonight, at the barbecue, we're going to have a little sit down with him. All we ask is that you share how his behavior has affected you, to remind him that his actions have consequences. Simple, from the heart, that kind of stuff. He doesn't respond well to preaching, believe me."

"Ah, an intervention, what fun!" Al laughed, "I hope you don't intend for us to be sober."

"We'd like to avoid the I-word," Greta replied with her schoolteacher voice, "but the comparison is there. We hope not to spoil the whole party, but a dose of temperance wouldn't hurt."

All eyes bounced around at that, trading glances of accusation and denial. Sure Maria's husband liked to drink, but Paul's appetites had evolved from an annoyance to a concern at recent events.

"And there is, of course, another variable in play," Paul inserted.

Bill was looking at Maria, and everyone else's gazes took the cue. Even Maria felt outside herself for a moment. How different would her judgment be if it were someone else's son implicated in this fiasco. Clear culpability—accomplice might not go far enough. She had raised Horace to be better, and her mind teemed with exculpatories, but she'd also raised him to think for himself, and any excuse, any downplaying of agency, damned him as much as it spared him. Would she rather he be a dupe or a scoundrel? What difference did that make?

"I had a chance to talk with Horace after the show, just the two of us," Bill revealed. "It was enlightening. I think he had the right intentions, and perhaps just got too caught up in the excitement of it all, getting in a little over his head. More than anyone here, if he were to speak honestly to Liam, to tell him what he told me, it would make a world of difference."

"But can we trust that he will?" Paul muttered unnecessarily, the thought on everyone's minds already.

"Can we trust that Liam won't storm out the minute you open your mouth?" Al shot back, pride on the line.

"Alright fellas, we all know it's a touchy situation," Bill soothed, "and ultimately events will play out how they do. The question is, Maria, do you want to tell Horace what we have in mind, or do you think it better he finds out as it happens?"

In other words, Maria thought, is he on our side or Liam's? Or no one's at all? Just a lonesome boy caught in no man's land. Lonesome *man*?

"No need to tell him. I know it will just stress him out. This is enough of a conspiracy already. What else did he say to you?"

***

"Um, so, why'd you write the screenplay?" Horace stammered out as soon as the door to the tech booth closed. Avoiding direct eye contact with Bill, he moved awkwardly to the far wall and ceded him the rest of the floor. He was getting it all wrong from the start, this moment he had been unprepared for since Liam had shared his confidences that early spring night. Horace had taken them to the tech booth to dodge his mother, but the implications of its total security were sinking in. Without Liam, who surely must be hunting them down, there were only his and Bill's words to be pitted against each other. Allergic to such confrontation, Horace found himself struggling to breathe.

"It was . . . an allegory, I suppose," mused Bill in what clocked as faux-contemplative hesitation to Horace. "I was expressing how my career made me feel. It certainly wasn't meant to be taken literally."

Already, Horace was at a loss for where to go next. He'd prepared for an uphill battle, but not a one-on-one fight. He was out of his weight class.

"Why won't you tell Liam what your firm really does? That's why he did all this, you know. He just wanted to get through to you. This doppelganger stuff—"

"—Is utterly ridiculous and you both know it. I never should have put up with it. We've been so patient and forgiving. Do you have any idea how hard this has been for me and his poor mother? You should have known better."

"I'm sorry," Horace mumbled, feeling foolish and shamed. Bill's words underscored what a mistake it was to have entered this locked room with him, and everything he said was made worse by it being true. The velocity of recent events had obscured these questions, letting Horace keep them at bay as he raced ahead, but now they filled the stale air of this tiny room. There was nowhere to run.

"We had a deal, you know, Liam and I," Bill said. "If he stopped playing make believe about this whole replacement theory, we'd let him stay in the guest suite while he finished this play and applied for jobs. Living in your childhood bedroom keeps you a child, that's what I was thinking. And here you are as more evidence."

"I'm really sorry, okay? This was all a big mistake. Liam explained his theory, about you being not you anymore, and asked for my help proving it. Just to watch your reaction to the play. I said yes, and then got roped into helping some more. I never really bought it, I just . . . I don't know. I wanted to be a part of something. I shouldn't have encouraged him."

"That's not enough. You've made more trouble than you could possibly realize. None of this was supposed to see the light of day. Did he go snooping in my files?"

"Uh . . ."

"Horace, I know he did. I just want you to confirm it. Start owning up."

Horace couldn't bring himself to speak, so he only nodded in confirmation.

"Of course. Shit! I just can't believe you did it in a place they own."

"They? What does Vein have to do with this? None of it's true, right?"

"Vein has acquired my firm. It's why I retired—I couldn't stomach working for them. And truth is irrelevant. In that world, it's only optics and what you can convince another to be true. That's why this play is a problem."

"I had no idea," Horace admitted, utterly shocked. How did this one company have so much control over his life? Were they targeting them, him, or just blanketing all of America? No, something personal had to be going on. Maybe it all centered around Bill—was this villain before him more of a victim, beset by the broader forces Horace had thought he represented?

"It's not something I've been publicizing. I was against it, but I just had to wipe my hands of it. They could carry on without me. But now I'm going to have to answer for this. God dammit all."

Three solid knocks struck the door. If it was Liam, Horace needed to let him in, but then this version of the conversation would be over. He asked Bill one more question.

"Is Chemical X—or Ten, I guess—real? Can it brainwash people?"

"You don't need a drug to brainwash someone," Bill replied coldly and without hesitation, "but you do need to give someone a reason to believe they've been changed. Vein understands this, and now that they have my firm, I think they can pull it off. That's a very, very bad thing."

159

The knocks came again with gusto. Horace's phone buzzed in his pocket.

***

Breakfast had left Maria in a foul mood, and she returned home to a considerable store of food no longer needed for tonight's new purpose. She decided to start cooking anyway, hoping some culinary absolutions might help wipe her slate clean, bringing her closer to divine concepts like forgiveness, patience, and wisdom. She curated herself a frictionless experience, Sinatra on the speaker, wine in an early glass, the kitchen wholly cleaned in advance of its next mess, Al entranced by TV till the afternoon, her kids likely to be asleep for just as long. She could be herself, finding direction through duty, hoping to translate the perfection of a single practice into emotional momentum. She transformed her ingredients indelibly into food, baked chicken breast never again to be raw, a corn salad never again to be discrete vegetables. Their fate was unchanged, either to be eaten or thrown away, but the fusion of elements made the stakes feel higher. What had last night changed, really?

"Hey Mom, good morning," Horace said as he entered the kitchen around 1 p.m., a running family joke from all his afternoon rises.

"Oh sweetie, hello, are you just getting up? Have you had breakfast?"

"Just got back from McDonald's." The kids resorting to fast food always registered as an insult to Maria, and it momentarily preoccupied her, but then Horace continued.

"I owe you an apology."

"Oh? Well, yes, I suppose you do. What was last night all about? What were you thinking? How could you lie to me about all this?" She had recovered her anger by the end, but Horace had caught her in a transitory state, the kind that left her staring out of windows when there were dishes to be scrubbed.

"I just wanted to help Liam, and I convinced myself what we were doing was worth it. It had to be kept secret to catch Dr. Hawthorne's honest reaction. That's what I first signed up to do, just to watch him, but I didn't think through how it all would play out. What a disaster. I'm sorry if I embarrassed you, and the Hawthornes too. I tried explaining it to Dr. Hawthorne, but I don't know how well I managed."

"It was a completely stupid idea. Imagine how I was feeling! I couldn't believe you would be so foolish, the shame of it all. This is not how adults settle their problems. They talk to each other. I just wish you had listened to me. I warned you, why didn't you listen?"

Without warning, in perfect daylight, four eyes were filling with tears, hers first and then his, with the sight of each other driving them both further.

"I knew you were right. I just felt like being self-destructive, I guess. It gave me something to do. That includes picking up the pieces."

She hugged him, discerning with her touch the feelings behind his tears, by now fully unleashed. Loss, helplessness, and the fear of change were knotted together across his heart like a tumor only now detected and classified but present all along. The play had been chemotherapeutic, poison as healing. If they couldn't stop the change, he and Liam, maybe they could spur it on, claim some control over it. At least that's how she imagined he felt. Still, those distances existed, barriers beyond sound and touch, even conscious thought. Some part of his heart would forever be kept from her, no matter how agonizingly she tried picking the lock.

"My baby bird," Maria said to break the silence, "why do you do this to yourself?" She emerged from the hug to face him. "It's never worth it, I hope you can see. Blowing things up just to have a clean slate. It's just like you with your Legos, how you would always tear them apart the moment you were done."

"Because if I didn't, someone else would. And to be fair, Dido did a couple times," Horace said, getting them both to laugh, breaking the tension with sweet relief.

"But I don't have to tell you that people are not playthings. These pieces will be much more difficult to pick up and put back together. I know I should punish you, but you've punished yourself, and consequences come whether someone assigns them or not. It's all so, so complicated. I don't know what to do."

Maria's didactic confidence slouched into timidity by the end of her statement, as she tried to communicate that it wasn't just his prospective restitutions that worried her. She also felt out of her depth and hated that her child had presented her with a problem she couldn't solve. To escape this discomfort, she turned the page to something about which she felt more clearly.

"As for Liam, ugh, that boy. He has serious issues. Look what he has put you through! You say you were just acting in his best interests, but can he say the same about you? That's something you need to ask yourself, and maybe ask him too. If he learns nothing from this, well, that would be a real shame. And between you and me, I do not know if the lessons his parents will teach him are the ones he needs. I do not understand what goes on in that household. I would always say that it's none of my business, but thanks to you it is now."

"This is gonna be some barbecue tonight, huh?"

The dos Santoses readied themselves for the evening with an exhibition of normality that betrayed superstition. Conversations, when they occurred, stuck only to the most mundane or essential of topics. No one knew what to say beyond that. Mostly everyone kept to themselves: Maria cleaning the kitchen like she was covering up a murder, Al with his beer in his chair watching TV, the twins party-prepping in their rooms for a night elsewhere, Horace playing video games to take the edge off.

After Horace left to take the twins to some party, Maria roused a snoozing Al, and they crossed together to the Hawthornes' home once more. There was too much to discuss to say anything on the short walk. Her better judgment hoped he'd stay checked out of this discussion, but part of her wanted to see him fight, against what or whom she couldn't say, but fight for Horace on her behalf at least. It wasn't for her to criticize what she couldn't improve, but that never stopped her Aloysius.

They assumed their places in the circle of chairs arranged around the Hawthornes' fire pit. Al and Paul strained themselves into chatting about the day's racing, the kind of observational talk that requires no listening even from the participants, and Maria gladly tuned them out. Liam sat across from them, performing a world-class sulk, daring someone to look straight at him and knowing no one would. Bill and Greta kept popping through the sliding door as if there was still a party demanding setup, and Maria accepted their offer of food and drink only out of politeness. To have an appetite in such a setting would be impossible. They were waiting for Horace, who at last stepped through the gate.

"Horace," Bill called, "your timing is perfect. As you can see, we've decided to scale down the party tonight in favor of a little pow-wow about your play."

"Please, take a seat," added Greta serenely.

Maria tapped the open seat between her and Paul, giving Horace a look too loaded to carry any meaning, her compassion restrained by an attempt at scolding propriety. Horace slid mutely into his chair.

"Well," continued Bill, "there's no two ways about it. Last night was unacceptable, if we're being objective about it. We all got together this morning and agreed that the best course of action would be to address things directly. Our hope is to demonstrate for our sons how to properly resolve conflicts."

"This is just a sharing session. Everyone will get their turn to speak about how they have personally been affected, and we won't have any arguing," finished Greta.

"Exactly. Greta can begin things and demonstrate."

"Liam, I want you to know that your actions have hurt me deeply. I feel lied to, and embarrassed, and unsure of where I went wrong as a mother. I understand now that you found the material for your play, and this whole theory of yours, from looking into your father's private matters while he was dealing with the worst of his health problems. I wish that you had spoken to us about what you had found and saved us all the troubles we have gone through. I also wish that my husband had admitted to me where your theories may have come from. Everything about this has made me feel so very alone."

Her speech sounded rehearsed and robotic, an empty vessel of content. She'd looked from Liam to Bill to straight ahead as if cued to them like cameras. She made no indication that anyone else existed. Maria regarded her son, who gave her an uncomfortable glance, and her heart stirred with pity for Liam, who was looking up at the sky, as if wondering whether it would rain.

"Thank you, my dear," Bill soothed. "I share your pain. For my part, I want to reiterate my apology to you for not having shared the connection between his theory and the creative project Paul and I had worked on some years back. I can't say that it didn't cross my mind, but I foolishly hoped ignoring the problem would make it go away. I was cowardly, and I hope to earn your forgiveness. I also appear to be reaping what I have sown, in the form of my son's behavior. Liam, you have insulted me—" Greta touched her hand to his leg. "Sorry, I feel . . . insulted by your behavior, not only the things you have said about me, but the way you have treated me for months now. I want to remind you of our deal that you have broken, and while it pains me to say it, you are now going to have to take care of yourself for some time."

As he paused, Al leaned to whisper something in Maria's ear, which broke Bill's momentum before she could catch his joke.

"Al, please." Al held up both of his hands and gestured for Bill to continue. "No, I think we've said enough for now. Would you or Maria like to speak next?"

"Well," Al began with vigor, putting more life into that single word than had been collectively spoken so far. Maria cut him off. The discussion called for her stability, not his chaos.

"No honey, please, I'll go. These last twenty-four hours have felt like a roller coaster. I think we all can relate to that. I'm upset with both of our sons, of course. And well, frankly, everyone, including myself. We're clearly doing something wrong, to have gotten to this point."

"Please, I would encourage you to avoid generalizations right now," interjected Greta placidly.

"Don't interrupt her," Al shot back, getting less able to contain himself.

"She's just trying to keep things from devolving into nonsense," Paul inserted.

"Nonsense? This whole thing is nonsense!" Al retorted. "I'm sorry, but why are you even here? What these two boys did, it's a joke. We're their parents, so we have to teach them a lesson, but we don't need any lessons from you."

Paul started sputtering and breathing heavily, but Bill cut him off before he could form any words.

"Gentlemen, enough. Clearly, this demonstrates the environment we are all in, our children included. And they are adults now, just like us, so they know how messy life can be, but unlike us, they may not know how to clean it up yet. I think it would be best if one of them were to speak next. Horace?"

Until Al and Paul broke containment, Liam had suppressed any reaction to what the circle was saying. Now, he picked his head up and stared at Horace. His face remained bland, but his eyes were narrowed as if to shield any feelings from spilling out. Maria could tell that he was only interested in what Horace had to say.

"Okay. I'm supposed to just speak about myself here? Sure. I— I'm sorry Mom and Dad. I really want to be a better son. I need to get my life in gear, like I don't want to spend the rest of my twenties living at home. Dr. Hawthorne told me last night that living in your childhood bedroom too long is bad for you, and I couldn't agree more. But I'm also really lucky. I've been jealous of Liam my whole life for so many reasons, like how smart, and confident, and capable he is? Like, I would wish that I had his life instead of mine. Even when he'd complain about his parents, I was like, buddy, have you met mine? Always in my business, on my case, worrying about me. You just get to do your own thing. But yeah, I was wrong. I feel really bad for him now. The play was a dumb idea, but what the hell is this? Why can't you talk to each other like a normal family? This public . . . spectacle is just dodging the issue. Like, Jesus!"

Everyone immediately had something to say, so nothing was heard until Liam yelled, "Shut up!" He stood and took the floor.

"You shouldn't have said that, Ace, but thanks anyway. I fucked up, and I know it. I am fucked up, and I know it. I don't need to be told that. But whose fault is that? Why am I like this? Why'd I try to kill myself? Nature? Nurture? Doesn't matter. All I can think is—I am who I was born to be, and who I was raised to be."

He closed his speech looking directly at his parents. Maria gasped. Paul, who had not stopped stewing and simmering, burst out into a rolling boil.

"How-how-ow-w dare you! I cannot believe you . . . you . . . youtilizerais cis chance pfour accuseh . . . eh . . . eck . . ."

Paul's trailing off caught everyone in confusion, including himself. Was he speaking French, or wait, was the left side of his face not moving with the right? In a moment, the implications of his symptoms dawned on them, and everyone jumped to their feet. Horace dialed 9-1-1. Al and Bill steadied him to ensure he'd stay in his chair. Greta burst into tears, and Maria paced about in helpless worry. No one noticed when Liam slipped away.

3.3 ~ The Cleanup

Flora got the call around 7:30 p.m. Readying for a night out, she was applying makeup in her bathroom, its vanity lights so bright she could watch, brushstroke by brushstroke, as she transformed herself into someone better. When she had time, she did one side of her face then the other, how her favorite makeup vlogger created a living before and after, because she liked to see both of her faces, even if she suspected they didn't like each other. She imagined her left eye judging the right side's haughtiness and pretentions, while the right eye dismissed the left side as homely and immature, yet also pretentious in its own way. At least they had that in common.

Music was playing from her phone, then it stopped, and the abrupt switch to buzzing and ringing rattled her. She'd been caught in a delicate state, not just in her own world but straddling the divide between two. She put down the brush and flipped over her phone to see it was Horace. He hated phone calls, so there was no good reason he'd be calling, but plenty of bad ones. She returned her gaze to the mirror as she answered, both sides of her face offering different flavors of sympathy, like she was some third thing they could both agree to pity. She saw her father on the left, his bags under her eyes, her cheeks scattered with his pocks and freckles, while on her right, her mother's strong cheekbones had been contoured into being, her mother's lashes waited for their cue to bat and beckon.

As Horace hurriedly explained what had just happened to her father, where they had taken him, and what they still didn't know, she watched the color drain from her left cheek, while the right side of her face was unaffected, cosmetically protected. She learned that her father had suffered a stroke, but the emotional adrenaline numbed any feeling. Instead of processing, she thought about what to do with her face. Removing it all was the sensible thing, but then she'd just be left with Paul, when she wanted herself to be Edith, shielded, removed. Edith who'd left them, or

Paul who might be leaving them soon. She called herself ridiculous as tears surfaced and wiped off her makeup before it could run.

When she got to the hospital, Paul was undergoing tests. Horace was sitting with his and Liam's parents, but Liam himself was absent. While they waited, she called her brother Louis. They talked briefly, neither the type to dwell on a point, a response to having been raised by their father. He wanted to know the facts, when it had happened, how long he had waited for care, data he could plug into his spreadsheet to measure expectations. Even when he asked her how she was doing, it felt like a survey to rate a service's quality. She was doing alright; she had no additional feedback at that time. Only once the call ended did the adrenaline run out. She sat down next to Horace, placed her head on his shoulder, and let a few tears drip onto his shirt. She wanted little else from him, or anyone, because she was self-sufficient. She didn't even need her father; they had a different relationship she struggled to name.

They waited for good news that never came. Not all of it was bad news, mostly the doctors hedged, but the benchmark for expectations declined with every update, each another missed opportunity for a positive turn. He appears stable, but they've ordered scans. Scans suggest brain swelling. Swelling calls for surgery. The surgeon is getting ready. The surgeon is operating on him. Surgery is complete. The surgeon did her best, always does her best, gives you the best chance. It couldn't have gone better, it could have gone worse.

Once Flora arrived, these updates were delivered to her alone, with others allowed to listen and nod. As she held her father's life in her hands, she found it a strangely light thing, like the string of a balloon that might slip away and never come back. The role of grieving daughter bothered her. It gave her permission to act however she wanted, separated from instinct and removed from some limiting principle she hoped existed. She cried because it was the only thing she both could and should do.

The other parents stayed until the surgery began, then Al took the women home, as it was well-past midnight. Flora and Horace in their own world and Bill in his, all sat in a waiting room for the news. Flora dozed on Horace's shoulder, while he sipped coffee that had long since lost its heat.

When the surgeon spoke with them after the procedure, she told them to get some rest and come back in the evening. They shouldn't expect any changes in his condition before then. She asked, as had several nurses, if Flora wanted any help contacting family members. Flora said she was handling it, but she hadn't told her mom yet. She wanted to ask Louis to, but that would be cowardly. She should be strong enough, and she'd wait until she was. The only help she would accept was from Horace, who offered to drive her home in her car. Bill left with them, and they said nothing but goodbye to each other.

They drove in dawn's light to Flora's apartment. The lurid sunrise taunted them, its beauty so indifferent to their problems, its nostalgic tones tinted by their tired eyes. They listened to classical music softly from the radio, and Horace kept rubbing his eyes, but Flora had no tears left to cry.

Horace collapsed on her couch and encouraged her to rest. Flora went to her room but lacked the appetite for sleep. She sat on her bed and tried meditating, desperate for some reconnection with herself. She longed to hurt, searching for aches in her chest, a storm over her eyes, rage in her fists, weakness in her legs. She checked in with her chakras and limbs but found them all empty, their essences drained. The only pain she could find was in these absences, but they were nothing to hold onto, the sadness of an empty house.

At some point, she realized she was flat on her bed and time had passed, sleep having mugged her. Annoyed with herself and disoriented, she got up without thinking, and her legs led her into the kitchen. She put the water on for tea. She also put bread in the toaster but never pressed down. By the time she realized, she was already sitting at the table with her mug and a book of nature poems. Too late to do anything about it. The bread would remain bread.

She'd selected the book at random from her shelf of favorites. She flipped through the pages till her thumb caught and one picked itself. The poem was about dead animals and grief, favorite subjects of that poet, and she decided to read it till she was properly grieving or dead. The poem also spoke of fertility, the only thing that could match death in pain and power. She thought of her father, first as a child, then as her child, the child she may never want or have, a child she may not have for much longer. And if he recovered, he'd be more childlike than ever, struggling with sentences, learning things anew, wide-eyed and confused with glimpses of joy.

"Now I'm getting somewhere," she mumbled to herself.

Horace stirred not long after. It was a holiday, but the next performance of *Solving for X* was set for that evening. After a moment of lazy adjustment, he checked his phone, which appeared to disappoint him somehow. He asked Flora for a ride home, which she was happy to provide. She needed something to do. They left with the bread still loaded in the toaster. Only in the car did the tragic humor of avoiding the smell of toast occur to Flora, who now took it as some sort of sign, though she couldn't be bothered to guess what it portended.

"I don't think Liam's gonna show tonight," Horace let out, once they'd merged onto the highway.

"What makes you say that?" Flora asked mildly, unwilling to summon the energy required by opinions.

"They found a note. Said he's going to stay with Ian Noone for a while. Remember him?"

"Liam's imaginary friend."

"More like his get-out-of-jail-free card. It was fine when he was messing with his parents, but not us. I've still heard nothing from him."

"Hm," was all Flora could offer. She'd never heard Horace sound so bitter.

"Sorry, I know you've got bigger problems on your mind," Horace added, bookended by silence.

"I still need to tell my mom," Flora finally verbalized, the thought having repeated itself louder and louder in her head till it finally spilled out. "Do you...I don't think...I don't know if she'll care."

"She cares about you, right? And Louis? She's gotta thank Paul for you two, at least?"

"She'll say he had it coming, and I don't think I can take hearing that."

"Would it help if I was with you when you called her?"

Flora took her time to answer. She knew he meant the offer genuinely, that he'd sit with her in silence, that he'd be there only to receive her reaction and help her process. He was always so generous with his presence, as if he had nowhere else to be. Perhaps that was often the case, but that made it no less selfless to her. He gave from all that he had. But unobtrusive as he was, he still changed things by observing them. Who she was with her mother upset her—her mind and her mouth at odds—and who she was with Horace confused her—all versions of herself stacked up and overlapping. It would be too much.

"Thanks, but I need to be alone for it. You understand. Text me tomorrow and ask me if I've done it yet."

"I will, but I bet you will have. You're the responsible one, remember?"

"I don't always want to be."

She dropped Horace off and continued to the hospital. She passed normally palatable food options on the way, but she was finding a perverse enjoyment in self-denial. It felt right given the circumstances, like a penitent nun. But more than pleasing her heavenly father, she worried how it served her devilish mother. If she had been meeting her mom in person for this, Flora could expect a compliment on how thin she was keeping herself. But Edith was far away, and the phone screen would protect Flora.

She knew it was unhealthy to only see a caricature of her mother, but the real woman rarely differed from that impression, in part because she hardly appeared in Flora's life at all. She could forgive her mom for cheating on her dad—hell, she hardly blamed her—but she'd never understand why her mom hadn't fought harder for custody in the divorce. It was mystifying to Flora at the time, but eleven years old and full of shame, it was too easy to accept it as somehow her fault that her mother didn't want her or her annoying brother. Only with time and a newfound capacity for self-respect did she come to appreciate how bizarre, how devoid of human instinct her mother's behavior had been during the divorce. Could her mother be a sociopath? She didn't know her well enough to disprove it, but her mother's absence might be evidence enough.

Instead, Paul kept the kids and Edith moved home to Montreal, where she and Paul had grown up. Flora navigated the end of her adolescence, most of puberty, and the rest of her life so far without her mother's aid. She had other women in her life to turn to, starting with the mothers and older sisters on the cul-de-sac, but she was too shrouded in shame to make much use of them. The internet became her new mother, a constant presence of infinite knowledge shared without judgment. Even the contact that she maintained with Edith, video calls and texts and the odd vacation, were mediated virtually, like her mother was an avatar of the greater internet, but only a shoddy, poorly integrated feature, capable of 3D manifestations once a year at best. Paul was faulty too, but at least he was unmistakably flesh.

Flora knew the longer she waited to call her, the more she'd open herself up to her mother's reproach. She parked her car in the visitor lot and went to find her father's room. He was asleep or sedated or unconscious when she came upon him. She wasn't sure the distinction and didn't want to ask. When a nurse came by to check on him, she asked if there were any updates to his condition since last night, and the nurse told her to wait for a doctor, who would be by soon. She took that as a no, or another nothing good. She also knew it was time to call her mother, while things were still unclear, before full verdicts could be rendered.

She called her while sitting by her father's side, his presence offering her privacy without loneliness. She counted the rings and prayed for the safety of voicemail, but her mother answered on the fifth.

"Yes, dear?"

"Hey Mama."

"What is it?"

"Papa had a stroke."

"What? You're mumbling."

"I-I'm with him in the hospital. Paul. He had a stroke last night. We're still not sure how bad it was, but it's not looking good."

"Jesus."

"I know."

"Paul had a stroke," her altered tone and muffled volume suggested to Flora that she was saying this to someone in the room with her. "Yesterday, you said? Why didn't you tell me sooner? No, never mind, I'm sorry. Is . . . is he going to make it?"

"I don't know. We're just waiting. It's bad, it's awful."

"Terrible news. Is Louis there with you?"

"No, he's figuring things out with work. He'll be down this weekend, I think."

"That's good, that he'll be there soon. Seeing him should lift Paul's spirits."

"Mama, he's not . . ."

"Your father will make a full recovery, I'm sure of it. God knows he's never been one to give up."

"Mom . . ."

"Look sweetie, I'm sorry but you've caught me in the middle of something. I'll have to go now. Please forgive me, and keep me updated. We'll talk again soon, okay?"

"Okay."

"Love you."

"Love you too."

The Cleanup

Flora had expected worse from her mother, and yet Edith not lashing out left more space for her lack of care to show. What Flora wanted from the call, what a normal mother would provide, was assurance that losing her father wouldn't leave her alone. Instead, her world felt smaller than ever, like nothing outside that hospital room existed, nothing outside herself mattered, her emotions throbbing so loudly, her body glowing so hot as if self-immolating. The last time she'd been filled with these sensations, they'd taken her to rehab, and now the trail, covered up but well-carved, was revealing itself to her again, beckoning. It didn't help that her first opioid high was administered in a room much like this one. She'd been planning to wait for the doctor but decided against it. She had to see trees and touch grass. The sight of a bird in flight might save her. She rose, kissed her father on his forehead, and departed.

The hospital grounds didn't do it for her. Pavement baked by the sun, trees and shrubs choked on medians, the approach of death wherever she looked. She escaped to her car and drove without knowing where to go. As she turned right at the first intersection, she realized it had to be to her father's house. When she thought of nature, it was those woods. When she thought of comfort, it was his large, leather sofa. When she thought of consolation, it was Horace's kindness. He'd be busy, but she could wait. There were others, she had plenty of friends, but she craved the company of someone who knew her father and could express kindred feelings, appreciate his imperfections.

She let herself into her childhood home, finding it frozen like a crime scene. A light mess in the kitchen he would've cleaned after the party. The ingredients for a Manhattan sitting atop a drink cart and a thin layer of amber water in his glass, the one ice cube he took with his drinks long since melted. The trash full of takeout and the recycling overflowing with bottles, while his fridge held barren shelves. The sight and sense of alcohol pervaded—her father's first love and second wife. He'd never dipped below functional, keeping up appearances like how he kept the home orderly and neat, but she knew he liked to clean while drunk. She'd told Horace her mother would say Paul had it coming because part of her thought that too, the part she associated with her mom, her functions of judgment and criticism that defended themselves as worldly wisdom.

She approached the cart, washed out the glass, and poured herself a rough shot of whiskey, topping it off with an ice cube. She'd never had a problem with alcohol but stopped drinking after rehab. She told herself this wasn't breaking her rules, that she was doing this to honor her father, but maybe her rules didn't matter anymore. She took a sip that stung her tongue, perversely pleasurable, and felt an instant, giddy intoxication as it hit her empty stomach. Then, a swirl and the threat of vomit, which appealed to her. She took another sip, and her stomach adjusted. She played music from her phone and danced lyrically to her reflection in the oven, holding her glass like the hand of a dance partner, seeing its liquid splash against the sides but not spill, feeling like a music box ballerina. She finished her drink and curtsied, then laid herself down on the cool kitchen floor, weak and empty and ready for death.

Like a spell had been broken, the discomfort she'd been enjoying started to reverse. The tile was too hard and felt dirty on her bare arms. Her stomach groaned, and responsibilities reasserted themselves. What had she come here for? She craned her neck and glimpsed through the window the birdfeeder she'd made in school and given to her father, some Christmas or Easter or Father's Day gift. She wondered if her dad still tended to it. If he died, all this would become hers and her brother's. That had always been the case, but only in future perfect tense, that one day it will have happened. She'd studied adults her whole life for their secrets, how they survived life's difficulties, and now she was presented with the ultimate test. Sick days and mental health days would not buy her time. She pushed herself off the floor.

She scrounged his fridge and pantry for sustenance, a search which yielded mixed nuts, olives, and an orange. Eating felt good and snapped her out of delirium, colors and sounds returning to full strength. Plans sprung into her mind to fill the void. She'd clean the house thoroughly. She'd call her boss and tell her she was taking the week off. She'd visit her father every day and read to him. She'd watch Horace's play again. She'd write poetry. She'd make use of her sadness. All these things were possible, and if she did them right, maybe her father would recover and come home to appreciate them and hug her and tell her how much he loves her, and she'd say the same though her actions had already shown it. She remembered that she'd wanted to go for a walk through the woods, but now that felt too aimless and reflective. She knew what she had to do. It was time for action. She opened a cider from the fridge and gathered the cleaning supplies.

She tackled the kitchen firstly and earnestly, emptying the sink, clearing the countertops, mopping the floor, sifting through the pantry and fridge, tossing expired goods, organizing the cabinets, wiping the windows, and leaving herself exhausted from the effort. She was too tired to have a third drink, which relieved and concerned her. Instead, she decided to take stock of the rest of the house and make a work plan for the week. She started with her father's bedroom, where she had spent the least time in the house. It was tidy with a made bed, although books overflowed his nightstand. Almost disappointed to not have more to do there, she decided she could at least run the sheets through the wash, in hopes he'd come home to clean bedding.

She continued to his adjoining bathroom, opening the medicine cabinet without thinking. A dozen pill bottles lined the shelves. Her mouth watered. She reasoned that you learn a lot about someone from the pills they take, things her father would never admit to her, so she was justified perusing them. He was managing heartburn, high blood pressure, acid reflux, and bad cholesterol. He had a variety of vitamins and minerals, and regrettably, some Viagra, which she shook to assure herself was far from empty. Her heart skipped at the sight of Ambien and Xanax, but it was the last bottle she got to, in the back because it was never needed, that stopped her cold. She held in her hands a half-full bottle of 10mg Vicodin, leftovers from her father's back surgery. She estimated it to have about twenty pills by weight. She popped the cap and looked inside. No one knew she was there, no one would care, no one cared about her, nothing mattered. No one. No.

"No!"

She dropped the bottle and fled the bathroom before the pills hit the floor and scattered. She ran downstairs and outside, leaving the door open, falling to the grass, hearing nothing but her throbbing pulse. She'd never been so close before to making that mistake. She was still close. But if she relapsed, her father would die, she was sure. She needed an escape, but she didn't feel capable of leaving, too close to quitting for her francophone brain. She needed help.

She called Horace. No answer, but she knew he'd be coming home soon. She called Liam. Straight to voicemail. She composed a text to Horace, taking a long time to settle on a final wording that captured the right amount of distress.

"hey!! I'm back on the sac tonight. been cleaning out the house. not feeling my best, can we hang out tonight? movie? i also kinda wanna smoke but idk if that's a good idea lol. anyway hope the play went great! did liam show?" She hit send then tacked on, "also called my mom yay me. no updates on papa =/"

Horace replied a few minutes later.

"Hey sorry I missed your call! Play just wrapped. I'll tell you about it tonight =) (it sucked lol). No Liam, so I had to stand in. I'm sorry you're not doing too great, but it'd be weird if you were tbh. I'm stopping at Chipotle first, you eat dinner yet?"

Flora couldn't help but notice he'd ignored her mention of smoking. She imagined him reading it and getting flustered, drafting and deleting a response, and she smiled. She also felt targeted by his mention of food. He hadn't asked her if she wanted something, which she didn't, but if she needed something, which she did.

"yay we can have a vent sesh <3," which she followed up with, "wouldn't say no to some chips and guac." Horace replied with supportive emojis.

He arrived an hour later. In that time, Flora had dragged herself into her father's study, placed a Crosby, Stills, Nash & Young album on his turntable, listened to the first side, and sat in silence for another forty minutes. At one point, she hummed that one Simon & Garfunkel song. Curled and twisted as tight as could be on her father's favorite chair, she scrolled through social media without reacting to anything. She briefly switched to her corporate account, having the authority to post on behalf of Vein's verified art foundation, just to view a world in which nothing was wrong, just businesspersons sharing their corporate successes, anodyne lessons learned, and days-old memes.

Horace let himself into the foyer and grinned at her through the open door, holding up his bag of fast casual like a prize rabbit. She hummed a hello that came out like a wince. Relenting to his efforts at comfort, she accepted the chips and guac and took polite sips from the bottle of organic strawberry soda. As he told her about the show, his stage high rubbed off on her, not quite reaching below her surface but dragging her upward and outward nonetheless. He related his embarrassing mistakes, complained about Russ while defending Gil, speculated about Liam's whereabouts, joked that he may have been kidnapped, and even admitted that he fancied the stage tech Mint though he was quick to add he'd never have the balls to approach them. He also unloaded his conversation with Dr. Hawthorne to her, how it was a failure but not a complete one, because there was something to fear about Vein, some weird connections to this Eden club he owned, maybe even some kind of brainwashing drug like Chemical X, though Dr. Hawthorne wouldn't confirm it. She thought about sharing the work rumors she'd heard about Mr. and Mrs. Vein, but she kept them to herself, unable to summon the effort.

She could tell Horace was still playing a character, the affable friend who could provide jester-like distractions from the day's oppressions, or the park ranger who vanquishes his fear to aid a wounded animal. He lured her in and warmed up her over the course of the meal, squeezing in questions to her between bites but never putting her on the spot about her troubles. Once they'd finished, Horace proposed a walk, insisting it was a summer night worth appreciating.

"I have a pre-roll I'm happy to share," he added.

"Thanks, I would, unless you think it's a bad idea."

"That's up to you. I'm the last person who can judge someone for smoking."

They agreed she'd only take a couple baby hits, then set out for the trail. She wanted to return his favor, rewarding him for the work he'd done to cheer her up, but her honest feelings were still a mystery to her. Instead, she opened up about something that had been troubling her, wanting to voice the thought before she got high.

"I don't think I'd love my parents if they weren't my parents. I don't know if either of them is a good person."

"What makes you say that?"

"It's just, I'm the mix of the two of them, right? A mix that did not work, like they were totally incompatible. They haven't done great on their own either. My mom's a cold bitch, and my dad's a workaholic drunk. It's mean but true. If I'm half of each, then what does that make me? The only thing that keeps me from admitting that is because I still love them, but love's blind and happens at random."

"I see what you mean, but that's not how I think of you. Lots of good people have bad parents. And I may not always like your dad, but I do love him, or he's at least worthy of love. He means well."

"I think the people who turn out better than their parents do it in spite of them, like in protest. But I always thought they were right and I was wrong. Now I just think my whole family's wrong, and a bit broken. Like why am I thinking about this when my dad's in the hospital?"

"Don't worry about that. You gotta let your mind wander, no use fighting it. Here, do you want some?"

She nodded and reached out a shaky hand to accept the joint, fixing her eyes on its smoking tip, watching the cherry glow brightly with her breath, tasting and feeling it enter her body and sweeten her spit, coughing, floating, stoning her like a sinner, either a witch or a prostitute. She passed it back and stared straight up at the sky, searching for stars, feeling herself be changed and unwound. They didn't speak for about a minute, then they reached the stump, on which she sat. Horace took one last hit of the joint and snuffed its flame to save for later. She felt within his power, someone she'd always cared for, the baby of the group. My, how he'd grown, how tall he now reached. She traced her hand idly along the stump's face, then found something new to talk about.

"H and F. I remember you showing me the change, you were so embarrassed. Feels like a lifetime ago. I hope you don't regret it. Not just this carving, the whole thing. I know it ended bad, but I'd never seen that side of you before. You seem more confident now, but not as happy."

"Not much to be happy about nowadays. It's been a rough couple of months and a terrible week. The play was helping, but now it's just another problem."

"I don't know about happy, but tonight has been nice. Thank you for being with me, you've made me happier."

"I'm glad," Horace said without looking at her, fishing in his pocket for cigs. He handed her one and lit both before continuing. "Can I ask you something? What are you supposed to do with those memories? The good times with an ex. All the photos on my phone. Even the ones from before we were together, back when it was just a friend crush. A fantasy, really. It's like they all turned to ash but still kept their shape."

"I've never known. You just carry them with you. I don't think trying to forget helps or works, really. You could talk about them if you want to. I'd love to listen."

*** *** ***

Horace was still unwilling to remember his good times with Dylan. How Dylan was there for him in his time of need. How they grew closer. How he laughed and tossed his hair. How it was when they first kissed. What they said in their goodbyes. He'd rather forget.

Yet through that wall, memories would still leak, and he'd be stuck blocking them out or else drowning in them. Sometimes there were triggers, like the stump, and other times there weren't, like his mind was a masochist. Though if there was pleasure in this pain, he had not found it.

There was the memory of first reunion, a sliver of intersection in their disparate lives. Both living at home and unemployed, but Horace had just dropped out while Dylan was celebrating a few months of freedom before Peace Corps deployment. The specific image was Dylan crossing the cul-de-sac when he spotted Horace forcing himself out on a walk. He was grinning and running over with the kind of grace that's meant to be given and that Horace felt he'd never received. After that moment, Dylan would tell him directly, with the humor only he could pull off, that he was thrilled to hear Horace had moved back home because he missed the local crew and wanted to hang, so they should. But in that moment, watching Dylan's approach, Horace felt afraid, already hating himself and seeing an old friend who might hate him now too.

There was the memory of first connection, the second time they hung out that spring, the prior having been dedicated to catching up, when Horace was already drinking and smoking again but at least he wasn't alone, and he found himself just staring at Dylan. That was the image, in the Falcos' carpeted basement, the place where he first felt something for Dylan years before, by then nearly empty save for a couch and television as the Falcos prepared to move, and he found Dylan was gazing contentedly back at him, like he was appreciating a decision he'd already made, one that he was waiting for Horace to make too. He'd definitely brushed back his long black hair, perhaps he'd even licked his lips, and at least one of his dimples was showing, not to mention his capable, tan arms resting by his purple tank top at a flattering angle, right before he leaned in to kiss Horace. The kiss and its rush of emotions were difficult for Horace to recall, but he remembered the moment before with clarity because it too was filled with fear, fear that he was incapable and unlovable, that not he but Dylan was making a mistake, and that they'd both suffer the consequences.

The rest could only be remembered like it happened to someone else. The sex like amateur porn, though the view wasn't much; the lounging and cuddling like a rom-com, too happy to be real; the dinners with their parents like a coming-of-age film, keeping such a silly secret from them. Dylan claimed he was proudly bi, but his pride and parents had yet to meet, though they soon would.

What kept it all from decaying into a dream, bringing it beyond the threshold of viewership, was his meager collection of evidence that it had all happened to him: the few photos, the superficial texts, and the two lines they carved into the stump. They'd been taking a joint for a walk, and Dylan was holding his hand, so Horace was smoking with his left and Dylan his right. Horace felt silly in the exact way he imagined lovers should. When they reached the stump, they stopped holding hands and started reminiscing. Dylan cracked wise about Liam and Flora's premature declaration of eternal love. Then he stopped and just looked at Horace, drinking him in, and Horace felt not fear but love. Dylan produced his pocketknife with a cheeky flourish.

"Why don't we correct the record? There's a new couple on the block."

3.4 ~ The Initiation

Mint reminded themself, yet again, that they had a job to do. A whole lot of sub-jobs were involved in this job, and the one they hated the most was babysitting. All babies do is crawl from one active hostage situation to the next, taking victims and threatening them with not harm but self-harm if their demands are not met. It's the worst because a baby never asks for you to be there, never intends to create disaster, and never knows how to clean it up when disaster strikes. There's no one to blame when something goes wrong except the victim in charge and the forces, parental or otherwise, that put this victim in charge.

Mint hated playing the victim because their preferred role was detective.

Yet here Mint was, charged with up to four babies. The number was uncertain because they weren't sure what to make of Russ and Gil. Both were employed in Vein's empire, but then again, so was Horace. They seemed guileless, and having seen their acting, Mint was skeptical they could commit to their roles as double agents. Yet Mint had only gotten here by following their nose for coincidences, and this one smelled like Axe body spray masking a deeper stench.

It was easy enough not to trust them because Mint wasn't there to trust anyone. Mint was there, inside enemy lines, to collect intel and compile a report. Journalism carried with it a code of ethics they felt unbound by, preferring instead the methods—ethic had nothing to do with it—of espionage. Though it was an outside chance, they had an opportunity to take down a man like Tevin Vein, or at least scratch his shiny armor, drawing attention to something ugly that no one could ignore.

Thoughts such as these sustained Mint as they sat at the switchboard watching this amateur hour, these four boys playing with spilled mercury stolen from a father's lab. They were going to get hurt, but Mint couldn't intervene because they had to witness the cleanup. Most of the damage was already done by the time Mint met them anyway. Liam's post was more than enough, and as dumb as it was, Mint had him to thank for getting them this far.

Mint had learned that Vein Holdings was acquiring Tyrellius, Dr. Hawthorne's firm, from a single line, barely more than a footnote, in one of the company's myriad SEC filings. As a private company, Vein Holdings wasn't open to individual investors, but as an individual, no one was more invested in Vein than Mint, who had read every piece of official literature, to say nothing of the unofficial, proliferated by the company. Mint searched these digital stacks for a hypodermic needle, some evidence of abuse, a trail that could be followed. At last, with the Hawthornes, they might have found it.

Years ago, before there was a trail or even the hunt for one, there was a podcast—as dumb as it sounds—and a community on a Discord server. Dedicated, surprisingly resourceful people, cloaked in anonymity, devoted to exposing the perversions and evils of various celebrities and miscellaneous bourgeois. Mint knew it was mostly LARPing, but they needed some fantasy mixed into their reality. Fresh off a gender transition that had taken an unexpected turn toward ambiguity (thanks to a realization that the grass was not greener but in fact yellow, and they too were yellow, not pink or blue or any combination of the two), they found class conflict to be the perfect channel for their rage amid the inescapable realities of social injustice and personal disaffection.

Tevin Vein, due to the ridiculousness of both his name and his behavior, was a popular topic on the podcast and in the community, a short-hand reference for dumbass billionaires, a frequently used reaction image, a meme in every sense. It was easy to forget he was a real person, rather than a name on buildings, a metonym for late-stage capitalism, and a gangly upper body and smug face appearing on Bloomberg TV and at Davos that you were never sure wasn't a deepfake. But real people bleed if you cut them. Billionaires die, or even better, they can be embarrassed, their mythos discredited. The market could lose confidence, and the value of their life would plummet.

So Mint started paying attention to him alongside the community, waiting for unsubstantiated rumors of impropriety—sexual, financial, whatever—to become corroborated. They started posting, made friends, posted more, learned some tricks of the trade, and gradually became something of a virtual gumshoe.

Mint alerted the Discord server to the curious matter of the Tyrellius acquisition, but no one knew what to make of it till someone got around to checking the social medias of the founding partners' families. Liam Hawthorne's post was instantly enshrined in their lore, and the tenor of the Discord changed from that day. When Liam posted a casting call for his play, when Vein was announced as the primary sponsor for the festival, when Mint discovered they lived within driving distance—when all those lucky stars aligned, they realized it was up to them to act. Sprinkle on top that Liam's play would be going on at a mysterious venue in a former-church-turned-real-estate asset of Vein Holdings, and it started to feel less like coincidence and more like conspiracy. But despite all the tangles, Mint hoped there'd be no one accounting for them, the meek stage tech who'd requested working with their dear acquaintance Liam Hawthorne.

Only now Liam was gone, and Mint was still here. A blubbering Horace had just told them Liam wouldn't be appearing for the show tonight. Made sense—opening night confirmed Mint's impression that Liam had never cared about the show beyond exorcising his daddy issues. Given Russ and Gil's reactions to Liam's no-show, how callously Russ argued that going on with it was pointless without him, how Gil appealed for the play not as a thing worth doing but a thing needing to be done, Mint felt only more comfortable writing them off as paid agents. Was Horace the only one who was here altruistically? His pathetic nobility garnered Mint's trust. The poor guy really seemed to be dreading the stage.

Yet whatever his motivation, be it semi-professional duty or a spite directed toward all involved including himself, he insisted the show must go on. Mint found his willingness to embarrass himself admirable. He cuffed the pants on Liam's costume, attached Liam's script to a clipboard, and stumbled through Liam's lines in front of a paltry crowd. It seemed they'd given up inviting people to the show, and Mint wondered why anyone had come at all. If the attendees were just amateur-theater enthusiasts who'd picked *Solving for X* at random, perhaps they could find some enjoyment in the different types of malfunction put on display: Horace trying and failing, Gil trying too hard to make up for it, and Russ not trying at all. It was Mint's favorite performance by far.

Mint was especially relieved the show continued because it meant they could keep their key fob for another week. They'd successfully cultivated a contact, one of the bouncers for the Eden club, a few weeks back when they'd snuck in by claiming they'd misplaced their invitation card. Everyone's happier to answer your questions once they've passed back your joint (smoking for Mint wasn't just an occupational hazard but an informational necessity), and this guy let Mint know Eden would be hosting an initiation party for its first class of members after the initial round of invites had run its course. Mint would be there to bear witness. To what and for what end, Mint still didn't know, but the trail was there to be followed, not blazed.

Mint's dream was to catch Tevin Vein himself in some compromising act, but there was little reason to believe he would actually be there. He had a vast corporate empire to maintain, within which Eden seemed little more than a gimmick. But that's exactly what gave Mint hope. Why would a private investment firm, with fingers in every high-margin pie under the sun, bother starting up some low-rent, piddly business like a nightclub? And why, judging by the goings-on inside, did they appear so uninterested in making money? There was simply no profit angle, so Mint turned to other explanations.

Well-versed in the psychological profiles of men like Vein, probable psychopaths with inhuman amounts of money, Mint's best guess was boredom. The boredom of having conquered the world drove others to space exploration, media production, or political office, but Mint suspected Vein considered himself more creative, more vulgar than that. Well, what's more fun than running a cult? The key to immortality is having youth around you whose blood (or whatever) you can suck. That's not a task you can delegate, either.

So, low expectation, Mint would try to get a copy of whatever NDA was included in this "initiation" going on that Saturday, and high expectation, they'd find Vein there too and do . . . something? Snap a photo for the Discord, at least. After following this beat for years as a virtual crusade, Mint found it weird to be re-entering the real world, preparing to face people who opposed them and their goals, knowing that decisions would be time-sensitive and crucial. It was hard not to be nervous, but Mint could live with nerves. What they could not tolerate was fear, any paralysis in a decisive moment.

In the meantime, they continued casing the joint, trusting that Russ and Gil would pay them no mind. But every time they arrived the place was spotless, empty save for the stacks of chairs. Whoever cleaned up after each night was frustratingly good. The fob only let them into the building, and the key to the tech booth seemed to be for that alone. The door to the right of the stage had to lead downstairs but was locked by a keypad, which yielded nothing from their impromptu fingerprint analysis or attempts with some common combinations. The planners behind this had done their job, but even the best security plans remain subject to execution, and Mint was determined.

Before each show, they searched through the bar, the one real fixture on the barren floor, looking for something that shouldn't have been left behind. They had no luck until closing night, which to Horace's credit he had performed off-book, although he flubbed a couple lines that messed up Mint's cues, especially whenever Gil veered off track to make up for it. His parents and sisters and a couple friends, two cute girls, had come again and seemed proud of him. A normal guy with loving family and friends felt so out of place here.

More important to Mint that night was the bottle they found, drops away from being empty, rolled away under a sink. They'd send it to a contact of theirs who was an amateur chemist, someone familiar with the synthesis and detection of drugs. Mint was convinced that there'd be Chemical X somewhere, maybe everywhere, if they only knew how to find it. But they'd have to wait on the results, given the timeliness of drug dealers.

After that show, once the few attendees had trickled out and Russ and Gil had bid adieu, Horace sat disconsolate on the stage like an ice block melting into a puddle. Mint spotted him from the tech booth as they were collecting their affects and letting their mind run wild with thoughts of the night to follow. He probably didn't know Mint was still there, giving them the option to slip out quietly, but they decided to check up on him, though passing comfort did not come naturally to them. As they walked down the aisle, Horace did his best to collect himself and cover his surprise. Mint considered hopping up next to him, but sensing his skittishness, they stopped short of the stage.

"Hey bud, nice work tonight. You're a better Liam's dad than Liam."

"No I'm not. But thanks. I'm just glad it's over."

"Heard anything from him?"

"Yeah. He left a note, told me to break a leg."

"Wow, what a bitch. I know he's your friend, but he seems like an asshole."

"Yeah, that's what people keep telling me."

"I don't know if we're ever gonna see each other again, so, it's been a pleasure working with you."

"Thanks, you too."

"No really, it has. You've got a lot going for you. You take responsibility, and you know how to treat people." Horace didn't reply, so Mint continued, "I think the best thing you can do is just forget about all of this. Move on. Leave Eden behind, take a break from crazy family conspiracies. Just focus on yourself for a bit."

At that, he let out a single, bitter laugh.

"Sorry. It's just funny cuz I got mixed up with this mess for the exact opposite reason. I wanted to help myself by helping someone else for a change. But yeah, you're right, back to the old strategy."

Mint could hear tears in his throat and remembered there was good reason they didn't give advice often. Who were they to tell Horace what to do with his life? When had they ever moved on from anything? They were giving the advice they ought to receive but would never heed. They had said enough. It was clear Horace was dealing with far more than just the show's close. After wishing him luck, Mint headed out, leaving him alone in the large, empty room he could fill with his cavernous feelings.

They returned the next afternoon, parking their car at the edge of some woods to stake out Eden's entrance. They timed their arrival for the end of the other City Fringe show running at Eden, brought snacks, put on a podcast, cracked open an energy drink, and started rolling some spliffs. They wanted to see how the space would transition, who or what would be brought in, and when the first guests would arrive. While they waited, watching the parking lot empty out and stay empty, they tried picturing Tevin Vein as he would appear in that space. It was easy to imagine a fancy car pulling into the lot, as a few had passed by on the secluded road while they waited, but they couldn't envision him stepping out of a car, his slicked-back hair, his entourage surrounding him, striding across the lawn and up the steps. A helicopter landing in the open field felt more right, but only as a movie would show it, the picture falling apart just outside the frame. Too much attention would be drawn. The outside world was not meant to be brought in.

Around 19:00, a sketchy, white van bucked past Mint's car and gave them a jump. They sunk down in their seat, keeping their head up just enough to watch it turn into the parking lot. The bartenders and bouncers, Mint recognizing a few of the dozen, filed out in a jolly mood and made their way inside. Once they had, the driver emerged from the van. A tall man, ungainly and ogrish, seeming grave and unnatural even from a distance. Someone to watch out for. Rather than heading for the stairs, the man loped around to the back with long, slow strides, like a giant's, though was he really that tall? Mint knew that door could only lead to the basement. If they found a way down there, they'd have to expect him. He was clearly not meant to be seen, and for that, Mint counted his appearance as progress.

Shortly after, one of the DJs showed up in a Lincoln, still wearing his cap and shades against the mostly set sun, and headed so briskly to the back that Mint barely caught a glimpse. More laboriously, the two seated in the backseat of the car, beefier guys, carried in his mixing equipment. The car pulled away. Mint found it curious that no one was expected to drive themselves.

That was all they got till the guests started to arrive, also in rideshares—though that was more understandable—several hours later. Watching them trickle in, Mint debated the best time to join the fray. They didn't want to look suspicious standing in a thin crowd, but they also didn't want to miss any key action. Then, someone familiar stepped out of a car, promptly vomited, and made the decision for them.

***

For the first time in his life, Horace was drinking with the intention to black out. After a week of blazing disaster set off by opening night and stoked by Paul's stroke, by Liam's escape, by Russ and Gil's apathy, by that empty theater and that awful stage, Horace had finally become intimate with the sober desire to black out the sun and all that memory could reveal. No accidental slippage, no casting of a gentle shade, he craved erasure. After a bottle of wine in his room, he stumbled down the stairs to his rideshare. For the fifth time in eight days, he found himself traveling the road to Eden, his living, recurring nightmare.

He puked the moment he exited the car, having barely contained himself on the trip, but he was not to be deterred. Disgusted with himself and slightly sobered, he popped a piece of gum as he crossed the lawn and climbed the steps to the entrance. They were done playing games, and his name was on the list, so there was no wait. Jena would be inside somewhere, having prepared for the night with some of her fellow initiates. He checked in with a bouncer smiling widely to welcome him as he inspected Horace's vertical ID.

"Thank you for joining us. Tonight will be incredible."

Horace nodded in reply, carrying himself with the shambolic resolve of a drunk on a mission as he entered. The fog and lights resounded, and the beat obscured thought. Not waiting for his senses to adjust, he checked himself into the bathroom, splashing water on his face, rinsing out his mouth, ensuring no vomit had stained him, and enjoying a nice long piss. He returned to the mirror, eyeing himself as he washed his hands, sticking adjectives on his portrait like gaunt, hollow, dangerous. Or maybe endangered. Now four months old, the scar on his hand could no longer be seen, and for that he was glad.

He paid for a cocktail at the bar, another splendid bargain. Then he swayed toward the crowd, which swallowed him whole. At some point he'd want to find Jena, but the strobes and smoke made active search impossible. Instead, he would find himself, get in touch with his limbs, connect his hips to the song and his feet to the floor, waiting for her to appear. He enjoyed dancing on his own, unheeded, solving math problems with the beat and his hips. The crowd tonight felt more interconnected than intraconnected, a singular outward focus, most of them facing the stage like some bohemian line dance. No one knew he was there, and so he smiled, and the fog sprayed like rain.

Someone spotted Horace, and they weaved through the crowd to him, smiling brightly as they hugged him. Horace had never seen this smile before, the way it changed the shape of their face.

"Horace!" Mint cried into his ear.

"Mint! Wha—," but the rest of his words were snatched by the noise-laden air. They grabbed his wrist—a physical command—and dragged him out of the crowd to find a spot where conversation was tenable.

"What are you doing here?" Mint demanded, having traded in that smile for their default intensity, not harsh but unshakingly direct.

"My friend is getting initiated," to which Mint raised their eyebrows, "and I want to fucking black out!" Horace said with attempted wryness, fumbled by his state and the required volume. Then, sensing his failure and noticing their lack of drink, "Actually, do you want some?"

"No. Look, I know you had a bad week—"

"—The worst week of my life! My best friend ditched me, I had to go on stage and embarrass myself, and my boss-neighbor had a fucking stroke!—"

"—I know, I know, woah. But you shouldn't be here. Tell your friend to get out, too. Actually," they eyed him up and down, "shit, just worry about yourself tonight."

"That's what you told me to do and that's why I'm here! Why are you telling me to go!?"

Mint looked around, then grabbed Horace by the shoulders to stop him from swaying. Their eyes locked, Mint's clouds pouring into Horace's puddles, inches away from each other. Horace felt a brief grace of sobriety break through.

"I told you to forget about this place. They're doing something here. I'm trying to find out what. I don't want you caught up."

"Vein?"

"Yes. He acquired a biotech company last spring. You can guess which one. Then this place pops up. I think they're linked."

"I know about that! Wait, do you think it's real!? Chemica—,"

Mint kissed him into silence before he could spit the rest out. There was pressure and movement, but more of a planting than meeting of the lips, Horace's stunned into stillness. It lasted just long enough for him to get hard, reinvigorating his drunken shame and confusion. He was attracted to them, yet unsure if he was supposed to be. Mint emerged coldly, but with the hint of a smirk.

"There's your stage kiss, actor boy, now zip it. We're probably being watched."

✳✳✳

Just what Mint needed, a third wheel on their date with destiny. Even if it was just a first date, both sides still keeping it coy, it was a serious impediment. But part of Mint's problem with babysitting was they couldn't say no. They knew choosing to protect Horace had a far more certain outcome than trying to get something on Vein, and to ignore those probabilities would be irresponsible. Kissing him—even having just seen him puke—made sense because it served both purposes, a rational calculation to minimize their exposure, and thankfully it hadn't been too bad. But now what to do with him?

Reeling from the kiss, Horace slumped against the wall, then started slouching toward the ground. Mint figured his head must be spinning, the room probably too, and they couldn't just leave him here. They pulled him up and tried shepherding him to the exit to hail him a ride home. He'd been carrying himself okay on the dance floor, but now that he had someone to support him, he grew increasingly shambolic, placing his balance entirely on Mint's shoulders. They reached the top of the stairs before they ran into a problem.

"What are you doing with him?" asked an attendant, hovering at the door like a hostess.

"I'm just getting him home! Had too much to drink," Mint replied with an easy smile, faking drunk enthusiasm.

"How do you know him?"

"What? Oh yeah, like, he's my partner," they replied, the lie coming instinctually, wanting to justify their inseparability, despite potentially complicating the reentry they had planned for themself.

"He's a cutie, hope you've been sharing!"

A decidedly uncute Horace, pale and sweaty and struggling to keep his nausea below his throat, picked his head up enough to look at both of them and register how weird a comment that was. Mint kept rolling as if unfazed.

"Period! I don't care who he kisses, as long as I'm the one to take care of him at the end of the night."

"We can do that, too. We have a house medic in our recovery room, can I take him there for you?"

She moved to his side as she said this, taking his other arm. For a second, Mint resisted, not liking this woman's intentions nor the implication they couldn't care for their fake boyfriend themself. But with this offer, the probabilities were shifting. Where could this recovery room be but down in the basement? What else might they see while accompanying him? And why was Eden so prepared for clubbing casualties that they staffed a medic?

"You're too kind, that would be great. Can I take him there with you? He's a little disoriented, I just want to make sure he's okay."

"Don't you want to keep dancing?"

"No honey, I insist. After you."

The hostess seemed taken aback, a bit disarmed by Mint's suddenly domineering attitude, but relented and led them back down through the dance floor. Mint felt their heart lift through their chest as they approached the door at the back. Sure, babysitting was a pain, but as previously only seen in adult entertainment, this part-babysitter, part-lover cover story was turning into a highly convenient excuse. Before entering the combination, the attendant turned around to address them. Mint casually drifted toward the wall, hoping to eye the keypad as she typed.

"Just so you know, the recovery room will be the first door on the left, but the rest of this space is for members only. Please respect our rules."

She turned, flipped up a panel, and unlocked the door with a fingerprint, dashing Mint's hopes of obtaining a mental key. The door opened to a stairwell lined with red LED strips, crisscrossing the walls with X's and marking the steps as well, and they began their dusky descent. As they were reaching the bottom of the flight, the door opened, and a giggling gaggle poured through and up the steps. There were enough of them egressing that Mint could only wait for them to pass. One of the women near the back of the clump stopped abruptly upon seeing Horace.

"Oh my God, Horaaccce, are you okay?" Then turning to Mint, "Is he alright?"

Mint regarded this enthusiastic blonde—her expressive eyes so open to inspection, her accent just slight enough to intrigue, her posture melting into concern without sacrificing her irrepressible happiness of being—and tried to figure why she looked familiar. Then they remembered: she'd sat with Horace's family for closing night. So, this was his friend getting initiated.

"We're getting him to the medic. Think he just didn't eat dinner."

"Ah, so sad, I will go with you," which Mint was unsure about till she added, "Maddie, is it good if I keep an eye on them? Then you can go back."

The attendant hesitated as if reviewing her training, and Mint held their breath, but she assented and transferred her side of Horace to the blonde woman, who introduced herself to Mint as Jena, Horace's coworker. Mint returned their name, while marveling that yet another Vein employee had surfaced in this small circle. Jena was doing them a favor, far more than she realized, but still couldn't be trusted. Together, they brought Horace out of the stairwell and into a tantalizing hallway, better lit with an administrative feel, doors scattered down the left-hand side.

They turned into the first door, which held a cozy room lined with a few rows of beds and chairs, awash with warm lighting, smelling of lavender and cleaning products. Sitting next to each other were two spaced-out partiers wearing headphones and sunglasses, while the man wearing a white medical coat stood by a computer in the corner. Jena explained the situation to him, another person she'd become familiar with, and he accepted custody of Horace, setting him down and handing him a Pedialyte and a bucket. Mint and Jena sat on the other side of the room to debrief further. Mint had so many questions they couldn't ask, given their present company. Instead, Jena got the first word in.

"Thank you so much for taking care of him. Are you his friend? Or maybe, more than a friend?"

"We worked together on the show," Mint said, but then worrying that Jena would cross-check this with Maddie, added, "and can we just say it's complicated and leave it at that?"

"Eeek, my lil Horace has a, um, special friend?"

"You could say that." They had to switch the topic fast before the lies stacked too tall. "So, are you a member now? Did the initiation happen yet?"

"I mean basically, but the official ceremony is upstairs at midnight, so I will have to run up soon! It is so wonderful here, do you want to join too?"

"I'm thinking about it. But what's it entail? Is there like paperwork and stuff, are there dues?"

"Paperwork?"

"You know like, I'm just wondering how official it is?"

"Very official. I am really not supposed to tell you anything, no offense. The mystery is part of the fun!" Mint thought they had touched a nerve and made Jena uncomfortable, but then she added, "Look I really should get up there, and you should come too! If you need to come back for Horace after, the door code is star-three-one-four-star." So Mint hadn't lost her entirely.

Mint thanked her, saying they would come up in a sec after checking in on Horace once more. Jena hugged them with surprising force, like saying goodbye to an old friend, then bounded away. Now with a moment to think, Mint processed how dilated her pupils had been, how that might explain the hug, and other things. Once they'd seen to Horace, who was hugging his lightly filled bucket, and checked in with the medic, who assured them he'd be fine in no time, they slipped back out into the empty hall.

They had a decision to make. Upstairs, some ceremony was about to begin that could be revelatory, but anything put on for the masses would be calculated and controlled. Meanwhile with everyone else upstairs, they had a unique opportunity to explore the basement. The decision took only a second, and they turned left down the hall.

The first door was locked. The second door opened to a bar supply room, which could be invaded by a barback at any moment. They felt uncertain and cursed themself for it, feeling the walls of time closing in on them. They resolved to come back to this door if the rest were locked, but as they closed it, another opened, the door to the stairwell. An unforgettable man stepped through, trapping Mint in the hall. He wore the dark jumpsuit of a maintenance worker or prisoner, which exaggerated his already strange proportions. He noticed Mint immediately and furrowed his brow while letting out a strange sigh, like an asthmatic groan. He stood there as if in contemplation, and Mint began to feel a curdled pathos for him, like a smell that makes you cry. How someone could end up like this, what had happened to him?

"You are not supposed to be here. It is time to go."

"Sorry, my friend was just—"

"—No, you must leave, now."

Mint was terrified, red-handed, and strangely mesmerized by the man. He threatened without anger in his voice, power emanating from his body, which took up the hall. He moved rapidly to them, closing the distance with a couple strides, and gripped their shoulder, causing Mint to flinch.

"If you leave now, I will not tell anyone I saw you here. There is an exit under the stairs. I will make sure your friend is okay. And gets home."

Mint had no choice but to comply. His arm still attached to their shoulder, he guided them forward and pushed them through the hall to the stairwell. Sure enough, under the stairs was the building's other exit, which Mint had missed. He shoved them through and slammed the door behind them.

Mint found themself alone outside at the bottom of a concrete stairwell. They wanted to think they could go right back up and through the front as if nothing had happened, but what if Maddie was still there? What if the man found them again? And even if neither of those was the case, Mint had to admit, they were terrified. They couldn't make themself go back. Their feet would take them only to their car, and so they went, hoping Horace would be okay.

3.5 ~ The Funeral

"Paul is dead."

Horace had been repeating this to himself so much in the week since he'd passed—just one week after he was admitted—that it had moved beyond reference to become a single word, paulisdead, loosed from its meaning and in search of a new one. He had suffered a minor second and fatal third stroke within 48 hours. Paulisdead. He'd received hospital care an hour into his first symptoms, Flora had read to him for an hour each day, and his doctor had expressed optimism an hour prior to the second stroke. Paulisdead, paulisdead, paulisdead. He'd been one, now he was zero; there was nothing left to save; his brain had no breath. Paulisdead.

Horace was there when it happened, giving Flora sour candy and company as she tended her near-constant vigil. Louis was on the way in to relieve them and convince her to get some rest. They were sitting in his room, attempting silly faces for reasons to smile, listening to his pitiful heartbeat on the monitor. Alarms disrupted their peace, nurses rushed in, orders were given, interventions were attempted, the line on the monitor squiggled up and down, up and down . . .

His body remained as connected parts: a bloody brain, an intubated mouth and nose, discolored flesh, sagging skin. He looked no different than the days before. Horace dared himself to look closely and see what had changed, why death was so special. All he knew was the lights had gone out in the house, never to turn on again. He couldn't divine any further.

That had been a week ago. Now, Horace dawdled in front of his mirror and fiddled with his tie. The suit he wore was a high school graduation present, and somehow this was his first chance to use it. Five years in closets, then a funeral. It fit the same.

Horace joined his family downstairs. His mother and the twins wore dark dresses, his father and older sister dark suits. Dido had flown home from Los Angeles for the first time since Dr.

Hawthorne's retirement party, which had happened to coincide with a conference she was attending. She'd missed her sisters' high school graduation for work. Even now, she was staying in a hotel but had joined them for breakfast. None of that mattered today, which existed outside time and narrative.

He'd never seen his family so uniform and severe. His mother hugged him and adjusted his collar. His father shook and clasped his hand just to do something. Sandy dangled her car keys with an impatient look on her face.

"We're late. Who's going with me?"

Cilla was already headed to the door, and Dido volunteered with nonchalance. Horace would rather go with their parents, where it would be easier to keep to himself. Since opening night of the play, he'd retreated into a dream state, voyeuristic and nonsensical but safely impersonal, that not even Paul's death could pinch. If anything, now he was sleepwalking one layer deeper. He couldn't imagine a pleasant way to pass a single second, so he let them trickle by, inert and indifferent.

Thoughts could still trouble his attention when he let them, and on the drive to the church his mind wandered as if channel hopping daytime television. What's on now, what's next, what was he missing? Present, future, and past were stuck in a rhyme scheme that was running out of words. He was ready for this verse of his life to close.

He looked out the window and dreamed of a road trip, but he couldn't picture a destination, and wherever he picked would make a big circle that finished where it started. The last time he'd planned an escape, it took him to heartbreak by the name of Dylan Falco. Maybe escape was the wrong way to think of things. If the trip to St. Pete's had been longer, he might have gotten somewhere, but they were parking after ten minutes.

Horace walked into the church with his parents, and Maria went to find her daughters and their seats. Sandy had been right to rush them, as the other pallbearers were waiting for Horace and Al. While Bill stood by in keeping with his recent daze, Louis greeted them, looking clean and tired in a well-cut suit. He resembled Paul more than Flora did, the Paul who been just handsome enough to win Edith's eye while knowing his place, with the slumpy, hunched posture of a keyboard warrior. He was showing signs of Paul's weight too, though the suit hid it well.

Jacques, Paul's brother (whom Horace had seldom met), served as the fifth man and was speaking to the funeral director. Horace knew the sixth should have been Liam, and his absence disgusted Horace. It had been two weeks without contact, and he was officially a missing person, thanks to Horace revealing the truth about Ian Noone. Liam would already have a lot to explain when he returned to their lives, but missing Paul's funeral verged on indefensible. What if the next time Horace saw Liam was in a casket? That image would surface in Horace's mind within waves of despair.

Then the sixth pallbearer appeared, wiping his hands on his pantlegs as he returned from the bathroom, moving with his characteristic jaunt, and casting his head about like a curious retriever till he spotted Horace, who received his arrival like a startled cat.

Dylan Falco was back early, and Horace's first thought was, "Paulisdead," which meant whatever's beneath rock bottom.

***

The last time Horace saw Dylan was the third day of his weeklong trip to Guatemala that spring. For that idiot, Horace left the country on his own for the first time, spending nearly a day in the air and airports of Panama City and Guatemala City, plagued by a swollen tongue of rusty Spanish and a stubborn bundle of nerves that spread through his body like cancer.

Horace got through the journey there by suspending himself in a memory, from almost two years prior, of the night before Dylan's departure when he held Horace in his arms and told Horace, "I love you." He'd been the first of them to say it, the first time anyone had said that to Horace and meant it like that, and he'd said it so easily. Horace had spent weeks thinking he loved Dylan, then thinking again. When he said it, Horace could only reply "you too," the missing word carrying magic too advanced for Horace to wield. "I wish we could keep dating," was Dylan's reply and the source of Horace's downfall, its meaning misinterpreted and destined for painful revision.

After that conversation, Dylan went upstairs to finish packing, while Horace slipped out the back door. Horace heard Dylan's words as almost a promise, a beginning. Only in the reflections of cervezas and hostel mirrors, killing days in Guatemala City after having seen enough of Dylan, did Horace realize it to have been an ending, wrapping a bow on the thing they had. For one perfect spring, they'd been lovers, and at the last possible moment, Dylan added the tag to confirm and archive it.

One reason Horace had been loath to discuss the trip upon his return was that its conclusions were obvious and unsatisfactory. Dylan Falco, the rogue with no trouble loving himself, the ex-lead singer of two garage bands, the fickle and voracious bisexual, had used him for a fun lay in his downtime before deployment. Not quite grooming but on that spectrum, not quite lying but leaving things unsaid, not evil but in the wrong. When Horace imagined telling his friends what had happened, the only response his mind could produce was the same question Dylan angrily asked him, "What did you expect?" He'd rather talk about anything else.

There were also nuances he felt silly holding on to. Yes, Dylan had withheld key details about Raquel from Horace, but would he have come had he known the truth about her? And yes, Dylan had withheld the full nature of their relationship from Raquel, but wasn't he better off having been received as an old friend than an ex-lover? Dylan wanted to see Horace and for everyone to get along. A sweet but selfish sentiment, Dylan Falco in a nutshell.

The whole visit fell apart in less than 24 hours, and the wheels were wobbling loose from the jump. As Horace disembarked the airport cab, which had provided his first nauseous taste of third-world urban driving, he saw Dylan standing outside their hostel, chatting with a pretty girl and making her laugh. Already concerning, his heart sank when they walked up and welcomed him together, depriving Horace of the initial moment with his first-ever ex-boyfriend he'd envisioned. Dylan's embrace was strong, but more earnest than tender. Then he broke it to introduce her.

"Horace, this is Raquel. Raquel, Horace."

That was it, Horace thought with a rock in his gut as he gave her a perfunctory hug—this small and smiley and frankly simple girl with sun-soaked skin and two French braids, so ready for action and ready even more for chatter, who was already peppering him with questions, delighted that she was meeting one of Dylan's oldest friends, oblivious that she could be intruding—it was already clear in the way he introduced her. Not as a fellow volunteer or even his best friend in the country, but as nothing worth saying beyond a name. It was exactly how Dylan would introduce Horace when he brought him along to gigs. They were an item.

Horace skipped tepid denial and went straight to molten paranoia, pre-heated through hours of exhaustive travel, weeks of pre-trip fretting, and years of self-doubt. They were an item, and he was a fool. He dropped his stuff off in a dingy, private room and returned to the lounge area to find them laughing, about him he assumed. Dylan asked if Horace was hungry, and Raquel jumped in to say she knew just the spot to take them.

"Back in training, we made it our mission to find the best croquettes in the city. I rank this place third, but Dylie said it was his favorite," Raquel informed Horace excitedly. Calling him "Dylie" nailed the coffin shut, all before Horace and Dylan had shared a private word.

After their meal, which Horace begrudgingly devoured, Raquel announced she had to pee and finally left Dylan's side. They were lounging at a picnic table outside the restaurant, and the air was scorching, stifling, adding to Horace's wrongs. March meant nothing in the tropics. Horace did his best to look agitated, begging Dylan to comment on the obvious, but instead he just asked what Horace wanted to do first. Raquel was back in time to announce that their next stop just *had* to be el Palacio Nacional. As they got up, she gave Dylan a quick kiss, and hand-in-hand they led Horace through the city.

At first, Horace chose not to press the issue because he'd already accepted it and moved onto disaster planning. But as the only thing he could think about was the one thing he refused to talk about, he grew increasingly taciturn. For a while, he got away with saying the barest minimum, but Dylan picked up quickly and even Raquel eventually, as they moved through the city's lively streets, ate delicious fruits, encountered national landmarks, and suffered the oppressive weather, that Horace was on some kind of conversational boycott. They tried engaging him, they tried ignoring him, but as the day wore on, Horace noticed with perverse pleasure, he was successfully bringing them down with him. Joy was beyond him, but schadenfreude was not.

No one addressed it directly till after dinner, when they returned to the hostel to shower and change before going out. As Horace watched them go off to their room together, he realized his fate was sealed from the moment Dylan suggested he book his own room. He'd missed so many details while planning their dream reunion and was unable to adapt to reality. He sat on his bed and stripped off his clothes, but he couldn't summon the effort to go shower. A knock came on his door. Horace didn't answer, so more knocks followed.

"Horace? It's Dylan. Can we talk? Are you able to?"

Horace sighed with an intent to be heard. He thought about answering the door in just his underwear but felt enough shame already.

"Yeah," he called out, while slipping back on his sweaty clothes. He opened the door then sat back down on his bed without looking at Dylan, who stepped inside but remained standing.

"Dude, talk to me, what's going on?"

Horace just shrugged, trying to look as pathetic as possible.

"Okay. Fine. I'll go first . . . We clearly got our wires crossed. I get that you're mad, I get that you're jealous, but like, what did you expect? We literally split up, and I have my own life to live. I was really looking forward to seeing my old friend, and I'm really bummed that I haven't. I don't know who you are right now."

Horace shook his head to suggest he didn't know either. His eyes were getting wet.

"I was so excited for this week," Dylan continued. "I mean, I haven't seen you in years, and I haven't seen Raquel in months. Not like we can just hop over to each other's villages ya know, and our vacation days our treasured. It's lonely out here, man. I thought we could just all have a great time together, but clearly not. Raquel's been so nice about it too, but it's such a bad look."

"Does she know about us?" Horace cut in, surprising himself with the force of his words.

"What? I mean, uh, look dude. So, not really. It's complicated. Like, she knows we were tight, but I didn't want her getting jealous or whatever."

"Tight? That's what we were?"

"Okay, grow up. I thought we could all just be adults about this. I told you a friend was joining us, you know. Raquel and I aren't even dating, we're just like, a thing sometimes. I'm sorry I didn't better communicate that, I guess."

"That's what you're sorry for?"

"Dude, I don't know, stop parroting me and tell me what you want! What can I do to make this better?"

Horace took his time replying, but he knew the one thing he wanted to say. It was just terrible and impossible, and he was saying it anyway.

"As long as she's here . . . I'm not going to . . . I can't do this with her here."

"Really?" Dylan scoffed, "That's what you're going with? Fucking Christ, dude. She's been so nice to you, what's your problem?"

"She sucks. She's sooo nice, and she sucks."

"No. That's not it. She's got nothing to do with it, maybe other than that she's a woman. Or would you be more jealous if I was seeing another guy? Wouldn't really fly here, ya know. But no, it's not her, and it's not even me. You need to get over yourself. Everything has to go according to your perfect plan or you're miserable. But what good would that have done you? If we'd spent this whole week fucking each other silly, would that make you any happier? I don't think so. You'd just go back home and be lonelier than ever. I wanted to show you there's more to life. I wanted to be your friend again. My bad, I guess."

Dylan's words, written across the day and released in a torrent, turned Horace's tears to ice and his blood cold, while a sick clarity of purpose possessed him.

"Get out of my room. I'm done with this. I'll just do my own thing."

"What are you talking about?"

"You're right. I'm miserable, and the least I can do is not drag you two down. Enjoy your lovers' vacation. I sincerely regret coming to visit you. I wasn't ready. Goodbye."

Horace got up, opened the door, and pointed for Dylan to go while staring at his shoes. There was no way he could bear eye contact without crying. For a moment nothing happened, then Dylan slowly walked out. The moment he passed the threshold, Horace slammed the door shut. That was the last they saw of each other.

Horace cried away the rest of the night and switched hostels early the next day. Dylan kept calling and texting him, wanting to try things over with him, but Horace's silence was complete. Horace considered blocking Dylan's number, but some combination of pettiness and safety concerns made him turn on read receipts instead. Dylan would know he was still alive, still seeing his messages, and still unwilling to speak. Horace didn't have enough money to rebook his flight, but he did have plenty to get drunk, so he did that for a couple listless days while rounding every corner with paranoia. He never ran into them and boarded his flight with the worst hangover of his life. Emerging from that intense pain, the kind of pain that remakes a person, Horace spent the flight erasing the image of Dylan he'd once lovingly constructed. Before that long day's end, he learned that Liam's dad had been replaced by a doppelganger.

✳✳✳

"You shaved your head," were for some reason the words that came out of Horace's mouth. Dylan's hair had been long enough for a manbun when they'd last parted. Now it was even shorter than when they'd dated. "It looks good."

"Thanks. Uh, your hair looks good, too," Dylan replied.

Horace's short, dark curls looked the same as ever. It was his one and only look since high school. He nodded and gave his hair a bashful muss.

With that, they took their places on opposite sides of Paul's coffin. Horace was reeling, but pleased that he'd spoken first, reversing the curse of the words unsaid and left behind in Guatemala. Or at least starting to reverse it. That's all he could hope to do; the day wasn't about them and their troubles. They were shouldering a shared weight, a large, dead neighbor in a heavy, ornate coffin. Dylan must have rebooked his flight when he heard the news, which Horace found surprisingly sentimental. They processed into the church, then took their places with their families.

Since moving home, Horace had attended mass at St. Pete's every Christmas and Easter, and not one time more. Full to the gills and dedicated to sacred joy, they were never the worst two hours of his year, a pleasant chance to sing poorly and zone out in anonymity. The mass today was served to four half-full rows of grief. He could look at each person gathered there and recognize how the day was wearing on them. Flora looked beautiful and broken and brave, a princess on her tragic coronation, arms linked with her brother. Both were lonesome next to their mother and her second husband, two people for whom and from whom Horace felt nothing. Bill and Greta sat apart from the rest, giving space to their multitudes of sorrow. Horace's mother was holding her twins' hands, and they were all holding their heads high. Jena sat out of place in the back row, one of the only workplace connections in attendance, looking around with a troubled mix of sorrow and curiosity. Dylan sat between his parents, his grave expression radiating a noble strength, while his mother had let her hair turn gray and his father's face looked thin and worn.

Only the priest, Father David, seemed unaffected, as weary as ever in guiding these lost souls toward a very specific understanding of what had befallen them. He'd known Paul, but even had he never met him, he'd still have assured them that his soul was with God, that his spirit was with us all, that Christ's love was in Paul's love was in our love for him and him for us, and that was all there was to know. Amen. Please rise. Horace had stopped taking the Eucharist years ago, but in that small, sad congregation he felt compelled to communion.

At the end of the service, the priest announced Bill Hawthorne would be giving a eulogy. Horace looked to his father with puzzlement, and Al quietly informed him that Jacques was "deathly afraid of public speaking, no pun intended."

"I had to write this speech without Paul," Bill began weakly, like he didn't trust his voice, "but I found I could turn to him still. We collaborated enough over the years we knew each other that, even though his soul has left his body, it lives on in mine and ours. A eulogy isn't about what we would want him to know, but what he would want us to think about and remember him by. He's been hard at work, as Paul as ever, inside all of us, presenting us with memories, asking for our reactions. Here's what he's been showing me.

"He showed me his generosity, helping me write about him even beyond the pale of me ever paying him back. And he showed me his love for all of you, something he struggled to convey at times in life. That's what brought the two of us together. He had the words he couldn't say, and I had a voice with nothing to fill it. So, one more time: he loved you all, Louis and Flora especially. He lives on in you more than the rest of us combined.

"He showed me his values, I must say American values, which I think even his fellow Canadians here can admit. Hard work and sacrifice, success and self-denial, expansiveness and unrestraint. They didn't make life easier for him, but he never cast them aside. He knew what those values were for, and what was worth treasuring.

"He showed me the world through his eyes, a world of sharp, righteous clarity. He looked at me and saw a man in need of a friend, but too proud to admit it. He recognized those parts of himself in me. He looked at all of you, everyone who came across his path, as a person of great potential, only partially realized. He looked at his son, and saw a better version of himself, but with the same struggles, some things he'd tried so hard not to pass on. He looked at his daughter, and he saw both a woman of unbelievable resilience and maturity, yet also a small child who once liked to curl up on his lap, and whom he had promised as she slept that he would never let anything bad happen to her.

"He showed me his regrets. Especially as we age, there is nothing more precious than one's time and health, and he failed to secure them both to his liking. He didn't want to retreat to within us all quite yet, but he knows, and we know, that he made the most of every moment he had.

"And, perhaps this is self-serving, but the last thing he showed me was forgiveness, which I sorely needed. I well know that I have been a source of stress within our community, just as I know well the adverse relationship between stress and health. He showed me that only the tightest bonds can be pushed so painfully far before breaking, and asked that I make things right, now that he won't be around to do so. Even in death, he's giving orders and restoring order. But I will, Paul, I promise.

"I share this to encourage you all to listen to what he's asking of you too. He's counting on us to finish the work he left behind.

It'll take all of us together to match him and make up for his absence. Thank you, Paul. I pray for your soul."

Bill's words concluded the service, and he moved solemnly to Paul's side. Horace rose with the other pallbearers and retook his place by the casket. They grasped their extraordinary, common burden and carried it out into the daylight. They returned to their cars after loading Paul's coffin into the hearse and followed it to the grave. Horace attempted to gather his thoughts about Paul, Dylan, Bill, Liam, Flora, Edith, his parents, God, Heaven, the soul, and himself, all without success. Desensitized to his sadness, the only thing he felt was a little bit hungry and in need of a smoke.

The cemetery was a forty-five-minute drive, as their suburb had little room for death. It reminded Horace of a country club golf course, with its expansive greens and winding paths. The hole was waiting for Paul, and a canopy with chairs waited for his mourners, protecting them from the July sun. Father David led them in a prayer, then Flora and Louis rose to say their goodbyes.

Flora delivered a poem she'd been reading to Paul every day in the hospital. Spoken flatly without emphasis, her words needed no amplification, traveling like tiny particles that pierced the hearts of those in attendance. Louis thanked everyone for being there, told his dad he missed him and loved him, and said they had brought one last smile to his father's face.

The funeral director gave Flora and Louis roses to lay on the coffin, and the rest of the congregation lined up to do the same. After Horace passed on his final deliverable to his boss and his final token of appreciation to his neighbor, he rounded the corner of the canopy and saw Dylan was waiting a short distance away, looking at him with something like apology on his face, softer and wryer than a look of sorrow. Horace approached him.

"Hey," they both said, followed with smiles and head nods for the other to go on. Horace took the initiative.

"I'm sorry for how I acted the last time I saw you. And thanks for coming back for this, it's nice to see you. You've missed a lot."

"Thanks. I've got just as much to apologize for, but I know this isn't the place to do it justice. And I would have done anything to come back for this, but I only had to move my flight up a week, so it was nothing. Living in that village for two years made me really miss mine. You never get another chance to say goodbye."

"I'm not sure that's true, but I get what you mean. I see it more as showing last respects more than saying goodbye. I had my issues with Paul, but I want to respect him."

"Hm. Showing respect, yeah. Which makes me have to ask—"

"—About Liam? We don't know where he is, or if he . . . we haven't seen him since Paul's first stroke. Left a note saying he was staying with Ian Noone, if you can believe it, so he could be anywhere. He was really going through it before that."

"Jesus, that's a throwback. He's unbelievable. How am I here and he isn't? I hope he's okay."

"Yeah. Me too, I guess."

Something about the formality of the occasion made this conversation possible, and Horace found himself relaxing, letting go of his aversion to Dylan. They were old friends mourning an elder's death, and from that zoomed-out view nothing else was wrong. The conversation stuttered, and Horace was ready to drift back into the fold, maybe give Flora another hug or check in with Jena, whom he'd been ignoring for some reason he couldn't bother to figure out, but then Dylan picked it back up.

"Do you agree with what Bill was saying, about Paul living on in you?"

"Definitely . . . Do you?"

"I don't know, just never thought about it like that before. Maybe we just weren't close enough, but like, even though I remember my time with him in the past, it doesn't feel like he carries through with me today."

Because you're already full of yourself, Horace thought reactively, and I'm empty, nothing but the reflection of other people's personalities. Others live on in me, Dylan Falco lives on in me, but there's nothing of me that lives on in anyone.

But he held his tongue till the thought passed and said instead what he thought Dylan wanted to hear.

"I'd keep thinking about it. Paul will come to you, tell you to work through the night or scold you for time fraud. You just gotta listen. C'mon, let's go back and join our village."

Act I

Act II

Act III

[Act IV]

Act V

4.1 ~ Posting

In the standard belly-to-Earth position, it takes about twelve seconds of freefalling to achieve terminal velocity. Once reached, that speed will not change until the skydiver pulls their parachute or otherwise hits the ground.

Horace had never been skydiving, but he was falling through a YouTube rabbit hole. First-timers, pros, and extremists alike reported the sensations of terminal freefall as simultaneous ecstasy and peace.

He envied these vloggers for the same reasons he avoided them: their lives were lived, their experiences were worthy of attention, and their viewers—such as himself—were jealous. But as he turned from browsing to binging, he found the skydivers relatable in a new way. Though it took him far longer than twelve seconds, he too was in freefall—the drag of his life caught up to the combined weight of his sadness and guilt. With those forces aligned he felt that same peace, though miserable, not ecstatic. The feelings weren't that different, just two sides of a coin.

A skydiver's freefall may only last a minute, he learned. Though he could not see the ground, he felt the approach of decision time. The two choices were to decelerate slowly or all at once. One choice, really—when to pull up. 1:36 p.m. seemed as good a time as any. He tossed his phone across the bed, flung off his sheets, and swung his legs to the floor.

It was Thursday, or maybe Friday. July lingered interminably but was on its last breath. The day after Paul's funeral, Horace's internship was terminated via email. Jena would be retained and reassigned, and their project was shelved. He didn't know about the others. Their website had never gone live. The new plan, so his dismissal email said, was for a conglomerated journalism app. Consumers prefer mobile interfaces. Websites are nearly archaic as print itself. Life closed a door and opened a window, out of which Horace fell.

It's not like Horace cared about his job, but he needed something to care about now that the play was over. He certainly didn't care about Liam anymore. His missing-person post was making the rounds on social media, and all were encouraged to share it, but Horace had not. He supported Liam's disappearance and didn't want him to be found. Plus, his network reached no one who didn't know.

Horace walked downstairs through an empty house. His parents had work. The twins were at the beach. He drove to McDonald's. He'd considered walking but was too weak and hungry for the heat. His appetite, when it surfaced, insisted on artificial pleasures. Breakfast had been over for hours, so he ate nuggets and felt disgusting.

He drove home, which greeted him with barely changed clocks and nothing to do. His gravity bong beckoned to him, a commitment to a ruined day. Instead, he paired health and abuse by taking his cigarettes for a walk. Greasy, sweaty, bloated, hungover, and dehydrated, he made it to 7-Eleven and bought a Gatorade, the bluest they had. He also pocketed an orange for the rush of theft as much as the nutrients. He peeled it in one piece that resembled an elephant, two big ears connected by a trunk, and smiled, thinking of grade-school lunch tables. A friend had once said it looked like a bra, and Horace had stopped peeling oranges that way for years.

He sat on a shaded park bench, considered a second cigarette, heard his stomach grumble a resounding no, and pulled out his phone to check Twitter. His timeline was full of quote tweets of an art foundation posting strangely. It was a verified Vein account. Chronologically, the first tweet was:

@artsinvein: petunia vein fucks young artistes and tevin watches
     The rest came as quote tweets to replies:
@artsinvein: tevin vein eats babies
@artsinvein: omg megarich artsy foundation is a tax dodge??
@artsinvein: its not even for eternal youth he just likes the taste

@artsinvein: y else do u think all r artists sign ndas
@artsinvein: petunia will ruin ur career if you squeal!!
@artsinvein: I HAVE NAMES
@artsinvein: tevin started a cult to harvest the blood of the young
@artsinvein: HE IS A SICKO!!
@artsinvein: he's turning them all into powerpuff girls #iykyk
@artsinvein: hahahahaha bc im hiiiiiigghhhgggg as a kite lol
@artsinvein: teehee all the p***words are changed ;)
@artsinvein: bc vein killed my dad and kidnapped my ex-bf
@artsinvein: omg this is alleged/parody btw ur honor im insane
@artsinvein: EDEN 2MORROW HELL ON SUNDAY

Horace already followed this account because Flora advertised her artist features on it, but it was reaching wide cross-sections of posting society, uniting tankies and reactionaries, independent journalists and shit-posters, avatars of anime waifus and roman statues. Responses, many of which @artsinvein retweeted without comment, ranged from anti-corporate glee to personal concern for the poster, though plenty assumed the account had been hacked. Horace wished that were so but knew better. He'd told her Eden was giving cult vibes. Were the sources for the other claims, the predation, just as flimsy? Did she really think Liam had been kidnapped?

He immediately called Flora, mentally catching up to the situation while the phone rang. Sucked back into his body, the urgent beads of sweat and his clumsily beating heart assured him this was real. He had a problem on his hands, and she wasn't picking up. Was she really getting high again? Was it his fault? Sure, her father died, but he shouldn't have given her that joint. He thought he was being helpful. He would have to make up for it.

He jogged toward home but ran out of breath and slowed to a walk, missing when he could run for days. Then, for the second time that month, he threw up. It came out of nowhere and landed on the curb, blue and nuggety. The first time had been that blur of a night at Eden. Mint kissing him and tasting it, so they abandoned him to the sick room. At least Jena made sure he got home. Or he assumed it was Jena—he couldn't remember the rest of the night, and he'd been too ashamed to ask for a recap the next morning.

He looked up and down the street. No one had seen him, so he carried on. His plan was to drive to Flora's, ring the buzzer till someone let him in. Maybe her roommate would have seen the tweets and left work to check on her. The plan changed when he saw her Prius parked a couple blocks from the cul-de-sac. He must have passed it from the front without thought. Choosing not to park it on their block, she was up to no good and knew it. That scared Horace.

He'd never known the Flora who used. Her fall and recovery had been so quick, so remote to his life, so unlike his understanding of her, that addict-Flora carried with it no mental picture. Post-rehab Flora was a person, someone different from pre-rehab Flora, and a hidden character spanned the distance like an underscore. That gap might soon be filled, or a fourth Flora would emerge.

The Neufchatel maison sat one house past casa dos Santos. Horace selfishly wanted to stop home and freshen up, brush his teeth at the least, but personal hygiene felt indulgent during an emergency. One last swig, swish, and spit of Gatorade would have to do. He was a garbage man cleaning up a mess. He'd get dirtier before he could get clean.

The Neufchatels' front door was locked. He knocked a couple times but barely waited for a reply. Walking to the gate to try the backdoor, his eyes caught on Brunhilde's house. He couldn't remember the last time he'd seen her, weeks at least. She'd been slowing down for years. The block was such a tight community, to which she was only an afterthought, a joke, or a source of complaints. After a childhood in Nazi Germany, one of the few facts he knew about her, she'd earned her distrust of community, and after the last few weeks, perhaps she'd been proven right. A curtain inside an upstairs window rustled, and Horace glanced away out of fear and respect.

He slipped through the Neufchatel's gate and tried, shook, and cursed the locked doors. Even the ground-floor windows wouldn't budge, and the curtains were drawn. She'd sealed off the house. Maybe she wasn't even home? You can tweet from anywhere, take pills anywhere. He moved to the back of the yard to get an angle on the upstairs windows. No information was gained, and he felt ridiculous. His friend was in trouble, he was on the scene, and he was useless. To whom could he turn? Calling Flora again felt like a waste of time, but he did it anyway.

He checked in nearby pots and under a gnome for a spare key while it rang. The search gave him nothing but the dust of sunbaked clay on his hands. Surely one of the other houses was trusted with a spare, but the Hawthornes were the last people he wanted to call. As he pulled up his mom's contact, he remembered one other person to try first. Louis Neufchatel picked up on the first ring.

"Do you know where she is?" he demanded instantly, accusatorily.

"Yeah, er, I saw her car."

"Where?"

"Near the cul-de-sac. I think she's home, but the doors are all locked."

"Fuck, of course. I'm on my way."

"Do you guys hide a key somewhere?"

"Yeah, but just wait for me."

"Louis, please."

"I'm just leaving her apartment. I'll be there in no time."

"What if she doesn't have thirty minutes?"

He groaned in anguish.

"It used to be in a frog by the back fence. Back-right-ish? It blends in. Call me if she . . . just call me when you know."

Horace traipsed through a dozen meters of brush and ivy to reach the back fence. The forest that bordered their homes was always creeping in, and without a Maria to repel trespassing vegetation, the Neufchatel yard was far more colonized. Or perhaps decolonized, Horace corrected himself. The plants were here before the homes, though not the invasive kudzu that swallowed much of the fence and spread across the ground where the frog ornament supposedly lay. For some reason the only plants he remembered from his mother's off-hand wisdom were the bad actors, the invaders to repel. He wondered what this patch of land had looked like two centuries ago. Perhaps he could have spotted a real frog.

Instead, spiky plants nicked his exposed legs, and the frog with a key in its belly was nowhere to be found. He kicked at some kudzu, and it absorbed the blow unsatisfyingly. Why they'd hide the spare key so well? From whom were they protecting themselves? The dos Santoses and Hawthornes rarely bothered to lock their doors. He doubled back along the fence to the left.

Horace found the frog in the far-left corner of the yard at the fence junction. Submerged in dirt, covered by detritus, perfectly camouflaged to avoid predation, placed in a precise location that would be easy to find if you knew where to look, but Louis had misled him. Likely unintentional, an error of memory, but still a waste of time. Delicately, he lifted the frog and popped open its back, only to drop it when a winged and leggy bug buzzed out in flight. The key spilled out and scattered. He spent another minute and earned another few cuts on his hand retrieving it from under the vines. The whole search had taken maybe ten minutes.

Assuming the locks worked like his home, Horace bet this key would only open the front door and skipped to trying it. It was important that he reach Flora before Louis arrived. There was urgency for her health, but he was aware of his secondary motivations, like competitive righteousness and heroic satisfaction.

When Horace emerged through the gate, the cul-de-sac briefly lost its familiarity. For a place he knew so well, he never looked at it. Years of stacked memories obscured change. Flora's blazing crisis cast this vantage in a new light. The houses were interlopers, cubist faces with dead-eyed windows and doors of jaw-dropped disbelief. The asphalt paved over a system of roots, and trees that never were rose like ghosts. Maybe they were the watchers he felt as he turned his back and stood facing the door. His neck hairs rose like someone was watching him. A Ring security camera recorded his face and assessed his threat.

The key unlocked the knob, but the door was deadbolted. The key also unlocked the deadbolt, but the door guard slid and caught the door's swing after a couple of inches. A father's paranoia now employed by his daughter, maximum security to house their shame. She must be home. Horace screamed Flora's name through the opening, startling himself with the scraggly sound. Even if she heard him, he might register as a hallucination or a threat. He called her name more pleadingly, and then put his ear to the opening. He'd never tried opioids, recreationally or otherwise, but was pretty sure a strong dose would cause her to pass out sooner than later. He heard nothing and slumped to the ground with his back against the door. The sun was shining on him like a spotlight.

As if it snuck into his hand, he was on his phone again, and Twitter was open. He checked if Flora was still online. @artsinvein's last activity was from ten minutes ago, retweeting a vague release from the official Vein Holdings handle that "we are aware of a security breach in one of our affiliate accounts and are looking to remedy the issue." Horace direct messaged @artsinvein.

"hey I'm at the front door. Let me in"

It was marked seen within moments.

"cant"

So she wouldn't answer his calls or reply to texts, but he could reach her inside the eye of the storm.

"please I just want to help"

"cant move"

"where are u"

"here"

She sent a blurry photo of a window that seemed to have been taken from the floor. The ornate drapes suggested Paul's bedroom. He stood up, took a couple steps back, and slammed his shoulder into the door. It held firm and shot pain through his back. He thought about doing it again because the pain felt right. Instead, he walked around to try the key on the side door, assured it wouldn't work until the moment the knob turned. How much time did he waste on his stupid assumptions? He raced through the kitchen and up the stairs.

Flora was sprawled on Paul's bedroom floor as if modelling for a chalk outline. Lying on her back, her hair splayed like a mane around her head, her legs were crooked in parallel, and her head was turned to face her phone, its dark display clutched with both hands. She was wearing only an oversized, ratty t-shirt and underwear, and Horace, himself feeling chilled by the full-blast air conditioning, worried she'd be cold. He rushed to her side, grabbing her wrist with one hand and putting the back of his other to her forehead. She had a pulse, likely slow and weak though Horace didn't know what would be normal, biased by his own pounding heart. Her skin felt cool and slick. She turned her head and mumbled at him. Her pupils were wide, and her eyes were wild. She smiled crookedly.

She's alive, now what? Louis expected a call. He also knew she needed emergency services. He rang Louis first, who again answered immediately.

"Finally! What's going on? I'm almost there."

"She's alive. She's in your dad's room. Come in the side door."

"Okay thank god. How is she?"

"Um, could be worse? Breathing. But barely responsive and running cold."

"Keep her awake, and warm her up somehow. Can you see what she was taking? I've got Narcan."

Horace stood up and looked around. There were a couple pill bottles uncapped on the bed, and a glass of whiskey on the nightstand. Not enough that she could've killed herself, a growing fear that might've been her plan. He read the labels, prescriptions for Paul Neufchatel, off to Louis.

"Vicodin. Ambien. Xanax. They're all on the bed. And some whiskey."

"Jesus Christ. Is she on her side? She could choke if she vomits."

"Sorta, hold on."

Horace put his phone on speaker and sank to her level. With her legs and arms already pointing left, it didn't take much to shift her onto that side. But rather than stay put, she rolled onto her chest with her right arm pinned underneath, her face in the carpet, and her left hand still holding her phone. In a moment of frustration, Horace snatched the phone away before forcing her back on her side. She moaned like a cranky toddler or a hungry cat.

"What's wrong?" Louis demanded to know.

"Nothing! She's just getting used to me being here."

"Be more careful. I'm getting off the highway now."

Louis ended the call. Flora groaned and clutched her empty left hand in pulses. Horace looked down on her and swallowed some revulsion. What was wrong with him, and what was wrong with her? He yanked the decorative throw blanket off the foot of the bed and draped it over her. She mumbled and appeared to snuggle into it slightly. Progress.

The Flora he knew was put together, composed, tightly wound. The Flora before him was a broken guitar string, snapped by over-tuned tension, curled by former demands but shapeless. He felt useless looking over someone so helpless. He stroked her hair and returned her phone to her hand to stop its clutching. She whimpered with appreciation, and her breath steadied to a shallow trickle. Maybe he wasn't useless. Paulisdead, but Flora was not.

A tranquil minute passed, during which Horace considered what he was good for. Then he remembered he should call 9-1-1, but it didn't seem like as much of an emergency anymore. A car door slammed outside. A thud from below resembled Horace's earlier struggle against the front door. Louis was never one for listening. Horace heard another door open, and a heavier echo of Horace's rushed footsteps moved through the house. Louis burst into the room.

"Flora!" he cried at the sight of her.

His anguished voice and haggard face startled Horace. Louis took to Flora's side and shooed Horace back with his hand. He checked the pulse on her neck and the temperature of her forehead, before tucking the blanket more tightly around her. They were both just playacting from television. Horace assumed the role of viewer.

On two knees, Louis withdrew the Narcan package from his pocket, and with practiced movements peeled off the liner, picked up the applicator with his first two fingers and thumb, placed the nozzle into Flora's nose, and pushed it up. He made it look simple, and Horace was appreciative of his training. As if reading Horace's mind, Louis addressed him.

"Always got this on hand since her rehab stint. Figured it'd be for bad coke and one of my buddies, not her again. What the fuck, man? Why'd this happen? How could she do this to herself?"

Horace was unequipped to answer such a freaked-out Louis's questions. He just shook his head and asked, "So should we call 9-1-1?"

"What? Fuck no. She's stable. This is a mental health thing now. Fuck hospitals, they don't do shit about that."

Horace wanted to ask if Louis was sure but could tell that he was, surer than Horace could be about anything. Horace nodded and swallowed, returning his gaze to Flora, whose chest was moving more visibly than before. He didn't know how long it took for Narcan to work, or even how it worked. He had nowhere else to be but didn't want to ask.

"I thought you were headed back to New York."

"Hm? Oh. No, I'm taking a month for bereavement. Got myself a dope Airbnb. This house is my job now, so no way I could stay here. There's just so much shit you gotta deal with when your parent dies, like you wouldn't believe."

"That's nice they let you take off for so long."

"They work us like dogs but treat us right when it matters. My boss assured me this wouldn't even affect my promotion chances, which were looking like a sure thing."

"Mm . . . That's cool. I got let go after your dad . . . well, y'know."

"That's so messed up. Fuck Vein. Everyone I know who worked there hated it."

"Even your dad?"

"He doesn't count. Deep down, I think he knew he deserved better. But he missed the memo that it's about the money you make, not the money you make for your company. He could have been so much richer."

Horace and Louis had never gotten along. Flora loved Louis as her brother, Liam challenged him as a foil, Falco respected him as a former club lacrosse teammate, and Horace related to him not at all. Despite shared friends and demographics and history, they spoke different languages. Louis's words tended to suppress or extinguish the ambiguities in which Horace crafted what he meant to say. Nonetheless, Horace wanted to work something out with him.

"What did you make of her tweets?" Horace whispered.

"That she's fucking crazy and delirious, and her life was in danger. What'd you think I made of them?" Louis did not take his volume cue.

"Right, yeah," Horace motioned for them to lower their voices. "But I mean, I'm just thinking about them now. If Vein's wife is a predator, there's a chance Flora would know about it from work. And the cult thing. There's this nightclub called Eden? I think she mentioned it in one of the tweets. I've been there, and it seems pretty sus."

"She's gonna be in so much trouble. I can't believe her."

"But like, do you believe her? What she was alleging?"

"I'm talking about court of law trouble. Slander. Or libel? Vein's throwing the book at her. She can't go saying that shit."

"Okay, but what if it's true? It's only libel if it's false."

"It's only not libel if it's proven true. We can't afford that kind of lawyering."

"I don't think she was making this stuff up. I think she really heard it. I just wish she'd told me about it."

"You're missing the point."

"Maybe we're making different points."

"Whatever. I'm just talking about what actually matters."

"Louis?" Flora interrupted groggily, snapping both boys to attention. Horace felt immediate shame that she might have been listening to them, but she seemed barely conscious, let alone aware. "When did you get here?"

"I came as soon as I could, Sis. You're gonna be okay, everything's gonna be fine."

"Good," she weakly smiled, closing her eyes again, at first peacefully then concertedly, squeezing her eyes and furrowing her brow, panting heavily. Her whimper picked up into a moan. "Oh my god, help me, oh my god, why does everything hurt, oh my GOD!?"

"This is withdrawal," Louis stated as much to Horace as her.

"I'm gonna be sick."

"Help me get her to the bathroom," Louis ordered Horace.

They lifted her to a seated position, slid the blanket under her butt, and dragged her by the shoulders to the ensuite bathroom only feet away. She protested the whole way, only to hug the toilet like it was an old friend and make immediate use of it.

"I can take this from here," Louis told Horace, who replied with a skeptical look at both of them. "I know how to take care of her, and this next part's not gonna be pretty. She'd rather you not see it."

"Are you sure?" Horace asked in disbelief. Louis nodded and jerked his head for Horace to leave. Horace looked around for some other way to be useful. "Do you want me to at least take care of the . . . stuff?" He was pointing at the pills on the bed.

"Don't worry about that. I'll take care of everything."

"Okay, thanks?"

"No problem. Thank you for finding her."

Horace crossed the bedroom and took one last look at Louis, still feeling this decision was wrong. Louis waved goodbye, then picked up Flora's whiskey glass from the bedtable and downed it.

"I needed that. See you later, Horace. I'll let you know how she's doing tomorrow."

Horace was shocked but could not protest. His rules were not for Louis. Horace's trauma defense meant putting up barriers and then peeking over them, exposure therapy in controlled glimpses. Louis seemed like the type to reckon with his problems head on, a cage match with his discomfort, with Flora's demons and, in this case, her spirits. Horace suddenly doubted Louis would get rid of the pills. But, like a coward or a paranoiac, that pushed Horace out the door. He accepted he was both.

4.2 ~ Playing

Back home alone, Horace took a long shower and felt no better. Then he sat on the edge of his bed, braced himself, and unleashed his agony. He made as much noise as possible in as many different ways: a holler, a yell, a shout, a scream, but more than anything it was a cry. He searched for a sound that satisfied him till his voice strained and hurt, till he dug deep enough in his chest to excavate a feeling and present it to his empty world. After that he felt a little better.

He took stock of his room, stripping away the years like layers of sediment. The clothes on his floor were recent additions, but the open drawer of his bureau revealed gym shorts from middle school. His full-sized bed and square-patterned rug came home with him from college. The desk had arrived in high school. The baby-blue paint covering his walls dated to fifth grade, and scratches along his bedframe revealed the beige behind it. Shelves of young adult literature, trophies for sitting on the benches of winning teams, posters of increasingly retro video game characters, a single art class project of which he was proud. For those who move on, he imagined childhood bedrooms to become time capsules. His he had never buried and was overstuffed with time, so nothing could be considered pristine.

There was a day he barely remembered when the room began empty. That day he met Liam and Flora and moved in his few possessions. It all built up from there. He fantasized about his next apartment, funded by his next job, being a fresh start. His clothes, furniture, and unfinished to-do lists could burn in a bonfire. Maybe he'd keep some ashes in an urn on the shelf as a tolerable reminder of his previous life, the only life he'd lived so far.

His next chapter promised independence, a studio apartment decorated with someone's taste, wine stocked in advance rather than by immediate need, an air fryer, and multiple plants. Maybe a cat. After all, he might need some company. He could torch the loneliness of his previous life, but its spores, rooted deeply within him, would return in a new growth.

At present, there was little he could do about his room, his job, or his future, but he could start weeding out his loneliness. Liam, Flora, and Dylan were respectively unavailable physically, mentally, and emotionally. That was for the best, he decided. There were new friendships to cultivate. He composed and sent three separate texts.

To Russ and Gil, he proposed they link up to game that night. To Jena, he asked if she was free to hang tomorrow. Then to Mint, after no less than 20 minutes of drafting and deliberation, he floated the idea of maybe wanting to grab a drink sometime.

"Fuck it," he said to himself as he finally hit send.

After minutes of scrolling, it sank in that replies were not immediately coming. He decided to clean. He put on a debut album released that year by an artist Jena had shown him, its sound reminiscent of his teenage tastes. The artist was younger than him and likely had the same tastes. He folded the pile of clothes on his floor and unshelved an even larger pile, destined for charity if not immolation. He went through his bookshelf and sorted books he'd never read again in stacks against the wall. He caught glimpses of his future in the spaces he created, the emptiness of anything rather than nothing. An unfamiliar, pleasant feeling soaked through him, but before he could name it, the music stopped and his phone buzzed. Russel Singh. Horace's new disposition vanished with the shyness of an imaginary friend.

"Yo, my guyyy!" Russ was either weirdly happy to talk to Horace or drunk.

"Sup Ace!" a muffled voice added enthusiastically.

"Ay, lemme get this on speaker first, Gil. Okay bet, you hear me alright?"

"Loud and clear," which was half true. Now on speaker, Horace detected a background of party-coded revelry. "Where are you guys?"

"Office happy hour. Every Friday, bro!" Gil answered.

"Oh-fish litty hour," Russ added.

"In litty titty tower!" Gil tacked on, leading both to howl like a rehearsed routine.

"Cool." Horace was worried this would turn into an invitation to bar crawl. "So, y'all wanna game later?"

"Ch'yeah bro. That's why I'm calling. Time and place, we mean bidniss."

"Wait, really? You can roll through whenever. I'm, uh, just finishing up work."

"Siiiiick."

"Illlll."

"Grotessssque."

"Never been to your digs before!"

At that, Horace doubly panicked. They genuinely might have missed that he still lived with his parents, plus his parents (his mother, at least) would not enjoy their ample presences. He thought of a way out.

"Actually, my CRT's really shitty. But the Hawthornes are all out of town, let's just meet at Liam's and use his."

"Word? That's bold dog, respect. Gil, you down?"

"Yeet!"

"Fuck it, I'm fiendin' for some Tbell. Let's bounce. Ace, one hour tops."

They hung up just as Horace put two and two beers together and realized Gil would likely be driving drunk. Oh well, not his problem...until he drank with them and they tried to go home. He'd encourage them to crash on Liam's empty bed. Would that be weird? If it really was Friday, Bill and Greta wouldn't be back for a few more days. And if Liam walked in on them, well, wouldn't that be a fun surprise.

Before heading over, he gathered his things in a drawstring bag. GameCube controller, water bottle, smokes, lighter, bowl, weed baggie, grinder. Russ and Gil might not smoke but that wouldn't stop him. He'd had a stressful day. Time to unwind, relax with friends, be normal. Or obliterate himself with substances.

Stepping outside, he enjoyed the light breeze and how the heat of the day had broken. He glanced next door to the window of the room where Flora should still be. He justified against checking in on her—he might just embarrass her now. There's always tomorrow.

Again, the corner of his eye picked up a curtain's rustle in Brunhilde's window, another trick of the mind. Or maybe she was watching him. It made little difference. He crossed the street.

Passing through the gate, punching in the keycode, walking up the garage stairs, and crossing the room, nothing was amiss. Only after he wheeled the dolly and its heavy TV over to the couch, while inspecting the power strip, did he notice the Nintendo Wii was gone. Horace's first thought was Liam could have moved it to his room, but even before he checked, he realized why that didn't make sense—Liam emulated all his games on his desktop. In his flight, he must have brought the Wii with him.

It wasn't an earthshattering revelation, but it flavored Liam's disappearance. Bringing along some comforts implied a greater plan. Maybe a friend from college was putting him up. Someone he trusted more than Horace. Horace could tell he was mad at Liam because he fantasized of contradictions: wishing Liam had entrusted him with his escape plans so he could rat on him, dreaming of saying he never wanted to see Liam again to his face.

When he pictured the world where he'd refused to be Liam's accomplice, he struggled to spot many differences. Bill still acquitted, Liam still gone, the neighborhood still shaken, and Paul one shock away from death if not still dead. He'd feel guilty either way, for inaction or action. But he wouldn't be waiting to play video games with Russ and Gil had he not gotten involved, so that was one thing. He wanted there to be more.

He returned home and packed up his Wii, fitted with an identical copy of the SD card in Liam's Wii. The only difference was the stats each had accumulated. It occurred to him that he should eat something, so he stopped by the kitchen. As he watched the leftover noodles spin in the microwave, his mother walked with her arms full of papers. She smiled at the sight of her son taking care of himself.

"How was your day?" she asked.

"Uneventful," he replied before realizing how wrong that was. "I'm gonna go play video games with Russ and Gil from the play in a bit, so having some dinner now."

"Hm. Two good things. Food and friends," Maria said without conviction.

"How was your day?"

"Oh you know, always another."

"For better for worse."

"Amen."

He ate at the table while she graded her summer-school students. He finished his bowl and put it in the dishwasher. She asked him when he was leaving and where he was going. He answered with "about now" and "to a friend's place," then slung his bag over his shoulders and headed out, worrying he hadn't done a good enough job convincing her he needed this. In what she didn't say, she seemed to understand.

Back above the Hawthorne garage, he booted up the Wii and warmed up his fingers against a CPU. He felt in tune with his controller, the precise timings and combo flows coming more naturally than usual. His generation had amassed an insane collection of skill for video games. Dexterities of forgotten ancestral purposes, put now to such little good use. He had the reaction time of a warrior but not the heart of one.

Russ and Gil barged in and bounded up the stairs some twenty minutes later. Horace could see the drunk in their eyes and pretended they'd gotten a ride.

They dapped Horace up and asked him how he'd been. He played along and talked some smack about how he was "gonna whoop them" while cringing inside. They accepted him and his challenge, and Horace backed his words up, winning four straight with ease. He was thinking about getting high to even the playing field when Russ put down his controller and said his fingers needed a break. Gil filled his other hand with a backup beer.

Horace realized he might have been taken things too seriously. He grabbed his beer, clinked it to Gil's, and tried to finish it, unsuccessfully. Gil appreciated his effort, and Russ asked Horace, for the first time ever, if he wanted to hit the vape. Horace obliged. It occurred to Horace that he might be having fun. It also occurred to him that he needed to pee, so he took his leave, practicing some smiles in the mirror while he washed his hands.

When he turned off the water, he heard whispering. The wall between the bathroom and the couch was thin. He couldn't make out full sentences, but he heard words like "Liam," "find him," "Horace knows," and "bitch," the last of which, clearly from Russ, could have been directed toward Gil, Horace, or even Liam. Horace stayed very still, the whispers stopped, and Russ barked something about getting another game going. Horace exited the bathroom with determination. He'd let too many opportunities pass him by.

"Were you guys talking about Liam?" Horace asked directly, walking into the center of the room.

Gil said "Eavesdropper," and Russ said "No," at about the same time. Horace relished the tension as they traded annoyed looks. They had something to hide.

"You wanna ask me? I'm an open book when it comes to Liam," Horace said.

"Okay," Russ picked up, "I mean, *do* you know where he is?"

"Nope. No clue."

"But like," Gil began, "he's not really gone, is he?"

"Your guess is as good as mine."

"Nah, we don't know him like you do."

"Yeah c'mon man, everyone's dying to know."

"Everyone? Who's asking about him?"

"Socials, bruh. You haven't seen all the people posting about him?"

"Right. Well you can inform 'everyone' I don't know. Out for cigarettes. Radio silence."

"That's so cold."

"You gotta let us know if he shows some proof of life. We're like worried about him, ya know?"

"So you can tell 'everyone' where he is?"

"Ace, you offend us. We're not snitches."

"And we're not bitches."

"C'mon Ace, maybe you don't know, but what's your guess?"

"Russ thinks the wrong people got to him."

"The wrong people? Who would be the right people?"

"Damn Gil, Ace is acting like he's onto us, what gives?"

"Yeah Ace, quit acting so sus."

"Why did you two agree to do the play?"

"Whadyamean?"

"I got roped in, but you two volunteered. You must have seen the obituary. Did you know that's what the play would be about?"

"Just thought it'd be fun. Like it's not that deep, bro."

"Then why'd you want to quit when he no showed? Why was it 'pointless' without him?"

"Did I say that?"

"No, Russ did. But you tell me, Gil. Was it your idea to do Liam's play?"

"No . . ."

"So it was Russ's? He came to you and said you two should be in a play again. Like, now's the time to get back into live theater."

Gil hesitated before saying, "Yeah. That's what happened."

"I don't believe you," Horace replied calmly, maybe even enjoying himself.

"Dude, you forget to take your meds or something? Why are you being such a schiz?"

"C'mon Russ, don't do him like that. What's it even matter anymore?"

"G-dawg, why don't you shut the fuck up?"

"Fuck you R-word. I'm gonna tell him."

"There's nothing to tell! Ace just caught Liam's crazy bug. What are you even hoping we'll admit to? I'd love to know."

"I have my hunch. It's just really lame you two won't come clean first. I'll put it this way. If I were as crazy as Liam, I'd write a play about how some corporation wanted intel on this guy whose firm they were buying, so they sent two employees to go hang out with his son on false pretenses and get a scoop. Then I'd invite you two to opening night and watch your reactions for evidence."

"Hold up, is that why Liam did the play?"

"Are you fucking kidding me, Gil?" Russ looked ready to fight. "You are the dumbest motherfucker alive."

"No, I thought Liam got the play from his dad. Why would he need evidence? I'm so confused."

"Obviously we were wrong on that one, dumbass. Which is why this whole thing was a goddamn waste of my time."

"I'm taking this all as an admission of guilt, by the way. May as well tell me the rest."

"You don't know shit, Ace. Useless know-it-all bitchass. I'm surrounded by idiots!"

Russ yanked his controller out of the Wii, wrapped up the cord with frantic sloppiness, and zipped it into his bag. Horace matched raised eyebrows with Gil.

"C'mon Gil, pack your stuff. We're bouncing."

Gil hesitated and Horace took initiative, stepping in front of Russ.

"No. You're too drunk to drive. You can crash here, but I won't let you go."

"First of all, try stopping me, coward. Second of all, we Ubered so save it with the sanctimony, broke bitch." Russ was right in Horace's face, or rather, just below it. Horace laughed it off.

"You Ubered all the way here just to ask me questions about Liam? What, are you not getting promoted unless you find him? I hope you expensed it at least."

Russ shoved Horace in the chest and sent him a few steps back. Acting on a never-before-used instinct, Horace ran toward Russ and tackled him to the ground. They wrestled and flailed for a few seconds before Gil pulled them apart with ease.

"Break it up! Break it up!" Once Gil was between them, neither combatant wanted to continue.

"Fuck you, Ace." Russ grabbed his bag and made for the stairs, flipping them off with both hands over his shoulders. As he stomped down the stairs, he called out, "Uber's here, Gil. Hurry up, or I'll leave without you."

"Sorry Horace," Gil said as he packed his bag. "I really liked doing the play. Russ is the one who cared about the bonus."

"Who asked you to do this?"

"Our boss's boss's boss? I don't even know. Word on high. I was just excited to visit the top floor. I don't think we gave them what they wanted, if that helps. But I'm sorry, I gotta go."

"Thanks for everything, then."

Gil ran down the stairs after Russ. After the door slammed, Horace exhaled and let his feelings sink in. He was onto something. Russ and Gil worked on behalf of higher powers. Liam's dumb play had garnered some attention after all. If they—this supposed *everyone*—were still interested, perhaps Horace had some more juice to squeeze too. The image of the pamphleteer returned to him, moonlighting as Eden's janitor. Horace still wanted redemption for his previous falters. That man might have answers he'd be willing to share. There was at least something he wanted Horace to know, and Horace finally felt ready to find out what.

Horace pulled out his phone and saw Jena had sent him a voice memo. Still no word from Mint, a disappointment he noted and swallowed. Horace played Jena's message to the empty room.

"Hello Horace! I miss you so much! And I so want to hang out with you. But, ugh, I am busy all weekend with this Eden stuff. I love these people, but they are so much, always more more more. It's like those stories where you get what you ask for in the bad way. But I always say no such thing as too much of a good thing, so it's funny. I don't know. This weekend is supposed to be my last big yoohoo for a bit and then I am chilling out. Maybe you want to come tomorrow? I know last time was no fun, but it can be much better. Please let me know! Or, how does next week look for you? I promise you I will be free for you even if I am busy for other people. That sound good, no? Okay talk soon, buh-bye!"

Horace did not want to go back to Eden, and next week felt like a different world. He couldn't think of a reply.

4.3 ~ Preparing

Horace returned home to his parents watching a European murder mystery show. He sat with them, and for an episode and a half he speculated whodunit alongside his mom and riffed with his dad about the absurd perils of Swedish shopkeeping. They'd been giving him a leash, an unemployment assurance that he was welcome to be a bum for a little while longer, but he knew his listless days were numbered. He wanted to spend what time he could with them, as thanks.

He went to bed dead-tired and fell asleep, awaking without an alarm around 10 a.m. He got himself out of bed and shuffled the few feet to his bathroom. Mid-brush, he heard his phone rattling on the windowsill and shuffled back to see Louis Neufchatel was calling. Horace rushed to the bathroom sink to spit out his toothpaste froth before answering.

"Dude, she's gone."

"What? When? Where?"

"I just got back with breakfast and she's not here. Should have fucking Grubhubbed. I don't know where, obviously."

"Shit. Fuck. What do we do?"

"Show me where her car is."

"Be outside in a minute."

Horace tossed on a t-shirt, slipped into his sandals, and bounded down the steps to his front door. Louis stood waiting for him in the driveway, pouting with a phone to his ear. He ended the call as Horace approached.

"I'm gonna keep calling her nonstop till she picks up or blocks me. I cannot believe her!"

"Did you call her roommate yet?"

"Obviously. She's on lookout."

They walked down the hill together. The car was supposed to be a couple blocks away, and they walked a few more blocks just to be sure it wasn't there. Louis wanted to believe Horace

237

misremembered where she'd parked, but eventually they called off the search. While she couldn't have gotten far on foot, her car could have taken her anywhere. Horace waited through another call with her roommate, who confirmed she still wasn't home. They headed back to the cul-de-sac.

"So, what should we do now?" Horace asked while they walked.

"Fuck if I know."

"How was she last night? Did you talk?"

"We communicated. She wasn't up for much talking. When she finally got lucid, she told me to save the lectures for tomorrow. I went along with it, not knowing she was gonna pull this type of shit. We ordered Chinese, and she fell asleep to our *Beauty and the Beast* Blu-ray, so I took her back to bed. She was still there when I got up this morning, and then she wasn't. I can't believe she tricked me."

Horace chewed on silence before replying optimistically.

"The more you need help, the less you want it. Until you reach a point. She'll come back to us. Not sure where else she could go."

"I just hope she doesn't know how to score any more stuff."

"Me too. So, what are you gonna do?"

"Sit around and wait for her to come back. It's that or drive around in circles. You got any guesses where to look?"

"Maybe she checked herself into a hospital?"

"Not a chance. She hates those places more than I do."

"What if she just went out for food and hasn't checked her phone?"

"Neither of those things sound like her."

They parted with a promise to keep each other updated. Horace felt like he should do something, so he cooked himself an omelet. It wouldn't bring her any closer, but he needed the strength. He felt everything should revolve around her, yet nothing was. His house, the neighborhood, the world were all indifferent as ever.

Unable to sit still, he went for an aimless walk and wound up at the stump. Seeing her carvings brought her no closer. That was the old Flora. He sat on the stump and smoked half a cigarette before losing interest. Lacking any inclination to be elsewhere, he settled himself among the roots of a tree and dozed off against its trunk, giving himself up to his stress and the summer air.

When he resurfaced, Jena had texted him again.

"Hey just checking in about tonight. Flora said she's in too!"

That woke him up. He called Jena.

"Jena, you've heard from Flora? Is she okay?"

"Yes, I think so? She was just texting me. She asked me to put her name on the list for tonight. I told her that the list does not matter for her, but I would be her personal escort if she wanted. Why wouldn't she be okay?"

"She relapsed last night and disappeared this morning. She went to rehab years ago, but it just felt like a blip till now. We've been worried sick about her."

"Oh my god, that is terrible. Is it bad I told her to come?"

"I don't know. Actually, it's good. Really good. We know where she'll be. I was leaning against it, but looks like I'm coming after all. Gonna tell her brother, cool if he comes too?"

"The more the merrier! Although this is no longer a happy situation. I'm so sorry."

"It's okay. You might help save her life."

"It is thanks to you for introducing us."

Had he done that? They'd met at the play. Jena insisted on seeing it despite Horace's protests. He'd told her how to find Flora, so they'd each have company. As far as introductions go, it was the definitive least he could have done. By the time he found them at the end of the show, they'd moved past any introductory phase into the rapport of good friends. Horace marveled at their amicability against his. The only friends he made were the ones who made it so easy.

"Yeah, well, thanks for coming to the play. See you tonight?"

"Yes. Oh, I wish I could just stick with you and leave when we find her."

"Why don't you?"

"It's not how it works. I have expectations now."

"Expectations? From whom?"

"The people in charge are so silly. They made us promise to party all night, as if I would ever get tired. Too many rules! Americans are always so intentional about these things. Like, I do not need training on how to have fun, and they are always watching. It's strange, but I go along with it because it usually means being myself. Tonight will be weird."

"Because of Flora? Or something else?"

"Many things. It is hard to explain."

"Try me."

"I don't know . . . I am sorry, but I have to go. We will talk tonight, no?"

"Definitely. See you tonight. Thanks, Jena. Please take care of yourself."

"I promise I will. We will be safe together. Bye Horace."

They ended the call, and Horace headed back up the trail. He pulled out his phone to call Louis, then put it away. He could knock on his door instead. He was growing accustomed to this state of emergency, which was currently at walking pace.

The wind caressed the leaves and flexed their branches. A squirrel hopped into his path, stopped, and looked up at him before darting off. Horace's vision blurred and his eyes misted, on the brink of so many emotions, yet he was not overcome. The tears, once they journeyed down his cheek, might be happy or sad, but now at the gates, they contained every potential.

Underneath this tranquil moment was a churning sea of questions. What would he do when he found Flora? What if she never showed? What did Jena mean by *everything*? Who was behind Russ's *everyone*? There had to be specifics, but what was he supposed to do about it all? He would show up and react. People accused him of always needing a plan, but his preparations often failed him. Intrusively, he thought about texting Mint again. Perhaps they'd like to know he'd be at Eden that night. But he didn't, because perhaps they would not.

At the Neufchatel door, he knocked. Then, feeling silly and old-fashioned, he took out his phone and placed a call. As ever, Louis answered abruptly.

"Did you just knock? Did you find her?"

"Yes. Uh, no. Er, sorta? Yes I knocked, no I didn't find her, but I do have a lead."

The door swung open to both of them holding a phone to an ear.

"What's the lead?"

"She texted my friend Jena about going to a club tonight. Eden, actually. Same place she was tweeting about."

"That's the last place I want her. But wait, no, that's huge. We can catch her there."

"Yeah, with a net?"

"She's coming home with me whether she likes it or not."

"Dude, I think she needs professional help."

"I'm telling you, she won't like that."

"Well, you can say it was my idea. When she's safe and alive."

"Whatever. Fine. Let's find her first."

"Well, doors are probably at nine. Want me to drive?"

"I'll call us an Uber. Be here at eight."

That gave Horace six hours, a horrible time to kill. The steady drip of action was stoppered, building a potential torrent. He was sitting in bed with his phone in his hand. What could he access with it? All the world's information had never felt less helpful. He searched for advice on how to confront a friend in relapse, refining his search with the specifics of her situation until it produced no new results. The purple links presented a uselessly generalized consensus, all the bullet points and listicles skipping over the part where you track them down while they're evading help, and their brother doesn't trust professionals, and you're hoping to catch them at a night club with opaque ties to experimental drug research. He may well be the first person to find himself in such a situation, but good advice was supposed to transcend specifics. To be alone on the internet was alienating.

He gave up, switched to a private browser, and jacked off, which affirmed with clarity how alone he really was. There were still five hours to go.

After showering, he went downstairs and flipped on the TV. Paralysis extended to his streaming options. Might his troubles have been chronicled in *Law & Order*, or one of those real-life-adjacent Hollywood shows? Even if he found a relevant recreation, the advice would be coming from writers with a mandate for drama. Sensible resolutions never made it to air. He chose the third *Lord of the Rings* film for inspiration and runtime.

His mother returned with groceries and began to prepare dinner. Without pausing the movie, Horace drifted in to watch and chat, and without thought his words were spilling from his mouth.

"Hey Mom, um . . . Flora relapsed yesterday."

Maria sent her knife through the onion with startled force then released the handle as if it were hot. The knife fell to the board, collapsing the dome of the half-chopped onion.

"Oh Jesus, that's terrible. That poor family has suffered so much."

"Well, it gets worse. Louis and I found her next door, but she ran away again this morning. We figured out where she's gonna be tonight, so we're going and getting her home, somehow."

"Where will she be?"

Horace was caught in two minds. He wanted to tell his mom everything—how Flora was going to Eden which might be a cult run by Vein to use Dr. Hawthorne's doppelganger drug as a brainwashing tool—but he couldn't imagine speaking those words out loud, let alone her reaction to them. "She'll be at a nightclub," was all he was willing to say. He could tell her the rest when it was over.

"Is this place dangerous?"

"I don't want you to worry."

"Of course I'm going to worry. Can I come with you?"

"No, Mom. Please trust me. I can handle myself, and I'll be with Louis."

"Hm. I don't like the sound of this. But I can't keep you home when Flora needs your help. I have to remind myself you're an adult now. Just get her home safe, and please, please be careful. We've lost enough already."

"I'll be who you raised me to be. A careful risk-taker. Though you know how to pick your battles. I would not have chosen this one."

"You still have a choice."

"I don't. Not at this point."

"If you say so."

Horace could tell his mother wasn't convinced, nor was she looking for convincing. Instead, he played to her Romantic sympathies.

"Alea iacta est, mater. Not much else to say. Do you want my help with dinner?"

"That's okay. If you see me crying, I can blame the onions."

"Well, let me know when I should set the table."

Tolkien really popped off creating the hobbits, Horace concluded. In a world of far mightier forces, their incorruptible bravery kept them relevant. One needn't be strong, skilled, or magical to be useful. But for all his rewatches, only now did it occur to Horace to question from where their bravery came. Was it, like a blindman's sharpened senses, that their bravery grew in deficit of other options? Or was bravery, like willpower, a mostly intrinsic gift, encoded by nature and enforced by nurture? Be brave and be strong. Was one more in Horace's control than the other? He took it for granted he wasn't strong. Tonight would be a test of his bravery, but wasn't choosing to take that test a more important measure than how he did on it?

His father came home and joined him on the couch. He'd read the books to Horace as a child, as much for his own pleasure as Horace's, but such love was either infectious or inheritable. Horace grew up believing in the virtues of high fantasy, only to learn with disappointment that wasn't how the world worked. He grew to understand it as an aspirational project, mythmaking for a better world.

When Al asked Horace how he was feeling, Horace replied, "Like Pippin."

"That means up to no good, you foolish Took?"

"Fool of a took. Yeah."

Once called to dinner, Al learned of Flora's relapse and what Horace had really meant. He took the news more easily than Maria, expressing his concern for Flora while affirming Horace's duty to intervene, proud that his son was acting like a man.

"It is amazing," Al mused, "the way a death of someone we love can change us. And not always for the worse."

After eating, Horace cleared their plates, and Maria asked if he'd like some tea. He could feel her delaying the inevitable and said it was time for him to meet up with Louis. She got up and hugged him goodbye, and Al started with a handshake but pulled him in for a strong but awkward embrace.

"Are you sure you do not want my help?"

"They're not letting you in the door, Dad."

"Ah, the ageism!"

"Get her home safe, my love," interjected Maria.

"I will."

"Or straight to a hospital."

"I'll try."

"And then you come right home and show us you're okay."

"I promise."

"I love you."

"Love you both too."

"And don't forget your cigarettes, you'll need them!" Al added mischievously, earning a slap on the shoulder from Maria.

"I don't, what . . ." Horace could barely stammer out a reply.

"Oh come on, sweetie," Maria soothed. "You think you could hide that from us? I only quit when I had your sister. I'll get mad at you about it later. Now go!"

Upstairs, Horace changed into all black and applied the eyeliner he'd recently picked up and been practicing while high. He felt a little badass and a little foolish. Furrowing his brow, his reflection looked fierce, tougher than brave. With lighter and smokes in his left pocket, phone and keys in his right, and wallet in back he headed for the stairs.

Horace made his way outside and over to the Neufchatel front door, knocked, and entered. Louis called out Horace's name from the adjacent study, and Horace heard another guy's voice say something too, inflected like a question. He opened the door to Louis Neufchatel sitting with Dylan Falco. Horace, immediately feeling self-conscious of his eyeliner, stuck his hands in his pockets to keep his fingers out of his eyes, which cried out to be rubbed and ruined.

"Hey Falco. You joining the hunt?" Horace volunteered.

"Yeah, Louis recruited me. I, uh, hope you don't mind," Falco grinned back.

"Why would I mind?" Horace asked with shit-eating serenity.

It occurred to Horace that Louis possibly didn't know about their history, or at least that one key blip. Louis hadn't heard it from him, and he'd asked Flora not to go telling everyone, not that she and her brother dealt much in gossip anyway. As for Falco not informing Louis, that was easy to believe. Louis's ignorance gave Horace the power here, and a decision on how to wield it. For once, he'd let Falco feel some shame and confusion. Horace sat on the couch with his ex and asked for one of what they were having. Louis was happy to oblige.

"Bit funny, isn't it," Falco jumped eagerly into conversation, "that we're pregaming an intervention?" He followed this up with a sip and some eye contact to show he wasn't complaining.

Preparing

"Less weird when you think of it as an extraction mission. You think soldiers fight sober?"

"Right, yeah, so where's the coke?"

"Not funny. I just didn't want to go to one of these techno shows sober. We're not getting wasted."

Louis handed Horace his drink, in which he'd dropped two ice cubes and poured a couple different types of liquor. Horace took a sip and guessed it was a Manhattan, or some trendy take on it. They toasted to finding Flora and getting the hell out of there, then Louis explained the rest of the plan they'd hashed out.

"I'll call an Uber for us in like 30 minutes. That should get us there before the crowd gets too big, then one of us can keep an eye on the door while the others go searching for her. Given what she tweeted, they might be waiting for her too, so we'll have to be ready for that. If we don't find her in the crowd right away, I'm thinking we take shifts on smoke breaks to watch the lawn. Horace, you smoke, right?"

Horace nodded and patted his left pocket. Falco smiled in appreciation, and Horace wondered if he was thinking of the cigarettes they'd split. Horace shook his head to clear the thought, then spoke to justify his reaction.

"That could be a lot of cigarettes."

"Good thing I've been practicing," Falco said with a compulsive smile.

"Well it's important, the most important thing really, that we don't look suspicious. That's what the drinking is for, too."

"What, are they gonna kick us out for being a bad vibe?" Falco asked with an unsteady laugh.

"They just might," Horace answered seriously. He filled them in on his call with Jena.

"Man, what did I sign up for?" Falco stated rhetorically, glancing out the window like he needed an escape before pushing out another laugh.

"Just getting Flora out. I don't care what else this place is up to, not my business," Louis said.

"And when we find her?" Horace inquired.

Louis looked at his phone before replying.

"We call 9-1-1, like you've been saying. That way she has two clear choices. Come home with us or go there with them. That work for you?"

"Seems reasonable."

It was a compromise, at least. Horace had a feeling that things wouldn't go to plan, so there wasn't much point arguing for a better one.

4.4 ~ Partying

In the Uber, Horace sat in the middle, and let his knees tilt to Falco's side. Had they been alone together, Horace would have iced him out, but in the presence of Louis, the unobservant observer, Horace relished the discomfort he could create. Falco perhaps shifted away a tad, certainly wasn't leaning in, but otherwise betrayed nothing. Horace never looked at him, determined to avoid receiving any private messages. He knew the look in Falco's eyes—Dylan's eyes—that asked why, and he wouldn't be able to answer. "Because I hate you and still like you and have a lot else on my mind," was the closest he could get.

It was a tense car ride, and the radio played advertisements that grated Horace's ears, until Louis barked at the driver to turn it off. The silence was instant and impermeable. Horace focused on the road ahead.

"Wish we had Liam with us," Falco brought up out of nowhere, talking just to ease his nerves.

"Fuck no," Louis shot back. "I hope that prick stays lost. As far as I'm concerned, it's basically his fault my dad's dead and Flora's using. He can go to hell."

"Sheesh," Falco replied. "Respect your opinion, but that seems harsh, dude."

"With all the shit he pulled, he's conservatively responsible for at least twenty points of my dad's blood pressure. As a marginal effect, that's basically fatal."

"Word. I'm just saying, if you wanna be a nerd and run a regression on why your dad died, there's a lot of factors that would go into it. Not like Liam meant to hurt him."

"You sure about that? Cuz the way I see it, he just wanted to cause trouble and make everyone as unhappy as he was. Horace, you were there for it. What's your take?"

Already stuck in the middle seat, Horace had been dreading getting dragged into this conversation and wanted it to be over as soon as possible. "Liam wasn't thinking about anyone but himself.

I don't know if that makes it any better. But we're giving him what he wants by still talking about him."

"Aight, fuck Liam, I guess. I'll get on board with that," Falco conceded.

They arrived at their destination and sidled out of the car. The night was young, the air was thick, and the building glowed, hummed, and throbbed, emitting gentle shockwaves that beckoned. Girls in shimmering dresses were entering the club, and two more rideshares were letting out. The trio briefly huddled.

"Eyes peeled, boys," Louis ordered. "Whoever finds her, do your best to get her outside. Then text the group."

"What if she never shows?" voiced Horace. "How late's our cutoff?"

"As late as there's a chance she might show. I'm not leaving till they kick me out. Could be a long night. You can call your own Uber home if you're tired."

"You're not watching the sunrise without me," Falco assured Louis.

"I'll be looking for my friend Jena, too. If we're lucky, Flora's keeping her in the loop, and we'll know what to expect."

The three musketeers advanced toward Eden. The liquid courage in Horace's blood made each step easier, as if swept along in a current, but did little to dull his nerves. A few weeks earlier, he'd crossed the lawn with a pit in his stomach, nauseously anxious about the prospect of performing in Liam's place. This anticipation burned even hotter, but he felt more in control of the blaze, not despite but because of the higher stakes. He loved having a job to do. His anxiety was made for moments like these, with every contingency worth considering.

One such contingency was Flora never showing, but Horace dismissed it as unlikely. From her tweets, she knew something was happening tonight. She was going to witness and embrace the chaos. She'd also predicted "HELL ON SUNDAY," a portentous claim no matter how he interpreted it. Instead, his mind turned over other pitfalls of various depths: what if she refuses to come with them, what if Vein's agents get her first, what if he's walking into a Jonestown-style cult massacre, what if he runs into the pamphleteer . . .

Horace ran these simulations as he ascended the steps, only to be jarred loose by the sight of Falco's powerful thighs climbing ahead of him. He shook it off. The occasional ogle and cheekiness aside, Horace commended himself for being so unaffected by his heartbreaker's presence. The high stakes provided scale and perspective. Romance can rise to any occasion, but matters between him and Falco seemed tiny in the rearview.

The bouncer collected their IDs together and took his time looking their cards and bodies up and down. His raised an eyebrow, pulled out his phone, and began to scroll. Horace tapped his foot and channeled a disaffected expression. Louis wasn't so patient.

"What's the problem?"

"Two of you aren't on the list."

The trio glanced at each other uncertainly, and Falco jumped in with earnest nonchalance.

"Ah, we were last minute invites. Bet the doc didn't get updated. Our friend warned us this might happen."

"Who's your friend?"

Falco made the briefest of eye contact with Horace, who kicked into gear.

"Jena. Jena Reus."

"Oh, Jena? Fuck yeah, she's my girl. Most of that crowd don't learn the bouncers' names, not Jena tho. I can make an exception, for her."

He handed back their IDs, affixed their wristbands, and asked for their phones to place stickers on the cameras.

"Enjoy yourselves in there. This is the big one. Didn't want any folks who don't get it, ya know?"

"Heard, yeah, much appreciated my man. Have a good night," Falco answered for them.

They opened the door, parted the curtain, and entered Eden. Out of night and into a dream, full of smoke and murky edges, dark but luminous, strobes like flashes of lightning, beats shaking the floor, and that smell rushing through Horace's nose and into his lungs, crossing his capillaries, filling his blood and pleasing his brain. He shivered and buzzed, charged with excitement, feeling the task at hand like his feet felt the ground, barely, as if both were lifted away and uncoupled. He kept his footing and squeezed his toes, stretching a thread up to his mind that carried a conscious, delicate purpose.

The scene assaulted Falco and Louis, who were taken aback and needed a second to adjust. After that moment, they gave each other nods of encouragement, Horace smiled an "I told you so" he had never voiced, and they took the stairs down into the fold, following Horace to the bar.

"Holy shit," Falco yelled into Horace's ear, gently tugging at his elbow, "this place is amazing. Won't mind if Flora takes a minute to show up."

He ended his comment with a smirk, and some genuine, melting eye contact. Horace felt a flutter and laughed back. He asked himself his first "why not" of the night, leaving the question unanswered. He and Falco—no, he and Dylan—could have some fun, if that's what Horace wanted. A side quest. They accepted their drinks, which Louis put on an open tab, and regrouped by a wall. Horace took the expositional lead, feeling the power of his knowledge over them.

"We got here at the right time. It's hopping now, but the floor is gonna get packed. Should be easier to search, though it's way foggier than usual."

"I don't know how people stand this shit. These lights are gonna give me epilepsy," Louis grumbled.

"Don't think that's the disease you gotta worry about catching here, Lou," Dylan cracked. "I think this place is sick." Again, Dylan smiled at Horace like he'd designed the lighting or deserved credit for anything beyond knowing Jena. "Let's dance our way through the crowd, yeah?"

"You two can handle the interior scan. I'm gonna do some laps," Louis asserted.

"Roger that, boss. Try not to look like a cop!" Dylan shot back, before downing his drink, voracious as ever. He placed it on a shelf before turning to Horace, whose drink stood half-empty. "C'mon Ace, let's boogie!"

With casual assent, Horace followed Dylan. As they merged into the outer layer, Dylan reached back for Horace's free hand, taking it firmly and giving it a squeeze. Once he found it, Dylan didn't look back, as if holding hands was the most natural thing. In some ways it was, and Horace didn't protest.

They made a good show of looking for the perfect place to dance and never quite finding it. From pocket to pocket, they traced a constellation across the crowd, using each point of light to take stock of their surroundings. Wherever Horace looked, he found ecstatic eyes pouring over him, begging him to stay and bond, but none belonged to those he wanted.

The sole eye contact he couldn't quite catch was from Dylan, like passengers on a road trip, taking the sights in together, trading glances in turns. Only near the front, under the DJ's covered eyes, did they turn to dance with each other. Nothing steamy, mostly playful, embracing the joke of the whole situation, but thrilling nonetheless. Horace could leave his night up to Dylan, whom he was thinking about more and more, and their mission less and less. Then Louis appeared and gracelessly interrupted their moment.

"Having fun? No sight of Flora."

"Yeah same," Dylan mouthed, while Horace withdrew his limbs.

Dylan tapped them both on the shoulder and grooved out of the crowd, which moved like water to fill the space. They regrouped and replenished themselves at the far end of the bar, in sight of the door to the basement. Horace kept glancing in that direction, not wanting to miss any comings or goings. Dylan announced his intention to take a leak, leaving Horace side-by-side with Louis, silently people-watching and nodding their heads to the music.

"What's up with you two?" Louis leaned over to ask, startling Horace.

"Sorry, we really were looking for her! Just trying to blend in."

"No, I know that. I mean, whatever. Forget it."

Horace would neither forget nor address it. Louis seemed immune to Eden's bubble of suspended disbelief, but Horace could hear the drinks slipping into Louis's speech. Louis had said he would wait all night, but who would he be by that time? Another addict needing saving?

The door to the basement sprung open, and a flood of eager bodies streamed out, saving Horace from speaking. Instead, he elbowed Louis and gestured for them to watch the flow. Halfway through, he caught his first familiar face, a radiant Jena, holding hands with two others, one who twirled her and the other who caught her. They were all laughing and sharing skin generously. Horace took a step toward her, looked back at Louis to hand him his drink, and pushed himself into her throng.

When she saw Horace, her face lit up. She untangled herself to embrace him, wrapping her arms tightly around him, kissing his cheek, clinging to his body like a life raft.

"Have you seen Flora yet?" Horace shouted in her ear.

"Who?" She yelled back while shaking her head no, an unsettling discrepancy. "I'm so happy to see you!" Pulling him in to dance, she brought their faces together, smiling with all her might, noses almost touching, and whispered coldly in his ear, "I need your help."

She crooked his arm with hers and shepherded him into the group. Her request had sent him reeling, and he squeezed his toes with each step as he followed them into a roped-off section at the base of the stage. The ropes came down, the crowd pushed in, and the DJ dropped the beat he'd been building. All Horace could do was dance and keep Jena in front of him, waiting for her to make a move.

She turned around, grabbed his face, narrowed her eyes—not with desire but determination—and kissed him. For a second, he thought she'd lost it, that her troubles were momentary and forgotten, but her lips weren't moving on his. It was another stage kiss, falser than Mint's. She emerged from the kiss with a satisfied smirk and wild eyes, a look of something barely suppressed, before again putting her lips to his ear.

"They must not know. I am so sorry."

"Have you heard anything from Flora?"

As if she didn't hear his question, she turned around to face the stage and fell into the lateral sway of the crowd around them. Sensing what she wanted from him, Horace followed her movements, put his arms around her waist, and leaned his head into hers, as if nibbling on her ear.

"How can I help you?"

Jena tossed her head back onto Horace's shoulder, closed her eyes in contentment, and grabbed his hair to tousle it and draw him into her. She kissed his neck and told him to keep following her lead. Their fellow dancers, coupled and tripled and dancing alone, menaced him innocently. Jena met his eyes, slowly blinked, and cast a look toward the stage. The DJ, even this close, was inscrutable. This man held so much power over them, yet he was nearly invisible, a wisp of darkness in the smoke, a floating torso hidden behind a table. When Horace returned his eyes to the floor, he saw someone dropping something into their own drink. Another did likewise, and they toasted to each other before swallowing deep gulps. Jena saw this too and turned to face Horace, grabbing both of his hands.

"Do you have any gum?" she loudly asked.

"I don't think—"

"—Then you must go look. Mint will solve my problems. Please. Find Mint, then come back to me."

She kissed him on each cheek and pushed him away. He hesitated, not sure who to help, everyone around him succumbing, surrendering themselves to obliteration. He looked back one last time, and saw Jena take a swig from someone's drink. He left her there.

Back at the bar, Louis and Dylan weren't waiting for him. He got a water and scanned the room that overflowed with strangers. He was looking for Flora, Louis, Dylan, and now Mint? Jena had met Mint the night they kissed, he roughly recalled. Or maybe they'd met at the show. Why did Jena need them now? Mint knew something about Eden that scared them, and that terrified Horace. Some connection to Dr. Hawthorne's firm, to Chemical X, to the doppelgangers. Was Jena going to be replaced? Would it happen tonight in some grand ceremony? Was it up to him, and perhaps Mint, to stop it and save her? His only evidence was the heavy feeling in his gut and the endless series of strange behaviors he'd witnessed.

He tried to act casual as he walked to the back, hands in pockets, taking in the edge of the crowd and the patrons of the bar. He checked out the bathroom and made use of it himself. His reflection appeared a little sweaty but mostly sober, and there were some red smudges on his neck he washed off. He splashed water on his face for good measure, then patted his pockets just to make sure he still had his cigarettes. It was time for some air.

On his way out, he checked his phone, and it still wasn't midnight. No inbound texts, so he informed Louis and Dylan he was stepping outside for a smoke. A new bouncer was watching the door, and a long line had formed outside, snaking along the grass. He skipped down the steps and settled to the side of a pack of smokers, relishing his buzz from the first puff. He tried scanning the line for Flora, but it was too dense to see deeply within it, and Flora was quite short. Somehow, he felt like she would skip the line.

As his cigarette reached the halfway mark, he felt a presence behind him and a tap on his shoulder. He turned expecting Dylan and instead there was Mint, looking scornful as ever. Horace felt a wave of embarrassment and a desire to apologize—for coming here again, for having asked them to drinks, for merely existing in their presence. Instead, he gave them nothing but an off-balance nod.

"I'm smoking with my friend over here," Mint stated. "You should join us. Not a good place to be alone."

Horace followed them around the corner, where the bouncer from before was lounging against the wall, enjoying a joint. It was the exact spot where Horace had stood and faced Eden's janitor. No one else was there, and he felt safe with them.

"This is my friend Horace. He's cool."

Horace was surprised to hear Mint call him cool, but realized they meant it differently. They were setting him apart from the others, the masses, those not to be trusted. The bouncer nodded and extended his hand, dapping Horace up and introducing himself as Curtis. The conversation haltered, then Curtis picked it up again.

"Oh shit, you're Jena's friend too, right? I let him and his boys in earlier. Coulda said you knew Mint, too. I like this kid. You got a good circle."

Mint narrowed their eyes but said nothing. Already, Horace could see a different side to Curtis. Big and Black, he fit the mold of a bouncer, but his off-duty posture was much friendlier. Mint, despite inviting him over, gave the impression they did not want Horace to be here.

"Yeah, I was just with Jena actually. She told me to come find Mint. Lost my buddies too, so figured I'd try my luck outside."

Mint took one last drag then stamped out their roach.

"I'll find her. You should stick with Curt, Horace."

"Nah, my break's almost up. You're good to chill outside though. I'll just be up there, looking bored as shit."

"Damn, right. Okay, you're coming with me."

Mint took off, and Horace crushed his cig underfoot then rushed to catch up. Once around the corner, they stopped on a dime and turned on him.

"You should leave. I told you not to mess with this place."

"I can't. My friend's in trouble. Several of them, actually. Jena asked me to find you. I don't know what's wrong. And Flora—"

"—Shh, lower your voice. Fine, let's go inside. Stick with me no matter what."

"Wait," Horace whispered, grabbing Mint by the elbow, "what are you doing here? Why'd Jena send me to find you?"

Mint sized him up, as if assessing his worth in a fight. He rolled back his shoulders and met even with their eyes. Mint, wearing combat boots, cargo pants, and a black tank top that advertised their intricate sleeves of tattoos, lived their days for nights like these, while Horace's skinny H&M fit cloaked him like a cosplay. But he felt ready too. Try me, trust me, let me help you—he stitched these words into his expression.

"I'm here for a sample," they finally whispered back. "My guy needs more for testing. Jena's my plug."

Horace nodded in appreciation and gestured for Mint to lead the way. He'd followed Liam into a dead end, only for Mint to pick up the trail from there, gathering real evidence like a professional. The play was Liam's cry for attention, and Mint had answered. Would Liam come back just to take credit? Horace was doing all the leg work, but maybe the reward he deserved was to fade into the background.

As Horace followed Mint up the steps next to the line, he snuck in one last scan for his friends to no avail. They flashed their wrists to the bouncer, who greeted Mint with recognition, and proceeded inside. Horace glanced at his phone to see Louis and Dylan still hadn't replied. He furrowed his brow, and Mint picked up on his concern.

"Your friends still lost?"

"I don't know. They're not replying."

"I can't save everyone. We need to find Jena. Where is she?"

"Front and center, where else?"

They stepped inside, and Eden greeted them with a higher BPM and redder lights. At a glance over the balcony, the crowd swelled to new proportions. Fresh air's clarity was replaced by a disorienting stench of raw humanity that was melting Horace's resolve. On the arduous path from the stairs to the bar, he fought with the night's intentions as he struggled to keep up with Mint. His focus was drawn to the people around him—happy faces, horrifyingly pleasured, drunken, twisted, living and dying.

The crowd thinned near the bar, and a gap appeared through which Mint vanished. Someone grabbed Horace's shoulder, stopping his chase. He turned back to see a sweat-soaked Dylan Falco, who pulled him into a tight hug.

"We found her!" Dylan yelled into his ear.

"Amazing," Horace replied. "Where?" He pulled back from the hug, but Dylan held onto him, sliding one hand down Horace's back while his other hand carried a drink.

"Up front. She's with Louis now, we did it!" Dylan told him, eyes drinking him in, smile widening, lips licked, pupils dilated.

"We should go find them?" Horace said, not meaning to inflect upwards.

"In a minute," Dylan charmed, knowing he was winning, that Horace wasn't even putting up a fight, the tired gazelle to his hungry lion. Horace braced himself for a kiss, but Dylan handed him his drink. "Try this!"

Horace did without a second thought, slipping back into Eden's permissions, watching Dylan out of the corner of his eye, taking a big sip for Dylan's approval, accidentally spilling some onto his chin. He smiled ruefully and wiped his mouth, and Dylan pounced. Dylan's mouth tasted like the drink, which was not the flavor a drink should have. After briefly enjoying the moment, Horace became preoccupied by the unexpected flavor, like licking a battery, as it spread from his tongue and mouth to his blood and brain. Horace broke the kiss.

"You taste like electric metal," he said with a teasing smile, though an alarm was ringing in a room several floors down in his mind.

"Yeah, it's whatever everyone's been putting in their drinks. Tastes bad but makes you feel amazing!"

"You put it in your drink!?" Horace asked with rising panic and nausea. Should he run to a toilet and pull trig? He shoved the drink toward Dylan, who clasped his hands around Horace's without taking back the drink.

"Ch'yeah, everyone is. Don't worry about it! We'll be fine, Flora's fine. Let's just have some fun!"

Time slowed for Horace as adrenaline flooded through him and numbed the moment. The music faded, his heartbeat picked up, and his mind rebooted as he stared at Dylan. Just when Horace was starting to trust him again, he'd gone and ruined it. That stupid, impulsive slut. Horace stoked his anger but kept his words short.

"Not cool. Let's find the rest. We need to leave." Dylan seemed taken aback and took a breath to launch into more cajoling, which Horace cut off. "You're a fucking idiot, you know that?"

"Whatever. You're such a buzzkill."

"I know."

Horace turned away and cast his eyes around for Mint, but they were long gone. He vice-gripped Dylan's wrist, a vengeful squeeze, and took off toward the front. The music fed his anger, pounding it into his skull, and he took it out on those in his way, bumping past shoulders and cutting through groups, while Dylan kept up with him like a stumbling slinkie. If he upset some partiers, so be it. They'd forget about him.

Nearing the front, Horace tried barging into the center, but the crowd, normally so willing to accept and embrace, rebuked them. Tightly packed bodies with no room for more. Shoulder taps that went ignored. Raised arms and swaying shoulders above planted feet, like a completed formation, an organism that could only grow outward, a critical mass ready to explode. Dylan tugged Horace back to him.

"Get with the vibe, dude. You gotta just go with the flow."

"There is no flow!"

"Just watch me, c'mon."

Horace wanted to be pissed with Dylan but felt a surge of relief at his suggestion. Everything was going to be okay, everything was okay, everything was good, he was feeling good. Where was that coming from? He didn't know, but it felt right. They switched places, and Horace changed his grip to a handhold. Maybe when they found their friends, they could dance for a bit before leaving, as a treat. They'd been through so much. He deserved a break.

As they neared the vantage where Horace last saw Jena, he was fretting again about finding anyone in this cloudy mass of humanity. In front of him, everyone looked the same—darkly clothed, ambiguously gendered, only varying in size and movement. Behind him, only the nearest faces were discernable—equally blank, many eyes closed, countless hands and bodies moving in and out of the way. But Dylan moved with assurance, and Horace felt reassured. Why be negative, why be anxious? A bright feeling was driving the bad thoughts away, playing good thoughts like reruns.

Horace closed his eyes for a second, just a second, and when he opened them everyone was there. They'd reached the front of the crowd, together under the DJ's shadow, Dylan accepting a drink from Louis, Mint whispering urgently in Jena's ear, and Flora dancing dreamily on her own. Joy coursed through Horace down to his fingers and toes. He hugged Flora and she clung to him, but when he looked in her vacant eyes it wasn't clear she recognized him. She'd have embraced anyone willing to show her such love. A white light flashed, and Horace glimpsed a shadow of himself in her dilated pupils, a paranoid and vulnerable face. He rejected the image, no longer recognizing that version of himself.

3

Joy was plastered on all his friends' faces, except Mint's, who sidled over to Horace and gave him a quizzical look. He grinned back and gestured to Flora—mission accomplished. Whatever the mission was. Mint zipped open their crossbody bag to reveal a baggie of pills, then zipped it closed and jerked a thumb toward the exit. Horace shook his head no. He wanted to stay. The music made thought hard and talk impossible. Mint gave him another judging look, but Horace didn't understand their negativity. Mint pointed at the bag, mimed taking a pill, then pointed at Horace accusatorily. Horace used his hands and face to say no thanks, he'd already had some, and pointed to Dylan. Dylan saw him pointing and gave a thumbs up—they were all having a really good time and wanted each other to know it. Mint's eyes narrowed as they flicked between Horace and Dylan. Their downer energy was starting to bother Horace.

Then Mint wasn't there, and Dylan was. They traded places, or the world moved, while Horace stayed put. Horace was too busy dancing to notice. The beat was dropping, and the fog was spraying, raining down on them, cooling and coating them. Horace took more sips from the drink in Dylan's hand, then kissed his hand, then kissed his face. He emerged from the kiss without shame. Flora and Jena were dancing together while Louis swayed to the beat, eyes closed and mouth open. Someone was missing, but Horace couldn't remember who. Liam? No, someone else. They probably didn't matter, whoever they were. Nothing mattered but that thin, infinite moment.

The music lulled as two beats merged. A woman's voice emanated from the speakers, sounding like an extended sample from some decades-old movie, sophisticated and beautiful, motherly yet erotic, mesmerizing.

"I am tired of the walls between us. Do you hear me? I am tired. I don't want you inside me or me inside you. I want to be one. Inseparable. Indivisible. So get over yourself. You are nothing. We are something. We are everything. Eat my body. Drink my blood. Snort it. Shoot it. Fuck it, baby. Be transformed.

Partying

Leave yourself behind. Believe in us. Believe in Eden. Believe in us. Believe in Eden. Live in Eden. Live in Eden. Live in Eden."

The track hooked and looped that phrase. The music built a castle in which all could live. Horace wanted to move in. All he had to do was leave his name behind. A fresh start sounded nice. What good was Horace?

Horace's leg vibrated. His phone never failed to torment him. He didn't want to check it, but its rhythmic buzzing insisted he slip it out of his pocket. Liam Hawthorne was calling him. How strange. He silenced and ended the call, placing his phone back in his pocket. The buzzing returned. He was in no position to answer Liam's call, and it upset him that Liam didn't realize that. He ended the call again. After a moment, Liam's text appeared.

"GUNS OUTSIDE EDEN LEAVE ASAP"

Bewildered, Horace tried to alert his friends by gesturing to the back of the hall. They shrugged off his concern and danced in ignorance, unable to imagine the outside from the safety of inside. Then the dam broke, and reality flooded in. Heavy men with body armor and large weapons broke through and swarmed the platform.

Like lightning followed by thunder, beams of bright light shined onto ear-splitting screams that rolled out from the back. The lights were blinding, searching, and innumerable as they slashed across the crowd, which turned feral in an instant, scrambling in every direction, shattering the collective. It was the end of a united world and the start of an American nightmare. The music's pangs sounded like gunshots, and Horace briefly lost his grip on reality. No one knew who was holding the guns, and everyone knew the price of their life was that of a bullet's. Horace got shoved up against the edge of the stage in relative safety, while before him bodies stampeded, tumbled, and writhed. The screams of terror morphed into cries of pain.

262

Act I

Act II

Act III

Act IV

[Act V]

5.1 ~ The Raid

The vans arrived without sirens. Mercedes Sprinters, Liam was proud to recognize. Zipping by Liam's car, parked on the wooded shoulder of the winding road, they tore around the bend and fanned across the lot, carving up the lawn to encircle Eden with frightening speed. The sight of two-dozen armed men piling out of the vans and signaling tactical movements thrilled Liam. He was so back, and just in time.

I'm sorry for running away, but you should have known I was holed up at Brunhilde's. I was half-hoping someone would notice me there, and I'm mad you didn't figure it out. That's where Ian Noone first hid! It was the perfect note, and you had the codex, remembering more of our lore than anyone. Or did you guess I was there and never let on, content with me rotting in my self-imposed jail? I'd understand if you didn't want to see me. Or were you just scared to knock on her door? She's asked me about you, and I only had good things to say. I know you're afraid of her and think she's a witch like we're all still kids. But I've seen you growing up. The past holds little good for you. I thought being gay meant rejecting all that and leaving the past behind. You still deserve a coming out party, of sorts.

Laying low in his car, Liam put down his notebook and pulled up Horace's contact on his phone. His thumb hovered over the call button. A photo of teenaged Horace, wearing safety glasses and holding a drill to his temple like a gun, stared back at him from its circle. That would've been an easier Horace to call. His phone was offering to update the photo, which Liam declined. Nostalgia was a waste of time. Today's Horace would be rightfully mad at him, and Liam had to accept that if he was going to offer his help. He swallowed his pride and tapped to call. After four rings, it cut off. He tried again, and only made it to two rings. At least he'd captured Horace's attention. He switched to text, which he composed and sent in growing knowledge of its futility.

"GUNS OUTSIDE EDEN LEAVE ASAP"

Where else could I go? I needed escape but didn't want to leave, so I turned to Brunhilde. She's been so kind to me. I disturbed her peace. She housed me, fed me, even clothed me with her dead husband's dusty shirts. She's gotten a terrible rap. It's so unfair. All because she wants to die in peace and solitude. I respect her. I've been happy to help, sorting her shit, her material life, into labeled boxes. Will I be the only one at her funeral? No, all our neighbors will turn up like they never shunned her. It'll look just like the morning I saw you all in your dark suits and guessed why. I'd heard the ambulance come as I made my escape. Even with my phone turned off, I was keeping an eye on things. But I was frozen. I couldn't follow you to the funeral. I couldn't make that day about me. I've done that too many times.

The armed men strafed toward the stairs, and a few split off to handle the smokers and stragglers, lassoing them into a clump with the gestures of their guns. The scene played silently under the steady beat seeping out through Eden's walls. Hands went up in pantomime. Two gunmen barked inaudible commands and performed thorough body searches. Some contraband was volunteered or found and confiscated. At the top of the steps, a bouncer, who was a Black man, showed slight signs of resistance and was the first to be placed in handcuffs. He made no further protest, standing resolutely under the entrance lights and shaking his head.

Do you think I bear responsibility for Paul's death? I'm tempted to say he killed himself, bit by bit, each day of his life. But if I hadn't started this, he'd still be alive. I'd have attended his funeral, one day. Dominoes and butterflies. I feel so, unbelievably guilty. I felt that way even before the stroke. But I also felt like nothing was in my control. Everything was spiraling. That's why I had to get away. Do you understand how I feel? I should have died so that he still lived. But who really cared about Paul? No one liked him, not even Flora. She just loved him, like she has a choice. Does anyone like me? Does anyone still love me?

After the men breached Eden's entrance, Liam expected the music to stop. He imagined the chaos and terror at the unexpected appearance of this lethal force. He thought of Horace, Flora, Louis, and Falco, whose phones reported being inside that building. Flora had just re-shared her location with him the day before. That notification, along with her tweets, brought him out of exile into that night's strange darkness. When he turned his phone back on a few days prior, a torrent of weeks-old concern—the countless undelivered texts and calls demanding his whereabouts—rattled his phone for a full, angry minute. He couldn't bear to read them and retreated back into his isolation. His phone continued undisturbed—people had given up looking for him—until Flora decided to show him where she was. He had considered sharing his location back or going next door to see her, but, peaking behind a curtain, he spotted Horace slunk disconsolately against the Neufchatels' door and decided not to intervene. Instead, he opened up Twitter and watched her words reverberate across the internet.

Does that mean I bear responsibility for Flora's relapse, too? One led to another, so if I caused Paul's stroke, I caused her fall. How can one person survive such a weight? Same as her dad, I could say she had it coming. I've always worried about her sobriety. She based it in virtue instead of weakness. At your lowest moments, the one thing you know is you're not good enough. But who am I to judge her? I'm so pathetic, so craven. I don't know how you stayed my friend, or if we are still friends. I'm thinking about going sober. This is as good a rock bottom as any. I ran out of weed a week ago. Scratch that, I lied. It's only been a few days, when I finally turned on my phone. I was just drinking Brunhilde's wine to be polite.

Liam got out of his car and crouched toward Eden with absolutely no plan. Loud and defiant, the music bumped on without relent. He stuck to the tree line as he made his approach. A small squad of operators battered down a side door and infiltrated the building. His warning was too late; his friends had no hope of escape. If these were cops, they were not the cowardly ones who waited around for hours. This was a tactical strike team, spectacular overkill for no clear reason. As he crept closer to the parking lot, the writing on the side of the nearest van became legible. Drug Enforcement Agency. They were after *drugs?* The federal government cared about *Chemical X?* Cared so much they were willing to make a scene confiscating it? Maybe that was the point. His friends and their fellow partiers were pawns in a bigger game. That made Liam the son of a bishop at the least. His father was a useful tool, already sacrificed to the board.

I'm sorry I told you I truly thought my dad was replaced. Part of me believed it, or believed it was possible, and telling you made it seem real. Belief needs momentum, and once you were on board, I felt I could keep going. Maybe you were just being kind to me. Whether you bought it or not, I'm still an asshole. You never stood a chance against my dad. God, I hate him. I hate that he worked for the American Empire. I hate that he still thinks he's a good person, or a flawed but noble one, or that he's anything other than a sellout. And he says he did it all for me, for our family, which makes me a co-conspirator. How can I repay that debt to the world? If my sister and I had never been born, maybe he'd have worked for good.

There was a thick stillness in the muggy air. After the initial flurry, the cops stationed outside simply held their positions, occasionally leaning into their shoulders for muffled communications. How had the music not been shut off yet? A floodlight in one of the vans clicked on and sent long shadows across the lawn. Liam could now see the disconsolate faces of the detained stragglers sitting against the building. One girl took out her phone, but before she could place a call, a guard brusquely snatched it from her. Liam was reminded of a teacher in school. These poor kids had no idea what they were up against, the arbitrary power of a man in uniform. Liam wanted to move closer, but he knew he'd just get roped in with them. He might not be of much good now, but his one power was to witness in secrecy.

My first step back into the world was to call my dad, and he picked up. I was sitting in Brunhilde's living room, looking out the window at the cul-de-sac. I don't know where he was, but his car wasn't home. They were probably scouting for a second home, maybe even to sell the first. A lake house retreat, avoidance until death. I didn't ask. He started with, "Where are you?" I told him I was coming home. He sighed. He didn't damn or praise me. He just said, "We'll be back tomorrow." I said, "See you then." I thought the call would end there, that my worst fears were avoided, or at least delayed, but he kept going. "Was Flora behind those tweets? Tell me everything you know." He saw those? It's forever weird to think of my dad as online. I said I didn't have anything to do with them, but yeah, they were pretty wild. "Think she'll get in trouble for them?" I asked. "We're all in trouble," he answered gravely. That spooked me a bit. "I talked to my partners about it," he continued. "They're livid." "With Flora?" I asked. "No one gives a shit about your friends," he said. "Well, maybe they do now. But no, this is about money and power and reputation, and you should thank your lucky stars none of you have any of that." I remember thinking that's not totally true, that Flora had the power of speech and virality, but I didn't say anything. I was cowed. He finished with, "Stay away from that damn club, and tell your friends the same." After that, I had to go to Eden, no doubt about it.

The music cut off abruptly. The boom of silence was slowly filled with crickets and other calls of nightly nature as Liam's ears adjusted. He waited for something to happen. Out of a van emerged three eager beagles on leashes and several large cans adorned with biohazard symbols. One dog was led around the back, while the other two took a detour through the detainees, finding a match in someone's shoe that prompted the night's second handcuffing. The handlers and their drug sniffers staged the landing at the bottom of the stairs, and other cops lined the steps with their rifles abreast in a domineering display. The arduous retrocession of Eden's attendees began. In forced march, frightened partiers exited the front door in twos. Many opened their hands over the bins to drop baggies or seemingly nothing—though Liam could guess loose pills—before being subject to the beagles' inspections. In the first wave, some withholding rebels were caught and detained, but the frequency dropped as evidence grew that these cops weren't fucking around. Those allowed to proceed spilled across the lawn in shellshocked uncertainty, cast from Eden to the earth, a harsh purgatory. Over countless minutes, the slow trickle amassed into a flood that flattened footpaths across the open space. Many stayed on the lawn, waiting for their friends. A few headed for their cars in the parking lot, though no one dared operate a vehicle. The rest headed aimlessly in both directions down the dark road. Liam recommitted to his hiding place as a group drew near, but no one paid him any mind. A cavalry of rideshares soon converged from across the city. The first driver popped his head out the sunroof, got a better look at the police presence, and drove off promptly without his passenger, earning a suppressed laugh from Liam. More took his place, either braver than the first or enticed by surging prices, and soon the road was nearly impassible with blinkered vehicles and stumbling escapees trying to match license plates. Distracted at first, Liam refocused his attention on the steady flow exiting Eden, determined not to miss his friends. He waited and waited. He checked his phone. Nothing came his way. He settled into a more comfortable position, sitting against a tree and watching the show. While the outflow from the building continued apace, the amassed pool was draining into the night. Two of the cops were directing traffic, clearly signaling they wanted people to leave. Liam's adrenaline was subsiding, giving way to a tired anxiety. He wasn't sure how many more times he could ask himself where his friends were, when Horace and Flora finally emerged from Eden and walked down the stairs with nothing to hide.

I know my dad was just doing his best. If we're all cogs in some terrible machine, does his higher leverage translate to greater guilt? Would the machine have run any differently without him? Does it run differently without me, currently a scattered part, molded for utility but bent out of shape? He claims his project failed, so does that make him a success by my standards? I don't know. It doesn't feel right. I want to leave the world cleaner, nicer, and prettier than I found it. National Park rules. I'm as guaranteed a failure as he was, only I get to see that going in. Lucky me, knowledge is a curse. He lived through the inflection point of progress, the beginning of the end. My life started on the downhill. I'm destined to be just another loser watching the climate burn and institutions collapse. Starting where he did, I wouldn't have done anything differently. Always easier to critique than to do.

Liam strode confidently out of the forest and merged safely into the edge of the crowd. There he lingered, milling among small groups, assuring himself he hadn't been noticed, and relocating Horace and Flora, whom he'd lost at ground level. He spotted Louis and Falco walking down the steps, both having emptied their hands over the bin, and tracked them to their reunion with Horace and Flora. A cop's harsh shout cut through the somber murmurs of the undeparted. Someone had passed by the dog's inspection too quickly and was being reprimanded. Liam recognized the concern on his friends' faces before he identified the rulebreaker as their stage tech, Mint. The dog howled and stuck its nose into Mint's crotch. They were ordered to hand over what they were hiding or submit to a body search. Mint cursed under their breath and reached under their waistband to produce the baggie. They were handcuffed and detained with the rest, who sat or leaned uncomfortably against the wall with their hands behind their backs. Mint's inexplicable appearance here was recasting their role in Liam's show, but he took it in stride as he closed in on his friends, who'd formed a closed circle of debate and distress. Catching them by surprise, he pierced the circle and wrapped his arms around Horace and Flora.

"Liam!?" the four of them said at once, in different flavors of surprise, joy, and distrust. Liam hushed them, not wanting to attract any more attention.

"Shh. Act surprised later. There's a lot to explain. My car's parked around the bend, let's get out of here."

"What about Mint and Jena?" Horace demanded.

"There's nothing we can do for them," Liam stated callously, unsure who Jena even was. He took a good look at his friends.

Horace and Flora's cheeks were flush with concern and scored with lines of evaporated tears. Louis and Falco's faces were pale and sweaty, and their eyes were unfocused, staring past Liam into nothing. "For the moment, anyway," Liam added. "We'll bail them out later if that's what it comes to. We need to get out of here."

Liam took several steps in the direction of his car and turned back to see his friends staring at him strangely. To be so unseen by those he loved filled Liam with despair. Something was wrong with them. They looked like his friends, but they weren't the people he knew. They were traumatized, and—it dawned on him—drugged. Unsure of their reality and shaken by his reappearance. To them, he was the doppelganger, an omen of their living nightmare. He had to pinch them out of it.

"C'mon guys. We're going. You can thank me later."

Liam hooked Horace and Flora by their arms, and they followed compliantly, though their heads craned back toward Mint. Louis and Falco stumbled along in tow. They marched across the trampled grass, past the shortened queue of rideshares, and along the shoulder of the road to his car in silence. Liam stewed with competing impulses of righteousness and guilt while observing his sullen friends. After helping them into his car, he came upon a satisfactory idea to salvage the situation.

"You know what we all need? A good meal and hot coffee. I'm taking us to Barnum."

"Aye aye, captain," Horace answered groggily for the group.

I've realized that my dad really messed up by giving too much to his work, not the work itself. He wasn't around for me when I needed it, and now I'm busting his ass when he's trying to make up for it. Yet here I am, having made the same mistake with my friends, especially you, losing myself in the work, leaving you in my wake, thinking only what I want matters. I gave you a purpose when you were aimless, but what a terrible leader I was. What a terrible friend. You deserve better, and I'll be better. Starting now.

5.2 ~ The Janitor

From the first sip of coffee, Horace knew he was going to be okay, but it wasn't until the pancakes hit his stomach that he began to feel like himself again. With a shaky hand, he'd given the syrup a heavy pour, and the sweetness clung to his tongue after each bite went down. He was at great risk of biting his cheek while he chewed, as if his whole body was sucking inward toward a singular point. He looked to his friends to save him, lest he disappear with a *pop* into a cloud of smoke that would leave behind only his chattering teeth and a polished stone, weathered into shape by his racing thoughts as they searched for an impenetrable understanding. His friends could take turns skipping that stone across the lake that lay between them, passing a message that was the mere act of communication.

They'd been a sorry, silent crew on the drive to Barnum. Liam, their steward and savior, couldn't wait to tell them where he'd been, how he'd hidden in plain sight, finding refuge first in the forbidden forest of their youth with Brunhilde and later behind the curtain of Eden's woods. The carpool received him with disinterest, as his nervous efforts to pave a zigzagged road to reunion were no match for their fractured mourning, collapsing deeper underneath the sloppy repairs. Liam gave up and turned on the radio, finding a DJ who was prattling on about jazz like nothing was wrong. Horace resented the serenity and dwelt on his regret, having lost Jena in the initial scramble and Mint to handcuffs and the risk they'd taken. Liam was a false messiah— he hadn't been there when the sky fell and the walls closed in, reducing everyone inside to their individual selves concerned with their own survival. Horace wasn't mad at Liam; he was estranged from him.

Horace struggled to understand the others, too, each absent in their own way. Falco, apparently convinced they'd been followed, kept his eyes on the diner's doors as he handled explaining their night to Liam, pausing abruptly whenever the entrance swung open or the waitress drew near, forgetting where he'd left off when he tried to resume. Flora, still blissfully unaware they'd come to rescue her, absorbed herself in the menu as if she'd never seen it before and almost ordered an omelet till Liam gently reminded her it wasn't vegan. Instead, she played with her fries, standing them up and parading them across her plate, choreographing a dance around a pool of ketchup. Louis was plain wasted, losing his battle with sleep several times before they gave up waking him. Horace supposed he was some mix of all of them.

But the pancakes changed things, bite by bite. The sticky, soggy sensations absorbed him, then grounded him, and reality constructed itself out of his pre-dawn breakfast. A reset. Having tripped before, Horace recognized the effects in himself, the looping thoughts, his spongy temperament, the mainlining of sound into feeling. When the cops stormed in, their commands manifested like loud, angry thoughts. Horace didn't have to agree with them, but they left room for little else. He wondered if Mint's disobedience came from their sobriety, but as the sugar and starch returned his strength, he accepted he couldn't have done anything otherwise.

He was settling back into himself, an old shape seen with new and weak eyes, like he was stumbling up to his room in the dark after a late and drunk night. Had that always been there—his unwillingness to rock the boat, his concern for the security of his friends, his sense of powerlessness and desire for permanence? Yes, just like there'd always been a tenth step at the top of the stairs. First you forget, then you remember. He considered his friends again and saw them stretched across time, zooming out until this blip of a night didn't register, and tried to find comfort in the flatness. Then he saw himself, in that moment, nodding and staring and being totally weird, maybe even muttering to himself. He gulped down some coffee and opened his mouth.

"Liam, what are we gonna do with them?" Horace was referring to the table.

"With them?" Liam answered skeptically.

"Okay, with us," Horace acquiesced, while jerking his head toward Flora, trying to drive home a distinction.

"I like the idea of a sleepover," Falco chimed in. "I'm gonna have nightmares otherwise." As he said this, he glanced at Horace, who recommitted to his pancakes.

"I'm all for sticking together," Liam replied. "Hey Flora, Louis, hello? Flora, can we crash at your, uh, family's place tonight? Do you have your key with you?"

Flora nodded vigorously, dug her keys out of her shoulder bag, and handed them to Liam. Her plate of fries was largely undiminished. Falco had wolfed down his steak melt and was eyeing Louis's neglected chicken tenders. Liam seemed to be saving his last bite of BLT. Horace's pancakes had gotten him this far, but suddenly they turned on him. He needed a different kind of grounding.

"I'm stepping out for a smoke," he announced to the table.

"Ooh, mind if I join?" Dylan eagerly asked.

"Sure," Horace said after some hesitation. Liam scootched out of the booth to let Falco by but made it clear he'd stick around to watch the sibling astronauts. On an impulse that suggested he was still a little high, Horace took his coffee along. He signaled his intentions to the waitress, who refilled his mug on the way out the door.

Outside, Horace fumbled with both the pack and lighter in his free hand before giving up and handing them both over to Falco. Falco—in one move becoming Dylan again—placed a cigarette delicately on Horace's lips and lit it before taking care of himself. Horace's cheeks flushed with shame, and he turned away, casting his glance toward lampposts down the road.

"Crazy night, huh," Dylan began.

Horace didn't reply, but he turned his face back to Dylan and breathed him in, blowing smoke in his direction.

"Man, y'all have been up to some crazy shit since I've been gone. Here I thought I was the one going on a big adventure and becoming a man in Central America. I don't even know what you got yourself mixed up in, but it's heavy."

Horace kept his silence, so Dylan kept going.

"Thank god we were there for Flora. Seems like she doesn't have a clue. Honestly, I'm not sure I do either, like in a different way. What on Earth was this all about? I'm so lost."

"I don't know," Horace finally answered. "It's over our heads. We think Liam's dad did some shit for the government. Then some rich fuck buys his company and uses whatever they were making to start a night club, and I guess some feds didn't like that. We were only caught in the crossfire. They're giants and we're ants."

"Fuckin' hell. That's wild. But Flora knew something, Liam was on to something, even your friend—uh, Mint?—seemed like they were up to something. And you, somehow you of all people ended up at the center of this?"

"Whole lotta good I did . . . All because I was so mad at you, y'know? And myself. And I just felt fucking crazy. Liam told me about the play right after I got back from Guatemala. I was ready to do anything. I guess that's what love does, when it's burned. There's so much energy in it, I had to channel it somewhere. Do you know what that's like?"

"I do. I think? Raquel and I broke up, ya know. Didn't see a future together."

"I don't know what I'm supposed to say to that. I'm sorry for you, I guess, and I still want you to be happy. Maybe we can be friends again, one day."

"Oh. Okay. I hope so," Dylan said hollowly, letting Horace's rejection show.

Instead of hugging him, Horace stamped out his cigarette and went back inside. Liam had already paid the bill and was wrangling the Neufchatels out of the booth. After returning his mug to the table, Horace left Louis to Liam and took Flora by the shoulders, squeezing her close for comfort. Flora put her arm around his waist and smiled at him, lucidly. For the first time that night, she seemed to understand. By the time they rejoined Falco outside, he had gathered himself and finished his cigarette.

As they were packing into the car, Horace's phone rang. It was Mint. He stepped away to answer.

"Hey, are you okay?"

"My wrists hurt, but no charges. They just let us all go. I don't get it. I'm at a police station. Can you pick me up? I need to get my car back."

"Guess they just wanted to scare you. Scare us. It worked. We're getting everyone home, but Liam and I can come after. It's gonna be like 45 minutes?"

"That's fine. There's a McDonald's across the street. I'll send you the address."

As Mint ended the call, a car turned off the road and bucked up into the parking lot, narrowly missing Horace. It brought him back to his roadside encounter with the janitor and his pamphlet. How had he known to approach Horace? Could such a thing be explained by coincidence? It seemed impossible, like everything else. Horace got back into the car and told Liam what Mint asked them to do.

"One last trip," Liam assented, "and then we're done with that place forever."

Horace knew, and figured it was on Liam's mind too, that Mint could've called a rideshare to go pick up their car. It seemed all three of them had unfinished business they weren't prepared to tackle alone.

Empty roads carried them to the cul-de-sac. As Liam unlocked the Neufchatels' door, he told Dylan to keep an eye on Flora in case she made another unlikely escape. Louis, fresh off his latest nap and cranky like a toddler, took unkindly to the remark.

"What, you think I can't take good enough care of her?" he snapped.

"Apparently not," Liam answered without looking.

"Say that to my face," Louis shouted as he advanced on Liam. Horace was standing in the way and held up his hands in peace.

Dylan put his arm protectively around Flora. "You get out of my way, and you get your hands off her!"

Liam turned around and moved Horace aside to face Louis. "Hey. I'm sorry. I'm sorry I dragged your family into this, and I'm sorry your dad's dead. You don't have to forgive me, but let's not fight right now. We're all too tired."

Louis was squeezing his fists, but he released them with an exhale and a grunt. He shoulder-checked Liam as he walked through the door. Liam brushed it off and shrugged at Horace, as if to say he had it coming. Falco mimed with two fingers that he'd be keeping an eye on Louis, too, before taking Flora inside and closing the door behind him. Liam and Horace returned to the car, and an empty highway took them into the city. Horace was keeping his thoughts to himself, but Liam eventually introduced a new conversation.

"I talked to my dad yesterday. Can't believe that was just yesterday. He said Flora's tweets got people's attention. I think she might've triggered the raid. He was worried for her safety. For all of ours."

"Was he mad at you?"

"No, but I'm sure he will be. On the phone, he was just worried and scared, in his own bravado kind of way."

"Still think he was replaced?"

"Nah. Dunno if I ever really did. It was just something to—"

"—Get people's attention?" Horace snipped as Liam trailed off. Dormant anger toward his friend chose this moment to assert itself, catching them both off guard, but Horace wanted to let his words flow.

"What if you were the one replaced? Or experimented on? Just something I've been thinking, while you were gone. Seems like you wouldn't put it past your dad, right? Honestly, maybe that would be the best for you. The Liam I know wouldn't have been such a bitch. The play, sure, that was a good prank. But why'd you hold back on me? And how could you just fucking vanish like that? Leaving me to pick up the pieces, play your role for you, explain shit to our parents for you, fucking carry Paul's casket while you were having tea and cake with Brunhilde? And now you're just back, saving the day? Expecting us to thank you for it? We would have been fine without you. We would have found our way home somehow. An app is way more reliable than you are. Jesus Christ. How can I trust you ever again?"

Horace was crying again by the time he finished, but Liam only cleared his throat and kept his eyes on the road as he calmly turned onto a residential street and pulled into an open spot. He shifted into park and looked at Horace. Shaken, he let out a long sigh, and his mouth opened and closed a few times before he found any words.

"I agree. You're right. I mean, in a funny kind of sense, I did get replaced, by you. Like, I got in over my head and just couldn't handle it. I didn't know how anyone could, and you did. I'm sorry. You deserve better, and the way you stepped up shows that. Actually, I wrote a letter to you in my journal, while I was waiting outside Eden. It's pretty manic, so I don't know if I should show it to you, but that was the intention. Do you want to read it?"

"I think I've had enough of your writing, for now. I just want you to be a better friend. I'm willing to forgive because, without you, I don't have much else. Especially with Flora now, and Dylan, I mean, I just, we're just—"

"—Yeah man, we're all fucked up. Maybe least of all you, Ace. Isn't that nice for a change?"

"Ah, fuck off. But yeah, you might be right, which means the end times are nigh."

"Also, back to doppelgangers, I know my dad didn't do shit. That's what I'm mad about, really, that he was a failure, and that he worked all that time for nothing, which makes him kind of a loser. And that I might be too, if we're getting Freudian about it."

"Honey, we're way past that. But I'm not so sure about your dad. If what I took tonight was his stuff, he might be a really good drug chemist. Maybe he can teach you how to cook."

"Sure, and I can teach him how to write. His screenplay was garbage, if we're being honest." They both laughed, breaking the tension at last, and Liam kicked the car back in motion. "We're still getting Mint, yeah?"

Catharsis was an unfamiliar feeling for Horace, but he might've felt it in the wake of their conversation. Something was unwinding, though he was still so mixed up inside. Yelling at Liam felt good, and laughing with him all the better. For a second, he likened it to the feeling after make-up sex, but he shook that off. For all his romantic confusions, even his worst impulses knew better than to view Liam in that way.

Plus, they were on their way to a more pressing romantic concern. Not that there was any chance he was on Mint's mind, in that way, in this moment. But in the wake of his final disillusionment with Dylan—it had set in that the idiot basically drugged him—and all the danger that followed, he was wondering if Mint would want to be held, and what it would be like to hold someone like them, so hard and mysterious and guarded. He wasn't dreaming of sex, just intimacy and comfort, the presence of a body so vital that it blocked out the rest of the world.

Mint was standing outside McDonald's smoking a cigarette when they pulled up, and Horace would've gotten out to join them had they not stamped it out and stepped over so quickly. The car was still moving when they slid into the backseat.

"Took you long enough. Let's go," they ordered.

"Didn't expect to ever see you again, Mint," Liam called back jovially, with a touch of smarm, as they exited the parking lot.

"Somehow I did," Mint replied in typical deadpan before livening up. "Thank you for picking me up. I didn't trust apps. *They've* got their fingers on everything."

"Oh yeah, what's your theory?" Liam asked, sounding too close to mocking for Horace's tastes.

"That everyone in is on this somehow, including maybe you," Mint shot back.

"C'mon Mint," Horace interjected, "you can trust us. You asked us for a ride, right?"

"I asked *you* for a ride. Hard not to be paranoid in times like this, but fine. I do owe Liam for the play and everything it kicked up. Even I don't think you're dumb enough to have put that on and still be on their side."

"Not that *I* should be the one telling *you* this," Liam joked with mild discomfort, "but you're using your pronouns pretty liberally here. Who's *they*?"

"Your dad. Tevin Vein. Any number of his employees, except for Horace and his friend Jena, maybe. Definitely your friends, uh, Roger and Gus, or whatever. Almost everyone working at Eden, like their freaky janitor. It's all a real-life conspiracy, whether you believe me or not."

"Heard that one before," Liam said.

"Liam, I think Mint knows way more about this stuff than even we do," Horace stepped in to say, trying to salvage the conversation. He felt silly for having just imagined Mint being happy to see him. But maybe they just hated Liam that much. "They were trying to get a sample of the drug, for testing. That's why they got arrested. And they, like, knew about your dad before the play, somehow."

"And here I thought you just hated my guts," Liam retorted.

"Don't rule that out," Mint replied.

"Whatever. You don't have to like me," Liam relented. "So, how'd you get on this beat?"

"Um," Mint hesitated for once. "I was getting tired of sitting by on the fringe. Like I'm paying attention, and I'm seeing the people in charge, these fascists who rule over us, the billionaire-climate-arsonist-pedophile class, they're getting sloppy. They think they're untouchable, so they're putting more of it out in the open. It started with some stuff I read on Discord servers, just rumors, about Tevin Vein and his wife. You know how it's impossible to imagine a billionaire going about daily life? Well, they don't live on Mars, yet. People meet them, get fucked and fucked over, and if they ever go public about it, they're done for. But stories were still coming from somewhere, brave people, that gave me the impression that Tevin Vein is a dumb-enough fucker who likes party drugs and young girls so much that one day he was gonna get got. I was obsessed, to be honest, but I didn't think I'd have a role to play till Vein bought your dad's company. Then the dominoes kept falling, and here we are."

"Wow," Liam said in earnest. "You're on a whole-ass quest against evil. I was just trying to stick it to my dad."

"Like I said, I owe you one," Mint admitted. "But without a sample of that drug, I'm not gonna have much of an exposé. I think Vein's been showing up at Eden, but I could never prove it."

"Maybe the huge DEA raid that just happened will make the news? Get people asking questions?" Horace added hopefully, though the silence that followed suggested none of them had much faith.

They all settled down for a bit, watching as the grid-plan streets lined with rowhouses gave way to winding roads with sprawling residences. While chewing on scenery in silence, Horace picked up on something Mint had dropped earlier.

"Mint, you met the janitor? Tall, long, freaky dude?"

"Yeah. He kicked me out that night you got wasted. I don't know what to make of him, but I don't trust him."

"I'd met him before. He approached me once, on the side of a road, tried to give me something, like a piece of paper, but I ran away."

"Weird. You should have taken it. Maybe he has answers."

"Yeah. I bet."

The turn onto Eden's road sent Horace's heart racing. The tiniest prick of cold wax formed on his nape, but it didn't spread. It was only a reminder, a warning. Or maybe it was just sweat, all along.

Horace steeled himself with deep breaths, and the sensation faded.

"My car's on the other side, but we should park here," Mint suggested. "Hedge our bets."

They parked on a bend just out of sight from Eden and progressed uphill on foot. Horace was on high alert, the kind of tired overdrive that gathers information compulsively but struggles with interpretation. Birds were singing out of sight. Dawn's light filtered blue through the trees while a creamy orange climbed lazily into the sky. It was nearly 6 a.m., and the world was at peace.

Horace was expecting a crime scene, yellow tape and red-and-blue lights, patrolmen to wave them along or take them in for questioning. He tried to think up an alibi, briefly sketching the entire conversation they'd have with a suspicious cop, but maybe honesty would serve them best. Why else would they be there, besides to retrieve Mint's car?

Hugging the shoulder, they rounded the bend and came upon Eden, desolate. The sight arrested them, the early sun kissing its steeple, early birds flitting across its field. Horace saw it again as an abandoned church, hallowed ground, like its desecrations were cleansed by the dawn. They resumed their approach, still cautious, but out of respect, reverence, mindful of their own intentions to disturb the serenity.

There was a windowless white passenger van in the parking lot. Horace knew who it belonged to, and it wasn't the DEA. He might've preferred cops, but it meant the cleanup wasn't finished. There may still be time for answers. Horace wished this could all be over.

"That's the janitor's van," Mint whispered. "I've seen him dropping off bartenders."

"Damn, does he live here?" Liam asked. "I can't believe I never saw this guy. Bet he was watching our play like Quasimodo, hiding up in the steeple."

"I don't want to think about it," Horace said quickly. "Should we just get Mint's car and go? What if he finds us?"

"I could be down for that," Liam seconded.

"I think we should find him," Mint responded with determination. "Worst he does is kick us out. But I wanna see if he'll talk to us. Don't you wanna know why he approached you on that road?"

"I do," Horace answered, trying to convince himself, to channel the bravery of his friends and heroes, to feel outside of himself.

"Lead the way," Liam encouraged.

Before approaching the steps, they swept the grounds for signs of life, but all they found were tire marks scoring the lawn in curved parallels. The fresh dirt and dewy grass clung to their shoes as they walked. Horace kept checking over his shoulder, feeling watched but never seeing who or why.

One of the side doors was battered in and hung half-open on its hinge like a broken jaw. Mint still had the key to the front door, but this seemed an auspicious opportunity to enter unseen. They approached the door obliquely, wanting to steal the first glimpse, not knowing what awaited them on the dance floor. They paused, flanking the door, listening.

"Do you hear that?" Liam whispered. "Like, swishing?"

Horace closed his eyes. At first, he could hear only his beating heart and his anxiety telling him to run away, but he focused on the spaces in between, drawing out a rhythmic swishing sound, long arcs matched with soft footsteps, something dragging on the ground, a clicking and squelching, perhaps even water dripping. Then came the whistling, the tune unrecognizable but the sound unmistakable, jovial and full-bodied, crisp.

"He must be cleaning," Horace realized out loud.

Mint placed their hand on the broken door and looked back at them. Horace glanced at Liam for assurance, but Liam was still scanning the area for potential witnesses.

"Go to the car if you're afraid," they whispered, almost inaudibly. They smiled at Horace, daring him. It was the kind of smile Liam had shown him many times in their childhood, anytime he proposed something dangerous. Today's Liam was standing hesitantly behind him, but he wasn't running either. Horace gulped and placed his hand on the door to show his commitment.

In his excitement, he miscalculated. The door received his indelicate touch with a groan and squeaked slowly open, grinding on its remaining hinge. Horace stepped back with panic, Mint glared back at him with disbelief, and Liam strode forward to make his entrance, shoving the door open and battering it loudly against the wall. Horace and Mint followed hurriedly. In the center of the dance floor stood the janitor, armed with a mop and yellow bucket. Facing them, he squeezed out the mop, docked it in the lower bowl, and used the pole to pilot the bucket over toward them.

"Do not take another step," he commanded. "Your shoes are dirty, and I just cleaned there."

Horace glanced at his muddy shoes and caught a strong whiff of bleach. The floor around him sparkled with residue. He looked back up, and the janitor had stopped only feet away.

"Why did you three come back?" the janitor asked. His deep voice and slow words gave an angry impression, but his expression was neutral. His long body imposed on them but did not threaten. His face looked tired, missing more than just one night's sleep.

"To find you," Horace blurted out, speaking on instinct, squealing to get out of trouble.

"I see," the janitor said.

"Can you tell us what's really going on here?" Mint jumped in.

"Nothing, anymore. I'm cleaning this place, and it will stay clean, and we will all move on," the janitor answered.

"Did you ever meet Tevin Vein? Was he here, was he drugging kids?" Mint pressed on. Horace and Liam exchanged worried glances, thinking this was the wrong approach.

"Why should I tell you? What good would that do?" the janitor said.

"People deserve to know!" Mint cried.

"If these are your questions, I can't help you," he replied, still unmoved.

"What happened to you?" Liam asked bluntly. "Why do you . . . look like that?"

"An excellent question, Liam Hawthorne." The janitor dropping Liam's name gave Horace a chill. "Do you have any guesses?"

"You know my name. Did you know my father? Did he do this to you?" Liam asked with trepidation.

"I do not blame your father, nor should you."

"Were you supposed to be a doppelganger?" Horace asked incredulously.

"I am not sure what I was supposed to be. I only am what I am now."

"Quit speaking in riddles, what happened to you?" Mint demanded. "We want to help you."

"You cannot help me. I was made to be a janitor. I clean. I do as I am told. I am content. First there were labs, and now there are dance halls, and soon there will be offices. There are always more messes."

"You approached me on the roadside, months ago. Why?" Horace finally got up the nerve to ask.

"That was a mistake. I was going through an unstable period. I am better now."

"But how did you know who I was? And who Liam is?" Horace pressed.

"I saw your photos. They leave everything up for the janitor to see. I never forget names and faces."

"What were you going to tell me? What was on that pamphlet?" Unnerved as he was, Horace refused to back down.

"I–I don't know. It was so long ago." Something was cracking in the janitor's façade, a light breaking into his eyes, searching inward. "I wanted . . . I wanted to warn you. To stay away. I saw your face, and it reminded me of someone. Mine? My child's? I can no longer say."

"Don't you want revenge on the people who did this to you?" Mint pleaded.

"I don't want anything. I am content. All I want is for you to go. To leave me alone. I am content. I have everything I need. I have nothing to give you."

"They're just gonna do this again, dammit. Save someone besides yourself."

"Mint," Liam half-whispered. "Give him a break. He's not gonna cooperate."

"Wait," the janitor said. He placed a hand over his heart, patted it uncertainly, and undid the button on his breast pocket. "I do have something to give you."

He took three long steps toward them, close enough for Horace to take in the scars riddling his face. From his pocket, he withdrew a folded and crumpled paper, red and glossy. He held it out for Horace to take. Horace looked him in the eyes, cloudy eyes that had seen so much and yet held no malice. He took the pamphlet. It was a Chinese takeout menu. Confused, he turned it over, and there was a photograph paperclipped to it. A picture from roughly a year ago of Horace and Liam, arms around each other, smiling for Greta's camera. Liam had posted it on Instagram. Horace slid out the photo to show Liam and Mint, which uncovered a message scrawled on the menu in thick marker.

"STAY AWAY FROM EDEN."

"You were trying to warn me," Horace stated in shock, as he passed the pamphlet and photo to a curious Liam.

"You should leave now," the janitor said.

"We'll leave, sir," Horace stammered. "I just want to ask one more thing. You tried to protect me, so I don't want to remember you as just Eden's janitor. What's your name?"

"Forget me," the janitor muttered, as he returned to his mop and resumed his task.

"Please," Horace insisted, "what do people call you?"

"They call me nothing! Leave me alone!"

The Janitor

From either rage or exasperation, the janitor kicked over his bucket, spilling the cleaning solution onto the floor, sending it racing toward them like the tide, lapping at their dirty shoes. Horace braced himself for the giant man to charge, but he remained in place, his shoulders heaving. Liam was already halfway to the door, and Horace ran to catch up, grabbing Mint by the wrist to take them with him. Breathless and delirious, they raced to Mint's car and were relieved to find it hadn't been towed. Mint offered them a ride around the bend only after Liam and Horace had already slid inside.

"I need to find out what they did to him," Mint said.

"I should ask my dad about him," Liam offered, less confidently.

"This isn't over," Mint asserted.

Horace wasn't ready to speak. Even after saying goodbye to Mint, watching them drive away, and settling into Liam's car, he found himself at a loss for words. It was a familiar feeling, with Liam already reviving his theories about his father's career and launching into casual speculation about the janitor's circumstances ("I'm thinking he was tall enough to body double Osama bin Laden. Or maybe he was too tall?"), but Horace felt an unusual dignity in his silence. Some things aren't meant for words, so we paper them over and describe the diorama instead. What lies underneath can only be felt.

Tuning Liam out, Horace watched Eden shrink in the side-view mirror. He lowered his window, stuck out his head, and blocked its final disappearance with a good look at himself. This is who he'd be traveling with for the rest of his life. Always moving forward, always looking backward. Always the same and never the same again.

Acknowledgements

On November 7th, 2020, I wrote in my journal, "I want to write a book about being in your 20s, which to me is defined by experiencing life not as it was promised but how it actually is, which for most people is extremely dissonant." At that time, Horace and Liam were set to be podcasters living in an alternate reality where Gore beat Bush. The following people made this book much better:

Olivia Comm, my editor; Lauren Meinhart, my first-draft reader and cover artist; Shawn Kerry, Dan Goff, Caroline Hockenbury, Thomas Roades, and Sam Lesemann, my readers; Levi Moneyhun, my cover designer and font consultant; and countless others for supporting my dream, providing ideas, reading snippets, advising on self-publishing, and generally putting up with me while I talked about writing a book for over three years. Lastly, I should issue the same acknowledgement as Liam: many characters and dynamics were inspired by my family, but they're not literally them. That would be weird.